DRAWN BY DRAGONBLOOD

BLOOD BORN 1

LYNN BURKE

DRAWN BY DRAGONBLOOD

A breeze from deep in the White Mountains reveals my intended female's sweet scent after years of giving up hope another dragonblood walks the earth. I soar through the skies in dragon form, intent on claiming my destiny.

I find her camping in the wilderness—in another man's arms.

My conscience battles my desire to tear the lovers apart, but my inner beast demands I take what belongs to us regardless of the cost to any human being.

But fate has other plans, ones I never dreamed possible.

Newlyweds Jon and Dakota agree to ride out a storm in my fire-hewn home atop a rocky peak. They don't understand the supernatural energy that draws them to me, nor are they aware dragon shifters aren't fantasy and that three of the ancient blood are required to breed a hatchling.

Revealing who I am and that a hint of dragonblood simmers within *both* of their veins uproots their existence and makes them question everything they believe.

Will Jon willingly submit to his alpha whose beast wishes to dominate him? Can Dakota accept she has no choice but to hurt the man she's loved most of her life?

My destined mates must find the courage to make

themselves vulnerable to me, or our legacy—and our species —dies with us.

CHAPTER 1

ELIJAH

I stood on my veranda, arms useless at my sides and my shoulders sagging.

The anniversary of my greatest heartbreak had once more arrived, ripping through my chest with talons sharper than any dragon's claws. I stared unseeing across the White Mountains where my cave-like home had sat unnoticed by humans for close to four centuries, my mind lost in past memories that intensified the ache my lover had left behind.

Samuel Barber's "Adagio for Strings" filtered through the sliding doors I'd left open behind me, worsening the intensity of my loneliness.

I had first heard the song in September of 1939 by radio broadcast and promptly fell in love with the haunting, passionate piece—and the dragonblood beta who had sat beside me at the time.

We'd had over seventy years together, and still, he'd left as though the time we'd spent as partners held no meaning. No letter or verbal explanation of where he'd gone or why, but I understood his unspoken troubles, what had kept us from bonding as we'd both been desperate for fate to allow regardless of the fact we weren't true mates.

I'd been born a royal alpha, intended to lead and protect. He was of a lesser family but a self-declared alpha all the same. He had never submitted himself fully to me in our bed and dungeon, but I'd felt sure if we had only located our third, a fertile female, we would have found fulfillment.

It took three dragonblood to create life, an accomplishment I would never be able to claim. I had let my three parents down—and every other Blood Born who'd perished over the years since my birth.

Releasing a sigh, I hung my head, my eyes as heavy as my heart.

Need.

My throat tightened at my inner dragon's quiet whimper that echoed the isolation I felt in my soul.

After ten years of searching for my lover, I'd given up hope of his return and had given in to my beastly desires to seek out release elsewhere. I had stuck to females since I would never trust another male who got on his knees for me.

The last woman I had allowed myself to enjoy ended up bruised and exhausted because I'd lost control to my inner beast's darker side. Even though I had left a large monetary gift to cover expenses while she healed from the cane she'd begged me to use, I'd yet to rid myself of the guilt for allowing my dragon to control my human's better sense.

There would be no more rope or pain play to give pleasure, I had told my dragon. No more fragile humans, and definitely no giving into my animalistic desire to conquer and dominate.

Wrapping my inner beast in mental shackles had kept others safe since that affair, but his daily pleadings for release beyond my own hand wore my determination thin.

As far as I was aware, I was the last of my kind. The only

ancient dragonblood with breath in their lungs. And I would die alone, never having scented or seen either of my mates that fate should have supplied for me to keep our kind from extinction.

My dragon snarled at my pessimism, but I'd given up hope after scouring the earth for proof otherwise.

"Enough," I muttered, my tone not allowing him to argue further.

Same as every year, I would wake in the morning, my mind once more set on making the world a better place for humanity since they would outlive the last of the Blood Born.

I turned from the edge of my veranda, intent on the numbness of sleep, my bare feet shuffling along the worn stone patio.

A breeze caressed my cheek like a silken fingertip—and brought with it a scent of sweetness that stirred my blood. The coolness wrapped around my heated, naked body, raising the hairs on my nape and arms and causing my pulse to thrum.

Yessss.

Spinning, I inhaled deeply, sensing the one I had longed for and never expected to find.

Mate.

"Our female," I agreed with my inner beast, elation making my emotions soar higher than my dragon's wings had ever physically taken us.

A rumble sounded in my chest as I once more filled my lungs —my heart and mind—with who she was. All the subtle nuances of her floating on the breeze revealed to my mind exactly as my alpha father had promised would one day occur.

Longer golden hair framed her pale face. Her eyes shimmered between blue and hazel green. I couldn't tell exactly which color and couldn't wait to find out that truth once I pinpointed her location and claimed her.

Lush curves and…muscular?

Eyelids falling closed to better sharpen my focus, I fought to retain the image her scent had brought. Wide, child-bearing hips, yet her thighs and calf muscles spoke of hours in a gym, more like those of a human man.

She would be sturdy enough to endure my dragon's darker desires.

A growl-like groan rose from the deepest recesses of my dragon, but I ignored him, grasping to retain more of what our mate's scent suggested.

My same six-foot-two height?

No.

I frowned, my inner sight hindered by murky, contradicting shadows.

She was not even five and a half feet tall, perfect for me to take her mouth while thrusting deep into her wet heat and breeding her.

Need rushed through my body, awakening hunger I hadn't felt in over a decade.

I often woke from dreams of my ex-lover who'd abandoned me—the intimate touches, the solidarity of two souls sharing themselves with each other in the most primal of ways, even if they would never be truly bonded.

Would I remember how to caress and stroke soft skin if fate gifted me a chance to know real love? Could I taste the musk between her thighs and open myself fully to a connection where no secrets hid? Or if she proved robust enough, might I allow my inner beast his own pleasure atop my human satisfaction?

Yessss.

Mine.

The pain of loving and losing wasn't something I desired

to experience again, but that didn't keep my cock from swelling as my dragon pleaded with me with his usual simplistic words.

Seek.

Take.

I opened my eyes and looked in the direction of the wind that had caressed my face. One of my intended mates lay northeast toward the highest peak. Using my dragon-enhanced sight, I scanned every swell of mountain and valley from my vantage point on my cliff home's veranda, my heart thrumming with growing excitement.

The idea that I wasn't alone, the truth a female of my kind roamed the earth with me, flooded through my soul, weakening my restraint.

Shift and fly.

Find.

Claim.

My dragon's insistence snapped through the shackles I'd mentally used to keep him contained. He threw me off the veranda, and I shifted mid-fall toward the rocks below.

The addictive burn of stretching muscle and bone pumped adrenaline through my system. A single flap of wings black as midnight caught the current along the cliff face, and we shot upward as one in a rush of wind, our pulse rushing and focus on finding what belonged to us.

The scales of our body reflected the sky around us, camouflaging our true form from human sight. If one stared closely enough, they might catch a bend of reality, of light around a creature who had secretly roamed the earth for generations without detection.

If only our ancestors had evolved their form of cloaking earlier, the knights of the medieval age wouldn't have taken us to near extinction. Our alpha father might still be the leader of our kind—we might not be the only dragonblood alive.

We're not *the last of our kind.*

My dragon rarely used full sentences as a means of communication, and my inner human grinned, relaxing as we ascended deeper into the wilderness.

Our gaze flitted from dip and valley to rock and cliff, the memory of our mate's sweet scent teasing us as we rushed through the sky. Mouth open, our tongue dripped saliva in hopes of tasting her on the late summer air once more.

But she escaped us.

The sun set to the west, streaking pink and purple through the sky as we flew high above the White Mountains. We caught sight of countless hikers setting up their camps for the night but none appeared like the vision her scent had brought to us. Nor did we feel the actual physical draw toward the one fate intended for us as my mother had promised I would someday experience.

After darkness fully fell, we returned home, my dragon disheartened and grumbling.

Inky darkness coated the land like a heavy blanket, but I stood in human form at the edge of my veranda. Breathing deeply, I hoped to fill my lungs with the hints of my fated mate's scent once more.

She escaped me still, the same way my ex-lover had done those years I'd searched for him before giving up.

But I wouldn't lose hope with my female. Having tasted her on the breeze, being assured she walked the earth as I did, renewed my dreams from childhood that fate would one day gift me my mates. Exhaustion demanded I rest, but I would continue my search in the morning.

I crawled between my silk sheets, the glide of them over my nakedness reminding me of the softness of another body. Flesh and blood.

My throat tightened. I had been so long without companionship or a gentle touch.

She would be sweet. A kind-hearted soul I would treasure forever. I would lay the world at her feet, give in to her every whim, and she in turn would love me. Remain loyal and never leave my side. My female would only ever know my softer nature. She would never experience the darker desires my dragon often whispered in my brain. She would be my love, and I would be her protector.

Would she enjoy a sweeter coupling? Or would she prefer I thrust into her like my darkness desired—wanting to split her in half, my teeth sunk into her neck? Would she ask for more? Beg me to take her harder?

Need.

I groaned in agreement and wrapped my hand around my hard length with a steely grip. Copious amounts of pre-cum oozed from the crown, slickening my moving palm and fingers. Remembering the hazy images her addictive scent had brought to mind, I continued to stroke myself, my hips lifting to fuck my hand as I imagined her pouty lips parting on a cry of ecstasy. Even without our beta, I would strive to breed her, fill her womb with my seed regardless of the action's futility.

Cum shot from through my aching shaft and coated my chest in thick, sticky ribbons. I groaned with every spurt, my muscles tensing until the fantasy of her sweet body milking my cock drained me dry.

More—need.

"Tomorrow, we will seek and claim," I promised him in a near silent whisper.

My dragon purred his approval.

CHAPTER 2

ELIJAH

For two days, I studied the mountains from the sky and on foot but hadn't located the one I sought. Had fate played an evil trick on me and I imagined our female on the breeze? Was she no more than a figment of my imagination born of heartache and loneliness?

A lazy trail of smoke snaked into the sky, pulling my gaze a couple of miles northeast of my veranda. The setting sun caressed my left cheek as I blinked, bringing into focus the smoke's origin. Two people sat beside the small fire in the far distance, but from the mile or so separating us, I couldn't tell their sexes.

The breeze shifted the trees around me, their rustling leaves hiding my cliffside home from view. I breathed deeply.

A blast of cooler evening air hit my face. Hints of the ancient blood ran in her veins, calling to me, and my pulse thrummed lava-like heat through my body.

Her.

"Our golden goddess," I agreed with a needy growl.

Mine.

I wanted to shift, shredding my jeans and long-sleeve T-shirt, and roar my savage declaration, but she was close enough to hear that I refrained for fear of scaring my precious gem away. Allowing my instincts to control us would be a mistake. I couldn't cause conflict for the female fate intended for me to protect at all costs.

I strode into my house, grabbed a pullover sweatshirt, a small pack, and a couple of water bottles. One of the two hikers out there belonged to me, and I would claim her by night's end as I'd promised my dragon.

My strides ate up the land, the rock and moss beneath my feet a blur as I hastened toward my destiny. Mind racing, my thoughts focused on the mostly-human woman I would soon see. Hints of fall cooled the air but it remained warm enough that being outdoors as the sun set wasn't bothersome. Not that I would have been uncomfortable either way. The dragonblood pumping through my arteries had been born of the earth's core and couldn't be cooled until death claimed my spirit and I soared through the cosmos with the others of my kind.

Less than an hour later, the breeze still at my back, I approached another outcropping perhaps two hundred yards from where I had seen the campfire. I pulled up short as the flickering flames came into view. Its smoke trailed away from me, not allowing my nose a hint of its scent or another tease of my female.

Two blond tousled heads peeked from beneath a double sleeping bag beside the ringless firepit—two writhing bodies in the throes of passion if their movements and moans didn't lie.

Rage roared through me, leaving my animalistic beast incapable of words.

I clenched my teeth, hands fisted at my sides, fighting off the push to shift and take what the human male had no right to touch.

Their erotic dance of two souls already connected held me rapt, arousal lighting a fire within me regardless of my burning jealousy. The female cried out her release, and the male followed with a groan so sensual and fulfilled that my heart stumbled in its beating. Blood rushed into my shaft with a swiftness that left me lightheaded. I palmed my swollen length through my jeans, squeezing away the need to spill my seed inside her. Claim and mark her.

My mate loved another, and he in turn worshiped that which he didn't own.

Another burst of anger from deep within threatened to reveal me, but I managed to keep my aggravation contained. Knees weakening from the inner battle that made my human side despondent, I slumped onto a rock hidden by the growing darkness.

The couple's murmurs reached my ears, however, their words remained indistinct as I fought to accept what I had stumbled upon, what fate had so cruelly dangled in front of me only to snatch away.

Mine.

Take.

Throat aching, I stared at the snuggling humans, my dragon obsessed and insistent in ways I'd never heard before.

The male tossed back the top of their sleeping bag, and the images I'd seen through their obviously combined scent I had tasted on the breeze came into view. Not just her with golden locks and lush curves but his muscular, taller form topped by a mess of similar blond, longer hair, the top portion of which he had pulled back into a ponytail.

He was gorgeous from what I could see, but my treasure stood, drawing my full attention.

My mouth dried at the sight of her.

Her petite frame showcased flawless, pale skin, and her perfectly formed breasts would fill my large palms. A small waist gave way to flared hips and a full backside I wanted to enjoy jiggling as I thrust into her slick heat from behind.

She tugged on her clothes, hiding her desirous body from me as joyous laughter reached across the distance to my straining senses. She smiled at her lover, the adoration in the curve of her lips like a knife to my heart. He caressed her cheek, her hair, his touch gentle on the one I was destined to pamper.

But she'd chosen him—and he held her heart.

Claim!

I ignored the inner growling, self-preservation demanding I contemplate rather than act on instinct as I'd done with my ex-partner. But my show of dominance hadn't kept Dolyn by my side.

Not ours.

I had to agree with my beast's silent voice, his reminder that a mate chosen by convenience rather than fate would eventually lead to heartache as we had experienced.

Would the one truly meant for me even offer a second glance my way? Would the bonding energy between mates draw her to me, steal her from the male she'd given herself to? Mostly human but for the tiniest fraction, would she even recognize the connection between us? Feel the insistent need to claim me in return?

An ache radiated through my chest. My dragon and I had barely survived when our ex-partner had left. The beast had nearly burned our home in the mountains to mere ash in his sorrow. How much more pain would being denied our *true* mate inflict?

Torn, I slumped where I sat, unmoving and watching as the two humans prepared a late dinner, their movements in sync as though they had spent centuries together even though they only appeared to be twenty-something. I listened to their indistinct words, their laughter. I studied them as the man banked the fire, and they both crawled inside their sleeping bag a short while later.

I swallowed my pain and jealousy as they curled together, two warm bodies intertwined, intimately sharing space as lovers did.

My dragon moaned his displeasure throughout the long night while I sat in silence, contemplating the situation I found myself in. I ought to leave, take us far from sure grief, but I couldn't bear to abandon her. Every cell in my body longed for my female mate, and had I been a younger, immature dragon shifter, I would have stolen her without a care for either her or her partner's feelings as many of my kind had done in centuries past.

But, how could I inflict on the human male the same pain I had lived with for a decade? The suffering, the loneliness of losing the one you shared your life with? I hadn't been offered a choice—my lover had left without allowing me the opportunity to beg him to stay.

I refused to do the same to another, but by the time the sun rose, my tortured mind needed *something* to appease both parts of my soul.

Resolution at the very least.

My dragon grumbled like a petulant child, but I held full control over his instinctive impulses to take without thought of another's heart.

As her alpha, it was my duty to protect her, emotions included. I would give her the chance to choose the mate she should be with or the one she had already attached herself to. It would be *her* decision as it ought to be, the male's broken heart her doing, rather than mine.

Weak.

My teeth gritted at my dragon's claim. Empathy was anything *but* a downfall. I'd become a better man because of my own misery.

Coercion is the only way.

I refused to bow down to his fears that also gripped my guts. We would show restraint and caution as always, allowing destiny to steer us toward a *real* bond that would last, unlike a forced one. Pulse racing and palms damp, I drew closer on silent feet, the delicious aroma of a mere hint of ancient blood in the air flooding my mouth with saliva. I could taste her sweetness on my tongue from a hundred yards away.

A low growl rumbled my chest, and I swallowed to silence my beast.

What would it be like once I closed the distance between us and touched her hand in greeting? Would energy crackle between our bodies or pull like a magnet enough to sway my mate into my arms?

Force.

"There will be *no* forced bonding," I whispered fiercely, demanding my dragon submit to my human side.

I was well aware being a Blood Born allowed me a way to make our female submit regardless of her hesitations. I'd promised my three parents I would be patient as they'd been with one another rather than manipulating as our kind had done in the past out of fear of our dwindling numbers.

Through all my years, I never believed in any god or higher being, but at that moment, I wished to trust in something bigger, something more than mere chance that my mate would want and accept me as her alpha on her own.

The closer I walked toward the couple, the intensity of the draw shifted to near impossible to resist. With every step, I cared less about the human man's heartache should my female mate choose the one she'd been destined for.

Those binds on my inner beast weakened as he strained forward.

Mine.

"Yes," I murmured my agreement, allowing him equal rein over our human form so his senses could at least enjoy her as I would in the coming moments. Shouldering the small pack I'd brought along to make it appear I hiked the mountain trail as the couple did, I moved into sight of their camp, my strides evident of my resolution on having what belonged to us.

The male squatted beside the fire, putting a small pot over the red coals, his pants stretched tight over thick thighs and a plump, peach-like ass made for plundering. My fingers itched to map out his backside.

I swallowed against the sudden desire for him, my pulse thrumming hot through me. "Hello," I called out, not wishing to frighten him.

His blond head jerked up, and he slowly stood, his blue-eyed gaze meeting mine.

Energy rippled like waves across the short distance separating us and wrapped around my body in a connection stronger than any I'd ever felt in my long life.

I stumbled to a stop as my heart slammed inside my chest, ripping the oxygen from my lungs.

Yessss.

My dragon purred his intense pleasure that flooded through my soul.

Our beta.

I fought to breathe, to accept what fate had gifted me after years of loneliness. The two humans were a bonded pair with ancient blood, in need of their alpha.

And I would find a way to claim them *both* exactly as my inner beast demanded.

CHAPTER 3
JONATHAN

The man standing at the edge of our camp held me captive like a deer in headlights. Couldn't take my damn stare off him. He had inky black hair and eyes so pale I couldn't discern their color. Wide shoulders and arms, even with the dark gray sweatshirt encasing them, hinted at muscles twice what I'd managed to build—and I wasn't exactly a skinny little shit.

His hello had caused goose bumps to ripple across my skin, some sort of inner buzzing like a light switch about to short circuit inside me.

Something about the stranger…excited me?

I couldn't quite figure it out, but the man exuded energy like a tractor beam, making me want to close the distance between us. Fall to my knees—

I blinked, shaking my head. That couldn't be right. I'd never been attracted to a man, but I couldn't deny the lust shooting through my balls.

Unable to find my voice, I dipped my head in greeting.

He took a few hesitant steps and paused less than ten feet

away from me. "Sorry to intrude," he said, his voice a deep bass, the kind women swooned over.

My legs went weak as visions of crawling toward him flooded my brain.

Frowning and locking my entire body up tight, I cleared my throat. "National forest is free to everyone."

His gaze flitted down over me as if sizing up all six-foot-two of me.

I should have been wary, my usual cynical self. Should have been on edge, but nothing about the stranger or the images flashing through my mind threatened me. I'd always been pretty good at reading people, and even though the man could probably bench press five hundred pounds, his demeanor or stance didn't appear alarming.

His pale eyes sat deep beneath thick brows. A thin, yet strong nose overlooked full lips, and a few days' worth of stubble covered his jawline. He was the type of pretty face found on a runway model, yet rugged enough to enter the World's Strongest Man competition.

Talk about intimidating—and hot as fuck. Even my straight ass couldn't deny that fact.

What human *wouldn't* want to be his sex slave?

We stared at each other for a full minute, neither of us moving. His nostrils flared a few times as though breathing the late summer air deep into his lungs, bracing himself for something. I swore his body heat emanated over the short distance between us, licking at my scruffy face and bare arms, causing goose bumps to rise along my skin.

Dakota's familiar humming traveled my way as she rounded the boulders she had gone to squat behind, and I tore my attention off the stranger to glance over my shoulder. Head down and rearranging her long-sleeve T-shirt over her leggings, my wife approached.

"Hey, Jon," she said, lifting her head, "did you—" She

pulled up short, her jaw snapping shut as her gaze landed on our visitor. Her pupils dilated, and the pulse in her neck I loved to see throb heightened. Even her nipples tightened into luscious buds. She stared at him, totally enthralled with a man like she'd only been twice in the years I'd known her. Once, when our eyes had first met, and the other with the blond douche who'd been the reason we'd broken up for a short time.

I tensed, waiting for jealousy to knife me in the gut, but nothing stirred, not even a hint. Instead, I understood her reaction to the dark man…there was no denying the warmth of want tingling in my own groin because of his close proximity.

Dakota crossed her arms over her unbound breasts and, blinking, turned her focus on me, gaze troubled. She waited for me to throw a nutty, get all caught up in my head over her looking at someone other than me with even a hint of interest.

But I did. Not. Care.

"This is…uh…" I turned back around toward the monstrous man, one eyebrow raised, my insides a swarm of *what the fuck*.

"Elijah Tolzman." He stuck his hand out.

My feet moved me forward as though he held me on his fishing line and reeled me in. "Jonathan Ebel."

Our palms meshed together with a slow glide, sending a buzzing jolt up my arm and straight down to my dick. I'd expected a battle of the manly squeeze, but he merely clasped his long fingers around mine in a firm but seemingly intimate shake.

Another fantasy lit in vivid color inside my mind from his touch but with darker tones…chains and cuffs. Pain with pleasure.

Lust radiated from my palm to my cock, and I swallowed

hard against the sudden lack of moisture in my mouth. Since when did that shit turn me on?

"Nice to meet you," he said, his low voice sending another bout of shivers across my flesh. His pale eyes—blue as a crisp winter day—skittered over my face as though searching out my thoughts, desperate for them even.

Although he'd clearly been surprised by *something* at first eye contact with me, the stranger had shut down all emotion on his face except for his inquisitive gaze that caused my body to want to drown in pleasure.

Dakota stepped forward, startling me back to reality.

I tugged my hand away from Elijah's, remembering that this man and I weren't alone. How the fuck he'd managed to make me even briefly forget the love of my life, I had no clue.

"My wife, Dakota," I rasped, putting my hand on her lower back, suddenly feeling the need to physically connect with her and let him know she belonged to me. Or perhaps I needed a reminder that *I* belonged to *her*.

"Wife." A frown flitted over Elijah's brow, so quick I thought maybe I imagined it. "A pleasure," he murmured with a slight nod but didn't offer her his hand.

Dakota's lips parted as she stared at him.

A sensual smile curved his lips as he studied her wind and sunburned face.

I rubbed my fingertips along her spine, and she glanced up at me, her greenish eyes unsure and hesitant as though fighting off her desire to continue drinking in the dark stranger.

Smiling down at the love of my life came easy when I should have been annoyed as fuck she'd been checking him out. I offered her reassurance while my footing teetered on what felt like the edge of a cliff. She had been mine since the seventh grade. My one and only, and three months earlier, she had vowed before a Justice of the Peace to love me in sickness and in health, in good times and bad—and bad they had been ever since.

We had planned a honeymoon in the Bahamas so she could search for the mermaids she wished existed in real life rather than just the fantasy books she read, but I'd been dismissed from my job mere days after we'd gotten hitched. Definitely not for a lack of work ethic or having been found at fault of jack shit.

My only friend outside Dakota had trusted me with being in charge designing software for a start-up company we'd dreamed to fruition and he'd financed.

He'd been a goddamned flirt, but I'd ignored my inner voice suggesting I put space between the three of us because he signed my paychecks. That poor choice led to my demise when he'd approached me about a threesome without Dakota's knowledge. I denied him even though we'd shared just about everything else, and he'd sent me packing the next day via a certified letter, dismissing me from his company.

The lessons I'd learned?

One, trust my instincts. Second, rich and powerful men took advantage of anyone and everything to get what they wanted. And finally, never start a new job without clearly lined expectations and a goddamned contract.

But Dakota didn't know the real reason behind my being fired, and I wasn't about to tell her the truth of why we struggled to make ends meet. All due to trusting the wrong fucking guy.

Finding work since then had proven impossible, and were it not for her support and love, I probably would have jumped off a bridge over my inability to provide for her. All because I couldn't stand the thought of anyone having a sampling of what had been mine since childhood.

She was the one good thing I had to my name, and I

wasn't going to open a can of worms by allowing a third person's lust to tear us apart.

My friend had claimed he simply wanted to fuck, but I knew better. One taste of Dakota, and he would have been addicted for life, same as I was. Her nurturing spirit was calming, her beauty breathtaking, and her sweetness impossible to ignore.

Dakota Ebel was craving personified.

"W-would you care to join us for breakfast?" Dakota asked, pulling me back to the present, her breathless tone betraying her unrest and arousal that should have had me raging with jealousy.

"I'm sure he's just passing through," I said at the same time his low, rumbled "I would love to" pebbled my arms again.

Dakota's smile didn't reach her hazel-green eyes as she slipped her hand into mine with a tight squeeze of reassurance. She peered up at me in question as though seeking my direction as she often did before making decisions, and being the sap that I was, I nodded.

Did she not know by now that I would give her anything she wanted, everything I could?

"Join us," I echoed her invite without looking at the stranger, my words easing the tension on my wife's face. "Please."

"We're just having instant oatmeal and some dried fruit," Dakota said, bending to rummage in my pack and putting her ass on display.

In my peripheral vision, I caught Elijah enjoying the view too.

Again with the lack of jealousy slithering through my guts, but I forced a frown and cleared my throat, feeling the need to show who the alpha was on the small, treeless hill we'd camped upon.

Elijah's focus flitted to my face. An intensity resided in his gaze, like an ancient wise one who could read souls and futures. The power in those unsettling orbs wasn't something new to me. I'd been too fond of fortune tellers in my younger years before responsibilities had settled in.

One palm reader had called me a beast, curiosity in her watery eyes as she'd peered at me.

Another had stated an aura of blue like she'd never seen wrapped me tight in its embrace, one she claimed would be covered by a much darker one. She hadn't been able to tell me what the vision had meant.

My foster mother, who'd been sitting beside me at the time, had laughed at the woman's words, but Dakota hadn't when I'd told her the next day at school. She'd been filling her mind full of fairytales about shape-shifters and elves long before I'd met her. She had also insisted she had a sixth sense about some people, and I hadn't made fun of her when she said she felt as though she ought to know something about someone but couldn't figure it out. Like a hazy picture in her mind, no matter how hard she focused on certain people, she couldn't discern whatever it was that teased her brain.

Even though her wandering eyes had never been anything sexual, it was that draw to other people that pissed me the fuck off. Dakota belonged to me and no one else. I even hated sharing her friendship. Call me an obsessed, possessive asshole, but I couldn't help myself.

When we were twenty, some douche had pulled her focus off me when I'd been mid-sentence about something I couldn't even remember now. She'd followed after him like he had her on a leash, and I'd gotten jealous as fuck. Once I'd caught up, my instincts demanded she stay away from him since that magical bullshit sixth sense she claimed made her spine tingle didn't actually exist, and I'd said as much. Our public fight ended in a breakup that had me ready to take my own life. We'd managed to talk through it a few days later after I'd calmed down, but I knew she still suffered from guilt when her gaze strayed on occasion.

Sometimes, I caught her doing a double take on a person on the street, her eyes narrowed, gaze thoughtful, but she never spoke of whatever she supposedly sensed anymore. I swallowed down my jealousy each and every time because I refused to make her feel like shit again even if no one had captured her attention like that guy had. She'd taken snapshots on her camera of all of the people she had a weird draw to except him, which I really would have hated. Dozens of pictures sat on her laptop, her "strange" file of random people who she claimed meant nothing to her but she felt connected to.

I would be fine as long as they stayed in pixel form and didn't come between us physically.

Like I imagined Elijah Tolzman doing.

Older and no longer a fan of the fantastical, I never wasted money on fortunes or palm readers, but the man intruding on our breakfast peered at me in a way that made me want to ask if he could see the future I'd always dreamed of. Plenty of money to allow Dakota a life of luxury, even if she claimed to not want it. All the babies she desired to fulfill her dream of having a real family with children who grew up with unconditional love and acceptance like neither of us had. Enough of a cushion that should I ever lose my income again, we wouldn't have to worry about the electricity being turned off in our one-room apartment. Cash on hand so dinner would be more than boxed mac and cheese—even if we both loved that shit.

Dakota stood, making me the one to break Elijah's stare.

She handed me the oatmeal packets and one of the tin coffee mugs we'd already used and cleaned, her attention flitting toward our guest like he was a train wreck she couldn't look away from. I recognized her curiosity and wondered how badly her fingers itched to pull out her camera and capture him from every angle.

Why the fuck didn't I *care*?

Turning my back on both of them, I hunched back down, emptying the oatmeal packets into the two bowls and coffee mug.

We'd been hiking for a mere four days, and I'd about had it with the camp food. Jerky, tuna packets, and beef stew made up the bulk of our meals, supplemented with dried fruit and whole-grain wraps that tasted like cardboard. I was so damn ready for a bloody steak and a fluffy baked potato, loaded with all the good stuff.

"So where are you from?" Dakota asked, sitting cross-legged on the ground beside where I squatted. She'd tugged on a sweatshirt, big enough to hide her braless, aroused state.

Elijah sat on my other side, his closeness warmer than the bed of coals in front of me. Something inside me felt that tug again, the need to sit at his feet and hope he gifted me a soft word or strong hand.

The fuck?

I blinked hard, erasing the picture from my mind.

"My home is just shy of two miles in that direction," Elijah said, pointing toward the southeast as his scent rolled over me. He smelled of fire and brimstone, spice and sex.

I stretched my neck side to side, fighting off the strange lust stiffening my dick, even though I wasn't exactly disturbed by the attraction I felt for him. Last thing I needed was to come untouched in my boxers. That would make for one hell of an awkward situation since I wasn't exactly quiet when busting a nut.

"I didn't think anyone lived around here," Dakota said, a smile in her voice. "Your own Castle in the Clouds like that mansion down in Moultonborough?"

"Something like that." That sensual smile played on Elijah's lips again, and I focused on pouring boiling water over the dry oatmeal, wondering why the hell I didn't care that he looked at my wife like he wanted to lick her from mouth to toes.

I handed Elijah one of the steaming bowls and a spoon while shoving my bitterness deep and attempting to not salivate over the man.

"Thank you." Elijah's full-on smile weakened my knees, and I sat with about as much grace as a two-year-old on ice skates.

At least I didn't spill my cup of maple and brown sugar oatmeal. Yay?

Dakota shifted so our legs pressed together. Her usual affection or a silent assurance of her faithfulness, I didn't know. Either way, I appreciated the action because my brain and body didn't know up from down.

"Just out for a stroll?" I asked and spooned up a mass of the grossest breakfast food on the face of the planet.

"Something like that," Elijah echoed himself, his voice softer with a hint of the smile lingering on his perfectly formed lips above a soul patch.

I ought to be suspicious of his lack of a real answer, but my usual caution had gone into hibernation or some such shit. What about the dark stranger made me comfortable over being sexually attracted to another guy? I shouldn't trust the man, but something inside me *wanted* to.

Fucking yearned for it so damn hard I swore I'd fallen into an alternate reality.

I tore my gaze off the dude's face and shoved the too-hot oats into my mouth. The burned tongue at least kept my twitching dick from swelling to the point of needing my hand.

Seriously. What the fuck was wrong with me?

Dakota was all I had ever wanted. Hell, I'd never even thought about another woman that way—let alone a masculine guy who would look fucking fantastic decked out in black leather and a harness.

I shook my head, blinking that image from my mind too.

From the first time I'd seen Dakota in middle school, I'd known she belonged to me and I to her. Like magnets, we had drawn each other in, and tearing apart at the end of every school day had been painful for me.

I found out later it had felt the same for her.

The first time we'd kissed, the longing for happiness that had haunted me every day faded as true joy flooded through me from the gentle brush of her lips and the sweet taste of her breath. And when we'd finally had sex? We had only been sixteen, but the stars had aligned, the off-its-axis world of my foster parent's home righted.

I'd found heaven and a different kind of magic buried deep inside Dakota's wet warmth.

It would be another two years before I could light out from where I'd spent my childhood filled with verbal and emotional abuse. An eternity of being told I was a worthless piece of shit, daily reminders that I was unloved and unwanted by the people who had created my sorry ass.

Whoever the hell they were.

I had no desire to find my real parents. They hadn't wanted me, so why the fuck would I go looking for them?

Like me, Dakota had grown up in a foster home, clueless as to her parentage and desirous of a husband and a bunch of kids to love. But at least she'd been lucky in having foster parents who'd nurtured and cared for her.

We were peas and carrots, just like Forrest Gump had claimed of him and Jenny, but so far, we hadn't been able to get pregnant. The push for that had ended when I'd been fired since I couldn't provide for the two of us let alone a third little human. We'd discussed IVF, but that plan got shot to shit when I'd lost my income. Even though my swimmers had failed for the previous handful of years in giving my wife what she wanted. Dakota had gotten an IUD to ensure didn't have a kid at an inopportune time.

"Are you heading toward Mount Washington?" Elijah asked, and I glanced over at Dakota rather than laying eyes on the man who made me question who and what the fuck I was.

The trip had been my wife's idea, and we'd been walking our feet sore up and down mountains I couldn't remember the names of. Washington, though, that had been one hell of a sight.

"We've been there already," she answered him.

"Back to civilization then," Elijah said, deducing we headed out of the mountains toward the south.

"I wouldn't mind getting lost up here." The longing in Dakota's voice, her eyes glowing with desire, made her even more beautiful to me.

My heart ached to hold her, protect and give her an easy life. Everything her heart desired.

Disappearing from the woes of reality sounded fine by me—if we'd been somewhere closer to the equator. A warmer location than where we'd been trekking the last couple of days. But Dakota loved the mountains. Who was I to say no?

If it lay within my power, everything Dakota wished for would be placed at her feet. She was my reason for living, after all, and no way in fuck would I ever allow someone to wreck the life we'd built together.

Even if the stranger led my thoughts down a dark, delicious-looking path I'd never dreamed of walking.

CHAPTER 4

DAKOTA

Need burned in my core, a desperate yearning for the man sharing our fire and breakfast. His presence was a magical cinch on every atom in my body, attempting to pull me closer from where I'd firmly planted myself at my husband's side.

A live wire of tension between Jon and Elijah sizzled and snapped in the open air as well, but I couldn't tell where it stemmed from.

Lust or jealousy?

Jon was straight, so I feared the latter as the minutes slid past and my unrest continued.

I hadn't been able to hide the instant connection I'd felt with Elijah like I would sometimes experience with complete strangers. That unvoiced whisper through my thoughts promised I knew him from a different reality. Or, rather, something about him hid from my mind like a fuzzy pane of glass when I tried to figure it out.

Years ago, a similar but not nearly as potent a situation as this had caused Jon's and my one serious fight that had left both of us brokenhearted. But the draw toward Elijah was a hundred times more insistent—and sexual in nature unlike the others' images I'd captured and stored on my laptop.

An all-consuming need owned my body to explore whatever it was that connected us on a different plane than anything I'd felt for a stranger before. My body urged—*begged*—to touch and taste. Become one with him emotionally and physically as I'd only ever done with my husband.

Jon had noticed my reaction. He could read me like an open book, always had, and he was well aware of my obsession with all things supernatural. Paranormal books lived rent free in my head. Daydreamer didn't begin to describe my state of mind most days.

I trusted Jon to be my protector in the real world. I always deferred to him to keep me safe since he was critical and careful in making choices while my head floated in the clouds. In my imagination, I was secretly a fierce creature rather than needy and insecure, a woman who didn't second-guess herself at every turn.

If only that other half of me existed in real life.

Even though Jon didn't appear angry or shift away from where our thighs touched, guilt like I hadn't experienced in years twisted my stomach. My body's reaction to the pale-eyed stranger must have hurt Jon, and like an idiot, I'd invited Elijah to stay for breakfast without thinking it through beyond my desire to feed and care for a guest.

I'd promised Jon all those years ago when my sixth sense nearly ended us to never hurt him again. That he was my one and only, forever and always. Jon was my reason for living and had been since we were young. There had never been a doubt in my mind that we were meant to be together. Best friends as children, we'd bonded by our similar home life, but we became so much more as we had grown into adulthood. Our bodies changed at the same time, mine much later than most girls. A late bloomer but perfectly in tune with Jon's squeaky voice and filling out.

I hadn't ever considered touching another man, hadn't ever *desired* anyone else in that way until the crystalline blue eyes of Elijah Tolzman met mine. My blood roused like I read about almost nightly on my e-reader. Unnatural, unquenchable desire even more than I felt for my husband flooded through me and refused to lessen as we ate.

The yearning to draw closer to the man disrupted more than just our peaceful hike through the White Mountains. He'd brought an unrest deep in my soul I couldn't categorize in my head. And although Jon had always been the one I trusted with my emotional well-being, I feared my need of his direction in that moment. Knowing how Elijah made me feel would prickle Jon's insecurities that stemmed from his never measuring up to the expectations his foster parents had put on him.

But what could I do other than defer to Jon's leadership?

I would find a way to squash the stirrings inside me.

Had to. Then Elijah would leave, and Jon and I could move forward in the life we attempted to build together.

My eyes strayed to the one who'd disrupted our peace.

Elijah was the opposite of Jon, bulky with muscles compared to the lithe, swimmer-like body I'd had wrapped around me all night in our warm sleeping bag. An alpha, rugged mountain man aura surrounded Elijah although his carefully groomed facial hair and the styled hair atop his head suggested refinement. He spoke with clarity, enunciating every word, his manners impeccable even though we sat on the ground beside a campfire. If I truly believed in time travel as I did magical creatures roaming the earth among humanity, I'd swear the man had been born and raised a century or two earlier.

I wanted to capture his beautiful face from every angle,

stolen images for me to ponder on as I often did over my laptop's strange folder in attempts to figure out why I felt drawn to complete strangers.

Not a single one of them had ever tipped my life sideways as Elijah had done though, not even that man from the streets of New York.

I sat on uneven ground in a figurative sense, fearing leaning fully one way or another would send me tumbling into an abyss. While the unknown caused my heart to race with sweet anticipation, dread of what awaited me through the fog clouding my future tightened my chest.

I continued to brush against Jon with my usual affection, seeking assurance. I also hoped he took comfort in my nearness, but he seemed intent on Elijah rather than focused on the jealousy that must burn in his stomach.

My eyes stung over my body's betrayal of my one true love.

How long would Jon be disappointed in me? Would I be given the chance to prove myself to him? Assure him of the faithfulness I'd pledged to him not that long ago before the Justice of the Peace that had declared us husband and wife?

Regardless of the tension among Elijah, Jon, and I, we remained social, Jon more gracious than I'd expected. Casual conversation flowed, all surface stuff that held no meaning beyond passing the time until we went our separate ways.

Hopefully sooner than later.

The three of us discussed the peaks Jon and I had climbed and the ones I still wanted to see and take pictures of. The White Mountains had always felt like home even though we'd both been born in upstate New York, and as with everything, Jon agreed to do what I wanted when it became clear we had to cancel our trip to Bermuda.

But would he forgive me this time since I'd gone *way* beyond my usual unusual interest in strangers?

I fought off tears all through our shared breakfast while faking a smile, my body and mind at war over arousal I couldn't stop. Soaked panties clung to my pussy, my nipples tight and aching because of one dark stranger whose presence tempted me to be unfaithful to the man I trusted to be my partner until death parted us.

The crisp morning air hinted at an approaching storm like the one raging inside me. The dark clouds crept toward us from the southwest and trailhead where we'd parked our old car for the week, matching my mood and unsettled emotions I fought to keep contained.

Elijah glanced at the horizon then at the double sleeping bag Jon and I had slept in the night before after stargazing while enjoying our usual pillow talk. "Do you have a tent?" he asked.

I squeezed my thighs together against the desire his voice incited like an alpha in one of my shifter romance books.

Me and my damned fanciful mind.

"Yeah we do," Jon replied, tucking an escaped strand of hair behind his ear, "but you know what they say, 'If you don't like the weather here in New England—'"

"—wait a minute." Elijah finished with a smile, his attention still on the approaching clouds as though he too was wary of what they might bring. "The storm was forecasted to pass south of us, but that appears not to be the case. And, with the flash flooding and dangerous winds they said would accompany the storm..."

"Maybe we ought to hike out of here," I said, setting my scraped-clean bowl aside, my feet itching to move.

Toward Elijah.

No.

Away from him, hand in hand with Jon who owned my heart.

My mind felt torn in two, my body doubly so. Eyes stinging, I stared at Elijah, wishing I could name what it was that drew me to him.

"You'll be soaked long before making it back to civilization, regardless of what trails you take," he said, his gaze on Jon, thank goodness, because I wouldn't be able to deny him if he looked at me with the same desire as he did my husband.

Jon shrugged as though unaffected by Elijah's blatant hungry stare, but I noted the tension in his shoulders and the tightness bracketing his lips. "Can't be helped."

"My house is a short distance away," Elijah reminded us. "You're welcome to wait out the bad weather there."

Jon scanned the mountains and rocks around us as my pulse thrummed at the thought of spending more time with Elijah. Nothing good could come from it even though my body begged otherwise.

"You really have a place in these mountains?" Jon asked. "I thought this was a national forest."

"It is, but my ancestors lived here long before the government made this protected land. We're the ones who sold most of it to them, in fact." Elijah spoke without any hint of bragging in his voice. "I'm the last of my line and have been able to keep the retained land in seclusion by a private road that I keep gated."

"What do you do in the winter?" Jon asked.

"Helicopter when the weather isn't too bad, Humvee when it is."

"You have power all the way out here?"

"Being off-grid these days is easier than most think," Elijah said, pushing up to his feet.

I tore my needy gaze off him and glanced over at Jon, who had tilted his head back to look at the man standing over us in a show of dominance that wasn't as threatening as it ought to be.

A flicker of something I couldn't name passed over Jon's face, but it was far from trepidation or even anger. He'd claimed to be straight as long as I'd known him, but...

I glanced down.

Jon was hard, a wet spot at the clear outline of his swollen cockhead firmly pressed against his jeans.

Swallowing a gasp, I couldn't help the pulse that clenched my pussy, causing an ache to radiate through my core.

"Want to take him up on his offer?" Jon asked me even though his gaze fixed on Elijah as though he was unable to tear his eyes off the man.

Mouth dry, I attempted to swallow and failed.

My gaze collided with Elijah's atop Jon's head, the moisture in my body pooling between my thighs at the barely restrained primal urge to claim residing in his eyes.

Fantasy. Not real, I told myself firmly even though my inner voice shook in time with the jitters inside my belly.

The man could prove to be a danger to my marriage if I didn't get my head screwed on properly. Forcing my eyes downward, I slipped my hand into Jon's.

"It's up to you," I managed to whisper, leaving the decision to him as I always did since I refused to be responsible for causing heartache again.

My husband finally turned his focus on me, studying my face. Did he see the war raging inside me? My fearful hesitation and hungry desire to say yes? Did he notice both?

Blue eyes, darker than Elijah's but no less potent in intensity, peered into mine. The world slowly faded around us as I wove myself in the cocoon of the comfort Jon and I had shared for as long as I could remember. I found myself smiling as I always did when drowning in Jon's love.

His unexpected double-dimpled smile made my shoulders relax even though sexual tension and energy lay heavy over our camp. There was no way in hell Jon would gift me that grin if he'd been jealous.

"Let's go." Jon squeezed my hand and stood, pulling me up beside him.

My heart thumping at the prospect of spending more time with the alpha god who had snuck up on us, I rolled our sleeping bag with shaking hands while Jon put out the fire. In five minutes, we started southward behind Elijah, his wide shoulders and sure strides leading us forward.

We didn't follow a trail, but I didn't sense any wariness from Jon who walked behind me.

"You've lived out here your whole life?" Jon asked as I fought to keep my focus on the ground rather than the flexing ass encased in jeans ahead of me.

"Yes. I've explored every inch of this forest and these peaks." Elijah swept his hand from east to west.

Thunder rumbled in the distance, and Elijah turned his head slightly, allowing me a glimpse of his strong profile. The straight nose, the full lips, and that sexy as hell soul patch beneath the lower I wanted to lick and capture on camera called to me on a deep level.

I shook my head against the otherworldly urge to crowd closer to his energy and focused on picking my way over rocks and tree roots.

Unease should have prickled the hairs on my neck over a complete stranger in the middle of government land claiming to have a house close by and offering to shelter us from a storm. My mind should have gone to what anyone would have thought—the guy must be a psycho mass murderer, luring us into his lair where he would chain us up, torture us...

Lust slickened the inside of my panties in a fresh drench of arousal rather than fear curdling my stomach. I bit on my lower lip to keep a moan contained.

What the actual *hell*?

Had Elijah put a spell on us? Drugged my libido with pheromones to lure unsuspecting victims like my sexy book boyfriends in the paranormal romance books I devoured?

Jon appreciated the aftereffects of my losing myself in stories, but that was *fantasy.*

Shivers wracked my body regardless of the truth, causing goose bumps to erupt over my skin.

Make-believe, I told myself yet again, focusing on Elijah's tight ass. He was nothing but a hot guy with empathy for strangers in his mountains. A kind man who wouldn't hurt a fly even though the muscle mass barely contained by his tight hoodie suggested he could take on a dozen Jons and still be standing—alone—when the smoke cleared.

The wind intensified as we descended a steep slope, neither of us hesitating to follow Elijah. We headed westward through a valley, sprinkles falling from the dark sky and dampening our clothing. A well-worn path with man-made rock steps once more took us higher into the mountain.

I pulled up abruptly as a stone patio opened in front of us. A wall of glass, sliding doors and reflective windows lay beyond, reaching up the rock face.

My jaw dropped.

Elijah's house was actually a cave. A gorgeous, what must have cost *millions* to create, house in the side of a mountain one would miss unless they'd taken the exact path we had. His home was like something out of Middle Earth but much bigger than anything a hobbit would need.

I couldn't see through the dark glass, and as my head tilted back, my gaze scanning the rock cliff, I noted a few other windows set in stone, a couple with small wrought-iron balconies attached.

"Holy shit," Jon said from behind me, echoing my exact thought.

I murmured a similar sentiment, eyes wide and still drinking in the striking beauty that promised safety and comfort regardless of being crafted from cold stone.

Elijah moved toward one of the sliders. Atop, etched in granite, lay writing unlike anything I'd ever seen.

"Welcome," he said, sliding one door open and revealing a sunken living room and dimly lit kitchen beyond. A classical tune played softly from somewhere inside, strings filled with sadness. The notes stroked over my emotions, thickening my throat.

I stumbled forward without hesitation, unable to withstand the draw of that imaginary cinch between me and Elijah, Jon close on my heels.

Rather than reaching for me as I half-expected, our host stepped back, allowing us entry.

I stepped into dry warmth that carried Elijah's alluring scent that hinted of fire and a sweet spice similar to cinnamon. My feet abruptly halted, jaw dropping while gazing at the high rock ceiling and the cut-in-stone stairs winding up the right side of the massive cavern. Two stairs directly ahead led down into the living room with its massive fireplace on the far wall.

"Sybil, music off," Elijah said from behind my left, and immediately, the haunting melody cut out, leaving us in near silence.

"Your home is beautiful," I said, my gaze flitting to the kitchen with its top-end appliances and vast counter space.

"Thank you." Elijah whispered words close to my ear, and I shivered as he grasped my backpack. "May I?"

I turned my head, our gazes colliding.

His pale eyes appeared to glow in the dim light coming

from who the hell knew where. My breath hitched, my pulse once more thrumming over his nearness.

Swallowing, I nodded and shrugged the straps off my arms, my focus flitting behind me to Jon, who pulled the slider shut while watching Elijah's every move.

Rather than scowling, he stared at our host with blatant hunger on his face I was well acquainted with.

The closeness of the three of us made itself known when I realized I could feel the heat of both of their bodies.

I should have been itching to run, insisting on leaving this strangeness that had tilted my world off its axis, but nothing about Elijah or his home raised internal alarms. That undeniable energy among us hummed through me with a deeper, richer intensity than when he'd first arrived in our camp. But it went far beyond mere lust for physical satisfaction, more along the lines of a sense of comfort, evoking a feeling of...

Home.

The word caressed my mind, and I studied the man who'd always been that for me.

Jon stood at complete ease as though unthreatened by Elijah and our surroundings. That hint of tension from his shoulders and mouth had vanished as they stared at each other.

Did he experience the same feelings of finding our place as I did? Why hadn't our tiny apartment in New York ever offered us the same?

My husband blinked as though waking from a trance and turned toward me with a smile, bumping my elbow with his own. "Hell of a lot better than trudging through the rain, huh?"

I attempted a smile in response that wobbled. "Definitely."

Jon slipped off his own pack but held it in his hands when Elijah didn't set mine down.

"Come." Elijah motioned toward the stairs with his free hand while moving away from us.

I was easily urged to follow his command—do whatever the hell he demanded.

"I'll show you to a guest room where you can shower. Would either of you care for coffee? Tea?" he asked, leading the way toward the winding stairs.

Same as down the mountain, Jon followed on my heels.

"Real coffee?" Jon asked.

"Freshly ground beans and French press real," Elijah replied with a light chuckle while climbing the stone risers.

"Thank fuck, and yes, please."

I laughed at Jon's mutter. He'd been full of complaints over the instant "shit" he had been sipping every morning on the trail. The man loved his coffee, piping hot and black as sin.

A hallway opened ahead of us, wide enough we could walk side by side without bumping. An occasional section of rock wall jutted out, man-made with stones so snugly stacked together I couldn't find a trace of mortar. I trailed my fingers over the strangely warm granite, realizing the overhead lights brightened as we approached and faded to dim behind us.

Maybe we *had* fallen into Middle Earth somehow, I mused rather than focusing on the fact a mountain rose above us. The ancient cave should have constricted my lungs, but fresh air filled the space, the high ceilings keeping my usual claustrophobia at bay. Rather than feeling closed in, I experienced tranquility seeping into my bones regardless of the continuing fire-like passion Elijah's presence had awoken inside me.

He opened one of the massive oaken doors lining the rock wall and motioned us inside. "This will be your room for the duration of your stay," he said, his low rumbling voice like a hot tongue lapping at my swollen, aching clit.

I squeezed my thighs together.

"There is a full bathroom to your right," he continued, unaware of how deeply he affected my body.

A glass slider ahead let in a bit of natural light as rain slashed against it. One of the balconies I'd noticed from the veranda lay outside with its wrought iron rail. Lightning flashed across the sky beyond.

A similar storm continued to rage inside me, a desperate need for release.

"Just in time," Jon said, setting his backpack on the floor.

Dangling lights slowly brightened as though welcoming guests but not by a dimmer switch. I glanced back at Elijah who stood by the door with his hands clasped in front of him.

A gentle smile lifted his full lips, hardening my nipples to tight points even my sweatshirt couldn't hide.

I tore my gaze off him and glanced around, taking in the wonder of his ridiculously crazy home that was just as alluring as he was. The rock ceiling soared overhead. A huge bed lay on the left, a small, antique bench at its foot. Two bureaus sat against one wall, thick throw rugs bracketed the bed's frame, and an open door on the right beckoned me.

I moved across the room, all too aware of Elijah's gaze on me, and paused in the doorway. The bathroom dwarfed our entire one-room apartment. It contained a large sunken bathtub, double sinks, and a shower big enough for three.

A shiver licked down my spine at the image of Elijah, Jon, and me beneath the spray together, steam and the scent of sex flooding the space as they both filled me to bursting, first with their cocks then cum.

Something inside me purred like a happy kitten, an inner noise I'd never heard before.

Jon cleared his throat, and I blinked the vivid, mouthwatering image of the three of us together away.

I don't want anyone other than Jon, I told myself, adding a few swear words for good measure to make sure my traitorous body got the hint.

The door to the bedroom clicked shut, and Jon's arms wrapped around me from behind, his chin on my shoulder. "You okay?" he asked, his breath hot against my ear.

It wasn't the right time for words—especially since I had no clue how to verbalize everything I'd experienced since Elijah had appeared in our camp.

I turned my face toward my husband and attacked his mouth with all my pent-up lust, my soul needing to connect with his again, to remind us both that I belonged to him alone.

CHAPTER 5

ELIJAH

Both of my mates felt the pull between us, of that I had no doubt.

Dakota fought it, feared it and the fact it might hurt her husband. Even though she and I hadn't yet bonded with my beta as the bridge between us, I experienced a hint of the emotional undercurrents rushing through her heart and thoughts. Desire, hesitancy, lust, fear, and a rightness she didn't yet understand teased at my mind due to the connection already forging due to our close proximity.

I longed to cradle her in my arms, offer comfort as her alpha ought to.

But one fingertip on her sweet flesh would snap my slight hold on the beast prowling and gnashing its teeth beneath my skin.

Jon recognized the attraction among all three of us and didn't seem to be bothered by his wife wanting me. If I had to guess, the discomfort shifting his gaze from me countless times since our meeting at their camp would be over the fact he found himself attracted to a man.

Mine.

I stared at the closed door to the guest room while silently agreeing with my dragon.

My darker side lusted to show Jon who the alpha would be between us. I wanted to chain him to the ceiling, make him shudder from the bite of pain. Teasing touches and fulfillment denied until he begged me to take him, mark him.

Own him.

My cock swelled inside my jeans, and I leaned my forehead on the door, eyes closed, nostrils flaring as I searched the air for hints of their combined scent I'd tasted on the breeze what felt like years ago rather than days.

Fate had never been so kind. I deserved the possible future she dangled in front of me for all the pain she'd inflicted over the centuries, but would she allow my mates to accept me? Love me as in addition to the connection they already shared?

A lust-filled moan filtered through the door, causing my heart to still for a harsh second before jumpstarting once more.

Dakota.

Yessss.

Want.

I strained to listen, almost sick with the desire to share her with my beta. My stomach cramped, and my fingers flexed and relaxed with the need to enter their room, to touch and taste them both, filling my senses with everything they were until fire and blood bound us together in an unbreakable bond meant from the beginning of time.

Their nearness comforted me, almost as if a part of myself bloomed back to life I hadn't realized lay dormant. The thought of them writhing together flooded me with a contentment I'd never felt.

The memories also heightened my need for release.

If their frantic coupling beyond the bedroom door was

any indication, they must have been similarly affected by my scent and presence. Within my home, their heightened need for sexual fulfillment—for *me*—would only intensify.

Feed them.

"I'll do no such thing," I muttered harshly since I wanted more than just their sexual submission. I needed all of them. Their insecurities. Every sigh and tear. I longed to hear their thoughts throughout each day gifted to us. They had to recognize the connection among us without manipulation and accept their fated roles so we could be properly bonded to share everything I hoped for as my parents had.

Jon's groan caused my ball sac to tighten up against my body, and I sucked in my lower lip to keep my echoed moan contained. Their combined grunts and gasps heated my ears and blood to the point I feared my scales and talons would erupt from my human skin. I squeezed my hard length through my jeans, my free hand flat against the door by my head.

"Oh, yes." Dakota's murmur nearly made my knees buckle.

"You like my cock deep inside you." Jon growled the declaration.

"Yes!" Dakota gasped. "Harder…fuck me hard, Jon, please! Deeper. God, just like that."

Her pleadings rang in my ears, the slap of their skin coming together tensing my body to the point of pain.

"Tell me you want me," Jon demanded. "Need me."

"Always!" Another gasp and Dakota cried out his name, hers falling loudly from Jon's lips mere seconds later as I fought to fill my heaving lungs.

The tips of my claws slid from my fingertips, ready to shred the wooden panel separating me from my mates.

Claim.

Own!

Trembling and half-mad with lust, I tore myself away, intent on my room and relief for both me and my inner beast.

I lusted for Dakota's soft sweetness between Jon and I as we both fucked into her, stuffing her full of our seed. Breeding her and creating life. I craved my mouth on her body and Jon's on mine. I yearned for us to be so damn intertwined we couldn't tell where one ended and the other began, our heartbeats and minds synchronized in beautiful harmony.

My bedroom door hadn't yet clicked shut behind me, and I tore at my jeans, shredding them until they fell from my body.

I palmed my aching shaft, silken heat over rigid steel. My slit oozed pre-cum in a steady stream, natural lubricant meant for me to take both mates without pain or difficulty. The moisture also contained a substance that would turn my mates into hungry sex slaves should they ingest a steady diet of it.

Yessss.

"No."

Leaning against the door, I closed my eyes and imagined myself with Jon and Dakota, loving them, claiming them in the *only* way I wanted to. With binding words and fire they willingly submitted to without fear or question over being tied to me until we breathed our last.

Cum abruptly shot into my fist, my teeth drawing blood from my lower lip to keep my beast's roar contained.

Lust sated for the time being, I changed into comfortable lounge pants and a T-shirt. I went to the kitchen to prepare the promised coffee. Dakota hadn't asked for anything, but she seemed more the hot tea type. I suspected green with honey and lemon.

"Sybil," I addressed my home automation system I'd designed, "music on, living area only." I placed the teapot on the stove to heat, and my heartbeat accelerated. The house's system picked up where it'd left off, Barber's "Adagio" caressing my ears.

Loneliness didn't echo in my mind, nor did heartache knife at my chest as it usually would with another haunting melody that reminded me of the past. Hurt over my ex-lover, Dolyn, and his abandoning me for good had eased somewhat in the face of having found the two fate intended for me. I would take the reprieve gladly.

I glanced around my cavern Dolyn and I had shared that would now hopefully become home to my intended mates. The sunken living room sat inviting with its leather, half-circle sectional, but rain slashed at the wall of windows beyond. Coffee percolating and tea steeping, I attempted to lock away reminders of my ex at every turn and decided to ensure my humans remained comfortable.

Not yet feeling their presence drawing near, I shot fire from my lips onto the tinder and kindling in the fireplace. Minutes later, cheery flames flickered light and warmth against the storm outside.

I'd had the entire cave—upper floors and all the ones below the living space—upgraded with the latest technology. Although an eighty-inch screen hung above the granite mantle, I rarely indulged in mindless entertainment. I preferred spending my time nose-deep in a book, learning of different cultures, their beginnings, and the tales and lore of creatures no one alive had ever seen.

Hardly any of the earth's original beings remained, and although ancient blood still sneaked its way into man's DNA,

I expected—or had, rather—that extinction lay in the dragon shifters' future.

Jon and Dakota...

Mine.

Need.

"I know," I whispered in attempts to soothe my impatient beast. "Remember our alpha father told us free will is key to a lasting bond?"

A grumbling rumbled beneath my breastbone.

Breed.

"Yes, one day we three will bring another life into being," I promised with a soothing tone even though I needed the assurance as much as my beast did.

While pleasure for both Jon and me, I wondered at Dakota having two mates inside her at once, flooding her with our cum. Filling her womb with our young. The size of me alone stretched every woman I'd allowed myself over the centuries, and I couldn't imagine an almost fully human woman taking two at the same time. I feared pain for my gentle female and promptly turned my thoughts into more pressing matters: that of making friends and creating a natural bond among us that would lead to what I longed for. Both required Jon and Dakota nearby for more than a few hours, and merely waiting out a storm wouldn't offer the proper amount of time.

Surely I could find a way—

My inner beast purred at the sound of shuffling feet at the top of the stairs as I scented their nearness. Both blonde heads appeared tousled and wet from showering, and their blue and hazel-green eyes turned my direction, not exactly unsure but curious at least.

Had they spoken to each other about the insistent draw among us?

They came down the stairs, hands clasped together as

though of one heart, spirit, and mind. Patches of scruff still lined Jon's jawline, but a young innocence clung to his slashed eyebrows, perfectly bowed lips, and the flash of dimples I'd seen back at their camp. The spattering of freckles across his nose solidified the thought of purity in my head. Skin kissed by the sun, his hair a myriad of golden and light brown hung unbound almost to his shoulders.

Much paler, Dakota's face had been reddened from the wind and sun, her hair a lighter blonde, and she was no less innocent-seeming in her wide eyes and parted lips.

What I had witnessed the night before and heard less than an hour earlier promised my mates were hardly innocent, but their fresh faces roused both me and my beast in a way I fought hard to keep contained. He thrashed at the hold I had on him, desperate to burrow deep inside both of our mates. Mark and claim so they could never leave us.

My lungs constricted, and I tore my gaze from their entwined fingers to move back into the kitchen.

"Make yourselves at home," I managed a calm tone once they reached the landing.

I busied myself with making their hot drinks as they moved behind me, settling onto the couch in a whisper of rumpled, comfortable-appearing clothing I'd rather have stripped off their bodies.

Once I had full control over my hungry beast, I gathered the drink tray in hand and turned.

The unique blend of their scents wafted past my nose. Dakota's sweetness settled over me like refreshing morning dew on grass, and Jon's more earthy musk reminded me of a brisk, fall day I enjoyed more than any other season. A perfect blend, delicious and groin-tightening.

Saliva pooled in my mouth at the thought of having their taste on my tongue, their warm skin beneath my fingertips. Sitting with them would prove an even greater temptation than outside where my home's energy wouldn't affect all three of us.

But I would bear the pain of shackling my beast for the sake of my future—or theirs.

Mine.

I wasn't sure what my dragon specifically referred to that time and chose to ignore his grumbling.

"Coffee," I said, handing Jon's mug to him.

Sitting before me, his bright blue eyes gazing upward into mine brought on images of him on his knees, submitting to me. Hands resting on his thighs, mouth opening, and tongue waiting to be fed.

Yessss.

I bit my lower lip to steady myself against the darkness prowling beneath my skin.

"Thank you." Jon's fingers brushed against mine, and that same electrical current I'd felt when shaking his hand earlier in the day at their camp sent a rush of blood straight to my groin.

I tore myself away from the tether hooking my libido to find his beautiful wife curled on the cushion beside him, legs tucked beneath her lush body.

"You seem more of a green tea type than coffee," I said, my voice lowered due to the strain from keeping my inner beast hidden and groin from fully rousing in a display of my rekindled need.

"How did you know?" Her dazzling smile was like the sunrise on my face.

Touch. Please.

Breath held, I offered our female the mug in a way that required contact between our flesh.

Her fingertips grazed over my knuckles.

The dragon inside melted rather than bursting free, and I

released a rushed exhale, half-giddy over the fact she would rule my feral beast with such ease.

Dakota stared up at me, eyes wide, lips parted from a quiet gasp. The pulse thrummed in her neck, and her nipples hardened beneath the oversized shirt she had donned after her shower.

I wanted *both* of our mates on their knees before me, gazing up at me with the world in their eyes.

But only because they chose to, not because they'd been coerced.

Moving away from them felt like muscle ripping from bone, ten times more painful than shifting into my true form.

Jon and Dakota kept their attention on me rather than the mugs in their hands as I sat on the other end of the sectional, angled to face them. Their gazes dropped to the semi-aroused bulge in my pants I wouldn't be able to hide even if I'd wanted to.

They both swallowed as though their mouths filled with saliva at the sight.

Feed, my dragon purred his suggestion followed by a slight chuckle. *They hunger.*

I ignored him. "Does the classical music bother you?" I asked, drawing my mates' attention to my face.

Dakota's tongue flicked over her lower lip before answering, her gaze once more troubled. "I like it, but it's not Jon's favorite."

"Yeah," Jon said, lifting his mug to his lips, "but I can deal." He sipped, and I stared at his Adam's apple as he swallowed.

Lust for him burned like hot coals, but my desire for learning about them was just as bright. I wanted to inquire after their pasts, their families, and home, but I got the sense Jon would better appreciate knowing about me before I pried into their lives.

"Would you like to hear the tale about this cavern and the creatures who crafted it into a home?" I asked.

"Creatures?" Jon echoed with a huff of laughter. "Go ahead and make my wife's day. Fill her mind fuller than it already is with fantasies about mythical beings that exist for our pleasure."

"Jon," she chided quietly, pink flushing her face.

"Dakota?" I murmured her name, enjoying how bumps rose across her arms as though my voice caressed her flesh.

"I-I would like to hear that story if you don't mind," Dakota said and sipped her tea while Jon settled back against the cushion, taking another swallow from his mug.

"Goddamn, that's the good shit," he moaned.

I grimaced over the fact he drank the bitter brew black while my inner beast whimpered his need for more of those noises to fall from our beta's lips.

My own sweetened and blond coffee in hand, I propped one ankle over the opposite knee and began. "Centuries ago, dragons ruled the land while man fought for existence."

"Dragons?" One of Jon's brows rose as he smirked, revealing his dimples I wished to lick. He glanced at Dakota. "It's like Elijah plucked that fairytale straight out of your brain," he said with a light chuckle.

"I love dragon *everything*," Dakota said, smiling at me, her eyes alight with glorious happiness.

The beast inside me purred. "Then you will enjoy this story."

Rain continued to fall. Thunder rumbled over the mountains, and lightning flashed through the one-way windows overlooking the mountains that usually flooded the interior with light, but my human guests sat in comfort as I shared the story of the Blood Born's downfall. Rather than openly declaring myself a direct descendent of those who lived in the cave before me, I spun the magical into the reality of inheriting the home my fathers had built for my mother—but kept the truth of me being the offspring of a triad rather than a couple to myself.

Leaving out that my birth occurred nearly five hundred years earlier seemed appropriate until they were ready to hear the truth of what I was—and who they were to me.

Dakota stared, her dreamy expression proof of her love of supposed myth. I could imagine her daydreaming I was the last of the dragonblood I'd told them about.

Jon seemed more settled in what humans saw as truth, one eyebrow arched again, a flashed grin over what he thought to be nothing but a false tale to perhaps enchant his lovely wife. "Dragons and fated mates—right up Dakota's alley." He laughed again, but his amusement didn't ring true to my ears. "It must have cost millions." He changed the subject, glancing around the massive cave I hid myself in when not needing to travel to Manhattan or Europe for business. Wariness had crept into his tone and eyes, making me wonder over his thoughts, insecurities, or suspicions.

"It cost enough," I agreed, thinking about the ease with which a dragon could melt and move rock.

I wondered—no, I *hoped*—they would both come to learn the extent to which I would reshape the earth to please them both given the chance.

CHAPTER 6

JONATHAN

"So, your ancestors were dragon shifters?" Dakota asked with a dreamy sigh.

"I'll bet he farts glitter and shits rainbows too," I said with a laugh while tugging on a few strands of her hair to keep her brain rooted in reality.

She glared at me and playfully swatted at my hand. "I happen to enjoy having my head in the clouds, thank you very much."

"I know, and I wouldn't have you any other way," I murmured, leaning in to brush my lips over hers.

Our gazes remained locked, our smiles fixed in place as I rested my forehead on hers. We'd had one hell of an explosive fuck in Elijah's bathroom. I'd taken her up against the door, both of us still mostly clothed. We'd been desperate for release, a shared hunger that flared brighter than we'd ever experienced.

Her sweet pussy had welcomed me with slickness and heat, a silken glove to milk my dick and drain my balls dry. I'd come so goddamn hard my legs went weak, but I'd managed to get her limp body into the shower and washed from hair to toes.

We didn't say more than two words to each other and only out of necessity. It was like my tongue was tied up in knots or some shit. Maybe a spell had fallen over us when we'd walked into Elijah's strange home. One meant to bind our thoughts, hearts, and goddamned bodies.

Couldn't deny that final idea kept my blood hot and sac heavy.

After showering in near silence, we'd dressed when I'd rather have gone naked. Everything about Elijah's home felt so fucking...natural. Right. Like we'd been meant to enter his kick-ass cave that comforted like a warm blanket on a cold night.

Elijah moved into the kitchen with our empty mugs. He'd never acknowledged Dakota's question about being a descendent of the Blood Born, ridiculous as it was.

I sat back, my gaze trailing after him. The carefully combed hair, the wide shoulders, and ripple of muscle across his back beneath his tight T-shirt tempted every cell in my straight body.

Was it any wonder Dakota lusted after the man?

Add in the tale about dragons and fated love, and he could be my wife's fairytale come true.

I chuckled to myself, wondering yet again why my insides didn't rage with possessiveness. If Elijah wished to get into my wife's pants, he knew exactly how to go about getting there. Not that she would give in to him.

I forced my focus back on the woman beside me and ran my hand down her arm as she leaned against me with another sigh. I wanted to pry, to ask what she thought of him, if she felt the need to take pictures of him to tuck away and ponder over, but again with the damned inability to voice the question.

"Tired?" I asked instead, not ready to discuss whatever the hell was making me reconsider more than I thought possible.

"You wore me out," she said, keeping her voice low.

My cock twitched at the memory of how she'd come around my cock like my rigid length had some magical touch that stroked more than her g-spot. Her cries had seemed louder than usual, the contractions of her pussy around my aching shaft pulsing with an intensity I couldn't remember feeling before.

Did the thought of Elijah do that to her? Was the fantasy of him while taking my dick able to turn her on more than I did? Was she growing bored with the same old, same old of hopping in the sack with me? Was I becoming only the man who hadn't been able to fulfill her desire for babies before I'd lost the ability to properly provide for just the two of us?

I'd only been plagued once by a lack of confidence in my relationship with Dakota, and I wasn't sure how to handle the emotion the questions roused. Sure, I had a shit ton of insecurities about other stuff from my childhood, but my relationship with her hadn't ever truly been tested before. Not even that one strange guy all those years ago we'd ended up fighting about.

He'd been nothing but a blip on our radar that had caused problems because we hadn't known how to communicate back then. Now, we did—but something hindered me from sharing jack shit.

Dakota rested her hand flat against my chest above my heart as though staking her claim. "Love you," she murmured, nuzzling her cheek against my shoulder.

"Love you more," I whispered my usual response, wondering if I really did speak the truth rather than tease like usual.

Elijah's story rang deep inside of me though, in places I'd long forgotten about. The child in me who had always dreamed of dragons, of the imaginary friend who soared the skies, keeping watch over me in my loneliness. Flickered images of that midnight-colored dragon had come to mind as Elijah's deep voice and his tale had rolled over me. Either I'd become so fucking hot for our host that I started imagining things, or I swore the man's eyes matched the memory of my imaginary friend.

I'd never wanted to kneel before the dragon who'd kept me company throughout childhood and even into my adult dreams on occasion, but Elijah?

Shifting on the couch didn't help my swelling cock. I'd never imagined myself to be a kinky fuck, but my body sure as shit wanted that man to string me up and consume every part of me. Even my skin itched to feel the scrape of his teeth, the bruising of his fingertips.

"Are you okay?" Dakota asked without moving.

Sure she sensed the increasing tension inside of me, I heaved a breath and rubbed her arm again, trying to chill the fuck out and relax. "Yeah."

"Want to go take a nap?"

I smirked down at my wife, but my gaze strayed to Elijah who stood at the sink, his back to us. A nap equaled a little lovin' in Dakota's language. Maybe making love to her rather than fucking her like a goddamn animal would lessen whatever the hell the strangeness inside me longed for.

I opened my mouth to whisper a question about how rude it would be to skip out on Elijah, but he cleared his throat, drawing my gaze. Dakota's head lifted from my shoulder. The sexual pull reached across the cave, tripping up my heartbeat and making the air too thick with tension to inhale a full breath.

That reel he had me on—fucking hell, I wanted to swallow down whatever had gotten me hooked.

"Please make yourselves at home," he said, his voice soft yet easily heard. "There's food and beer in the refrigerator and a wine cellar downstairs." He shifted his pale gaze to Dakota. "If you'd rather, rest for a while. I've got some work that needs my attention."

"Thanks," I said as Dakota murmured the same.

With a dip of his head, he turned, disappearing behind a door beneath the stairs that led to the second floor.

I imagined him heading down to a dungeon, complete with whips and chains. Ball gags and cock rings.

My skin burned to be touched. Tortured. Devoured.

The fuck?

Biting back my groan over shit I'd never actually considered before, I pushed off the couch. "How about that nap?" I said, pulling Dakota up to her feet.

Her nipples and pebbled skin betrayed her.

So why didn't *I* feel betrayed?

An hour later, somewhat sated and wide awake, I stared at the rock ceiling above the massive bed we sprawled over. The rain had stopped, and streaks of afternoon sunlight cut across the sky outside the lone window. Dakota slept beside me, her light snores barely heard through the tangled thoughts in my head. I'd worn her ass out.

And hadn't been able to stop thinking about Elijah while enjoying all she'd offered.

My dick swelled at the image of the damned man in my head, overshadowing the guilt nagging at my stomach. Imagining cheating was the same as doing it, wasn't it?

Jaw clenched, I climbed out of bed and pulled on a pair of

shorts and a T-shirt. Maybe a couple of beers would take off whatever edge I rode.

Barefoot, I slipped into the hallway. Silence lay heavy over the cave, but the lights welcoming me with every step and fading behind me strangely gave me that sense of home again I'd never experienced before stepping into Elijah's domain. I should have been unsettled thanks to the truth of my upbringing where I had never belonged. Elijah was a mere stranger with an odd living space in the middle of nowhere. So why did my soul rest and freedom from the hardships of real life wrap around me with every breath filling my lungs? Even the continued sexual tension riding me didn't threaten that sense of serenity.

The quiet, main living area opened up before me, and I wound my way down the stairs into the kitchen with no answers whispering in my head.

As promised, cold beer sat in the fridge. The chilled bottle against my palm cooled my hand but not the heat Elijah had stirred to life inside me upon first entering our camp.

Had it only been that morning?

I twisted the cap off and glanced at the door he'd earlier disappeared through while chugging down a few swallows.

Should I find him and figure out what the fuck was going on or ignore the tension and light out with the sunrise like Dakota and I had agreed to do, leaving Elijah Tolzman and his hotter than hell *everything* behind? Not used to dealing with temptation, I didn't know what the fuck to do.

I stared at the door and finished off my beer, some sort of energy rippling over my skin and pulling me into the bowels of his cave castle. My feet moved as though on their own, and I slipped behind the door beneath the stairs.

It was the damned fishing line he had me on, I swear to fucking god.

A staircase led down into the dark, but the second I

stepped onto the first tread, lights shimmered into existence overhead. Similar to the stairway to the second floor, some rock had been cut for more headspace. Another cavern opened at the bottom, smaller than the living area above with two doors on either side. The hallway continued on ahead, but I stopped at the bottom of the stairs and listened.

Not a single sound caressed my ears, no hint of Elijah's boring as fuck music, not even dripping water expected inside a cave. My exhales broke the stillness as I strained to listen for the slightest noise. My gaze flitted to the door on the right, and like my body knew Elijah was on the other side, I found myself moving in that direction.

The door sat ajar by a few inches, and breath held, I peeked through the crack.

A weight room, I noted from a quick scan of what I could see, but my focus honed in on the man lying on a bench beneath a barbell in its hold, his laced fingers atop his forehead as his chest rose and fell.

He rested between sets, most likely.

I'd never found a man's bare legs attractive before, but the defined calf muscles and bulge of his thighs peeking from beneath the shorts were damn fine. I imagined Elijah standing and ordering me to kneel before him.

My dick twitched at the idea of him tugging on his cock inches from my face. My mouth watered over the thought of him rubbing the head slickened with pre-cum over my lips before telling me to open. His low voice rumbling to take him deep—swallow it all.

Fuck.

I bit back a groan and adjusted my swelling dick, even though the thought of Elijah's spunk on my tongue should have grossed my straight ass out.

Guess that label needed to be tossed in the trash. I wasn't bi or pan. Elijah-sexual? That sounded about right.

He reached up and grasped the barbell, readying for another set.

Like a sick fuck, I continued to watch him, every lift of the bar flexing his massive pecs and pulling a grunt from him. He was a beast. The amount of weights on the ends bent the fucking barbell. Thank Christ he had a safety bar slightly above his chest, but the man really should have a spotter when benching that kind of weight.

With that excuse in mind, I pushed the door inward and approached him.

Elijah grunted one last time and set the bar on its handles before I made it halfway across the room. He sat up, his focus landing on me. Sweat beaded his brow and every inch of his bare upper body. Like the stone around us, his muscles were cut, defined, and I expected hard as granite.

The intensity in his gaze twisted my stomach in a way that only one woman's perusal had ever done.

"Is everything all right?" he asked as I forced myself to meander to a pull-up bar bolted into the wall.

I tried for my usual carefree grin and probably failed while wrapping my hands around the bar. He had every weightlifting apparatus imaginable, and most of it appeared brand new. "Guess when you live this far out, you need your own gym, huh?" I asked rather than answering.

Deflection at its finest, something I'd learned from my not-so-lovely foster parents.

Elijah's low chuckle as his stare roved over my exposed midriff sent a shiver rustling over my spine. "I probably spend too much time down here."

I bit back the compliment that almost rolled off my tongue about every minute obviously being worth it but couldn't keep from sliding my eyes over his seated form again.

Forget the six-pack I sported—his was a fucking eight.

The rippled muscles disappeared beneath his waistband with a hint of dark hair leading southward. A large-as-fuck bulge filled those damn shorts, and I swallowed against the rush of lust swarming me. My asshole should have clenched not relaxed with the need to be stretched.

What the actual fuck?

I closed my eyes and gripped the metal in my hands, a simple contraction of my upper body muscles pulling me upward. A few reps cleared my head a bit and kept me from tenting my shorts, and even though my eyes remained closed, the heat from Elijah's stare seared my skin.

I had to face the truth. My brow furrowed as the reps became tougher. I was thoroughly sexually attracted to a man and had to get the fuck over it…it was no big deal. Dakota and I would be gone tomorrow, back to our non-cushy little life and never see him again.

Why did that idea make my gut clench?

I lowered my body, the cool rock meeting my bare feet.

Elijah hadn't moved from the bench, but his bulge had swelled and lengthened.

Averting my eyes as though they burned, I fought for something to say, anything to break the need-to-fuck tension flooding the room. "I had a dragon as an imaginary friend when I was a kid," I blurted the first nonsexual thought I had.

"What did he look like?" Elijah asked the question as though the beast had been a real being rather than make-believe.

"He was huge and black as midnight. Pale eyes." I tightened my grip on the bar and, unable to help myself, glanced over at Elijah while shifting from foot to foot.

He studied me until I stilled as realization settled in. His eyes were a blue so pale, so damn *familiar* that goose bumps broke across my arms.

"I think I need another beer," I muttered and forced my feet to move toward the door.

"Don't go." His quiet command pulled me up short, but I didn't turn.

Couldn't.

Elijah released a slow exhale. "It's...nice having someone share this space with me."

Not exactly what I'd expected—or hoped? I turned, an eyebrow lifted. "No roommates or family?" I asked the question my usually cautious self should have done hours ago.

Elijah shook his head and turned away from me to grab a towel off the floor. I tried like hell not to stare as he wiped his face and chest free of droplets of sweat that my tongue lusted to taste. "No," he finally answered me, wrapping the towel around the back of his neck, fisting the ends in his massive hands.

Hands I wanted on my body. Mapping every inch, tying me up, and taking what he wanted.

God*damn.*

I cleared my throat, fighting off a boner again. "How long have you been alone?"

"What seems like an eternity." His lopsided smile didn't reach his eyes as he stood. "Would you like a turn?" he asked, motioning toward the bench. "I find that physical exertion does wonders for restlessness."

Maybe pumping some iron would help. "Why the fuck not—but you need some serious tunes going on in here if I'm going to hang out in your dungeon."

I swore a growl echoed through the cavernous room, and my heart tripped.

Elijah's chuckle sounded forced. "What is your preference?"

With a dominant man like him? Bottoming, no fucking doubt.

I swallowed hard at the needy ache in my asshole before clearing my throat. "How about some heavy metal?"

Elijah grimaced but asked his genie in the hidden speakers to play what I'd suggested.

CHAPTER 7
DAKOTA

I clutched the spines of a dark dragon as we soared through the air, the wind whipping my hair behind me. Rather than laughter bursting past my lips, I moaned, every shift of my hips rubbing my bare pussy and clit against warm scales. Riding the beast took me to the edge of a climax that would pitch me so far into oblivion I fought against my impending doom.

My breath caught. Body quivered. My toes tingled as my release rose upward, rushing toward the massive need deep inside of me. I should have fallen and been swept up in the vortex of the wind, lust, and euphoria awaiting me...

I opened my eyes.

The bamboo sheets of Elijah's guest bed tangled around my legs. I reached for Jon, so damn aroused a mere flick of my clit would send my pussy into spasms as it had before I'd fallen asleep.

The bed beside me felt cold to the touch.

"Jon?" I called hoarsely, lifting my head, hoping like hell he would be up for another round to sate the ungodly need storming inside me.

The room sat empty, the door to the bathroom open and revealing darkness beyond.

A brief moment of panic caught my breath.

Had he left me? Made love to me one last time before taking off because I lusted after another man? My throat thickened and eyes stung.

Jon's backpack sat by the door, his sweatshirt thrown over the back of a chair.

He was still here. Somewhere.

Expelling a huge breath, I let my head fall back to the pillow. He hadn't seemed upset by my traitorous body, but Jon had always acted carefree, arrogant almost, around others. As if nothing in the world bothered him, when I knew the skeletons in his closet and loved him even more because of them. Was he putting on a front? Hiding pain I had caused him?

I chewed on the inside of my lip, sure his eyes and smile hadn't lied.

He'd worshiped my body earlier. There was no possible way he'd faked the emotion on his face while filling me. My core pulsed with the desire for another dose of dick but for more than my husband's.

Mind racing and stomach unsettled by my thoughts, I climbed off the bed, needing to move.

Our combined cum from before napping sliding down my thighs. "Damn." I frowned and cupped myself while awkwardly walking to the bathroom. "You'd think he hadn't come in two weeks rather than two hours." Shaking my head at the amount of Jon's semen leaking from me, I sat on the toilet, my arousal easing slightly.

Cleaned up but still naked, I meandered back into the bedroom, hands on my hips. Hunger clenched my stomach, and a glance out the window revealed it had to be past our usual suppertime.

How long had I slept?

Sex twice in one day and still feeling decidedly naughty, I didn't bother pulling on panties but went straight for the only pair of clean leggings I had left. I strapped the girls into a bra, however, since I wasn't about to reveal to the world for one more minute what our host did to my libido.

Neither man sat in the living room or kitchen, but the thump of music spilled from the ajar door beneath the stairs leading to the lower reaches of Elijah's home. I pulled it open, the warm light beckoning me deeper from the top tread.

Another stairwell with magical lights enticed me downward. A similar hewn cavern lay at the bottom but less than half the size of the kitchen area. The door on the right stood open spilling a Nine Inch Nails song, its beat one Jon and I had fucked to plenty of times. Heavy breathing and grunts reached my ears—and immediately a jolt of lust shot between my thighs.

My mind having a heyday over thoughts of Jon and Elijah tangled together, I hurried across the smooth stone floor, my bare feet silent. Fingers itching for the camera still buried in my bag, I peeked through the slightly ajar door. A workout room lay beyond but didn't reveal anything sexual. My breath left in a rush as I realized I had hoped to see the opposite.

I *wanted* to catch Jon's hands on Elijah and vice versa. I also lusted to be between them, all three of us a tangle of legs and arms and grasping hands.

Face hot and heart pounding over the image in my head, I filled my gaze with the two men doing dumbbell curls. They stood with their backs to me. One blond and wearing a sweat-stained T-shirt, the other dark-haired, the bare skin of his torso on display. Both had broad shoulders and were ripped enough to flood any hot-blooded woman's mouth with a rush of drool.

Muscles flexed in their upper arms and shoulders. Tight asses clenched beneath thin cotton.

I would never be able to hear that damned song again without imagining a sweaty, man-on-man sandwich with me squashed between. I also should have worn the panties as wetness smeared against the cotton lining of my leggings.

Elijah was the first to put down his dumbbells and turn as though he'd felt my hidden presence and stare.

Our gazes collided, and I found my lips parting but unable to form a word. A sheen of sweat covered his cut chest and matted the spattering of black hair. The happy trail of a lifetime cut between those lush muscles that created a V at his hips and disappeared beneath his low-slung shorts.

My mouth dried.

"Dakota."

Caught in the act of lusting, I jerked my head toward Jon, expecting the worst. Heat flushed through me from head to toes.

His dimpled smile melted my damn heart and allowed me to draw a breath.

He *had* to know what Elijah did to me. Hell, there was no way to hide our host turned me on, and same as earlier, Jon acted as though he didn't care. Then again, perhaps his own guilt over being all hot and bothered by Elijah swayed his emotional response.

Unsettled by the energy between us, the shame, and the longing for Jon's cock—again—caused such a shitstorm in my brain, I couldn't think straight.

"There's too much testosterone in this room for me," I said with a breathless laugh, trying like hell to keep from fidgeting and making the moment even more awkward.

One of Elijah's eyebrows popped up, and he glanced over at Jon. I did the same to find him still grinning at me.

"How'd you sleep?" my husband asked.

"G-good." I returned his smile, but it wobbled as I glanced at Elijah again. "I dreamed about a dragon." The words tumbled out of my mouth, reheating my face as the vivid images of riding the beast swept through my head.

Soaked, rubbing against its warm body, my arousal coating its scales...

My pulse thrummed, and I licked my lower lip while forcing my attention back on Jon. "I—I'm going to heat up a can of stew," I stumbled hastily to get the words out. "Do you want some?" I ran my hands down my thighs, my skin itching for someone else's touch.

"I already planned to prepare something for dinner," Elijah said, his low, sexy voice pulling my focus again. "You're welcome to join me."

"Thank you." If my body didn't betray me, my needy voice sure as hell just had.

Elijah didn't return my strained smile but continued to stare at me with an intensity that weakened my knees.

Mumbling something about needing a drink, I spun and hightailed it back up the stairs on wobbly legs. Jon's quick footfalls sounded behind me, but I didn't stop until I stood in the kitchen.

He wrapped his sweaty arms around me and nuzzled my neck as though he was starved for affection. "You wear the rumpled, I've-just-been-fucked look so damn well, baby. I want to sink into your sweet pussy again."

I sagged into his embrace with a sigh as he licked from my collarbone to my ear.

"Pretty sure Elijah was thinking the same damn thing," Jon whispered. I tensed to pull away, but he tightened his hold on me. "The man has good taste." He suckled my lobe into his hot mouth, and a shiver of goose bumps rose across my arms.

Rather than question his lack of jealousy over another man wanting me, I breathed a partial sigh of relief. If only I could turn my body off toward Elijah, we might be okay.

"You wear the post-workout body damn well," I said, my voice still loaded with arousal.

"Mmm." Jon nuzzled my neck again. "What about Elijah?"

My heart stalled out, and I swallowed hard. "E-Elijah?"

"Mmm," Jon murmured again, his tongue flicking my ear. "All that hard muscle. Dripping sweat..."

"He's all right, I suppose," I managed past the quaking in my stomach.

"Just all right?" Jon chuckled and grasped my chin, turning my head toward him. Rather than anger burning in his crystal blue eyes, a whole lot of lust leaked from his steady gaze and liquified my bones. "Admit it. The man is hot as fuck."

"The man is hot as fuck," I echoed on autopilot, my voice a mere whisper.

Jon captured my mouth with a ferocity I hadn't felt from him since we'd first started fooling around. His tongue swept into my mouth, laying claim to what already belonged to him. I hadn't admitted jack shit—I'd only echoed his words out of surprise at the factual tone he'd used.

Jon thought Elijah was hot as fuck.

I moaned against my husband's mouth, lifting my hands up to grasp his unbound hair. Damp strands stuck to my fingers, and I held tighter as he slid one hand over my front to cup me through my leggings.

"You're soaked," he said against my mouth.

Murmuring my agreement, I rubbed against his hand, seeking the release I'd wanted upon waking.

The thought Elijah might climb the stairs behind us and catch us in a lust-crazed embrace only made me burn hotter.

"Touch me, Jon," I whimpered my plea while yanking on his hair.

He worked his hand beneath the waistband of my leggings and groaned. "No panties."

Freshly shaven, my body didn't hinder his fingertips as they glided down over my pelvis. My swollen clit throbbed, and I gasped as he grazed over the nub. He thrust two fingers deep inside me, and I pressed against him with a desperate whimper. "More."

Jon pulled his fingers out and plunged deep, his thumb finding my clit and rubbing.

That doom, that edge of euphoria crashed into me like a tidal wave, and I bit my lower lip to keep from crying out. A deep moan rose, but Jon captured my mouth again, swallowing what was left of my release.

Feet shuffled up the stairs, and Jon slipped his soaked hand from my leggings. Panting and trembling, I held onto the island and slid onto a stool as Elijah's large frame filled the doorway. He glanced at my heated face then at Jon, who smiled at me and sucked his fingers clean one by one.

Holy fuck.

I wanted the floor to open and swallow me whole.

CHAPTER 8
ELIJAH

The scent of Dakota's release threatened to be my undoing. My mouth flooded with drool, and my inner beast roared, causing every muscle in my body to tense. I wanted to lay our female on the table, devour her pussy, lap up every trace of her cum that Jon had enticed from her body—because that was exactly what he'd done.

He sucked her essence off his fingers, teasing both halves of my being.

My dragon growled, and I struggled to contain the rumble in my chest rather than let the noise escape as it had earlier in the weight room. Jon had heard and seemed unsettled but had brushed off the sound without questioning it.

I glanced between my mates, want rivaling my sanity and my human side's desire to keep them safe. Sexual tension radiated among the three of us regardless of our female's orgasm. Sated seconds earlier, she still hungered for her husband. For me.

And Jon?

A tempting glint rested in his eyes as he turned his focus toward me, and his pinkie popped free of his mouth. He adjusted his bulge like a tease, begging to be tortured and sated.

Take.

Claim.

I breathed deeply, slowly leaking the exhale from my flared nostrils in attempts to calm my beast. My mates required true sustenance, not to be exhausted by my insatiable need to taste their flesh and feed them my cum.

And my human side desired emotional connection as much as my beast did the physical.

Dakota's face remained bright pink as her focus flitted between her husband and me like a frightened hare ready to bolt.

"Would you help me with dinner?" I asked her, forcing a level tone and nonchalance to hopefully set her at ease.

"Yeah." She cleared her throat and slid from the chair. "Sure."

I tore my stare off her alluring curves I longed to have beneath my fingertips and focused on gathering what we would need to prepare our meal, the scent of her sex still thick in my nose. "How does homemade marinara and angel hair pasta sound?" I asked, glancing over my shoulder at Jon, envious he'd had the pleasure of tasting her.

He leaned against the island, arms crossed and a sexy smirk dimpling his cheeks. "Anything from scratch sounds fucking heavenly to me after the shit we've been eating since climbing into these mountains."

I grinned over his lack of refinement, enjoying the fact he came from a different era than I had gotten to experience while his age. His blatant honesty and adding curses to get his point across strengthened my desire to dip my tongue between his lips and lick.

Taste him.

A low hum of agreement escaped at my dragon's sugges-tion, but I focused on the task at hand.

Dakota chopped an onion, and I preheated a sauté pan with olive oil before retrieving a pot to water to boil.

"Would you mind grabbing a bottle of red from the wine cellar?" I asked Jon, wanting Dakota all to myself for a few moments since I'd had her enticing husband alone for close to an hour.

"Sure," he said, straightening from where he watched us work, his stare as potent as his musky scent in my nose.

"Downstairs, end of the hallway—another set of stairs and door on the right," I told him.

"Got it."

He stepped behind Dakota, pushed her pile of hair to the side and planted a kiss on her neck while smiling at me. "Be right back," he murmured against her ear, causing a shudder to ripple through her.

His attempt at stating he was the sole mate of her tickled me and made my inner beast growl. Jon would learn. Eventually.

A small grin stretched my lips as the door shut behind him leaving me and my female without another's presence for the first time.

"Sybil, music on," I said, my smile widening as 2Cellos's rendition of the *Game of Thrones* theme song began.

"Don't you get lonely up here?" Dakota asked, her voice breathless and hasty as though she was uncomfortable without Jon's presence. He wouldn't be gone very long but hopefully just enough I could calm her spirit and make her receptive to the energy of my home and the blood calling to blood.

"A bit at times," I admitted while pulling a few cans of organic diced tomatoes from the pantry. "I keep busy though."

"With?"

"Work. Reading."

"TV?"

I shrugged and set to opening the cans. "I'll watch the news and weather on occasion, but find TV shows these days to be mostly nonsense."

She nodded as though agreeing and pushed the diced onion off the cutting board into the frying pan. "Garlic?"

"There." I pointed to the basket I'd gotten the onion from, and she moved across the kitchen on steadier legs as she grew a little more comfortable in my space.

Our space.

My insides purred at my dragon's declaration. Everything around us, every part of me, belonged to Jon and Dakota, same as they did to me.

"Oh!"

I turned to find her smiling, her hazel eyes twinkling with happiness.

"This song is from Game of Thrones, isn't it?" she questioned.

"It is," I agreed, dipping my head.

"Jon loved that show."

Cans of tomatoes opened and ready to go, I rifled through my spice drawer. "You've known him a long time." I didn't ask a question since their interactions a closeness most humans could only ever hope for.

"We met in seventh grade." Her voice held a hint of sentimentality beneath the pure joy of having found what she'd probably thought as the one fate had intended for her.

Two.

The voice inside me stated yet another fact that made my soul soar. "And you've been together ever since?" I asked, unable to keep my eyes off her.

Cheeks tinged a deep pink once more, she nodded.

"When I first saw Jon, I felt connected to him—like a sense of belonging, you know?"

She hadn't really asked a question, but I nodded regardless.

"And the first time we talked to each other, I had this feeling that he was mine too."

My heart ached with sudden desire to be seen by her in the same light. I swallowed, forcing another nod. How could I possibly put myself between them and intrude on the love they shared? Even though Jon didn't seem the jealous sort, I feared heartache for one or both when the emotional barriers eventually came down between us.

Because they would. Being inside stone walls hewn by my ancestors would ensure the outcome given time.

Dragon grumbling beneath my breath about my *weakness* and refusal to speed up the process with manipulation, I went about getting plates and flatware to set the table. Equal measures of being torn and tempted warred inside me. "It's a beautiful thing to find your person," I murmured.

I felt her stare and glanced over to meet her gaze, ready for her questions.

"It is," she agreed. "Have you—I'm sorry. It's none of my business."

"Go ahead," I encouraged, turning to fully face her and give her whatever she desired of me. Information for now since she wasn't yet ready for physical touch that would bind us that much faster.

"Have you ever fallen in love? Enjoyed the connection with that one person you were meant to be with?"

I nodded, having experienced similar sentiment upon walking into her and Jon's camp earlier that morning. Fated mates didn't always equal immediate love, but the tether proved equally as strong from what I remembered of my parents.

"It's like…" She looked over my shoulder out the tall, glass windows letting in the beauty of the mountains freshly bathed by the rainstorm. "It's like coming home where everything lines up in your life, like you recognize that other soul is a part of your future."

My chest aching, I nodded again.

Dakota went back to her task, crushing the cloves of garlic with the flat of the blade before peeling them. "How long have you been alone?"

Her question hit me like a rushing gust of winter wind, stealing my breath.

I took a few moments to gather my thoughts and tear them off the heartache Dolyn's leaving had inflicted. In our early years together, he'd often asked for time alone which I'd agreed to. Even though I'd found my true mates, the hurt of his complete abandonment a decade earlier hadn't disappeared as expected.

My inner beast curled up deep inside, quiet for a change, allowing me a moment of human connection without his needy influence.

"I fancied myself in love once, but they didn't feel the same," I finally answered, keeping the part about a lack of our true bond to myself. Answering truthfully about my lonely existence would reveal I wasn't wholly human. Dakota might have a fanciful mind, but I didn't believe she was yet ready for the truth of who we were.

"I'm sorry."

Empathy radiated from her words and the gaze I felt on the side of my face.

"Fate has a way of weeding out what doesn't belong, and while I grieved for a long while, I've come to realize that person wasn't for me." I glanced at Dakota with a smile that wasn't quite genuine.

"I'm still sorry, all the same." Her whispered declaration

and the pain in her eyes soothed me in a way nothing ever had. She offered comfort only my female mate I'd been seeking for years could.

My dragon lay quietly beneath her soft words when the lingering scent of her cum should have kept him restless with his need for us to mark her with ours.

"Thank you," I replied, my voice low and rasped.

Cheeks turning pink once more, she returned to her task, the fall of golden tresses hiding her face from me.

The scent of Jon's approach, the quiet shuffle of his feet on the stair's treads reached me, rousing my dragon from his near slumber.

"So your taste in music isn't *all* shit," Jon said about the theme song at the top of the stairs, two bottles in hand.

Dakota whispered an admonishment, but honest, rare laughter burst from me.

"Good fucking show right there," Jon continued, sauntering into the kitchen as though he owned it. Little did he know, I would lay the world at his feet if that were his wish. "Wasn't sure which kind you'd want, so I grabbed a couple." He set one of the bottles on the small island. "I'm not usually a wine guy, but if it's this old," he said, glancing at the label on the bottle still in his hand, "I'll give it a try."

I took note of the Penfolds Grange 1951 he'd brought upstairs, humming my approval of his choice. "The glasses are there." I pointed to the corner cabinet on the far side of the kitchen.

My gaze glued to Jon's backside as he moved toward where I'd indicated. Tight glutes flexed with each step in the shorts I'd been wanting to rip off his body with my teeth since the moment he'd walked into the gym.

Mine.

I swallowed the growl, wanting to declare dominance and demand he submit to my beast.

Unaware of my inner struggle, Jon opened the cabinet and reached up toward the top shelf, his T-shirt lifting to tempt me with a peek of muscled, golden skin, same as when he'd done pull-ups and roused my dragon's desire to dominate and mark.

Jon turned and met my gaze, one of his brows rising. "Corkscrew?"

He knew I stared. Must have.

"Here." I tore my focus off him and rummaged in the drawer in front of my hips.

Like a warm, fall breeze, Jon moved close, his earthen scent flooding my senses and swelling me to full length within a matter of heartbeats. I bit down on my tongue to keep my groan contained.

Our fingers brushed as I handed over the gadget, and his lips parted on a caught breath.

Once tied in my ropes, how many stripes would it take before he leaned into my cane? How long before he begged me to fill him? Allow him release?

Dakota stared at us, knife poised in her mincing of the garlic. Even the strong scent of the allium didn't overpower the combined pheromones dousing my kitchen.

She was hesitant.

He was tempted but not enough for me to risk her or his heart.

"Sybil—2Cellos, 'Thunderstruck'," I commanded, my voice strained.

Jon's brow furrowed as the cellists began playing the AC/DC song, but recognition lit his eyes within seconds, easing the dent between them. "Get. The. Fuck. Out."

Smiling at pleasing my beta, I returned to my task in willing my groin to relax. "That wine is predominantly made with shiraz but includes a bit of cabernet sauvignon. One of Australia's finest." I didn't add that the bottle had cost me close to fifty-thousand dollars. I would give my mates everything I owned if it meant they would stay of their own accord where fate intended.

Ears tuned in to their every move, I listened as Jon pulled the cork and filled three wine glasses while Dakota placed the garlic in the pan.

I had watched the two of them making dinner the evening before by their campfire, and I found myself feeling as though my presence didn't hinder their harmony. Like a well-rehearsed orchestra, we worked together to create our meal.

Onions translucent and garlic perfectly fragrant, I added the remaining ingredients for a marinara I had been making for tens of years.

Awareness of Jon's presence tingled my skin. "Here."

I turned, my gaze landing on his crystalline blue eyes. No boundary hid him from me, no wall of hesitancy or self-preservation. He peered at me with naked honesty, glass of wine in his outstretched hand as if to say, *I see you. I know you.*

My soul shifted as though the mountain trembled beneath my bare feet. Did he mean it?

Truly?

Jon moved away before I found my voice and handed Dakota her glass. He kissed her temple and murmured his love. Grabbing his own glass off the island, he faced us both. "I've been trying to come up with some fancy-assed toast for this old vintage but fuck if I can think of jack shit."

I smirked as Dakota coughed, clearly pained by his lack of refinement in front of me.

"To new friendships," she said, her words almost void of tone as she glanced at me.

"To lovers finding their fate," I added, lifting my glass.

"Hell, I'll drink to that! To good fucking music too." Grinning, Jon tipped his wine back and drank down a large swallow rather than sip, which would allow him to appreciate its richness. "Damn." He peered into the glass as he lowered it. "That's some good shit."

I swirled my wine inside the glass and lifted it to my nose, inhaling—and completely missing out on the red liquid's aromas. Jon's face, pure enjoyment, and laid-back attitude held me captive.

Want.

Dragon teeth gnashing to bite into my male mate's flesh, I sipped without really tasting. My beta's blood would be sweet on my tongue, a heavy bouquet that would soothe the beast prowling for release inside me.

But would I have that chance? How could I entice him and our female to stay longer than a single night without resorting to physical manipulation?

Unable to give myself an answer, I sat down to dinner after serving the two I wanted to spoil forever.

Dakota's lack of control over her body's response to both of us men delighted me throughout our meal and created an ache in my groin I longed to ease between her thighs. The scent of her arousal wafted through the air more often than not, adding to the musk of Jon's pre-cum that seeped from his hard cock hidden beneath the table between us.

While dining, they spoke of mundane things, the wheres and whats of life. Information exchanged did little to douse the hot embers of desire among the three of us.

They'd married three months earlier and had rented a one-room apartment in New York. Jon had just lost his position at a tech company, but Dakota's freelance photography job and their savings would see them through for a time. She liked hiking and the outdoors. He enjoyed gaming, something I wasn't fully familiar with, and Dakota's bragging of tournaments and titles he'd won revealed her pride—and his embarrassment.

Jon and I finished our pasta, drinking our wine while our female continued to pick at her food. He lounged in his pushed-back chair, legs spread and hands clasped behind his head. The move stretched the T-shirt tight across his defined pectorals and biceps. It also put his bulge on display.

Between his blatant need for release and the sweet scent of Dakota's continued wetness, my dragon hissed and spat, fighting against my control to come out and play.

"But what about you?" Dakota's question as she placed her fork upside down on her plate tore my focus off her husband and the dark thoughts his beauty inspired both halves of me to bring to fruition. "What do you do for work?"

Talking about myself wasn't something I enjoyed but had relented to while we'd been briefly without Jon's presence. Bragging, even more so. I shifted on my seat at the intrusion into my personal life even though I wanted them both to share in every year I had left on earth.

"I hold a few degrees and put my gained knowledge of them to the test almost daily," I replied.

"Degrees? Plural?" Jon asked.

"Chemical Engineering—" I only named one of three "—but my newest love is robotics."

"What do you build?" Dakota asked, reaching for her wine glass.

"Offensive types. Weapons and those sorts of things."

Jon snickered, his appreciative gaze sliding over my shoulders and chest. "You're a modern-day Tony Stark?"

A smirk curved my lips. "Something like that."

"You're a government agency's wet dream," he said, his eyes twinkling—without a doubt flirting.

I shared in his light chuckle but didn't answer.

"Fuck." His gaze narrowed, even though his dimples remained. "You're government, aren't you?"

"I'm not, but I'm hoping to close a deal with our military in a few days."

"Shit." Jon's eyebrow rose. "You work with any other countries?"

"One or two," I said, standing to gather our plates, "but if I tell you anything more, I'll have to kill you."

Jon snorted a laugh at my blatant lie I'd offered with a wink.

"Let us help," Dakota said, rising to her feet and sending a fresh waft of her spring-like scent past my nose.

My cock throbbed even as contentment swelled in my heart.

"More wine, Mr. Tight Lips?" Jon asked, finally moving from his sexy pose and reaching for the second bottle on the table. He hadn't been forthcoming either, leaving answering my questions to his wife.

I dipped my head, hardly bothered by his read of my similar character as his own. I wondered who had caused Jon's careful nature. "Please."

The new moon had attempted to light the sky, but nothing other than stars dotted the darkness beyond the windows once we finished cleaning up after our meal.

Mere embers remained of the once crackling fire, and empty wine glasses sat upon the coffee table in front of us.

Dakota curled against Jon's side, and same as earlier, I positioned myself a bit away from the couple, angling to face them.

Her hand and cheek lay on his chest, but her attention focused on my face. Jon trailed his fingers though the long tresses draped over her shoulder but kept his gaze on me as well. As one, they stared my way, probably unaware the other did the same.

I explained the sensors behind the lights system, the home automation system I'd created, the natural spring in the deepest parts of the cavern that fed the entire house with fresh water, and the solar panels with enough battery backup to power the entire space for a week. I realized I might have droned on too long in answering Jon's questions about the technology that made the cave a comfortable home when Dakota's eyes glazed over and her hand slid down to rest on Jon's thigh, mere inches from the bulge in his shorts.

Not having showered, both of us men emanated the musky scent of having sweated while working our muscles. Given the chance, I would have gladly licked every inch of Jon, lapping up the salt lingering on his skin, drawing him so deep into my lungs he filled my soul.

And Dakota...

The addictive tanginess of her desire filled my nose with every inhale. Would her folds be swollen and pink? Fragrant as a summer morning, full of life-giving nectar I was desperate to gather on my tongue, swallow, and claim as my own?

My saliva glands roused at the thought of licking between her thighs. Nibbling on her sensitive flesh. Dragon rumbling deep in my chest, I realized I needed to escape the draw to my mates before I took things too far, much too fast.

No—take.

"I believe I shall retire," I said, standing suddenly as my dragon growled his displeasure at me. "Feel free to linger as long as you wish."

Stay.

Feed and breed!

My neck hairs stood on end as I strode away, my beast's desperate pleadings wrangled and tied up tight. Body tingling with the need to taste and claim my fate, I hastened up the stairs and into the hallway intent on the privacy of my bedroom where I could find my own release, unsatisfying as it might be.

Jon's shuddered sigh brought me up short, just out of sight of the downstairs.

"Yes," he whispered, and I imagined Dakota's hand trailing higher up his thigh, grasping his hard length through his shorts. "Just like that, baby."

Silence fell for a few seconds, my heartbeat thundering in my ears. No bribe, monetary or physical outside of my mates, could have torn me from my spot in the middle of the hallway.

"Aw, *fuck.*" Jon groaned.

Had she pulled him free? Licked the pre-cum from his swollen cockhead?

I glanced over my shoulder, scales fighting to shimmer over my skin. I clenched my jaw to keep my true form from revealing itself and crept back until the back of the couch and their heads came into view from my high vantage point.

Dakota had leaned over Jon's lap. I envied him and his hold on her hair as her head bobbed over him. Did she take him deep? Swallow around his sensitive glans?

Need.

I grasped at my own length through my shorts while wishing for a clearer view. My cock was hard and aching, same as Jon's must be. I longed to plunge into Dakota, Jon's shaft tucked alongside mine within the clutches of her tight heat.

Filling her full until she overflowed, seeping our combined seed from her body.

Yessss.

Lower lip between my teeth, I tugged down my shorts, tucking the waist band beneath my drawn-up balls. One hand cupping my sac, the other smearing my own pre-cum over my length, I fought off echoing the groans rising past Jon's lips.

"Don't want to come in your mouth," he said, pulling her head up. He claimed her lips with his own, causing them both to moan.

Dakota's hand took over where her tongue had left off, the flex of her arm within vision feeding my imagination while moving my own with the same rhythm. Down and up, swirl over the crown, thumb across the slit, and to the root once more with slickness.

Mouth still fused to hers, Jon pushed Dakota onto her back on the other side of the sectional, settling between her thighs. His torso and wide shoulders hid her from my hungry stare. His hand moved between them, causing Dakota to gasp against his lips.

"Your pussy is soaked for me." He hummed his appreciation. "But I want your ass."

"Yes." Dakota whimpered the word, sending a shiver through me.

"Lube—"

"Don't need it," she rushed to say. "Just use the wetness from my pussy."

Jon sat on his haunches abruptly and yanked her leggings off.

A heartbeat later, Dakota moaned.

The back of the couch hindered the erotic sight of whatever he did to her. "Let me prep you, baby."

My cock throbbed as I imagined him stroking deep inside her sopping core, gathering her slick arousal.

She grunted. "Jon."

"I know, baby." His arm flexed as I imagined he worked her open to take his cock.

"I'm ready—hurry."

He leaned over her. "Relax and let me in." His perfect peach of an ass flexed.

"God!" Dakota's cry clenched my balls.

My beast growled, clawing for release, attempting to shred my human form from the inside out. But I needed to stay in control—watch my beta fill our female and bring her release.

"Fuck, your ass is so tight." Shorts resting beneath his flexing backside, Jon took his wife's offering.

Like a true pervert, I stared and masturbated, every inch of my human flesh vibrating in desperation to keep my dragon contained.

Her cries spurred Jon on and hastened my sliding grip along my throbbing length. Her hands grasped at his shirt, his hair, and I squeezed my hardened balls.

"M-more, Jon." Dakota's legs shuddered around his waist as she gasped, a moan following seconds later. "Harder. Please. Want to feel you every time I sit for the next week."

"Fuck, baby—the shit you say sometimes. Goddamn your ass is so fucking hot. Silky smooth."

He grunted and groaned words of love, his hips pistoning toward her, his ass flexing with every thrust. The combined scent of their desire rose, filling my home with the most divine bouquet.

Dakota shrieked, and Jon captured her mouth, muffling the glorious music of her release. Seconds later, he followed, his low growl of her name tingling deep within my groin.

I bit down on my lip as my dragon roared. We overflowed my fist with the seed that was meant to mix with our beta's, breeding our female mate.

CHAPTER 9
JONATHAN

Focusing on Dakota while fucking had proved harder than usual because Elijah's fire and brimstone scent permeated damn near everything. He'd left us, but even the air simmered with the strangeness I felt between us whenever he stood close by.

Whispering endearments, declaring my love to Dakota over and over again didn't diminish the truth I cheated on her mentally. Growling out her name when finally coming deep inside her ass, both of us sweat-drenched and out of breath, didn't lessen my shame.

I collapsed atop her, completely spent. She still clutched at my ass with her heels, her hands holding tight to my back.

"God." She swallowed loudly in the sudden stillness. "What *was* that?"

Burying my face in her neck, I fought off the truth about the situation I found myself in and how it made me feel.

Tempted.

Guilty.

"That was me loving you," I lied.

She giggled. "You've got to start loving me every day, then. Holy shit, that was hot."

"I *do* love you, Dakota," I stated, more for me than to assure her.

"I know, baby." She kissed my cheek and lifted my head, her soft hands cradling my cheeks. Lit only by the waving light of the fire's embers, her face wasn't readable. "You're my world." She whispered the statement, but I caught the hint of a question in her voice.

We shared everything, every thought, but mine toward Elijah, and hers as well, wasn't something I was ready to or even wanted to discuss if I'd been able to. That shit made me too uncomfortable. Same as how he called to me, pushed me to lower my walls and let go of my usual caution.

The man scared the shit out of me, but my body couldn't help but crave his nearness.

Best just to enjoy the guy's generosity for the night and light out with the sun. Back to our shit car at the trail head, New York, and my jobless, bleak life I wasn't sure how to move forward in.

At least I had Dakota to walk beside me and hold my hand when I stumbled in my inability to be a real man like my foster father had attempted to mold me into.

That sense of failure I'd had riding my shoulders for months crashed into me with renewed strength. Seeing all Elijah had, hearing of his accomplishments even though he'd spoken of them humbly, made me realize what a loser I really was.

A long-haired hippy who would rather slouch with a game controller in his hand while staring at a huge screen on a wall rather than sit in a cubicle somewhere, fingers banging away at a keyboard for some rich CEO who treated his employees like slaves.

Envy over Elijah's accomplishments snaked through my

blood but did absolute jack shit to erase my lust for the rich-as-fuck man housing us for the night.

"Let's go to bed," Dakota murmured, and I gave her my weight to plant a slow, soft kiss to her mouth, counting my blessings.

Attempting to, at least, but a hole gaped open inside my chest.

Why was I suddenly feeling as though something… lacked? She'd always been enough for me, so what the actual fuck? And how had we gotten to this point where some heavy shit lay between us, but neither of us seemed able to bring it up? Since when did walls erect between me and Dakota?

She grimaced when I pulled out, my cum seeping from her swollen asshole.

I ripped my shirt off and pressed it between her legs, wishing I could do so much more than care for her physically after taking out my aggression on her sweet pucker. "I'll carry you up to the shower."

Dakota snuggled against my chest, clinging to my neck as I held her in my arms, and I was thankful as fuck for her love. We would make it. Somehow, we would overcome whatever this moment was, same as we'd done that last time we'd fought almost a decade ago.

That shit had gotten left in the past where it belonged, and so would Elijah.

Eventually.

Hopefully.

A grimace marked my face at the conflict in my damned chest over my head. Talk about a fucking tug-of-war.

The large cavern's lights faded to darkness behind us as I climbed the stairs, my steps heavy.

Fire and brimstone along with something decidedly

sweet and mouthwatering hit my nose once I reached the landing, causing my spent dick to twitch.

Dakota swallowed hard as though her drool factory had been flicked to life as mine had.

Fuck.

I shifted her slight weight, clinging to her a little tighter, starting to wonder if there was some sort of supernatural bullshit going on to make us both horny as teenagers.

That idea lingered long after our shower where I'd washed my exhausted wife, both of us lost in silent contemplation. Usually, we would talk about whatever had stolen our thoughts so thoroughly, but for me, I needed to figure shit out before spewing anything that would lead us down a path that I feared would turn dark.

I couldn't sleep and lay staring into the night long after Dakota passed out snuggled up against my side. The seemingly magical energy of Elijah's home did more than act like a little blue pill to my dick. As if I'd had three shots of espresso, my body and mind buzzed, electrified and ready.

For what, I could guess at and lusted for all while hating myself for it.

Dakota's steady breathing beside me let me know she didn't suffer from the same wakefulness, thank fuck, because when the wife was dead on her feet, she became a sullen bear, best left untouched and unspoken to until she slept a solid ten or so hours.

I found myself grinning at the dark ceiling of the guest room. Even when in bitch mode, she was magnificent. Those were the only days I loved her from afar, biding my time until she rested, had some food, or her hormonal swings passed. The IUD she used to prevent pregnancy kept her from the lovely womanly cramps and stuff I didn't exactly enjoy hearing about, but not the fluctuations of happy one minute, sad the next once a month.

She claimed fucking helped to keep her blues away, and I was always glad to assist, but I waited for her to initiate during those five to seven days. Thank fuck that had been the week before because I wouldn't have been able to keep my hands off her the entire day spent in Elijah's company.

My dick swelled again at the thought of him, and I wondered not for the tenth time what the fuck was wrong with my body with how easily I'd gotten hard all damned day. An unnatural phenomenon but something I wouldn't mind lingering after we left come morning.

I glanced over at my wife. She must be sore as hell because I hadn't taken it easy on her the three times we'd fucked in the previous twelve hours. But she'd also been a slickened, sopping mess before my pre-cum added to the lubrication between us. Hell, we'd both been so turned on I hadn't needed anything other than what our bodies produced to slide into her ass earlier.

Elijah's doing?

I wondered yet again but with fewer insecurities clanging in my brain. How could I attempt to rouse jealousy I ought to feel when the mere memory of him made me hard as fucking steel? I hadn't realized I'd palmed my dick, but the involuntary thrust of my hips causing me to fuck my hand brought the reality of temptation crashing into me.

I wanted him—in my mouth, in my untouched ass—I didn't fucking care where. And that goddamned driving force, that tractor beam-like draw insisted I move. Slipping out of the bed would be an easy feat seeing as how Dakota slept like the dead once she passed out. Elijah and I could fuck each other out of our systems, and I could crawl back into bed with my wife none-the-wiser—

Fuck.

Releasing my grip on my cock, I flung my forearm over my eyes, scowling at the sickness of infidelity. Fucking him wasn't an option. Period. How would I feel if I found out Dakota had snuck into his bed and begged him to take her in every hole, in every way imaginable while I slept?

Oh fucking hell.

I fought off a groan, visions of sitting on a chair in the dark corner, watching him stuff my wife full of his dick filling my mind. She would whine to come but only release when he demanded it from her. Then he would tell me to come in his low, growly voice, and I would black out from busting a nut so goddamned hard I couldn't breathe.

Blowing out a steady exhale, I focused on relaxing my body.

But it was another hour at least before I finally passed the fuck out.

CHAPTER 10

DAKOTA

My eyelids popped open, and I blinked at the gorgeous sunrise through the window. Usually, I lingered in bed, enjoying the sleepy warmth of waking to a new morning, but as though caffeine already swam in my system, I found myself wide awake, ready and itching to move.

Jon snored lightly from behind me, and I rolled to take in my sexy husband. He was a vision of tanned limbs tangled in rumpled sheets, mussed hair, and parted full lips that had been kissing me senseless for years. The gentle rise and fall of his chest cradled a heart I all but worshiped.

I smiled while climbing out of bed and pulled on his T-shirt from the day before that had been soaked with his sweat, his natural scent—and Elijah's.

The man's essence covered everything like a magical creature from the books I read. I wondered if Jon could smell Elijah on me even though our host hadn't touched me beyond a graze of fingers. Was Elijah's scent the cause of Jon's sudden insatiable lust?

Is it mine?

A shiver slid down my spine as memories of the last shifter book I'd read created too many fantasies in my mind. Being claimed. Bitten. Owned and bred. Warmth rose in my core, a hot, achy need that required a dick to sate. Even better would be two—

I blinked the image away, released a slow exhale, and tiptoed from the room.

Coffee for Jon, I told myself to keep my thoughts contained to the sanctity of our marriage. Wake him in bed with a sleepy kiss only he deserved. Maybe enjoy one last ride on his cock before heading back down the mountain toward our car and home.

Something inside me hated the idea of leaving. Almost a…hiss of sorts spitting in anger like a pissed off cat with its hackles raised.

But I was no witch with a familiar.

The welcoming illumination rose in the hallway, but as the great room opened below me, the need for artificial light disappeared. A spectacular view of the White Mountains, the lower ones with fog kissing their bases, filled the wall of windows. Pink and gold etched across the sky, promising a new day.

A new beginning.

Smiling, I hurried down the stairs into the kitchen, needing to finish my task so I could capture every view from Elijah's mountaintop home with my camera before Jon and I left.

Coffee grounds already sat ready in the French press, along with the makings for my green tea beside it.

My smile widened as warmth spread through my chest.

I turned on the stovetop, ears straining for a hint of our host's whereabouts. The only sound stirring the stillness besides the simmering teapot was the ticking of a clock. Once the water neared boiling, I poured it over the coffee grounds and into my waiting mug. There was still no hint of Elijah's whereabouts or noise from Jon upstairs.

Needing that first couple of sips before pouring Jon's coffee and heading back up to him, I cradled the mug in my hands, breathing in the steam. Piping hot with a swirl of honey, the tea was perfection.

I made my way to the sliding doors leading onto the veranda, drawn by the beauty beyond. Thinking I would take a few minutes to enjoy the brisk morning all to myself, I grabbed a fleece throw off the couch and followed where my body led, sliding the unlocked door open and stepping out onto the veranda.

My breath fogged in front of me, but I slid the door shut and shuffled across the cold stone of the patio to the wrought-iron fenced edge. A sheer drop fell away before me, and a stairway of natural stone led down to the right, opposite of how we'd approached the day before.

Another smaller stone outcropping lay to the east at the bottom of the stairs.

Elijah stood in the rising sun's rays, his upper body bare and glistening with sweat. He moved through some sort of yoga-type fighting stances—tai something or another most likely—with beautiful grace, the muscles of his body flexing and stretching with the preciseness of a machine.

I clutched the throw around me, forgetting all about the steaming tea in my other hand as every cell in my body honed in on him. My desire to freeze the image in my camera's lens to drool over later grew as strong as the one insisting I draw closer to him.

The sunlight glinting off his damp skin brought to mind the dragon from my dream, the scales I had writhed upon, and the story Elijah had told us about Blood Born walking the earth. Arousal, thick and wet, rose between my legs, and I should have turned away, taking my focus and thoughts off Elijah.

My feet remained rooted to the cold stone, growing numb as I continued to stare at his liquid movements and the powerful muscles of his thighs. The bulk of his shoulders rippled as well as the muscles lining his stomach. The bulge hugged by tight shorts came fully into view as he turned sideways.

Shifting weight on his bent left leg, arms stretched out, he lifted his gaze.

Pale eyes met mine, stalling out my ability to breathe.

Elijah held the stance, unmoving as we stared at each other in the morning light, the sexual tension spanning the distance between us and intensifying that need to draw closer to one another.

I could taste his sweat on my tongue, could smell the brimstone and cinnamon scent of him in the air. My body leaked arousal down my thighs.

For Elijah, not my husband.

Heart squeezing as though in a vise, I spun and hurried back inside. I felt like a cheating whore, drooling and dripping over another man when the love of my life—

Jon stood at the top of the stairs, shirtless, bleary-eyed, and scratching his balls through his shorts. His face lit as his gaze landed on me, his slow, easy smile with flashing dimples lovely and so much more than I deserved. "Looks cold out there."

"Mmm," I hummed an affirmative and, tipping my head down to hide my hot cheeks, hurried into the kitchen. "Coffee?" I asked, my voice shaky.

"Fuck yes."

I poured the rich brew into a mug, my hand trembling.

Jon wrapped his arms around me, resting his chin on my shoulder. "Morning, beautiful."

"Hey, baby." I couldn't turn, couldn't let him read my face. God knew what he would think of the desire crashing around inside of me and without doubt showing in my eyes in the thin press of my lips.

My husband nuzzled beneath my ear, his hard length resting against my lower back. "Missed you this morning."

I snorted. "Your dick did, you mean."

"Not just this." He nipped my lobe while grinding against me. "The bed was cold. Empty."

"Sorry," I whispered, my guilt intensifying even though I'd left him with good intentions.

"Don't be. Enjoy the fact I'm addicted to everything about you. It's a good thing I can't get enough of my wife, isn't it?"

"Mmm," I agreed, my eyelids fluttering shut as he licked over my neck.

"Why are you so goddamned delicious?" He groaned the question.

I laughed lightly as he nibbled on my flesh, my insides jittery, an absolute mess.

"Want to take a bite out of you. Mark you with my teeth so the world knows who you belong to."

The possessiveness in his tone made my pussy pulse but also rekindled that worry in my head.

Was he quietly staking his claim, reminding me I was his alone?

I should have turned in his arms and assured him of my love, but the memory of how Elijah's presence had seemed to call to me from the sunbathed cliff made my soul restless.

"Gotta pee," I said, slipping out of Jon's hold as he reached for the coffee I'd prepared for him.

And wipe the evidence of my lust for another man from between my thighs.

I hurried up the stairs, Jon's trailing gaze lifting the hairs on my neck.

But I couldn't help craving Elijah. His assured touch. His dick.

The sound of my husband's hurried footsteps behind me heightened my pulse and my need to be filled. This time, I would focus on him alone and ignore the fantasy itching my thoughts about a mythical creature and threesomes I'd never even considered until meeting Elijah.

CHAPTER 11

ELIJAH

I knew the second Dakota had stepped onto the veranda. With every passing second she had stayed at the railing, the more her arousal had filled the brisk air and roused my dragon to wakefulness when he usually slumbered through my morning ritual. Her presence had overridden my focus, and I couldn't help but glance up at her. Frozen in Single Whip pose, everything but her pull on me had diminished to static in my mind.

Lips parted, pupils huge, she'd stared.

Come to us.

My dragon's command to our female echoed between my ears, and I'd held my breath, waiting, my selfishness wishing she broke her husband's heart in that moment.

She'd spun away.

My arms had dropped to my sides as my beast groaned his misery, and I'd straightened, head tilted back in hopes she would appear above me once more. Some time had passed before I accepted she'd denied us.

I grabbed my towel before heading back through the hidden lower entrance near the wine cellar, pondering the desire among the three of us and Jon's insecurities he'd silently revealed the evening before. Being in his alpha's house would call to the dragonblood in him, make him want to submit to me, but he didn't seem the type to bow down to another man's command.

Same as Dolyn.

I clenched my jaw, refusing to think on the man and how his name echoing in my head still caused a sting in my chest.

The longer my real mates remained in my presence, the better. If only I could figure out a way to get them to stay of their own accord.

Shackles.

"No," I grumbled under my breath.

Rope.

I shook my head at my dragon's insistence I take what belonged to us rather than wait for their initiations as was required for a lasting bond. I refused to lose my humanity to instinct no matter how badly I ached to claim my mates.

I found myself alone in the main living area when I passed the staircase threshold leading from the lower levels. A deep breath and careful listening assured me they hadn't yet left. Jon's cup of coffee sat untouched on the counter, Dakota's barely-sipped mug of tea beside it.

Did Jon catch her watching me? Could he smell her thick arousal as I had? Did jealousy eat at him this morning when it hadn't seemed to the day before?

Moving up the stairs toward the bedrooms, I focused on the sound of running water. They showered, I realized while passing their cracked-open door.

My foot stumbled at Dakota's soft whimper of pleasure.

Want.

Jaw clenched, I continued on toward my room even though the unclosed door suggested it'd been done as an invitation to join them.

Get ready for the day and think up a way to make them stay, I told myself, trying to shut out the sounds of my mates and the resulting images my brain created that only heightened my dragon's desperation to own them both. My mind didn't offer the answer to the conundrum I faced, and until I returned downstairs, intent on a cup of coffee and seeing both of their faces, my palms sweated and heart raced at the truth they would leave me shortly.

Abandon me to loneliness I'd barely survived when my ex-lover had disappeared all those years ago.

Steaming mug in hand, I stood in the kitchen, listening as Jon and Dakota exited their room and made their way down the hall. Backpacks loaded and in hand, neither met my gaze while walking down the stairs. The thumps of their dropped bags sounded loud, like a dead weight falling to the ground—exactly as my heart did.

No one spoke.

Jon peered at me, Dakota's gaze flitting between the two of us. Although freshly showered, their hair still damp, the scent of their combined cum clung to them. My dragon wanted to smear mine over both of them, chain them up, and force a mating they might not want.

Yessss.

Take.

Keep.

My throat tightened as my stomach twisted. Why did they need to return to New York now? According to what they'd said, another week of vacation lay before them, and Jon was unemployed.

"My job," I said, my voice higher than usual as an idea shot through my brain. "I have to go out of town earlier than expected. It's the government contract I spoke of." Mind scrambling, I blurted the first thing that came to mind. "I'm unprepared for a last minute absence and can't leave things left undone here at home. Solar batteries and the like."

Neither moved.

"I don't suppose I could talk you into housesitting for a few days while I'm gone?" I focused on Jon. "I could show you what needs to be done while I'm away."

He still didn't speak, but I could see the desire to stay—and the hesitation over accepting.

"I'll pay you," I tossed out when Jon glanced at his wife, beyond desperate for him to agree to remain where my essence would hopefully entice them to linger even after I returned.

"What do you think, Dakota?" he asked, his voice low and full of caution as I'd expected.

"Your call," she whispered, glancing over at me, "but I don't have to hand in the photos I took for *North Woods Living* for a couple more weeks."

Jon returned his focus my way. "When would you get back?"

"Friday." If it earned me the time required for my mates to realize they ought to stay indefinitely, the lies would be invaluable.

The blue eyes I'd once thought innocent stared into mine as though reading into every word. A smile hinted at Jon's lips when I'd thought he would sneer. "Any chance we could hang a little longer and you could use your chopper to fly us back to our car so we don't have to waste time walking out of these mountains?"

A rush of breath I hadn't realized I'd held expelled through my parted lips. "I'll do whatever it takes for you to agree to stay," I stated honest words for the first time since they'd descended with intent to leave.

Please, my human mind called out to Jon through the

energy already seeming to connect us even if dragonblood would never visibly make itself known. *Submit to my request.*

"You got yourself a deal, friend." Jon stuck out his hand, and I clasped it in mine, the hint of ancient blood in his veins sending a charge up through my arm and straight to my groin.

Mate.

Mine.

"I need to pack," I said, forcing myself to pull from the hair-raising desire between us. "I—I'll find you before I leave."

Jon dipped his head, his gaze unwavering from my eyes until I turned my back on them both and hastened up the stairs, the coffee I'd desired left forgotten on the counter.

I threw a bag together, only half paying attention to what went in it. My meeting in New York wasn't scheduled until Thursday, but I could always get some other work done to pass the time.

And watch from afar.

While my guests breakfasted, I made my way to the lowest level where my tech room sat. Countless screens showed images from the various cameras I'd installed throughout the cavern the year before even though no one— dragonblood or otherwise—could enter my home without being invited past the ward etched in granite over each entryway.

Jon and Dakota still sat at the table, both of their gazes flitting toward the stairwell leading to the lower levels where I lingered.

My chest ached with desperation to be near them, but enjoying the sight of them on-screen would have to suffice.

Double-checking the live feed could be accessed by an app on my cell, I exited and locked the room behind me. The door directly across from me drew my gaze, and I paused. I hadn't entered the room for years.

Would the scent of my ex-lover still linger? Would the toys I'd used to bring us both pleasure be dust-covered? Unusable? Would the wall my dragon had melted with fire in our overwhelming grief over his leaving fully resurface the heartache I'd felt a decade ago?

I had imagined Jon cuffed and bared for me in my dungeon, his wife tied down and unable to escape the vibrator I had strapped to her clit, but the memory of every device, each carefully crafted crop and whip, brought fresh ideas to my darker side.

Cock swelling, I punched in the key code to gain entrance when I hadn't considered doing so in over a decade.

CHAPTER 12
JONATHAN

It had been Dakota's idea to go traipsing through the mountains for our honeymoon, a contracted offer of good money for photographs of the White Mountains at the most opportune moment. But the hope glinting in her eyes over Elijah's request made the decision to accept his offer as easy as that from *North Woods Living*. She wanted to stay but would insist I choose what we ought to do, same as always.

Elijah's words held manipulation I recognized all too well, but he'd been ten times softer—kinder—than that of the narcissistic asshole from my childhood who'd taught me how to erect walls to protect myself from that shit.

Elijah had scaled them with ease, the crafty fucker.

I, too, yearned to say yes, but fear over trusting the wrong person heightened my inner bullshit scanner.

Elijah wanted something from us, far beyond sexual gratification I felt sure, and although living with Dakota for so many years had somewhat eased my defensive, suspicious nature, Elijah brought it to the forefront with the lies spilling from his delicious-looking lips.

But my pampered love wished to stay, and it wasn't like Elijah would be around to tempt either of us into writhing between the sheets of his bed wherever it lay on the second floor.

Even though I preferred having a little while to think shit through before agreeing to anything, I'd taken him up on his offer of money in exchange of caring for his home. At the clasp of his hand, my dick had swelled at a rate that left me lightheaded.

Dakota and I ate some natural, cardboard-like cereal while Elijah moved about—upstairs then down—both of our gazes glued to him when he shared the room with us for those brief moments before disappearing into the lower cavern. He returned upstairs to the second floor for a time but emerged once more, bag slung over his shoulder.

We had finished breakfast and nursed new cups—mine with coffee, Dakota's, her tea.

"I can show you where the batteries are," he said, drawing me to my feet as though his words were a leash demanding I follow like a well-trained dog.

I had to bite back a damned groan at the idea of crawling after him on hands and knees when I should have been grimacing with disgust. Guess I could add another kink to my *I wouldn't mind giving that shit a try* list.

"I'll take you on a complete tour of the lower levels on my way out if you'd like," he said to Dakota as a request for her to join us.

Funny how he was softer with her and more demanding of me.

Not that I had issue with either. I appreciated his kindness toward my wife and secretly got off on the bossiness leaving his tongue.

"Sure. We'd love that," she said, standing and taking my

hand, keeping me rooted in the here and now rather than a fantasy of infidelity.

Elijah's brow furrowed for a split second as he glanced down at our entwined fingers.

That's right, buddy. United we stand, I muttered inside my head.

The thought didn't hold the anger or resentment it should have toward the man who threatened my resolve to stay faithful to the love of my seemingly damned existence. Instead, I found myself wondering at his loneliness. The lack of love in his life I expected Dakota felt empathy for as she tended to be toward those who hurt.

Hell, even if both she and I invited him into our bed, we would leave him shortly afterward anyway, and he would be alone once more.

But what a few days those could be…

Shaking my head at the turn of my thoughts toward being united in *desire*, I followed Elijah down into the bowels of his caverns, through winding passes and the occasional smaller open areas. He showed us the solar panel system, the part below ground, the shutoff for the water pumps, the natural hot spring he had enclosed as a sauna-type room.

Dakota's eyes lit up upon seeing the steaming water, and I knew we'd be visiting there again before long.

Elijah ignored flanking doors as we passed through another hallway, and I wondered at what lay beyond.

"The garage," he said, pushing open the one directly ahead.

He flipped switches on the wall, flooding the room with light. A Humvee and sleek Audi—both shiny and black—sat in the room that appeared hewn out of rock. A steel garage door hung at the cavern's far end.

"This faces west," Elijah said, motioning us across the garage and up a few steps through another door. "And this is my pride and joy." Lights shone down on the helicopter he'd told us about. It rested upon a raised, steel floor, and as he flicked another switch, sending a similar door to the one in the garage upward, I realized exactly how he accessed the air from beneath a mountain.

"Come along," Elijah said, motioning us forward onto the dais-like platform.

Gears shifted, natural light flooded the room along with the cool, morning air, and the floor beneath us started to roll out into the shade of the mountain.

"That's fucking cool," I said, grinning at the technology that hung the platform over the road disappearing down into the valley on our left and leading to the garage door on our right.

A cold wind whipped at my hair, and I tugged Dakota close as I realized she'd wrapped her arms around herself against the chill.

Elijah turned toward us, fished something from his pocket, and tossed it to me. Keys jangled as they landed in my hand. "For the Humvee, just in case."

My smile widened.

"The same switch will pull the platform back in and shut the door, but I can close it remotely from the helicopter," he said, opening the chopper's door and tossing his bag inside.

"I'll get it," I said.

"Will you remember how to return upstairs?"

I rubbed over my chest from a sudden, strange ache. "I'm sure we can figure it out."

"We might need to stop by that hot spring on the way, though," Dakota said, a smile in her voice even though the suggestion sounded somewhat strained.

And breathless as fuck with obvious intent.

My dick bucked inside my jeans.

I held out my hand, and Elijah hesitated a few seconds

before clasping mine again. The same energy shot up my arm and straight south to my cock. "Safe trip," I said.

He dipped his head, pale eyes intently studying mine. "I left my cell number on the table. Call if you have any questions or problems."

"Will do."

Stepping back, he released my hand, leaving me feeling… bereft I believed the word was. "Dakota." He nodded toward her, and Dakota whispered a "safe travels" as he turned without touching her.

I laced my fingers through my wife's, seeking comfort, and we stepped back into the garage, far from the aircraft and the whirl of wind as the blades started cranking.

Headset in place, Elijah busied himself with whatever it took to get that beast in the air, and when he finally glanced our way again, a small smile tilted his lips up. We both waved, and he lifted away, leaving us in a thunder of noise and whipping wind from the rotor blades.

A sense of sadness crashed over me, a tugging toward where he disappeared on the horizon.

Dakota absently rubbed her chest as though she felt it too.

"Come on," I croaked, pulling her back into the warm cavern that remained flooded by Elijah's scent regardless of his absence. "Let's go check out that sauna and see if we can make it any hotter."

CHAPTER 13

DAKOTA

Elijah hadn't just left his phone number on the counter—he'd set a couple of hundred-dollar bills there as well.

"Maybe we ought to head to civilization and party today," I said with a laugh while thumbing through the Benjamin Franklins. We'd visited the hot springs as Jon had suggested but hadn't burned the roof down. Unlike I'd expected, we didn't have sex in the steaming water but sat and conversed about the normal issues as we'd done so easily before meeting Elijah.

Our future.

Having the children we both longed for.

Him finding a job first so he could properly provide for us.

The topic of Elijah himself, neither of us touched with a ten-foot pole. It was obvious we both skirted what immediately bothered us, and while I knew a simple spilling of our thoughts would clear the air or at least give us a path forward together, I weirdly wasn't able to discuss it.

Fantasy bordered on reality. Dreams in wakefulness and while asleep alike silenced my tongue.

It was as though something outside our control, some greater power demanded we both work through our issues as individuals for a change, that no outside influence—even each other—would be tolerated in deciding our individual fate.

The lack of Elijah's presence eased some of the tension in my shoulders, but hints of his alluring aura and energy remained behind. My libido lingered on edge, making me continue to long for what I shouldn't.

"You really want to go out for the day?" Jon asked, pulling open the fridge.

The idea of leaving Elijah's home made me squeamish for some reason. "No. Not really."

He handed me a beer, and we twisted the caps off and clinked the bottles together. His blue eyes twinkled down at me as he flashed his dimples. "Let's get drunk and break in every piece of his furniture."

"Probably doesn't get much action," I mused quietly, feeling sorry for our host but not so much it killed the mood. Add in the remnants of Elijah's brimstone smell that clung to everything in his cave-like house, and I was insatiable.

"Probably not."

I held Jon's gaze while taking a big swig. "Kitchen table first?" I asked, one brow raised, my body primed and ready for him when we'd have been better off sharing words rather than bodily fluids.

"After that, I'm bending you over the couch," he promised, heat kindling in his eyes and causing my pussy to pulse.

I swallowed another mouthful of the bitter hops, humming my agreement.

"Then we can christen where he and I were lifting weights—"

"And every other room we find behind closed doors," I tacked on, some strange part of me wanting to cover Elijah's belongings with Jon's and my scent.

"What if they're locked?" Jon asked, his grin infectious.

"Maybe those keys will let us in," I said, raising my beer and nodding toward the ring of them Jon had tossed on the counter.

"Maybe."

We downed our beers, and Jon grabbed us a second cold bottle each. Another cheers, and we mentioned the wine cellar and the front seat of the Humvee for our future sex-capades since we didn't have much else to do and we both were feeling the horniest of our lives.

"What about his bed?" I blurted a sudden thought and slapped a hand over my mouth, snickering and cursing in my head at the same time.

One of Jon's eyebrows cocked upward, a hint of mischie-vous devil in his eyes. "Think he would know if we did?"

I shrugged, believing if he did find out, he'd probably jerk off to fantasies of us fucking where he lay every night. "Who cares?" I said, a breathless bundle of hormones while hopping up onto the island ready to get started. "Come here." Setting my nearly empty second bottle of beer aside, I reached for Jon, snagging his T-shirt in my fist.

"I need to do some laundry," I said, nuzzling my nose against his hard, warm chest and breathing in Elijah as well as my husband.

"Later," he said gently pushing me back enough he could pull my shirt off overhead. "And no damn bras or panties while he's gone either." He cupped my throbbing core through my leggings. "I want this pussy available to me all day, every day. Pulsing around my cock after I give it the lovin' it's so damned wet for."

"God, ye—"

He swallowed the ending of my word with his mouth crushed to mine, and we began our plan to fuck our way through Elijah's house.

I had wrapped my legs around Jon as he'd carried me to the living room. He'd lifted me off his hard shaft, spun me around, pushed me down over the edge of the couch where Elijah's head had rested, and fucked into me so damn hard we'd jostled the couch out of its place.

Elijah's scent had swarmed my nose as it pressed against the leather, the thought of him being there with us, shoving his cock down my throat making me come harder than ever before.

Mind on replay of that euphoric climax it took a good half hour to recover from, I tossed our laundry into Elijah's washer. I'd stolen the clothes Jon had worn while he lay sprawled on the couch butt naked, flicking through the few TV channels Elijah's satellite offered.

Since I wasn't allowed a bra or panties, I'd told Jon he couldn't wear clothing—at all. If my pussy had to be accessible at all times, his cock had to be a hand or mouthful away, no hindrances.

He'd agreed without question, making both of us burst into carefree laughter like we used to do before Jon had lost his job and the world had seemed to crash down on him.

Eyeing one of Elijah's button-down shirts hanging nearby, I pulled off the tee I'd had on earlier and donned to gather our laundry and tossed it into the wash as well. After starting the wash, I pulled Elijah's shirt off the hanger and buried my nose against the expensive fabric.

God.

A whimper rose past my lips.

It smelled like him. Fire and brimstone, cinnamon and… *something* flooded my lungs and mind. Where did the moisture coating my pussy come from? Constantly aroused since having first met Elijah, my body seemed to have an endless supply of wetness. All the sex Jon and I'd had and I could walk with no problem. There was no twinge of discomfort between my thighs—unless one counted the sudden need making my pussy throb.

A few minutes later, panty-less and warmed through, I rounded the still-askew couch. Jon's gaze landed on the shirt, but he didn't say a word as I curled up on his lap. "I didn't have any clean clothes," I explained while pressing against his hard, warm front.

He scooted down a bit, wrapped his arms around me, and buried his face in my chest. "Christ, do you smell good," he said, his voice muffled against Elijah's shirt and my left breast.

His cock swelled against my leg as he continued to breathe deeply, nuzzling my tight nipple.

I certainly wasn't the only insatiable being in the cavern, but was it possible Elijah affected Jon in the same way he did me? The fanciful idea magic actually coated Elijah's home only made me wetter, and I rubbed myself against Jon, seeking friction for my needy clit.

He growled, his teeth nipping at me, his hands yanking up the edge of Elijah's shirt to access my pussy. "Christ, you're soaked already."

I whimpered as he shoved two fingers inside me.

"I want you again," he growled around a mouthful of my nipple and fabric.

"I can tell…" I'd meant to let out my giggle at his drive when we'd finished fucking not an hour earlier, but he clamped his teeth over my nipple, ending all thoughts on a deep moan. "More," I whimpered, yanking on his unbound hair. "Harder."

He obliged, stroking my aching bundle of nerves with his thumb while finger fucking me. "You like that, baby?" he asked between nips, and catching my lower lip between my teeth, I jerked my head in a sharp nod.

"Hmm." He backed off, his gaze searing my face. "Maybe we ought to get you some nipple clamps."

Another rush of arousal coated the fingers he still worked inside me.

"My baby likes that idea."

"I'm game—" I gasped as he pulled his fingers from my pussy and pinched my clit, "—if you are."

"You know I'd do anything for you," he whispered, settling between my thighs.

"Fuck me."

He claimed my mouth and body with one thrust, giving me exactly what I'd asked for.

CHAPTER 14

JONATHAN

For three days, all we did was eat, sleep, drink wine and beer, and give each other orgasms. I did leave Dakota alone long enough that she had time to click off a hundred pictures or so of Elijah's home and the mountain views from the veranda. We ran low on fresh produce—not that I gave a shit—and even Dakota didn't want to leave our hideaway to replenish Elijah's stock since he'd said he would bring some when he returned. We fucked like a couple of horny teenagers, and I took every hole she offered, but Christ, I felt like something was missing. There was a shit ton of unspoken things between my wife and me, thoughts and feelings I still couldn't quite get a grasp on in order to name even if I'd been able to. I secretly appreciated I couldn't speak since doing so would make Dakota think she wasn't enough for me, and she always had been and would be.

Even though a sense of being unfulfilled haunted me, living in Elijah's house was like finding Elysium. A wine cellar disappeared into darkness, countless cases of beer on hand, free food when groceries were expensive as shit, the most gorgeous woman on earth, and Elijah's scent everywhere.

I caught Dakota sniffing his shirts, which was on a daily basis because that was all she'd been wearing since the man had left us to our own devices. Something about the thread count, she'd said. Whatever. She looked sexy as hell and smelled even better with his scent on her.

The fuck is wrong with me?

Scrubbing a hand down my face over the question ringing between my ears since first meeting Elijah, I stared unseeing at the TV. Dakota started cleaning up the dinner dishes behind me. She'd insisted on doing the job herself, and I'd given her what she wanted— same as always—even agreeing to go naked while Elijah was away, but that wasn't a hard choice.

Nothing better than living life the same way you came into the world. But what I really needed—

I bit back my groan at the warring thoughts in my brain, tearing me apart. I lusted for Elijah with a yearning so damn harsh my entire body ached. Couldn't stop thinking about him, even while making love to my wife. Guilt ate at me like a medieval fucking plague to the point I checked my torso on occasion for blistering evidence of some sort of disease.

My feet itched with the need to move, and like that magnetic pull from Elijah drawing me to him, the urge to go downstairs propelled me off the couch. I didn't evaluate the why, just went with my instincts.

Using the excuse of retrieving a couple bottles of wine for the evening, I made my way through the dim corridors and into the cellar, doing exactly as I'd said. But I set the bottles of red on the floor outside the door and made my way deeper into the caverns rather than returning upstairs. Lights brightened and dimmed behind me, and with every step, I knew I needed to find whatever it was that slowly heightened my heartbeat and drew me forward.

I approached the end of the final hallway that ended at the garage door. Two wooden doors flanked me, both with keypads which Elijah had ignored when giving us the tour of the main caverns and rooms beneath the living area. The door on the left didn't open when I turned the doorknob beneath the keypad. The one on the right didn't either, but I couldn't release my grip from the handle.

Yes.

Something inside me whispered a single word, a voice that tickled at my memory, but I couldn't place. Shaking my head, I pulled my hand away, my gaze landing on the numbered squares above. I brushed my fingers over the pad, pressing when the keys warmed beneath my touch.

The lock clicked, and the knob gave way beneath my other hand.

I glanced up the hallway, adrenaline pumping through my system, but the magical pull of Elijah didn't caress my skin. His scent, while lingering in the bowels of his home, didn't make me salivate like when he was nearby.

Palm on the door, I pushed it inward, not leaving my spot on the threshold. Soft light flooded the area as the door swung open, illuminating a cavern-like room that looked hewn by centuries of water or fire.

Singeing heat raced through my blood like a kick to my groin as I realized the room's purpose.

I'd found Elijah's dungeon.

The one I'd been fantasizing about, the chains and harnesses hanging from the ceiling, the black Saint Andrew's cross against the far wall, along with a spanking bench and peg boards where all sorts of toys hung. Canes, whips, floggers, and dozens of other implements I didn't have a clue about.

My focus returned to the cross and the shackles at its four corners. On instinct, I walked across the dungeon, my hard cock leading the way, until I stood before the large X. Hand shaking, I reached out to touch the scale-like material covering wood, the slightly bumpy yet satiny soft finish warm beneath my tingling fingertips.

An image flashed through my mind of me strapped tight in its bindings, my head tipped back and mouth opened on a groan as slashes of pain radiated through the fronts of my thighs and straight to my dick.

I palmed myself, finding a slickened mess dripping from my slit, and I moaned for real while sliding my grasp down to the root and back up again.

I knew who wielded the flogger in my imagination, and my body ached for the fantasy to come true. Unable to help myself, I jacked my straining length, the wet sound of the hand fucking and my sharp breaths the only noise in the room.

Yes.

The voice whispered again, and I gripped harder, jerking with a frenzied passion I didn't understand but didn't want to stop no matter how wrong it might be.

"Fuck." A growl rose from my chest as my balls swelled and tingled, and my eyelids fell shut, bringing his eyes to mind. I moaned. "Elijah..."

Cum shot from my shaft with such force my knees buckled, sending me to the floor. One hand on the ground, the other milking my spurting cock, I hung my head and panted as wave after wave of euphoric, pure fucking *bliss* rolled over me.

My dick pulsed to completion, and I groaned.

"Christ." I swore a few times, realizing I'd shot my spunk all over the cross and floor. Shivers coating my body in goose bumps, I sat back on my haunches and glanced around, my heartbeat pounding in my ears. Towels were stacked on a bench by the door but looked like they'd been sitting there a long fucking time.

Sure enough, by the time my shaking legs got me across the dungeon, I found a good-sized coating of dust on them. I scanned the room, paying closer attention. Everything from the toys to the larger apparatuses appeared unused for a dozen years or so—except the cross, and a swept path leading to it from the door.

My focus honed in on the black covering. The lack of dust on the cross's four shackles. I grabbed a couple of towels from the bottom of the pile and wiped myself off while returning to the X. Every inch had been recently cleaned.

I leaned forward and sniffed along one of the upward-reaching arms—Elijah.

My dick actually fucking twitched again. Jaw clenched, I cleaned up the mess I'd made and left the room, vowing to shut the memory of what I'd just done deep in the recesses of my mind, never to be thought of again or talked about with another soul.

I tossed the towels I'd used into the washing machine, retrieved the two bottles of wine from the hallway, and made my way back upstairs.

Dakota was putting the dried dishes away as I walked through the door. She smiled at me, righting the axis of my off-kilter world. "I set out glasses," she said, glancing at the island.

Forcing a smile as though happy as hell like I'd been the previous couple of days, I went about opening the first bottle, pouring a glass to the rim for myself. A few gulps revealed the wine was expensive as shit and would quickly fuzz the memory of what I'd done.

"Sybil, play 2Cellos," I said, wanting Elijah yet not.

I poured a half-glass for my wife as the duo slid out in a

song I didn't know and meandered to the couch where I tried to relax, focusing on Dakota as she puttered around Elijah's kitchen. She curled on the couch beside me a few minutes later, her and Elijah's combined scents like a soothing balm to my tense muscles.

"Are you happy, baby?" I asked with my lips against her temple, her hair tickling my nose.

She hesitated for a second. "Yes."

"Best vacation ever," I said, not wanting to question why she hadn't answered immediately because if I'd been the one asked, I'd have done the same damned thing.

"Better than Bermuda could have offered, that's for sure," she said with a sigh, snaking an arm around my naked chest and resting her cheek on my shoulder.

I huffed a snort of laughter. "This place is like a Bermuda Triangle," I said. "It's like we've disappeared off the face of the earth and found heaven." A flash of the black cross filled my vision, and I bit the inside of my lip, a frown denting my brow.

"It is perfect here, isn't it?"

"Just about," I mumbled, my body longing for Elijah as the low strings of some classical shit played overhead. "Wish I could give you something like this."

Dakota sat back and cupped my scruffy cheek in her hand. "I don't need this to be happy," she said, her greenish eyes shining in the flames flickering from the fireplace. "I'll be content wherever we go—as long as you're with me."

"You're my world," I told her, more for my own peace of mind than hers, because I always thought stating something made it true. "You're everything I'll ever need."

She kissed me gently, and fuck if guilt didn't rise like bile up the back of my throat.

CHAPTER 15
ELIJAH

The days dragged by, and I only managed to stay away from my mates because of the live feed I pulled up on my phone every second time allowed. Lounging in my Manhattan apartment, I dined on takeout and, like a pervert, studied Jon and Dakota as they made themselves right at home where they belonged.

The dining room around me hinted of bleach and lemon cleaners, but I imagined the scents of my mates, their mingled cum dripping from Dakota's pussy.

I'd heard them a few times in those twenty-four hours we'd spent together in my home and had gotten a glimpse of them fucking, but fully watching them from start to finish on nearly every surface in my cave filled me with a voracious hunger I couldn't sate on my own.

Relieving myself as they found their release took away some of the tension, but didn't satisfy in the way I needed. Thursday night, long after the dinner hour and finally getting the government officials to agree to my terms at my downtown office, I returned to my apartment, ripping off my tie and swiping over my phone's screen to turn it on.

I had been plagued by memories of my mates all day long while trapped in an office building making the sale of my life —and in the process, creating the perfect job for my beta. Thoughts of the contract for remote robots covered by my patented armor similar to dragon scales flew from my mind as the live feed from my living room filled the screen.

Jon and Dakota lay in front of the fire, making love with slow, sensual touches rather than in desperate hunger as they'd been doing since I'd left. I slumped on the edge of the bed, elbows resting on my knees, cell clutched in my hands, my heart pained by their erotic dance. He pulled out and kissed every inch of her body, worshiping her with lips, tongue, and sometimes nibbles, making my mouth flood with drool, my dragon growl with the need to use my own teeth on her silky skin.

Dakota held Jon's head in her hands as he licked her breasts, sucking her nipples deep into his mouth. I couldn't hear the sounds coming past her lips but could pull them forth from my memory. Gasps and the sweetest moans that made my blood heat.

Our female's back arched off the floor and head tilted to the side, her eyelids fluttering upward. Her gaze latched onto the camera positioned above the kitchen sink I'd thought hidden from sight.

Did she know I observed their love making? Lower lip between her teeth and focus seemingly right on me...

Did she *hope* I stared, entranced by their display of pleasure they offered each other?

Jon rolled her over and positioned her face down, ass in the air. He gripped her hips and slowly sank into her body, his head tipping back, his mouth moving as though whispering all sorts of loving or filthy words to make her come around his cock. My balls tightened as he fucked into her harder, lowering his head and watching his length disappear into her body. Faster, his hips pistoned, flexing his ass I wanted to mark with my teeth.

Dakota shuddered beneath him, her hands grabbing at the rug beside her face, eyes clenched shut, lips parted.

Jon lifted his head, his gaze pinning me in place as he too focused on the camera, same as our female had done.

He must have felt my steady gaze, his alpha looking on with longing and aching need.

I swallowed and immediately darkened my screen.

Had the two of them gotten into the control room while I'd been distracted with work and seen the wall of live feeds from the cameras I'd placed throughout the cave? If they'd gained access to that area, nothing would keep them from my dungeon across the hall.

But my phone would have alerted me to someone attempting to open both doors without the proper code. I had access to my cameras while I'd been in and out of meetings the previous two days but didn't have time to check them until returning to my apartment.

Jaw clenched while willing my cock to deflate, I tossed my stuff back into my bag and strode to the elevator. The urgency to return, to see what else they might have figured out, sent a rush of adrenaline through my system.

Home.

Mates.

I swiped my cell's screen to text my driver but paused, my need too great for a car ride to where my helicopter waited to whisk me back to the mountains. I made my way upstairs, not stopping until I melted the lock on the door leading to the roof with a single flame between my lips since I didn't have a key.

I let myself out into the night, breathing shallow to avoid filling my lungs with exhaust and the stench of the city, every inch of my body vibrating with a desperation above what I'd felt when first catching a hint of my mates' combined scent on the breeze days earlier.

Desire for my ex-lover had never owned me like this.

Thoughts of Dolyn banged through my chest, and I hated how I still hurt, how some part of me couldn't seem to let him go. Grief over not knowing where his body rested, of not having closure, continued to haunt my mind.

But the memory and ache for him didn't lessen my desire for what fate had put in front of me.

Stripping in the cold night didn't affect the heated blood coursing through my veins either. I stuffed my shoes on top of the rumpled suit I'd worn all day, zippered the bag shut, clutched it in my hand, and threw myself off the building.

Shifting mid-fall came as easy as breathing, and a single flap of our wings sent us shooting upward into the sky. An approaching plane slipped past beneath us, mere feet from our talons and the tiny bag dangling from one claw.

The rush of the aircraft's exhaust faded as we flapped twice more, sending us northward faster than any plane could fly.

Hurry.

Darkness coated the land beneath us, but we didn't bother with enjoying the beauty of night flying. Our focus lay on the mountains in the north, every harsh flap of our wings rushing us closer to our destiny. What would take a human pilot over an hour was less than half that in dragon form.

We made almost no noise while touching down on the road outside of our garage, and I quickly shifted back, forcing my inner beast to give way to our human side that would fit through the door. Not bothering with pulling on clothes, I punched in the alarm code for the entrance off to the side of the garage's stall door and let myself in. The

Humvee and Audi sat untouched without a hint of my mates' scents clinging to their exterior.

A few seconds later, I stood between the two doors a key code required to unlock.

Only a slight, lingering scent of Dakota remained in the hallway, sending a rush of blood to my cock. She hadn't been down in that area of the cavern since I'd left, but Jon?

That curious man had been snooping. Not that I was surprised by the fact. He was as wary and careful as I tended to be.

My gaze swung to the door on my left, the room I had visited the day before deciding to head to New York. The room was coated in dust, unused for far too long. Something had propelled me to clean the cross I'd imagined strapping Jon onto, and I'd done so, unmoved by all other hazy memories from before when another had given himself to me but refused to submit how I'd dreamed of.

But Jon—he was fated to be mine.

Yesssss.

Take.

My shaft hard and aching, I keyed in the code and pushed the door in. A wave of Jon's scent filled the room, and even though he had cleaned up after himself, the sweet muskiness of his cum hit my tongue, flooding my mouth with saliva.

A low growl, desperate and full of yearning rumbled in my chest.

As an alpha, I'd never desired to taste a man's seed before, but Jon made me want in ways no one ever had.

Need.

My gaze snagged on the wall my dragon had ruined with fire, the rock melting and resolidifying in droplets that reminded me of the many tears I'd shed after Dolyn's disappearance.

Not ours.

I grit my teeth, hating the lingering ache in my chest. Spinning away, I shut the door on my past and, brow furrowed, let myself into the tech room. I scanned over the screens lining the far wall.

Jon bent over deeply, rifling through the refrigerator, his bare backside and puckered hole on display, causing my mouth to water and another groan to my lips. I wanted to lick and suck. Plunder and own.

Yessss.

Dakota let herself into their bathroom—one room I didn't install cameras in. The door closed behind her.

A war raged in my head and heart, instinct and reasoning clashing like I'd never experienced before.

Should I stay put until the following morning when I'd claimed I would be home or head upstairs and fill my eyes and lungs with the two drawing on my soul to mate? I wanted to fill them in every way imaginable.

Need—own.

My dragon thrashed against the bonds I attempted to control him with—but I still refused to take without consent as his instinctive nature demanded we do.

Jon straightened, backed out of the refrigerator, beer in hand, and glanced at the doorway leading down to the lower floors. He lifted his head slightly as though sniffing, his focus on the stairwell that would lead him to me.

His cock thickened slightly between his thighs, and my heart skipped a beat. Was it possible the dragonblood inside him had begun heightening his senses from time spent surrounded by my scent? Did he feel the same tug toward me, the alpha who would dominate him yet lay the world at his feet?

I held my breath, but Jon eventually moved to the windows, peering into the dark sky, going from pane to pane. He donned a pair of shorts he grabbed off the floor and lounged in the corner of the end of the couch where he could keep watch on both the door beneath the stairs and the hallway opening at the top to the second-floor bedrooms.

He sipped his beer, gaze flitting from one to the other as though waiting for which of us would arrive first. His wife—or me.

I pulled on the clothing from my bag, uncaring of their rumpled appearance. Bag in hand, I slipped back into the hallway and made the trek up the stairs, my heart pounding and inner beast purring over my giving in to the need to be nearer to my beta.

A last check of my phone's app revealed Jon still lounged on the couch, but his focus honed in on the door I stood behind, his nostrils slightly flared in awareness I was close by.

Simmering satisfaction coursed through me as I shut my phone off and hesitated a moment to tighten the leash on my dragon's need to moan his delight.

Not only had my dragonblood drawn Jon to me, but it had without a doubt awakened his as well.

I pulled open the door and stepped into the kitchen.

Jon had already started my way, his blue-eyed gaze taking me in from head to toes, the desire swirling in his orbs not lost to me. The fact he wasn't surprised to see me solidified my thoughts on how the ancient blood simmered in his veins with heightened awareness.

Want.

My hold on the beast within me slipped slightly, and I blinked to keep my eyes from shimmering, shifting to reveal that something more than human stood before my beta.

I dropped my bag on the island, and Jon came close, hand outstretched.

"Welcome home," he said, a smirk on his lips and hunger in his stare.

I clasped his hand, and he yanked me in for my first ever bro-hug, his palm hot and possessive on my back, his chest pressed against mine.

His heart thrummed in time with the one beating beneath my breastbone.

My inner beast whimpered rather than raging to take what was ours.

Eyes closed, I breathed Jon in, the wildness of the outdoors on a crisp fall day soothing when I'd expected the explosive need to fuck to own my human form.

We lingered in our hug longer than was usual of acquaintances or even friends as though hesitant to put distance between us. Lust and longing filled both of our faces when we finally pulled back slightly. There was no way Jon didn't feel the connection to me—didn't see that he belonged to me.

He cleared his throat and stepped away, breaking all physical contact between us, leaving me cold and empty.

Dakota appeared at the top of the stairs, but I'd been so caught up in Jon that I hadn't heard or scented her. Head down, she fumbled to undo one of the buttons on my shirts she wore. The cotton gaped across her breasts, and she lifted her head with a satisfied smile that quickly dissolved when she saw me and stumbled to a stop on the second step. The color leeched from her face. "Y-you're home," she sputtered, her voice breathless.

My dragon growled, a low note of pure need escaping my lips. Swallowing it down a second too late, I nodded. "I am." Opposite of her reedy tone, my voice rumbled louder than I'd intended, my grasp on my dragon slipping as fire flooded through me.

A flush swept up over our female's chest and neck, prettying her cheeks.

Lick.

Taste.

My gaze slid down over my shirt to where it caressed the tops of her knees. From our vantage point below, the apex of her thighs drew my focus, stiffening my half-swelled cock to the point of pain in a single heartbeat. Her sex was bare to me, the edges of her pink, swollen labia and the hint of her clit beneath its hood.

Breed.

I licked my lips, unable to keep back the beast's groan rising unhindered from inside me.

CHAPTER 16
DAKOTA

I should have fled from being caught half-naked by our kind host. At the very least, I should have clenched my thighs together, hiding the view beneath Elijah's shirt. But I couldn't move.

Didn't want to.

Jon's stare was like fire on my face, but Elijah and his energy rippling off in spine-tingling waves held me captive. He stared upward, the view of my pussy unhindered.

A second low, animalistic groan from his chest caused my core to spasm.

"I—I should go put something on," I barely whispered the words, my desire unmistakable.

Elijah snapped his mouth shut and swallowed hard, glancing at Jon.

My husband—a slight smirk, of all things, lifting his lips —looked over at Elijah. No anger, no words of jealousy or reminder of who I belonged to left his lips. He simply stared at Elijah as if to ask the gorgeous man, *now what?*

I stood stunned, unsure what to think or how to feel outside the yearning to lose myself between the two.

Clothes, I told myself and forced my feet to turn away and take me back the way I'd come. I was a shaking, horny mess with arousal pulsing through me. From my body's state of need, no one would ever believe Jon and I had fucked less than an hour ago.

Elijah had returned home a day earlier than he'd told us, and I wasn't sorry in the least. Every inch of me had been yearning for him. The energy seeming to permeate the cave without his presence no longer seemed enough to satisfy my craving.

Properly covered but hardly calm, I returned to the stairwell and found both men, beers in hand, sitting on the couch. They lifted their attention my way as I paused, my face heating over the realization I hadn't changed out of Elijah's shirt or buttoned up to cover my cleavage.

Jon's smile melted my heart.

Elijah's intense stare turned my bones to ash.

Between the two of them, what was the point of even wearing underwear? Soaked through from mere glances at their faces, and what chance did my leggings have of hiding the evidence of what I wanted?

My knees knocked as I started down the stairs, and Jon and Elijah resumed their conversation from before I'd arrived. I grabbed myself a bottle of beer and curled my legs beneath me on the couch beside Jon, very aware of the wetness soaking the cotton between my thighs.

He set his hand on my leg and gave a slight squeeze. "Elijah seems to think he has a solution to our problem."

My heart seized. "P-problem?" I glanced between the two men but focused on Jon when he didn't answer right away.

"My lack of a job." Jon stared at Elijah, although he'd spoken to me.

My breath left in a rush at the realization the issue he referred to wasn't the sexual attraction eating away at my body. "You need an IT geek?" I asked with a shaking voice while turning to face Elijah fully.

"Actually, it's his gaming abilities I'm most interested in."

I stifled my sudden snort of laughter with my hand. *"What?"*

"While in New York, I began looking into his past accomplishments you told me about," Elijah replied, "and the contract signed just this afternoon created a job he could probably do with his eyes closed—if indeed his skills are as good as you claimed, Dakota."

"You're kidding," I said, my eyes going as wide as my smile.

"Not at all."

"Oh my God, Jon!" I turned to find him still studying Elijah, a light in his eyes I hadn't seen since our wedding day when all in our world had been right.

"Imagine being able to game for a living." I burst out, breathless and giddy with happiness. "You can't be serious," I said, my focus flitting to Elijah again.

His steady gaze told me he didn't lie.

"But how? I mean, gaming..." Was something I'd always teased Jon about, even if he excelled at the hobby that had seemed like a waste of time other than bringing him joy.

"I signed a contract with the government for something I can't discuss without either of you having the proper clearance, but I think Jon's abilities will help me test the final product in ways I'm unable to."

I sat back, blinking, my jaw unhinged.

"I've offered him a trial period of four weeks," Elijah continued, leaning forward, elbows on his knees, his pale eyes seeming to reach straight into my soul and tug in attempts to pull me closer. "I can get him started as soon as tomorrow."

"Tomorrow?" My voice squeaked over the sudden tightness in my chest. "But how..."

"I have a computer lab down nearer the garage where he can work remotely—for me—until the government approves him to move onto what's been contracted."

I glanced at Jon who hadn't yet torn his focus off Elijah. "But we need to go back to New York?" I tried for a statement but it came out more like a question. "I—I mean, I have to get those images into the magazine," I offered the only reason we truly had to return home.

"Can they be uploaded to my computer and sent via email?" Elijah asked.

I nodded. "Yeah—definitely."

"That you may do from the lab as well."

"He invited us to stay here during the trial period," Jon stated quietly, still not taking his stare off Elijah, but I could hear the excitement in his voice. "We would house-watch for him while he travels in the coming weeks."

Zero thought for our tiny apartment and the life we'd built for ourselves in the city clashed with the idea of remaining in Elijah's home. Our car could easily be retrieved and parked alongside Elijah's Audi.

I stared at my husband, breath held, waiting for him to make the decision that I felt sure would change our lives. We stood together on the edge of that abyss, hand in hand. But rather than push like I longed to do, I left the choice to him as I'd always done, my fingers crossed.

"I want a contracted offer written up," Jon eventually stated firmly. "I also insist on the right to counter any part that pushes my boundaries or doesn't seem in mine and my wife's best interests."

I blinked at my husband. He'd been hurt by his friend firing him, but I hadn't realized steel had slid into his spine.

"As you wish," Elijah agreed quietly, his tone soft.

I almost snorted since my ears heard Westley from *The Princess Bride*.

"That's it, then." Jon stuck his hand out in a display of trust—for now. "I look forward to your offer."

My pulse thrummed as time slowed, every beat of my heart loud in my ears…a gong declaring the time had come.

For change.

A dive into the unknown.

Elijah reached for my husband's hand, their palms gliding together, creating static electricity that shot across my skin and lit me up from the inside.

Waves of heat radiated from the men, burning me clear through. I bit my lip as they stared at each other as though lost in their own little world. They didn't war for dominance. Elijah held the alpha status as clearly as the freckles scattered across Jon's nose and flushed cheeks.

He wanted Jon

My husband wanted Elijah.

I wanted them both.

The truth of all three statements settled inside as I studied them, and the feeling of absolute rightness, the same as when I'd first met Jon in seventh grade, slowly leaked through the cells of my body.

My heartbeat slowed to its usual strong cadence, my mind placid like the water of a pond.

We belonged to each other on a deeper level than seemed humanly possible.

Something stirred deep in my soul, far beyond mere arousal. A bone-tingling sense of awareness I couldn't name or place. I clung to the addictive feeling, wanting to keep it as close to my conscience as I did both men to my body.

But how to bring up a conversation to explain my desires? How could I voice the topic of my fantasies without making Jon feel as though he wasn't enough for me?

I can't hurt him again.

Biting the inside of my lip, I fought off the sudden tears stinging my eyes at the memory of his face when I'd told him I needed some time alone after that public fallout all those years ago. I hadn't wanted to break up with Jon, but our argument—all thanks to that gorgeous blond god of a guy—ended us on a jagged, agonizing note. We'd parted ways for two days before an intense craving, a desperation to connect with my other half had sent me crawling back to him.

Jon had cried in my arms when I begged him to give me another chance. He'd sobbed, pleading with me to never rip out his heart like that again.

I swallowed thickness from my throat as he and Elijah finally released hands, and Jon swiveled his head my way. A slow smile starting to reveal his dimples dissolved when his focus landed on my face. "You okay, baby?"

I jerked my head in a quick nod, desperate to squash the remembered pain and guilt that lingered regardless of his forgiveness. "J-Just happy," I managed to whisper as a tear slid down my cheek.

"Come here."

I did as told, curling up on Jon's lap, my bare foot brushing across Elijah's thigh. An electrical-like charge swept up my leg straight to my clit, and our gazes locked as I laid my head on Jon's chest, my heart no longer calm or steady but erratic in its beating.

Our host's pale eyes didn't even try to hide the truth of his want as his gaze slid down over my hard nipples poking out from his shirt.

But it wasn't simply lust radiating off Elijah. The intensity in his crystalline blue eyes held unspoken promises and declarations that sent me floundering in a swelling sea of emotion.

Desire roused, but so much more than a mere yearning for physical release.

Jon was no longer enough—I bet my life we'd been meant to have a third. Felt sure of it in the deepest reaches of my psyche.

The fire crackled, and I flinched at the intrusion of the tense silence that had settled over us. Jon rubbed his thumb in circles on my thigh, but the action only heightened my need to be touched and taken by them both.

Jon's cock swelled against my side when he should have tensed with anger over the fact another man looked at me the way Elijah continued to do.

Before I could figure out the why of Jon's lack of jealousy, he shifted sideways to face Elijah, pulling my back to his chest, his hard cock resting against my ass cheeks. He swept my hair off my shoulder and nuzzled my neck. My heart skipped a beat—and another as he flicked open a button of Elijah's shirt, revealing more of my breasts to the man I craved as much as I did my husband.

I trusted Jon with my everything, but I couldn't melt into his embrace without knowing where his thoughts were.

CHAPTER 17

JONATHAN

The tension had pulled tight among the three of us, and something had to give or I'd lose my goddamned mind.

"What are you doing?" Dakota whispered as I started on another button, my gaze set on Elijah's face.

He stared at my hands baring my wife to his hungry gaze, his nostrils flared, lips parted.

My intentions?

To give my wife what she desired because doing so would lessen my guilt for wanting the same. Was it infidelity for us to indulge in a threesome?

I didn't believe so, especially since Dakota didn't fight my instigating an affair all three of us had been dying for.

I'd made the right choice in denying my supposed friend a taste of my wife, but doing the same with Elijah, who respected us enough to not even dare ask, didn't sit right in my head. No red flags waved, no booming voice insisting I whisk Dakota away from Elijah's potent virility.

Sharing her with him felt *right* in that moment, and I needed him just as badly as he appeared to want both of us.

Another button popped free beneath my fingers, causing Elijah's shirt to gape open, and I reached beneath the fabric, palming Dakota's full breast that overflowed from my palm.

"Jon?" She questioned me again, her whisper cut short as I brushed my thumb over her hard nipple.

"I'm offering Elijah what he's been drooling over since the moment he laid eyes on you," I finally answered her, my other hand running over her stomach to palm her hot, soaked pussy through her pants. "What *you* want but haven't been able to voice, sweet wife of mine."

Her audible swallow sounded loud in the heavy silence hovering over the living area, but she didn't argue the truth I'd spoken.

I licked the shell of her ear and slid my hand beneath her leggings, down over her silken pubic bone, straight to the wetness seeping for me—for him.

Yes.

That damned voice again.

Same as earlier in the day when I'd submitted to my instincts and found Elijah's dungeon room, I gave over to the need driving Dakota and me crazy. Putting my wife on display hadn't been planned, but the second I'd made the move, something clicked inside me, erasing all doubt about what had been brewing—and that guilt that had been riding me since laying eyes on Elijah.

I was meant to be the catalyst I realized in that moment, the one to bridge the gap between them, but I also needed both of their consent.

"Do you trust me, baby?" I murmured against the soft skin of my wife's neck.

"In everything," she whispered, her words more along the lines of a pant than bold declaration as she melted against me.

Elijah's gaze didn't leave my hand as I moved beneath

Dakota's leggings. His body tensed, hands fisted at his side as though he fought off the need to pounce on what my wife and I wanted to experience with him.

"I..." He let out a rush of air and groaned, grasping the bulge in his slacks and squeezing while I slipped a finger into Dakota's pussy. "Fuck."

His low, rumbled curse, the first we'd heard pass his lips, had Dakota clenching around me. Her head tipped back to rest on my shoulder, my dick pulsing against the lush globes of her ass.

"I didn't—" Elijah swallowed audibly "—I didn't offer you shelter from the storm nor a job in expectation of anything in return." His voice strained, low and rumbly.

Hot as fuck.

My dick bucked against the material separating me from sinking into my wife's warmth.

"I know you didn't." I slid a second finger inside Dakota, and she gasped, following my favorite sound in the world with her throaty moan. Hand stilling against her sopping heat, I waited for Elijah to meet my gaze.

Dakota whimpered and dug her fingernails into my forearm in attempts to make me move, but I held her still on my lap, refusing to give her what she needed until our host agreed to what I'd started.

Elijah finally lifted his attention to my face as though hearing my unspoken request.

Promise of relief I'd been chasing since first seeing him lay in his pale eyes, and remembering that damned black cross in his basement, my balls seized on the verge of nutting without skin-on-skin contact.

"I want both of you." Elijah's quiet, low bass confession caused pre-cum to ooze from my throbbing cock.

I shuddered beneath my wife over someone finally laying out on the goddamned table what had been burning among the three of us since we'd shared oatmeal beside our campfire.

As far as I was concerned, there would be no stopping the train barreling us toward a completion I sensed would be life-changing.

"Do you want Elijah to make you come?" I rasped against Dakota's ear, completely ensnared by Elijah's intense stare promising me the kind of satisfaction I hadn't thought would fulfill me but now craved more than another sip of oxygen into my lungs.

If he wished to string me up with chains and flog my body until I sagged in spent elation, I wouldn't deny him.

"Mmm." Dakota writhed in my arms, and while I was aware of what the sound meant, perhaps Elijah didn't.

"Is that a yes, baby?"

"O-only if it's what you want. If you're absolutely sure."

Not the simple yes I'd hoped to hear in that moment, but I knew my wife's body, the fantasies she'd always shared with me when she was in the mood to fuck.

I slipped my hand from beneath her clothing.

"Wh—"

"Elijah is going to remove your leggings," I cut off her sure complaint and flicked open another button of Elijah's shirt. "Then he's going to do what he's been watching me do to you the past couple of days—eat your juicy pussy until you cream all over his face."

Elijah and Dakota's lust-filled curses hit my ears at the same time, the tension between them zapping like a live wire.

Our host didn't deny what I'd been wondering about with those cameras he had placed around his home. I'd found one by accident and had gone looking for more. He had them in every room except for the guest bathrooms. Turned out Elijah had five empty guest chambers upstairs along with his master suite Dakota and I had decided to not fuck in during his absence.

"Dakota?" Elijah whispered her name, his need for her verbal consent assuring me of his respect and care for my wife.

"Yes." She gave without hesitation what both of us wanted.

Elijah reached for her with trembling hands, and Dakota lifted her hips in offering.

She whimpered, and he growled as he slowly peeled the leggings down her legs, revealing her pink, glistening pussy. Her sweet aroma flooded my nose, and I ripped at the final button, yanking Elijah's shirt wide.

He showed more restraint than I, gently pulling the spandex off Dakota like she was a gift, an old vintage wine to be savored.

The second he released her second foot from the leggings, I pressed her thighs wide with zero resistance on her part, my own legs keeping her spread for both their pleasure.

Fixated on her pussy, Elijah shifted back enough to lean his torso on the couch and slid his hands beneath her ass, both of his pinkies caressing my hard-as-fucking-nails dick pressed against her backside. I groaned, and he sniffed her pussy like she was a glass of fine wine. Rather than sipping a mere taste as I expected, he growled and dove into her hole like a starving animal, gathering up her wetness to swallow down like her arousal was the sustenance his body craved.

Every wet smack of his lips, every gasp and moan from my writhing wife as he lapped at her slit was like a shot of adrenaline to my overheated blood.

Yes.

I groaned the whispered word in my head and rubbed my cock against the back of Elijah's hands as he clasped her plump cheeks.

I'd never come without direct stimulation before, but goddamn if I didn't feel like my nuts could erupt from the friction of the shorts rubbing against me.

Why?

Why the *fuck* had I waited so goddamned long to get this show on the road? I should have spoken up sooner—we could have been doing this shit for days on end, lost in a haze of sex and cum, sated libidos and empty balls that would be more satisfying than me and my wife going at it like a couple of bunnies.

Elijah's low groans and throaty growls over my wife's taste filled my ears. His scent brought a potency of arousal the likes I hadn't known existed.

And I was fucking here for it.

Dakota's breath caught, and I jerked open my eyes, not having realized I'd closed them, lost in the waves of desperation for completion pulsing through the air around us.

I pinched both of her nipples, parting her breasts so I could better see Elijah's head against the milky whiteness of her legs. She had her hands tangled in his hair, her thighs now pressed tight against his ears.

He lathed up through her pussy with his tongue, circled her clit, and latched onto the protruding nub.

"Going to c-come." Dakota half-choked on the word, her body tensing with a telltale sign she approached climax.

"Give it to him, baby." I pinched her nipples hard enough to send the sting down to her clit she'd claimed to like. "Come on his tongue—give him a taste of how sweet you are."

Her knuckles went white where she clutched Elijah's dark hair.

"Oh, fuck!" She shrieked and bowed in my arms, breath catching between groans while riding out her release.

His low moan, the sight of his ass flexing as he humped

the air had me clenching my jaw to keep from blowing my load in my shorts.

"So fucking sexy," I hissed through teeth, my balls tight against my groin, the throb fucking *unbearable*.

I heaved for breath, my ears ringing, body strung to the point of explosion as Dakota finally relaxed against me, loosening her hold on Elijah.

I wanted to fuck my wife.

I wanted Elijah to fuck me.

He shifted back into his seat, creating distance I lusted to leap forward and close.

Our gazes clashed, and I swear to fucking god, the black of his pupils swirled, but I couldn't give a flying fuck beyond my need to come—lick my wife's cum off his full lips.

Dakota slid off my lap and kneeled on the floor before I could decide how I would find release. Her gaze moved from my face to Elijah's, and I recognized the hunger in her eyes.

I stood over her and shoved my shorts to my knees with one vicious push. My gaze flitted down to her still-pebbled nipples flanked by the sides of Elijah's shirt while palming my cock. "We're going to come all over your gorgeous tits, baby," I rasped, my voice ragged with want for so many things I couldn't fucking fill my lungs.

"Mmm." She hummed her agreement and pressed her breasts upward, creating a plump shelf for me to blow my load onto.

"Come with me, Elijah," I begged.

He stood beside me in a wave of heat and energy, and I glanced at his face, squeezing my dick to keep from shooting too soon. The pulse in his neck throbbed, the scent of his pre-cum slamming into me like a wall as he pulled his massive dick from his pants.

"Together," he said, his deep voice sounding as tight as my body.

"Yes," Dakota whispered, peering up at us, worshiping us with lust in her blown pupils.

I stroked down my length, my balls throbbing. "Fucking hell—gonna come so goddamned hard." My taint spasmed, and I groaned. "Fuck. Can't—" A string of cum erupted from my shaft, spurting across Dakota's chest.

A rumbling growl left Elijah's parted lips as his shot atop mine, marking my wife.

Dakota gasped, her gaze on Elijah's face as our cum laced over her chest.

A few more curses flew past my lips as I milked myself, the sight of our spunk on my wife's skin sending a rush of satisfaction through me. I'd only instigated the whole scene with the intent to relieve tension, but my obsession for my new boss took root in my goddamn head—and cock.

I'd either seriously screwed up or had started us on a path toward heaven on earth.

CHAPTER 18

ELIJAH

Spent but not nearly finished, I tucked my still-hard cock back into my slacks, my attention riveted on the ropes of my cum across our female's breasts.

Still, Dakota stared at me, her mouth parted, a hint of wonder in her eyes. "It tingles," she whispered, finally glancing down at the mess we'd made on her flushed skin.

Feed.

I clenched my jaw. Walls had tumbled to dust between us, but I wouldn't force more than they were ready to consent to.

My cum would give my mates what they needed to extend their human lives for longer than nature intended, and the desire for more would override rational thought until they bore my mark.

Unwanted or otherwise.

I could command Jon to lick her clean, and I expected he would. I could tell Dakota to suck my essence off her husband's tongue, and there was no doubt in my mind she would obey.

Yessss.

My jaw clenched.

They would choose me of their own volition, not be forced by their dragonblood's instinctive desire for more.

"Taste him." Jon's command—oh, how I loved his desire to be alpha if only for a moment—roused the dominant animal inside me.

I opened my mouth to stop the action, but my inner beast strangled my voice with a cackle of glee. Helpless, I could only watch as my two humans made their own decisions.

But if they knew the truth—

Dakota smeared her finger in the cum on her skin and sucked the digit clean. The widening of her eyes, her rapid blinks, the pink flush to her cheeks incited renewed need to course through my body.

Yessss!

I whimpered against the beast roaring inside me.

Jon studied his wife swallowing our seed while I stood rooted, trembling from the effort to regain complete control once more.

"Do you like it?" he asked, swiping his own finger through the sticky mess and offering it to her.

I wanted to tell him to stop but still couldn't find my voice.

"Yes." She flicked her tongue out and licked some of the thick fluid from his finger.

Another cackle lit inside me.

Jon shoved the digit into his mouth and swallowed what remained.

Feed.

More.

"Fuck." Jon's brow furrowed as he blinked at his finger. "I can taste...goddamn. I thought you said cum was salty and gross, baby."

"His is..."

"*Sweet,*" they both stated together.

Their alpha's seed would be ambrosia on their tongue, and even though I'd studied biology for close to a century, I couldn't begin to explain why they would hunger for what would bind their minds to mine and prolong their life.

Command to eat.

The damned beast didn't have control over my vocal cords other than shutting them down.

My mates hadn't ingested much, but I didn't know the effects even a simple sample would have on their mostly human blood.

"Fuck." Jon huffed and pulled up his shorts rather than falling to his knees and licking his wife clean like I'd expected. "I just tasted a dude's cum."

"It was hot." Dakota breathed as though still in need of dick as Jon would say, but a rush of air deflated my lungs at their lack of falling to consume more as I'd feared.

The small bit they'd consumed hadn't been enough to cause addiction or take away their consent.

My inner dragon muttered his disappointment and seemed to slink into the background, giving my voice back to me.

I reached for our female, but Jon beat me to it, pulling her up into his arms.

She clung to him, flushed face pressed against his neck where I couldn't see her eyes and assure myself she didn't regret what we'd done.

"We need to clean you up." Jon carried her toward the stairs, and I followed on weak legs even though no verbal invite had been voiced.

I'd finally gotten my hands on our female, her flesh soft and delicious on my tongue. She was sweeter than all of earth's natural sugars meant to assist in sustaining life.

I craved more of her, an addict clear through every cell in my body.

But would I be gifted the opportunity to gorge myself on her arousal again? Was getting my hands on my beta a possibility as well?

My inner beast rested quiet, seemingly drunk on our female's release they'd both allowed me to taste.

"Let me get that for you," I said, sliding past them as we neared the guest room they'd occupied. I pushed their door inward and moved across the room to open the bathroom's as well.

Their scent had infiltrated the area, and I wanted to roll all over their sheets and add my essence to theirs.

I forced my steps toward the bathroom where I turned on the shower.

Jon set Dakota on her feet by the time I turned around.

Longing to care for them both ached through my chest, but for the first time in my life, I faltered, unsure of what to say or do.

Jon shucked his shorts and picked Dakota back up, smearing our cum across his chest. "Damn, it *does* tingle." A hint of awe lit his words as he glanced at me.

Dark pupils dominated the blue of his eyes, and I pushed hard against the desire to give him more. Coat his skin with my seed. Drown him in the fluid that would prolong his life so he would never be able to abandon me as Dolyn had—

I stepped back at the thought of my ex and the sudden sting of sorrow that accompanied it.

Why was it he haunted me mere minutes after finding release with my mates? Shouldn't sharing intimacy with them have wiped him from my mind?

Half of me yearned to join my beta and female in the shower, to continue exploring how we might pleasure one another. The other part of me wanted to lick old wounds and sit in a dark corner while feeling sorry for myself.

But I would do neither as I wished more to move forward.

If only the memories of my ex allowed me to do so.

The empathetic area of my human brain reminded me the married couple standing in silence before me would need time alone to discuss the line we'd crossed, so I prepared myself to leave them.

Would they regret their choice? Come to the conclusion they needed to put distance between us?

They didn't yet know about fated mates, how creating another Blood Born required three with the ancient blood.

Not ready.

I agreed with the whisper even though he'd been insistent on forcing a bond. Now wasn't the time to reveal the truth.

"I'll be downstairs," I said, glancing between Jon and Dakota.

Our female's eyes swam with varied emotions, but her lack of regret eased the tension in my shoulders.

Jon nodded in agreement. The absence of wariness in his gaze suggested he too was okay with the choice he'd made to set us on this path.

I turned away, that sense of pain ripping muscle from bone as strong as when I'd flown to New York over leaving them behind. More potent than when I'd found Dolyn gone from our home that final time.

Dakota's flavor lingered on my tongue, the scent of Jon's release still in my lungs regardless of where my thoughts travelled.

My body ached to return to my mates' sides.

How much more pain would I suffer should they come to the conclusion they'd made a mistake and decide to go back to that tiny apartment neither sounded attached to?

How badly would I wish for death to finally come and claim my weary soul?

I made my way to the kitchen and grabbed a beer from the refrigerator, my heart heavy.

Telling Jon and Dakota the truth about me—and the blood in their veins—should have been a priority for me from the start, but the fear of rejection, the sure agony of being abandoned again paralyzed my lips.

Although the need to fuck them both still raged through my body, causing my dragon to shimmer beneath my skin, he finally seemed to understand the fragility of our situation.

We'd made gains in a natural connection with both mates individually as was necessary for a lasting bond, but the taste of our female's release had softened my beast to a greater degree than I'd expected.

Fear of losing her now that we'd shared intimacy caused him to prowl beneath our skin—but he no longer demanded force.

Not once in my nearly five centuries had my inner beast shown a hint of insecurity, and his distress shook me to my core.

Help.

A hard swallow bobbed my throat at his whimper. "They need to love us of their own accord," I murmured, my eyes clenched shut at the memory of the man who'd claimed to do so a decade ago. "Desperately, that the thought of living without us is not an option."

But how to accomplish such a task?

Being under the same roof for four weeks would provide plenty of opportunity to strengthen our growing desire for one another. I could keep my travels to a minimum—

The helicopter.

They might wonder how I'd returned from New York if they noticed it missing.

Another lie about someone borrowing my toy and having dropped me off ought to work should the need arise.

Lies.

"I know," I muttered and took a long pull on my beer.

Manipulation.

I clenched my jaw over being called out when I'd denied him the right to do the same.

Revealing the beast inside me that wanted to tie our mates' souls to ours for eternity with an unbreakable bond would send them rushing down the mountainside.

Hadn't Dolyn left me because I'd been desperate to do that very thing with him? I'd tried to coerce and sway him into giving me what I wanted—a declaration of submission in every way even though we hadn't been fated for each other.

Or a female I had desperately longed to share with him.

A forced triad wouldn't stand the test of time. Each individual needed to come to their own conclusion, face and accept the fact they were meant to be shared in equal measure among the three of us.

Luscious hints of spring and fall flooded my nose, pulling me from my musing.

I glanced to the top of the stairs.

Jon and Dakota stood freshly showered with no hint of cum on either, which meant they hadn't fucked in the shower as I'd half expected them to.

My shoulders relaxed at their proximity and the fact they hadn't sought release without me.

A pink blush flushed Dakota's face, making her eyes appear greener in the overhead lights I had dimmed. She led the way down the stairs, Jon close behind her, his wet hair hanging to brush over his shoulders.

He wore a pair of lounge pants and nothing else while

Dakota, our sweet female, had donned yet another of my button-down shirts.

My dragon purred his delight in seeing her cloaked in material soaked by our scent.

I couldn't help my smile as our gazes met. Dakota was the first to look away, her cheeks even redder. The usual cocky smirk on Jon's face didn't appear. He studied me with every step bringing him closer, a calculating glint in his eyes.

Now what, he must wonder, but I had told them the truth of my feelings, that I wanted them both, and I had no intention of rescinding my words.

Dakota retrieved a couple of beers from the refrigerator, and they both sat closer to me on the couch than I'd expected. Jon lounged as usual to put his lean muscles on display, his arms and legs sprawled out in comfort. Dakota perched ramrod straight on the edge of her cushion, hands wrapped around her bottle.

The flames I'd breathed to life in the fireplace while they'd showered crackled as Jon peered at me. I held his gaze until he shifted, his focus flitting to his wife. Once more, her nipples strained against the crisp cotton of my shirt, and I breathed deeply, catching a hint of her rekindled arousal in the air.

If my dragon had hands, he'd have been rubbing them together in anticipation.

"Thank you," I said, my gaze on our female although I spoke to both her and my beta. "It has been a very long time since anyone allowed me to partake in such passion."

Dakota finally glanced up at me through her lashes but not in a coquettish way. Her natural shyness around me made me want to strip her bare, body and soul, so I could feast on all that she was.

Breed.

I swallowed hard at my beast's insistence we do as fate

intended to keep the ancient dragonblood from disappearing from the earth.

Jon ran his fingers through his wife's long, damp locks. "I would do anything for her," he said, his voice so sincere and filled with love that my heart ached. I longed for him to think the same of me, and the honesty of my thoughts twisted my insides.

One man had taken clear advantage of my giving nature, and I dreaded a similar outcome.

But my mouth opened, spilling my truth. "I would do anything for either of you as well. Ask and it shall be freely given if it's in my power to do so."

Even if their desires eventually led them to leave—and doom our species to extinction.

CHAPTER 19

DAKOTA

E lijah spoke to both of us but peered at Jon while making his claim. His low, vulnerable voice was potent enough to thicken the sexual tension between the two men as they stared at each other.

Jon and I should have talked over what we'd done. How our world tipped, taking us out of our comfort zone. How he'd shaken hands in agreement to a job when he should have been wary, considering how his best friend had let him go without notice.

It seemed he trusted Elijah, his spirit definitely boosted by the decision he'd made.

I should have told him so while he'd washed me clean of Elijah and his cum. But my tongue remained tied because I couldn't figure out what the hell was happening among the three of us.

And Elijah's claim about giving us whatever lay in his power to do?

His words couldn't have been a declaration of love, so what was it? An offering of his body to satiate the obvious lust that continued to simmer and zap in the air around us?

Or was it something insanely *more*? A promise that went beyond human instinct and desire to seek out sexual fulfillment?

The two men continued to study each other, and I almost felt like a fly on the wall—and suddenly wished that I was. If I didn't sit between them, would they act on their need for each other? Would Elijah grasp Jon's neck and yank him close, claim his lips like he seemed desperate to do?

I had no doubt that was how it would play out between the two—Elijah, the alpha, my Jon his submissive. Hot enough alone to dampen my panties, but put them together in what I realized were their natural tendencies?

Sexy as fuck, Jon would say, even if he'd never shown a hint of interest in bending to any man's will before let alone someone as powerful as Elijah's presence radiated. The images of Jon giving himself to Elijah flashed through my head, renewing my hunger with aching force.

I whimpered, and quickly bit my lip as both of their gazes latched onto me as though my needy noise broke the little world they'd been encased in. I hadn't meant to intrude, but I couldn't quiet my rising arousal.

"What's on your mind, baby?" Jon asked, his pupils blown.

My face heated as I imagined him on his knees before Elijah, peering up with him with blatant hunger only Elijah could satisfy.

And I didn't care that I wasn't enough, that Jon had desires we needed a third in order to sate.

Elijah had brought something to life in both Jon and me, meant to be shared in equal measure. Acknowledging the truth made a hint of my hidden inner fierceness rise to the surface, stretching at its newfound freedom from insecurity.

Jon had taken a step on his own, and it was time for me to do the same and make a choice without leaning on him again.

"Dakota?" Elijah pressed, but it wasn't the command in his voice that opened my mouth.

It was a yearning for fulfillment of things I hadn't realized I wanted until that moment—and the figurative balls to speak my desires.

"If I wasn't here..." I glanced between the two, unsure of how to word my thoughts in a way that didn't make me sound like a sexual deviant.

"You want to know how we would act on our mutual desire?" Elijah questioned quietly without a hint of judgment in his tone.

My insides jittered with sweet excitement that bordered on anxiety. "Yes." My reply sounded more definite than I'd expected, considering my past inability to speak up. I glanced at Jon, breath held.

"Well, well, well." He smirked, flashing his dimples. "It seems we have another voyeur on our hands."

A rumble escaped Elijah, but I couldn't tear my focus off my husband's glinting baby blues.

"So, if Elijah and I pretended you weren't here, and we got it on, you'd be a sopping, panting mess? Even more than you probably already are?"

My thighs pressed tightly together as a wave of lust pulsed through my core. "Yes," I repeated with the same assurance.

A twinkle lit in Jon's eye as he took my full bottle of beer from my trembling hands and sat it on the coffee table.

"Sit back, baby," he murmured with a wink. "We're gonna reward you for speaking up."

Jon had always claimed he would give me the world, and his words suggested he'd continue doing so if I continued to ask for what I desired.

My inner giddiness intensified, making my breaths come in pants. Oh, the power sitting on the edge of my lips...

I glanced over at Elijah.

He didn't move from his seat on the couch a little ways away from us. Nothing about the man's presence hinted at submission, but he seemed acquiesced to let Jon lead for the time being.

Perhaps I could test that assumption later.

Jon stood and turned toward Elijah.

God, how I wished to be that fly so I could buzz around and see his face. I no longer existed for Elijah—he only had eyes for Jon as my husband approached him.

Jon stepped between Elijah's spread knees, and he sank down to his own, offering me a view of both of their profiles.

A low rumbled growl emitted from one of them—Elijah, I guessed, considering how he stared at my husband.

I gulped and whimpered again, my pussy pulsing. "Holy shit, this is so hot," I couldn't help but whisper encouragement for them to continue.

As if they would stop having been given the green light.

My man had willingly dropped to his knees for the obvious dominant male in the room without having to be commanded to. Had he dreamed of kneeling before Elijah? Had he wondered how the man would react?

Elijah shifted to the edge of the couch, his shoulder muscles bunching, hand shaking as he reached for Jon. His fingertips caressed with gentleness rather than the blatant display of animalistic hunger that seemed to seep from his pores whenever he stared at my husband.

"Don't hold back," Jon rasped, the urgency in his voice making me curl my fingers to keep from touching myself and getting off long before either of them did.

Elijah grasped Jon's neck and yanked him close, their mouths coming together in a rush.

"Oh, God." I squeezed my thighs together and bit my lower lip at the rough way their lips meshed.

Teeth gnashed, and groans flooded my ears as they acted with desperation to sate their hunger for each other. Jon's fingers dug into Elijah's thighs as he yanked on Jon's hair, angling his head to better plunder my husband's sweet mouth. They both gasped for breath, lips parting momentarily, before crashing back together again.

Arousal leaked from my core, and I couldn't find it in myself to care I would leave wet evidence on the couch of what their appetite for each other did to me.

Like a violent storm bent on breaking everything in its path, the two men's passion crashed into me, igniting something deep within my soul, an unnameable yearning that went far beyond lust and mere need for release.

The storm inside me swept me toward the abyss, and I was powerless to stop falling into the unknown.

How did one return to normal after sharing intimacy outside marriage?

I was convinced Elijah was meant to be our third, but would Jon recognize the truth of our connection with him?

He lusted for Elijah, but was it possible for him to bond in the way I swore I could feel along my skin? Like energy wrapping itself around me, drawing me closer to the man who I somehow knew would fulfill us in every way.

The truth of what the three of us could be went beyond fantasy. My mind wasn't simply in the clouds this time.

Something real—*tangible*—drew us together.

Need to be a part of what the two men experienced in front of me singed along my arms, and I unintentionally moaned loud enough they became aware of my presence once more.

Jon tore his mouth from Elijah's and glanced at me. Black pupils dominated the sky blue of his irises. Lips bruised and swollen asked if I was okay, but I didn't hear his voice past the rush of blood in my ears.

"Don't stop. Please, don't stop," I heard myself whine, writhing in my seat, hands fisted at my sides to keep from reaching out and begging to take part in what they shared.

Elijah yanked Jon's hair, pulling him back to claim his mouth again, and when he reached between them and grasped Jon's hard-on, I bit my lip. As though the strength left Jon's body, he sagged forward, his forehead resting on Elijah's as the man shoved Jon's shorts down.

Elijah spat on his palm and wrapped his hand around Jon's cock.

"Ah, fuck." Jon gulped and thrust into Elijah's hold, wetness beading at his slit.

"Touch me." Elijah's growled command rumbled clear through me, springing every hair follicle to life.

My body tensed, cells vibrating to do as told even though Elijah hadn't voiced the order to me.

Jon reached for the button of Elijah's slacks, gaze ensnared by intense pale eyes as he unbuttoned and unzipped what hindered him from obeying.

My breath left in a rush at the sight of Elijah's hard length, flushed and straining upright. Pre-cum leaked from his slit in unnatural steady pulses, making my mouth water as it coated Jon's fingers.

Forget the gentle glide of hands touching and learning a partner for the first time. Elijah and Jon's forearms both flexed, rippling with muscle as they jerked each other off. To the root and back up, palm over the head and down, they moved in sync, their hips pressing up on every downward stroke.

The temptation to touch myself, fuck myself with my fingers while they worked each other over, made me dig my fingernails into my palms. I refused to get so caught up in my own need that I missed out on the hottest thing I'd ever seen.

A shudder rippled over Jon's back. "Jesus, fuck." He gulped.

Elijah yanked his head back and leaned in to devour his mouth, the combined scents of their arousal thick and heady in the air.

I found myself on my knees, crawling toward them, so far gone in my need I didn't care I would interrupt what I'd claimed to only want to watch.

Elijah pulled away, and blinking, Jon glanced at me, his blue eyes hazed over.

"I—"

Jon tugged me forward and between them, tearing the words I'd intended from my mind. "Suck his cock, baby."

I bent forward to do as told, my gaze snared by Elijah's. Jaw clenched, he gently cradled my head in his hands as I placed mine on his thighs. At the first swipe of my tongue across his slit, the sweetness of his pre-cum flooded my senses. I licked and lapped, my pussy dripping with abandon in response to his flavor.

"Does he taste good?" Jon asked, leaning over me and reaching between my thighs. I widened my legs, desperate for his touch where I needed him most.

"Yes." The word gasped past my lips as he cupped my sex.

"Take him deep," Jon said, his voice rasped to hell. "Show him how talented your mouth is while I empty my balls inside your needy pussy."

I whimpered and closed my mouth over Elijah's crown.

He blinked twice as though trying to stay focused on my face and leaned back, giving me more room to work—and watch. Swirling my tongue, I moaned as another burst of his flavor smeared over my tongue. I swallowed the rush of saliva, stuffed my mouth with his cock, and closed my throat around his girth.

He growled, his jaw clenching, nostrils flaring.

"Mmm." Jon lifted my hips, yanked my leggings and panties to my knees, and filled me with one thrust.

Soaked, swollen, and so damn ready for him, I didn't do more than moan around Elijah's girth.

"Her pussy is like silken fire," Jon said, breathless, like he rode the edge of his orgasm. "So damn wet." He slammed into me over and over until I couldn't hold to a rhythm of lifting and sinking my mouth over Elijah's length.

I whimpered, my eyes closing against the onslaught, the need to come.

Elijah's hold on my face tightened, and he began thrusting in time with Jon, filling me, his control, both of their grunts, the glide and thrust of Jon's cock deep inside me, causing a tingle to sweep up from my toes to my thighs—without a single touch to my clit.

Light exploded behind my eyes as my body detonated, and I arched my back, lifting my ass and moaning around Elijah.

"Christ!" Jon stabbed against my womb, his cock pulsing, filling me with his cum.

Elijah yanked my mouth off him, and grabbed hold of his cock, jerking his length in front of me. Two thrusts, and a deep groan rumbled from him as thick ropes of cum shot up across his stomach rather than on my face like I'd hoped for.

Still, at the first wave of his release shooting over his abs, I fractured anew as though connected to him. A ripple of throbbing pulses clenched my core around Jon's cock emptying deep inside me.

My heart pounded, euphoric tingles rushing over my skin as we finished, both men's hands gentling on my body. With a shuddering sigh, I draped over Elijah's lap, my cheek on his thigh.

Elation soared through me far beyond what I'd expected or even dared to hope.

We had shared in release at the same time, bringing a sense of satisfaction I hadn't know existed.

And to think we'd only just begun.

CHAPTER 20

JONATHAN

Elijah's and my gaze met over my wife's back. I felt sexually sated for the time being but hardly satisfied. Longing for so much more knifed at my chest, making me want to lean into him and kiss his soft-as-fuck lips. Inhale the sweetness of his breath and give over to the firmness of his grasp and the command of his voice that almost had me nutting before burying balls deep in my wife.

His eyes mirrored the desire in my head—in my fucking soul.

One taste, and he had me by the fucking balls. Fucking owned me in a way Dakota never could.

Still buried in my wife's body, I pulled her back against my chest, smoothing her hair away from her face. The love of my life, my person, my better half...

How could it be Elijah had taken a piece of me—without even taking *me*?

Unease slithered down my spine, but I couldn't pinpoint why.

Past trauma?

Emotional damage from childhood?

Whatever the fuck supernatural desire to kneel before another man coursed through me should have at least left me unsettled with my suddenly changed sexuality.

My dick preference in the moment, I didn't give a shit about.

It was the making myself vulnerable by submitting that worried me, considering how I'd been manipulated by the foster fucker who'd raised me.

With Elijah, I'd offered myself as a gift. I'd been the catalyst again to span the distance between him and Dakota, and strangely, *that* truth gave me a sense of purpose.

My dick still rested inside my wife's warmth, and I had zero desire to shift her off my semi and end the moment among the three of us even though Elijah was no longer physically connected.

I could still feel his touch as though he'd burned marks on my skin.

I ran my hands over Dakota's stomach, loving the softness beneath my fingertips and how Elijah's gaze tracked the movement with a different type of longing in his pale eyes.

My heart ached for him even though I had no fucking clue why.

Lifting Dakota off my dick sent a rush of cum down over my balls, but I shuffled forward on my knees, placing her on Elijah's lap.

"I'll get something to clean us up," I said, standing on shaking legs. I made it to the kitchen sink without glancing back.

Thank fuck for thirsty paper towels. Dakota—or I—had made a hell of a mess. She'd never come so hard around me in all our years of fucking, and her second climax right on the heels of the first had sent another rush of liquid to drip down my balls.

"Damn." I tossed the used towels in the trash and grabbed a few more handfuls before turning.

Elijah cradled Dakota to his chest, his eyes closed, lips pressed against her hair. One hand soothed down her arm, the other wrapped around her legs, clutching her close in a possessive hold that didn't inspire jealousy like it should have.

That damn ache knifed again, and if it weren't for my handfuls of paper towels, I would have scratched my chest in attempts to lessen the weird as fuck pain that didn't actually hurt in a physical sense.

He cradled her while I knelt in front of them and cleaned between her thighs. Her shuddering sighs while resting against Elijah's chest, eyes closed, furrowed his brow and stirred some sort of weird satisfaction in me. Both of us cared for my wife, and the connection I felt for the two of them—I didn't have fucking words as I watched him look at her as though she was the spring sun that chased winter away.

I understood the sentiment. Fucking experienced it in every cell of my body. She was an addiction, and the need for more of her could never be sated. And I didn't blame Elijah for experiencing her sweetness and yearning for another dose along with me. Would do it again should either of them hint at wanting more.

Elijah finally looked me full in the face, and for the first time since meeting the man, he allowed me to see him in ways I had yet to offer to him.

Complete vulnerability. Desire. Grief.

He gifted me a glimpse into a soul tortured by shit I couldn't begin to imagine, but contentment and thankfulness oozed from his eyes as well. My sense of satisfaction over my role in helping him and my wife find theirs intensified.

I'd given him that when I had a feeling he could have

pushed for shared release without a fight from either of us. Hell, he could have commanded it, and Dakota and I would have given until we bled dry, no fucking doubt.

Another shiver of unease tingled my spine, but rather than be truthful of my feelings, I flashed my dimples at him.

"You're welcome," I stated with a wink and enough snark one of his eyebrows raised. A shudder ripped through me, making my cock twitch with interest.

Elijah shot out his hand and grasped my neck, his palm hot and branding. I stilled, breath held, the moment intense as fuck, energy rippling between us like tinder smoldering, ready to ignite with a flash. He didn't speak a word, but promise rested in his stare. For what, I wasn't sure, but fuck, did I lust to find out.

Later. After my wife rested.

Somehow, I managed to deny his dominant hold on my soul, tearing my focus off his searching gaze, that sense he peered straight into my head and knew every thought brewing there.

"Come on." I pushed up to my feet, refusing to give him my eyes again like that newly awoken submissive part of me desired to. "You can carry her upstairs since your tree trunk thighs can't be goddamned Jell-O like mine, and she's complete toast."

He actually chuckled, and I led the way, feeling like the fucking king of Elijah's cave-like castle.

Elijah laid Dakota on our bed and stepped back while watching her curl on her side, eyes still closed, a smile on her lips. Emotion warred on his face as he looked down at her.

Had he fallen under her spell already? Gifted her his heart on a platter? Fuck knew that was easy as shit to do, since she was so goddamn perfect.

A heavy sigh sank his chest in as though resigned, a battle inside having been won.

He turned away without a word when I'd expected him to ask if he could stay.

Or demanded it.

I opened my mouth to call him back but hesitated from inviting him into our bed. Allowing Elijah to become a part of our lives outside of fucking, for however long, would be hinting at wanting something long-term. Definitely messing with fire.

I locked the door behind Elijah and slid under the covers to spoon Dakota's backside.

"He's gone?" she whispered.

"Yes." I kissed her shoulder and wrapped my arms around her.

"I-I wasn't sure what to say or do afterward and felt...I don't know."

I nuzzled my face against her hair, relieved the bind on my tongue had faded. "Do you regret what we did?"

"No." She didn't hesitate to answer, thank fuck. Another sigh rippled over her, and she settled in my hold. "Want to do it again."

"Same," I murmured against her hair, every cell in my body agreeing.

So many damn emotions and thoughts flooded through me, and even though I felt sure I could finally find the words we needed to share, I didn't have the balls or energy to further discuss what had taken place on Elijah's couch. Pretending it hadn't happened wouldn't work—I definitely still wanted Elijah's hands and mouth on me. Initiating anything further wouldn't be the best way to—

Ah, fuck.

—start my new job.

I slammed my eyelids shut at the thought that should have been forefront in my mind *before* making a decision to fuck around with Elijah.

I'd let my soon-to-be boss taste my wife. Possibly lose his heart to hers. At the least, his body already craved his newest addiction.

Goddamn it all to hell.

I'd been offered the opportunity to make money to support the love of my life again.

Had I thoroughly fucked shit up?

CHAPTER 21

ELIJAH

I had wanted to take Dakota to *my* room, lay her on *my* bed, and demand Jon join us—and never leave. And even though I fought my dragon, teeth gnashing, at the memory of finding release with them, I'd left them alone in their own bedroom, shutting the door behind me.

Dakota had lapped at and swallowed my pre-cum that didn't contain seed like a human's. The slickness intended for easing my mate's ability to take me didn't have the potency to rob her of consent like the spurts I'd shot upon my own skin rather than hers.

They had retained their freedom to choose and would need space. Time to assure the other of their love, dedication, and all the things a committed couple needed to do after involving another person in their sex life. For I had no doubt that would be the next step in our relationship—and I couldn't wait to taste them both again.

Jon's strong grip on my cock had been the biggest temptation for me. The alpha in me needed to establish the beta's position before I had any hope of mating with the female. She would have to come to her own conclusion about where her heart rested, but if Jon gave into my dominance first, I expected her choice would be easier.

She wanted sexual gratification, but I couldn't yet tell if she felt drawn to me in the same way Jon was. He, at least, recognized the connection enough to kneel without being told, but his position on the floor had only gone that far. There'd been no submission in his eyes. Or in his kiss.

Dakota had gone along with what her husband had put into action, but was she ready to submit to me, to recognize she belonged to me as much as she did to Jon?

Yes, she'd spoken of her wish to see the two of us together, but I'd yet to get a clear read on her desire outside of climaxing due to my touch.

Humans and their misconstrued notions of love and same-sex relationships... So many in the non-human world had evolved centuries earlier from one male, one female. The humans would eventually catch up to the other creatures of the universe, but I believed it would be hundreds of years before that happened.

Strict religious teachings, like leading lambs by the powerful, the manipulative, had gotten humanity to a point of closed-mindedness that didn't leave room for the truth of evolution. Besides world religions through the ages, I had also studied psychology and recognized the symptoms of a man having spent his childhood beneath a narcissist. Both Jon and Dakota had told me they'd grown up in foster care and didn't know their birth parents. Neither had said much beyond that, but I was well aware of when to let a matter lie.

Jon's childhood with such a caretaker would explain his love for Dakota. She accepted him and built him up with words of edification.

What I needed to do in order to win his affection was to show my unconditional love.

Yes, love, I admitted to myself while my inner beast grumbled about our weaker human side.

I thought I had experienced what that emotion was, but I'd never felt the all-consuming need to shelter, nurture, and protect like I did with both of my mates. And what a welcomed feeling it was.

I stepped into my room, believing I might have found a way to true happiness but couldn't imagine the joy of bonding would fully bring.

The sight of my bed drew me up short.

I'd been fantasizing about having Jon and Dakota both there, but memories of another swamped my mind.

Bonds tying him to the frame.

A massive plug in his ass to ready his hole for my cock.

His denial to taste my cum, his fear from being forcefully made to submit his beast to mine.

My other half's grumbles escaped as a rumble in my chest.

"I can't help how the human heart feels, the grief that his leaving us still holds over me," I murmured in the stillness, tearing my focus off my mattress and heading for the bathroom.

Dolyn had only been meant to share a short time in my existence, and we'd enjoyed years together, creating mostly beautiful memories.

I'd been hesitant to accept his demise after failing to locate him, but I no longer would live in denial of his death. Closure would have eased my transition of transferring my loyalty and love to those intended for me. Perhaps knowing his final resting place would allow me the freedom from grief that lingered longer than was healthy.

Hot water pelted me from all sides as I stood in the shower, arm against the tile, my forehead resting alongside.

A heavy sigh released some of the tension still riding my mind.

I'd been too domineering, too demanding with Dolyn, in attempts to cling to what I'd longed for.

A mate.

Now, both rested in my cave, and I would not overstep bounds or make another mistake.

Remembering Jon's hand on Dakota's stomach, caressing her womb, caused my cock to thicken, but I ignored it, choosing instead to focus on the longing to sense life there.

My soul shredded at the truth that as dragonblood fated mates, they would never conceive without me.

Own.

"Shut up," I muttered.

Alpha.

"As if I don't know that." I swiped my shower gel off the shelf and proceeded to wash myself with clinical efficiency.

I set out the makings for coffee and tea the next morning before sunrise, intent on my ritual of greeting daybreak with mediation.

But the veranda still overshadowed by darkness called.

Yessss.

The window of the guest chambers where my mates rested remained unlit due to its one-way glass, but I didn't have a sense of watchful eyes. No hint of their scents suggested they'd left their room either.

Shift. Fly.

I would give him freedom, but only for a short time while those most precious to me weren't in close proximity.

Once stripped down to bare skin, I threw myself off the cliff, muscle and bone stretching until our wings caught air.

We shot upward like a midnight rocket, the beast in full control over our body.

Rather than cackle or taunt our supposedly weaker half, the darker side of us remained silent as contentment roared through our heated blood.

Speeding through the predawn, cold air rushing against our face, we soared and dove, leisurely stretching as we hadn't since before I'd caught the combined hints of Jon and Dakota on the breeze.

We had made promising steps toward strengthening the connection among us the evening before. And we'd barely restrained from shooting cum down our female's willing throat. The way she had sucked and probed at my slit as though desperate for life-giving—

A gale of wind slammed into our left side, catching us unaware, and we rolled through the sky.

Our mind flashed to memories of Dolyn's golden body flying alongside us. How he would play, roughhouse in the air, testing how far he could go in attempts to show dominance fate hadn't intended for him.

The last time we'd flown together, he'd crossed a line by nipping at our hind quarter.

We'd chained him to the dungeon roof once we'd returned and shifted back to our human forms. My whip had reminded him of his place.

Dolyn's mind fought submission even though he'd given himself to me, but his body had responded, gifting us his release. He'd hated every second, declaring his human half had betrayed him, and wouldn't allow me to pamper him with aftercare.

Anger and bitterness had rolled off him, his golden eyes wet while peering up at me and declaring he was meant to be alpha—he'd had zero thoughts otherwise in his heart. We'd kindly reminded him of my beast's royal lineage, that there had been no denying who'd been meant to lead between the two of us.

The next morning, I'd woken to find Dolyn gone from the home we'd shared.

Tears whipped from our blinking eyes, and the beast roared his anguish he continually denied into the rising sun.

My human half huddled in silence, long having allowed myself to grieve. If only the feelings would abate for both halves of us.

Surely, once we mated, the pain of our past would dissipate, and we would be free to live and love without further hauntings.

While the beast battled to enjoy stretching our wings as we'd been doing moments earlier, my other half required a break from emotion. Forcing my human mind on the project Jon would be laboring over helped me focus.

Testing of the now-contracted robots had been done at the New York office over the previous six months, but with what the military wanted me to upgrade, I would need to do more.

However, I refused to return to the city and leave my mates again. I hoped Jon had the skills to do the testing required remotely and we could stay holed up in the cavern, exploring each other and deepening our bond for when I had no choice but to go back to New York.

We would do everything within our power to drag out the days and hours, taking advantage of every minute allowed to us.

Pink and hints of red streaked across the sky before I returned home, keeping toward the backside of the mountain lest Jon and Dakota were awake and watching for me from the northern side where all the windows overlooked.

I took on my human form outside of the garage before letting myself into our home. Silence hung over the cave, so after retrieving my clothing from the veranda, I made my way down to the lower outcropping for my morning ritual of tai chi I was in a better headspace to enjoy. Within minutes of meditating through motion, serenity descended, easing my mind of all stress. I flowed through each pose effortlessly until sweat poured from me and the sun kissed my face.

My skin pebbled a second before the scent of Dakota swept past me, but I continued my practice, fighting my cock's desire to swell. The click of her camera sounded loud in my ears, but I pretended I wasn't aware she captured me with her lens.

A second shiver licked at my spine. Jon watched as well. Unable to concentrate any longer, I lifted my head.

Dakota stood at the railing above me same as before, alone, a blanket wrapped around her. Cheeks flushed, she stared at me, her camera lowered, hands trembling.

Come to me, we silently bid her, but lower lip between her teeth, she turned away.

My attention roamed upward, seeking out Jon. I could sense him looking down at me through their darkened bedroom window, but he disappeared a heartbeat later. Quickly. As though he couldn't bear the sight of me.

Stomach tight, I grabbed my towel and entered the door leading into the lower cavern. Did he regret our actions from the night before? Did he hate that his wife watched me? Took pictures of me?

Heart racing, I donned my T-shirt and hurried upstairs in fear of the sure conflict ahead of us that could very well tear my mates away from me.

CHAPTER 22

DAKOTA

I'd felt Jon's gaze on me while I stared at Elijah through my lens and finally captured images of him with my camera. Guilt swamped me even though we'd stepped beyond friendship, and I had no reason to feel that way. What had transpired had been Jon's idea, after all.

We hadn't spoken of what took place the night before, and Jon snored when I'd climbed out of bed and grabbed my camera. I'd hurried downstairs, intent on the veranda, only remembering at the last second to grab a throw from the couch to ward off the cold morning air.

I'd sensed Elijah before I'd seen him, and I once more questioned the magical air of his mountain. Fanciful I had always been, but something about his cavern home made me believe perhaps the paranormal world wasn't as much fiction as humans believed.

How else would someone other than Jon catch my eye?

My breath had stalled out at the sight of Elijah—hair dampened by sweat and glinting in the rising sun. Sweat slickened his bare torso and brow, and my tongue had tingled with the need to lick him from head to toes. The memory of the sweetness of his pre-cum, the silken glide of his cock against the back of my throat had caused my too-empty pussy to clench. Pulse thrumming in my neck, I'd bitten the inside of my lip and clicked away, focusing in on the light and shadows of his luscious body.

Elijah had lifted his head, and desire rolled over me at the need in his crystalline eyes.

My body had longed to go to him as though he'd made a verbal command, but the hairs on my neck stood on end. I hadn't needed to look above me to know Jon peered down at me. I'd turned without attempting to meet my husband's gaze in the one-way glass and walked inside, trying like hell to focus on the preparations Elijah had left out for our morning coffee and tea rather than the unease standing the hairs on my nape.

Would Jon be upset that I'd gone down to watch Elijah rather than waking him as I'd done the previous three days? Every morning, I'd had my lips around his soft cock, sucking, licking, and nipping until he lost control and flipped me onto my belly, hand tangled in my hair, fucking me from behind until we both lay spent.

Lower lip between my teeth and hands shaking, I poured boiling water over the grounds in the French press and into my mug with the tea bag Elijah had placed in it.

"Morning, baby." Jon's sleepy and calm voice from the top of the stairs encouraged me to tip my head back.

His slow smirk warmed my belly.

I smiled back, the lack of anger or judgment in his eyes easing my anxiety. "Morning."

Scratching his balls through the shorts he'd pulled on, same as every morning, he moved down the stairs, and I turned away, chuckling. Why had I worried myself? Jon was the love of my life, and he knew it.

He wrapped his arms around me from behind as he was

fond of doing and kissed my neck, a slight scent of soap from our shower the evening before clinging to his skin and filling my greedy nose. "Missed your mouth this morning."

I sighed and pressed my ass against him, a thrill of that newfound sexual prowess seeping into my blood and giving me the desire to be bolder than usual. "I'll make up for it after coffee if you want."

"Pretty sure I'm supposed to start work, but I can tell my boss I'll be a little late." He ground his hips against me, making me aware his cock was interested in what he'd said.

"Probably not the best way to start a new job, though."

"Yeah," he muttered beneath his breath.

I turned and draped my arms over his shoulders. His eyes appeared troubled even though the usual chemistry between us had him staring at my mouth. "It's going to be okay, Jon," I stated quietly, my heart starting to race at my boldness in bringing up one of many conversations we needed to have. "I can feel it—somehow know this thing with Elijah is right."

He nodded, but his eyes remained wary.

I waited for him to offer his thoughts or expand on his agreement, but he remained silent, simply holding me.

Perhaps it wasn't time. At least I'd made an effort. If Jon couldn't find the words just yet, I would be patient for him to settle his thoughts on what was transpiring between the three of us.

"Anyway." I smiled, hoping to put him at ease. "Are you excited?"

One of his eyebrows rose, and a twinkle lit in his eyes.

I rolled mine. "Forget I asked, you horndog." I leaned up on my tiptoes, raising Elijah's shirt enough for Jon's hands to cup my bare ass, and pressed my lips softly against my husband's. "Love you," I murmured, rubbing my nose across his.

"Love you more." He squeezed my ass and pressed me against his semi but stepped back. "Coffee?"

Huffing on laughter, I turned and poured him a cup.

Jon cradled the mug and, eyes closed, breathed in the rising steam. "The man has exquisite taste in coffee, wine, and women."

Heat flooded my face, but fortunately, Jon didn't peer at me as though gauging my reaction to his declaration. He sat at the island, sipping, having simply stated a fact as he'd seen it.

Butterflies flitted in my stomach, bringing another smile to my face. Turning back around, I added a teaspoon of sugar as I had noted Elijah enjoyed to the second mug before lacing my tea with honey.

The luscious scent of Elijah and the tingling over my skin let me know he drew near. I glanced at Jon. He stared at the door leading downstairs from where I could feel Elijah approaching.

Surely, magic resided here.

Elijah stepped into the kitchen, his body dried of sweat and a T-shirt hiding his upper body, but my drool factory set to work regardless. Forcing myself to focus on the mugs in front of me was like peeling my eyelids from my body it burned so bad.

"Good morning." His low rumble caressed against my ears.

My knees went weak.

"Hey," Jon said at the same time I squeaked a "Morning."

My body tuned in to every shift of Elijah's energy as he sat at the island. Breath held, I placed his coffee in front of him without glancing at his face. I took up the third chair and held my mug in both hands, eyes closed as Jon had done, wishing I could smell the tea over the scent of fire and brimstone, soap and sex emanating from Elijah's skin.

"What time did you want to get started this morning?" Jon asked.

Guess that means the elephant isn't going to get discussed with Elijah either.

I peeked at Jon, unsurprised considering how he'd stayed close-lipped about it a minute earlier.

He lounged, seemingly relaxed on his stool, smirking as though he hadn't a care in the world—or that the man beside him had his face buried between my thighs the night before.

I finally looked at Elijah. A flicker of something unnamed crossed his face as he glanced at me then back to Jon. Unease, maybe? Perhaps he'd been expecting us to regret our affair? Or *he* did?

My chest went tight at the thought, and I flitted my focus to my husband who stared at his new boss.

"I'll meet you in ten?" Elijah's deep voice pebbled my nipples and sent a pulse through my pussy.

"Sure." Jon lifted his mug and sipped, holding Elijah's stare until the man gave us his back.

Elijah climbed the stairs with sure steps, coffee in hand, and Jon kissed the top of my head before heading off to the shower.

Jon had set wheels in motion that I wanted to roll down-hill—damn quick—but the thought he or Elijah had zero plans to continue pushing us forward had me chewing the inside of my lip to death. I sat and stared at my steaming tea, relieved Jon wasn't upset but beyond bummed one of them hadn't initiated our picking up right where we'd left off a handful of hours earlier.

Perhaps I was the one meant to act. Take a step without direction or gentle prodding from the man I always looked to. Maybe the awakening creature inside me needed to grab the reins and steer us around the boulder blocking our forward motion.

The idea dried my mouth and left me shifting on my chair at the same time.

Wield my sexuality and get more fantasies fulfilled? Explore what I felt sure would lead to something more than sating lust? Elijah had wormed in between me and Jon—but not in a negative way.

Something about the man…

My camera in the middle of the island caught my eye, and I pulled it toward me. Image after image on the screen caught Elijah paused in motion, muscles flexed, sweat dripping. His beauty was other-worldly—as though generative AI had finally crafted perfection. I focused in on his face, the memory of his full lips laying open-mouth kisses between my thighs causing my core to pulse with need.

"Damn," I murmured, tempted to finger myself.

A whisper of sound reminded me of where I sat, and I glanced up to find him at the foot of the stairs. How he'd descended without my awareness proved I'd been caught up in fantasy.

My breath snagged, and the sexual energy between us caused my heartbeat to heighten and my belly to flutter. I sat frozen, ensnared by his unwavering gaze as he stalked toward me in near silence as though unable to bear the distance between us.

He pushed my hair over my shoulder, his fingertips brushing along my neck and sending a shiver of goose bumps down my body. "So beautiful," he murmured, laying his warm palm against the side of my neck.

I breathed in the scent of fire and cinnamon and found myself leaning into his warmth, all thoughts but the right-ness of his hand on me having fled my mind. My lips tingled to touch his and assure him he wasn't alone. My nipples strained against his shirt, desires of the heat of his mouth or the tug of his fingers, accepting the pleasure he longed to give me.

Frozen in time took on a whole new meaning as I floated in an ocean of desire, of physical and emotional need so intense a soft whine escaped me.

"The memory of your mouth on me and the taste of you lingered on my tongue far into the night," he whispered, his voice lower than usual while sweeping the pad of his thumb across my lower lip. "I couldn't sleep for want of you. To bury my cock in your slick heat. Hold you in my arms while flooding your womb with my seed."

Arousal leaked from my core as his words captured and set me on fire with unquenchable flames.

I whimpered at the steady pulses in my pussy, the desperation to squeeze and milk his length until he did what he said.

"You long for the same." Elijah's words weren't intoned with question, but I found myself needing to answer.

I swallowed, knowing it wasn't the time to steer us toward fulfillment like I'd considered doing. "I— Jon's w-working for you now…"

"That's not a no."

Silence hovered, and I stared into his swirling pupils, damn near lost in my desire to feel him inside me. Owning me. Claiming the part of my soul where he'd made himself at home.

I could be more open with my husband and push for what I lusted for, but interaction without him, however right it felt, *wouldn't* be right.

"I-I'm not free to take what I want. It has to be Jon's doing," I whispered, hating I couldn't fully grasp my inner fierceness, yet proud of myself for remaining faithful to the man who I'd committed my life to. I would sacrifice my desires to prove he was enough, more than worthy of my affections all on his own.

Elijah's shoulders fell as though my words disappointed him.

"The decision must be *yours*, Dakota." His hand dropped to his side, and he stepped back, putting space between us when every part of me except for my brain demanded the opposite.

"But I..." I couldn't voice the riotous mess in my head warring with that in my heart.

"You both must come to me of your own accord," he stated quietly and with finality, reminding me of old men quoting scripture or ancient text. His tone also hinted of inner turmoil. Longing so intense I couldn't breathe.

My throat swelled shut at the tightness in my chest.

"I don't understand," I whispered.

His pale eyes burned bright, as though some inner light wished to snake from his body and mark me.

Fantasy, I reminded myself.

Shaking my head, I slid off my stool and headed toward the stairs, every shuffled footstep away from Elijah like peeling skin from bone.

Assurance of my husband's presence upstairs alone made my escape possible.

CHAPTER 23

JONATHAN

I hopped in the shower knowing time ran short, and I didn't have a spare minute to relieve the ache in my balls Elijah had caused from a mere three minutes in his presence.

How the hell was I going to work with him every day for the next four weeks without giving in and dropping to my knees to beg for more? The temptation to deny my lips after tasting him, to keep from feeling his cock swell in my hand, the squeeze of his hand on my dick?

Goddamned torture.

Sating my lust last night had only made me want him more. A mistake, for sure. The three of us together, even if we hadn't fucked, had been the single hottest night of my life, and it could be even better if I gave in to my body's strange, sudden needs.

But initiating would cause issues with my employment. Never mind weirdness and jealousy would eventually come into play and fuck up my marriage—and my job. Couldn't live without the one person who loved me as-is. Definitely refused to put that at risk.

But fucking hell, my body yearned to crawl to him—hell, I would pay to kiss his goddamn feet and suck his toes if meant I had his devotion in return. I wanted the same for Dakota too.

I should have been behaving like a possessive lunatic considering how I'd responded to my ex-best friend requesting a taste of my wife, so why the fuck was I thinking this shit about my new boss?

My body sure knew what it was after. My head? Not so much.

I'd studied Elijah doing his fancy yoga-still-my-mind-shit for a full minute before I noticed my wife on the veranda below capturing him on camera.

How long had she watched him? The thought she'd gone to drink her fill with her eyes rather than wrap her lips around my cock like she'd been doing every morning didn't even nudge the sleeping green beast inside me. Why wasn't I jealous? Any other man would be raging.

She walked into our room as I dressed, and I could literally feel the tension radiating off my wife as she stripped to get in the tub. Lust or unease? I couldn't decide, so add that shit to the fucking cluelessness making a mess of my thoughts.

And I needed clarity for the new job I was about to start.

I pulled my wife into my arms before she stepped into the water, her curves melting against me, same as always when I held her.

"Love you so goddamned much," I rasped, my throat attempting to close off. Didn't deserve her though. Elijah could better provide and probably be able to plant that baby in her belly I'd failed to—

I shut that shit down and kissed the top of Dakota's head, eyes closed, thankful as fuck to have another day with her even if it hadn't started out the same as it had the previous three.

There didn't need to be dick sucking or fucking for me to be content with our relationship.

But lately?

Something seemed to be missing.

A specific someone.

"You're going to be late," Dakota whispered even though her hands clung to the T-shirt she'd washed for me that still smelled of Elijah.

My cock twitched at the truth I wore his scent.

"Yeah," I muttered, torn on whether to stay or go.

"Get a move on." Dakota slapped my ass and pulled away from me. "Go show that man your mad skills with a keyboard and controller, and I promise he'll give you a raise after this four-week trial is up."

Her confidence boosted me, same as her making the decision for me to take a step when usually shit was the other way around.

"Fucking love you," I swore.

"Love you more."

I doubted that, but whatever.

Grinning and second cup of coffee in my hand a few minutes later, I took the stairs down to the cavern's lower levels. I didn't need anyone to tell me Elijah had already gone below. His smoldering, fiery scent swarmed my nose the deeper into his lair I travelled.

Lair.

I chuckled at the word my brain had chosen. His cave-home felt like that exact thing, and I was the unsuspecting victim falling prey to his pheromones. Dakota would get a serious kick out of my brain right now.

She'd sat in the sunken tub surrounded by bubbles when I'd left our room. Had she touched herself yet?

Taken care of that sweet pussy I had shared with Elijah? He'd been the only other man to taste her. The idea of anyone but him putting their hands on her had me clenching my jaw against a sudden growl rising from my chest.

Surprised by the animalistic noise, I coughed it away.

Was I turning into a beast, for fuck's sake?

I reached the flanking doors—the dungeon I'd jerked off in and the computer lab, I realized while peeking into the wide-open door to my left.

Screens lined the far wall, showing feed from the cameras I'd located throughout house, and a quick glance revealed every room but the bathrooms. And the dungeon across the hall. He must have watched us, just as I'd suspected, but I needed to know.

"Get live feed on your cell?" I asked, lifting my coffee cup for a sip.

He turned, glancing over my clothed form with heat in his eyes, causing my dick to twitch beneath his perusal. "I do."

"Did you enjoy your daily and nightly shows while in New York?" I asked without a hint of anger over his Peeping Tom antics without our consent.

"I did." The dude didn't even have the grace to glance away, blush, or apologize. Those pale eyes of his stared at me, so light blue they twinkled like a diamond.

Fucking fanciful mind.

A grin popped my dimples. "My wife is hot."

"As are you."

Well, fuck.

My cock swelled further, but I was determined to focus and start off on the right foot because this job was important as fuck. I cleared my throat. "So. About that contract."

A corner of Elijah's lip quirked, and he turned away.

"Please have a seat, and we'll go over what I had my legal team draft overnight."

It was obvious the guy had money, but to keep lawyers working late into the night for a three-page agreement to entice me to sign on the dotted line? As if my ass hadn't already known the truth of his wealth once I had seen the helicopter and the mad technology that allowed him to hide it deep inside a mountain.

Nothing about my first read through of the papers in front of me suggested Elijah had any intent to swindle me. Nor was he a cheap bastard. Full benefits. Sick leave. Retirement fund. Bonuses. Maternity leave should Dakota and I ever have a child.

An ache raced through me over how I'd failed to give her the world in that regard.

A slower, second read confirmed nothing lay in fine print that would fuck me over. No red flags waved, and when I'd brandished Elijah's pen, that sense of rightness I'd been feeling too often lately rushed through me.

I signed my name without hesitation, no usual instinctive wariness creeping over my skin.

For two agonizing hours afterward, I sat in one of the kitchen chairs beside my new boss. He said he'd get another office chair on the next trip to New York in a couple of days, but I didn't even notice the discomfort of the hard back and wooden seat.

Elijah was an AI god who built robots.

Like, fucking real-life humans, two legs, arms, ten fingers and toes. And I held a controller in hand, moving one of the high-tech models around in a huge laboratory all the way down in his New York office. Three-hundred some miles away, and I had the fucking thing sprinting, leaping, and spinning like a world-class gymnast, its motions fluid as though blood pumped through muscle beneath the fake skin covering the frame.

"Holy fuck, this is cool." I stared at the monitor, my mind blown. His invention appeared more lifelike than any robot I'd ever seen, unsexed, but with agility enough to make me think the damn pile of metal and plastic *was* a human.

Elijah's on-site employees had set up a dozen obstacles to test my ability to control the robot. Once I got the hang of how quickly the limbs responded, I raced that motherfucker around the lab like he owned the place.

A smaller remote controlled the hands, and after a few dexterity tests, I dismantled a fake bomb, snips and all, just like in the movies.

"Well done." Elijah's murmur after I completed the final test warmed me through.

"Coolest fucking shit I've ever played with." I put the remote controller on the desk and sat back, watching as the New York staff in their white lab coats and bootied feet began checking the robot over.

"I have a dozen other prototypes—"

"Shit."

"—but this is the one the American government decided on."

"How much does it cost to build one of those?"

A wry smile twisted his lips. "Too much, but if they will save lives while not endangering others..."

"Damn worth it," I said, glancing once more at the creature he had created. "Are they going to clothe the damn thing or let it run around naked?"

"There's armor which you'll be testing various designs to see which best suits each prototype."

Grinning, I tipped the chair onto its back legs, hands behind my head. "When do I get to see these in real life?"

"I have to go to New York in a couple of days." Elijah flicked a few buttons and spoke into a mike, telling the lab tech to outfit the robot in the first suit of armor. "You're welcome to come along with me if you'd like," Elijah said, returning to our conversation. "I'm sure you'll be wanting more of your belongings from your apartment—if you're still planning on staying here with me for the four weeks we agreed upon?"

The contract I'd signed hadn't even hinted at living arrangements. "Better fucking believe it."

My gaze snagged on his lips as he turned to face me. Full, perfectly bowed, sexy as sin and so fucking soft...

I sucked in my lower lip, remembering how he'd owned me with that mouth. The slickness of his tongue fucking mine, the sweet scent of his breath filling my lungs when I'd expected the tang of embers.

"Jon."

"Hmm?" I tore my gaze off his mouth, and my dick jerked fully to attention at the hunger in his eyes.

"Last night..." He glanced away, his brow furrowing.

I waited, my body tense, jeans trapping my hard cock that throbbed for his touch. "Last night, what?" I pushed when he didn't continue.

Elijah heaved a breath and stood. "Run the same course with that armor," he said, nodding toward the monitor. "I'll return in a few minutes."

My gaze trailed after his backside—his tight, round ass in jeans I wanted to rip off his body.

"Fuck." I growled under my breath at the lost opportunity and picked up the remote, my knee bouncing while the lab techs strapped on black, scale-like armor. The breast plate glinted in the lab's light, sending a shimmer of rainbows across its surface.

A tickle of a memory shifted in my mind, but I couldn't bring clarity to what it was my brain tried to tell me.

I leaned forward, mesmerized by each piece of material the lab techs strapped to the robot. They looked like scales. Black, fucking *dragon* scales like my make-believe friend—exactly like those on the cross I'd been dreaming about being shackled to.

"No fucking way." I actually touched the screen, my fingertip trailing over the robot's body.

"Whenever you're ready, sir." The tech's voice came through the speaker, jerking me back to the present rather than flying through the skies like I'd done in my mind as a child.

I cleared my throat. "I'm ready."

For fifteen minutes, I set the robot through the course, only slightly hindered by the armor they'd added. The techs took over, readying the next suit of armor, and Elijah still hadn't returned.

I stood and stretched the kinks from my neck and back. Without meaning to, I strode up the hallway, drawn as though tethered to a life-giving energy I couldn't escape—and had no wish to.

CHAPTER 24

ELIJAH

Both Jon's and Dakota's actions baffled me. I'd sensed his disappearance from the window earlier that morning as though he'd been angry, jealous perhaps, at finding his wife watching me, and I had expected so much more than a mere question about work over coffee.

But nothing had transpired as I'd been waiting for.

His seeming disinterest in expanding upon what had happened the evening prior sent a lancing through my chest so painful I was reminded of my heartache with my ex.

My inner beast growled his annoyance at me.

"I'm unable to move on as quickly as you," I reminded him quietly while striding away from the office.

Weak.

I ignored his mutter.

And Dakota…

I'd had a moment of vulnerability earlier in the kitchen and hadn't been able to contain the truth in my soul about what I longed for. Her desire for me couldn't be hidden, yet she'd outright refused me. While I should have been pleased by her strength and wanting to remain faithful to her husband, I couldn't help my own jealousy over the emotions she held for him. I longed for both of my mates to experience the sense of ownership I felt toward them, for their desires to bond to match my own.

Breed.

"That too," I agreed with a mutter, my heart heavy.

Two hours trapped in the room with Jon, my mind replaying the kiss he and I had shared and the stroking of each other's bodies, had taken my human side to the breaking point. My cock swollen and aching from close proximity, I'd needed to distance myself. Gather my thoughts and rein in the steaming dragon within before I lost the constant battle against his renewed push to claim since being patient didn't seem to be working in our favor.

I sat on the weight bench, my head in my hands, trying to find the serenity I had while practicing my tai chi but failed. Breathing deeply and flowing through the poses in my mind cleared my head slightly but didn't lessen my yearning for my mates to love me fully and without manipulation.

At least my dragon half remained quiet rather than pushing against my boundaries like he had in Jon's presence.

Still, I felt as though a thousand-pound weight lay upon my chest, suffocating the life in my lungs.

I sensed Jon moving up the hallway, and I straightened, arms dropping to my sides.

He appeared in the doorway, his gaze focused on me, a slight frown furrowing his brow. "Break time?"

I shrugged, at a complete loss of words. Would telling him the truth in my heart sway him toward accepting what grew between us? Would doing so plant thoughts in his mind he wouldn't have considered otherwise, thus taking away his free will?

The beast within me growled over being too careful, but I

refused to mess with fate's intentions and perhaps lose the two people I desired most in life.

Jon sauntered to the pull-up bar and grabbed hold, his T-shirt lifting and revealing a stretch of golden skin. The V of muscles alongside his hip bones above his low-slung jeans ensnared my focus. He flexed his arms and hauled himself upward without effort. Five steady reps, and I couldn't tear my gaze from that peek of skin, the tease of what lay below.

He lowered his feet and stood but kept his hands clasped around the bar. "See something you like?"

My groin throbbed in response.

The smirk in his tone—on his face when I glanced up—confused me, considering his lack of interaction or words before work when I'd expected some sort of negative outcome.

"Why are you doing this?" I asked, my tone wary even to my own ears.

"Doing what?"

I ran my hands through my hair, the urge to move toward him, slam him against the wall, and claim what belonged to me wreaking such havoc in my body I shifted on the weight bench.

Take.

"Tell me what you want, Jon," I demanded, knowing he would obey—but only sharing *his* thoughts, unswayed by my own.

His smirk faded as he held my stare. "Fuck if I can figure it out. I want to see my wife happy—content." His jaw ticked to the side as though he considered a deeper truth. "But I yearn for *more.*"

Yessss.

I was on my feet and approaching him before I realized my inner beast moved my human legs, but I quickly regained control. Heart pounding, I hovered in front of my beta, breathing in his heightened exhales bathing my face.

Arms still overhead, he didn't shy away or even flinch at my unnatural speed to close the distance between us. Jon held my gaze as though unsurprised, his blue eyes unshuttered and revealing a vulnerability that made me want to weep.

Submission lay in his gaze when it'd been absent the night before while peering up at me from his kneeling position.

He longed to give up control—stood on the brink of doing so.

I lifted one hand and caressed his neck, gently wrapping my fingers around his nape.

"Tell me, Jon," I repeated with a ragged whisper, begging rather than commanding as my beast demanded of me.

Admission would open doors, break down walls, allow us to move forward in building the right kind of bond I yearned for. Sexual energy rippled in the few inches separating us, radiating outward in an all-consuming vortex of need.

Lips parted, Jon tilted his head back as I fought to keep from tightening my hold on him in a display of dominance as the dragon within me pushed to do.

"Please—" My word cut off and nostrils flared at the sudden energy and sweetness wafting toward us from the doorway. Pre-cum released from my slit in a throbbing pulse, hard enough I grunted. My inner beast whimpered. "Your wife is watching," I growled at Jon, my mouth flooding with drool over the fact she'd taken the initiative to seek us out and let herself be known when she'd hidden the last time she'd stood outside the gym's door.

Jon's gaze flitted to my left, but I didn't need to turn to know she stood in full display on the threshold. I could taste her in the air, the memory of her musky arousal on my tongue causing my mouth to water.

"She wants this as much as you do," I made the statement without intent to manipulate. Unable to help myself, I leaned forward to nuzzle Jon's neck and sniff my beta's scent deep into my lungs alongside our female's. "Don't you, Dakota?"

My balls firmed as the desire to breed seared my entire body with flaming heat regardless of the fact she'd denied me mere hours earlier.

"Yes." She whispered her submission truthfully and without prompting from her husband as I'd hoped for—exactly as Jon needed to hear.

Appreciation of her owning her sexuality and finding the strength to choose her own fate flooded through me, causing a sweet hiss to steam inside me from my beast's pleasure. My heart soared, attempting to rip through my breastbone and fly free. Unknowingly, she'd allowed her longing, her inner dragon, to claim what her codependent human half hadn't been able to until that moment.

"Good girl," I murmured to our female.

Dakota moaned at my praise, causing another ooze of wetness to smear inside my slacks.

"If only you could find the courage to be so honest," I told Jon, pulling back to meet his gaze.

His blue orbs hazed with his wish to do the same, but he remained stubbornly silent.

"Jon."

He swallowed hard, searching my eyes I fought to keep from swirling with my supernatural half shrieking to be set free. "Why do I want this?"

I slid my other palm down over Jon's abdomen to the rigid length in his pants. His body had clearly already accepted his fate. He just needed to tap into his own inner beast to understand. "*This* or to give into the yearning to submit to me?"

"Fuck." He cursed through gritted teeth, fighting his body's need.

Same as Dolyn had done.

My skin threatened to burst—expand and make way for the muscle and bone beneath screaming for release.

We *are alpha.*

My dragon had stated as such countless times, but the words in that moment hit in a different light. Clarity radiated through my brain, offering me truth I hadn't considered in my single-minded determination to dominate without coercion. The tight restraint I'd kept on my beast eased, and my shoulders relaxed.

I released a slow exhale.

My darker side had been wanting to force my mates to accept their places when I'd been unwilling to do the same with mine.

Owning my position in our triad would not be taking without consent *or* manipulation. It was my responsibility to lead, and I'd been doing my mates a disservice by refusing what my other half had tried to remind me of.

I could take my place as was intended before time, and in the process, Jon would find peace in his. And willingly accept his fate as his wife had chosen to do without his influence—or mine.

"Touch yourself, Dakota," I requested of our female, peace settling deep inside my soul in knowing she had gifted me the right to command her actions. "Slide your fingers deep inside your sweet pussy and show your husband how much his submission turns you on."

CHAPTER 25

JONATHAN

I held onto the bar with all my strength, my white-knuckled grip keeping me upright.

Elijah's hand around my neck, his low voice in my ear wracked shudders through me.

And the sight of my wife obeying him without hesitation, unafraid for the first time to make a choice without my influence? Her independence only turned me on even the more. Seeing her take what she wanted…

Goddamn, the heat flaring among the three of us was going to burn my goddamned skin to ash.

She slid her hand beneath her panties, my voice echoing the moan leaking from her lips as she reached deep into her pussy.

"Show him, Dakota," Elijah repeated his request.

Already panting, she pulled her hand from her leggings and lifted her fingers. They glistened with her wetness, and I swore the addictive sweetness of her teased at my nose across the distance separating us. Widened, her luminous green eyes showed, regardless of her owning her desires, she feared hurting me.

But she didn't have to worry. My need for Elijah had to be twice as much as hers.

"It's okay to want this, baby," I whispered, my tone ragged.

"Just as it's the same for you to desire me, Jon."

Blinking, I tore my gaze off Dakota to find Elijah peering into my eyes, a satisfied curve lifting his lips at whatever he read on my face.

Definitely lust.

Yearning for a connection I couldn't fathom yet craved.

And goddamned submission—to his desires, to his leading.

In that moment, I would have offered him anything. Everything.

Because I didn't doubt that my wife would be right there with me, sharing in mutual need and fulfillment that I somehow knew only Elijah could give us.

"Please touch me," I whispered.

Eyes darkening, Elijah reached inside my pants and wrapped his large hand around my dick.

My knees went weak, and I clutched at the bar with waning strength.

"Fuck." I groaned at his strong grip, unlike Dakota's or my own, so damn potent my balls seized up tight.

"You wish to please your wife."

"Yes," I panted even though he hadn't asked a question.

"And me?"

"Fuck yes—anything. Jesus, fuck, Elijah." I thrust into his grip, my entire body tensing.

"Finger yourself, sweet female," Elijah murmured to Dakota without taking his focus off my face. "Find your pleasure in watching me make your husband come."

He shoved me toward the wall at my back, and I let go of the bar. My fingers found purchase in his hair as he quickly yanked my jeans to my ankles. Standing once more, he squeezed my cock in his fist, his other hand holding my neck in a possessive yet tender grip. Energy radiated off him, licking at my skin, setting me on fire regardless of the cool stone pressing against my spine.

I couldn't look away even if I'd tried.

Dakota whimpered, the needy noise causing my dick to buck in Elijah's grasp.

His chest rumbled as pre-cum oozed from my slit and coated his palm. He leaned in close, beginning to work up and down my length. "Watch your wife, Jon. See how your submission makes her burn."

It fucking hurt to tear my focus off his pale eyes overcome by black pupils, but I did as told, only needing to shift my head slightly to take her in.

Dakota stared at me, her mouth parted on quick inhales, already close to coming. Her eyes were wide, vulnerable yet wary as her hand moved inside her leggings. Blonde hair hung around her shoulders, brushing over her tight nipples poking against the shirt she wore.

"You're fucking gorgeous, baby," I gasped as Elijah thumbed over my slit. "So goddamned perfect. Love seeing you like this—fucking love how you respond to your fantasies coming true."

She whimpered, her gaze dropping first to Elijah's grasp on my neck and down to where he smeared more wetness over my swollen cockhead with the palm of his hand.

I thrust into his grip, hissing. "Jesus—you're fucking killing me."

"Tell her how you're feeling, all you've been holding back."

I groaned instead, and he pressed harder against my neck.

"Jon." His tone promised I might not like the consequences of disobedience.

"His hand feels so damn good, baby." The words, strangled as though ripped from me, hung heavy in the lust-filled air.

Dakota began to fuck herself with her fingers in steady rhythm, stroking in time with Elijah's along my aching length.

"Goddamn." I clenched my eyes shut, willing away the too-soon tingle in my balls. "Been dreaming about him touching me. Touching you. Fuck." I gritted my teeth, breathing deeply through my nose. Fire and brimstone filled my lungs.

Not a single part of me escaped Elijah's presence, and I still lusted for more.

Images of the three of us entwined, flashing through my head. Heated skin. Desperate hands. Hungry mouths.

"Need to blow my load. Want you." I gasped out every word. "Jesus—come, baby. Give us your climax."

"Oh, God." Dakota whimpered.

I forced my eyes open.

She leaned against the doorjamb, legs widened for access to her sopping pussy, frantically finger fucking herself.

My eyes started to roll back into my head, but Elijah pressed tight against my neck.

"Wait for her," he murmured in my ear, his hot breath burning my skin with a delicious sting I could easily become addicted to.

"Fuck." I panted, trying with all my might to focus on Dakota, will her to come so my balls could explode. "Please, baby, *please.*" I begged, my hips jerking with Elijah's downward strokes to my base and tight sac.

Dakota's telltale whine built in her chest.

"Yesss," I hissed, half-delirious. Fucking mad with need for release.

"O-oh!" Dakota cried out, slumping against the doorjamb, and my eyelids slammed shut as I let loose.

My balls pulsed and shot cum up through my dick with every euphoric noise leaving my wife's lips.

Elijah growled as I twitched and jerked against his fingers, my cum spilling over his hand. The pressure on my neck lessened as I sucked in wind, one last spurt ripping a grunt from me. His pale eyes, intent as ever, peered into mine, and I swallowed at the heat still pouring from them.

"Take off your pants, Dakota," he said, his voice rumbling with the type of command no one would dare defy.

Regardless of his dominant nature and tone, we had agreed on our mutual want of him. Obeying came easy as breathing in the scent of smoke and sex emanating from him.

Elijah held my gaze captive as Dakota's rustling of clothing reached my ears.

"Lie back on the bench and pull your legs to your chest." He continued to quietly steer us toward mutual fulfillment. "Your husband is going to lick the cum from between your milky thighs." Elijah stepped away from me as she obeyed in my peripheral vision, but he didn't take his gaze from my face. "Crawl to her on your knees, Jon. Clean and fuck her with your tongue until she comes again."

Embarrassment should have burned my face, but I wanted to hear similar words of praise he'd gifted my wife.

I'd voiced some of my thoughts while he'd held me captive against the wall, but desires far beyond what I'd admitted to still lay in the back of my mind.

And I was pretty fucking sure he'd seen in my eyes what I hadn't been able to speak.

Something potent had ignited among the three of us, and I didn't hate how Elijah had finally taken the reins in guiding us forward together since both Dakota and I had been tongue-tied and unable to make another move.

I would swear on my wife's life that we'd been meant to run across him in the White Mountains, that fate had somehow led us to his lair when we'd planned on the Bahamas.

And I wanted this. Him.

I dropped to my knees, and a sense of rightness flooded through me.

"Good boy."

Jesus fucking Christ.

I swallowed hard as his words lit me up from the inside out and once more made my dick hard as granite.

CHAPTER 26
DAKOTA

Jon had quickly kicked his jeans off and crawled toward me at Elijah's command. Although he'd just released over Elijah's hand, Jon's unfocused, lust-filled gaze on my pussy made my breath catch.

I'd been brutally honest in finally admitting what I wanted, but lingering fear over my husband's reaction erased from my mind at the look in Jon's eyes.

He prowled across the rock floor like a predator, his hair falling around his face. Lips parted, he stared, his blue eyes intent upon my swollen folds as I grasped the backs of my knees and bared myself fully. Arousal leaked from my pussy down my ass crack.

Awareness of Elijah's gaze on both of us caused my pussy to pulse and kept my heart thumping at a rapid pace.

Jon's hands closed over mine, our fingers lacing behind my knees. He lifted his gaze up to my face.

Undying love shone from him as our souls connected on a deep level in the way they always did. Assurance of his love rushed through me.

He flashed his dimples, and I shuddered.

"Please," I whispered, my throat tight.

Holding my gaze, Jon licked me from asshole to clit, his tongue like silken fire in lapping up my cum.

"G-God..." I bit the inside of my lip as he repeated the motion.

With lips, teeth, and tongue, he showed me how much he loved me, worshiping every inch of my swollen labia and protruding clit. I wanted another release—needed it like my panting mouth did water, my lungs, oxygen.

"Jon," I whimpered his name, writhing against his hold on my thighs.

"Come for us." Elijah's command worked like the flip of a switch.

I detonated, arching and crying out.

Jon groaned, shoving his tongue deep into my pulsing pussy until I went lax, sprawled and barely able to keep my thighs spread.

Elijah advanced on us, erection freed from his slacks, Jon's cum all over his hand acting as lube as he stroked himself.

Another rush of lust swept over me, tingling my toes and earning a growl of appreciation from Jon as he lapped at me.

Too much...I couldn't... My mind tumbled, lost in a swarm of emotion so overwhelming tears leaked from the corners of my eyes.

Need.

The quiet whisper in my mind gave voice to the desperation I felt in the deepest parts of me.

"Take her, Jon," Elijah said, barely suppressed aggression in his pale eyes as he halted alongside us.

I couldn't look away from his intense stare and the darkness swirling in his pupils.

Jon lifted his face from my throbbing pussy and shifted closer on his knees.

No way he was hard again already—

Jon filled me with one thrust, causing my back to arch on the low-weight bench.

A gasp tore from my lips at the sudden fullness, but no stinging pain lanced me. Like an animal, he pulled out and thrust into me, grunting with each stab into my body, his hands like a vise on my thighs, holding me open, doing exactly as Elijah had told him to.

I gasped with each slam against my womb, the sight of Elijah jerking himself with my husband's cum beside me causing my toes to tingle with yet another impending climax.

"Open my shirt covering your breasts so I can paint them with my release."

I tore at the expensive fabric in desperation to obey Elijah, uncaring a button pinged across the floor.

A deep growl rose in his chest as I bared myself fully to him.

"Come with me, beta," Elijah whispered the words, but Jon clearly heard the order.

As one, both men released.

Elijah's cum laced over my aching nipples with tingling heat.

Jon cursed, veins in his neck throbbing as his cockhead pulsed against my womb.

Elijah's second shot landed on my lower lip, and when I licked his cum into my mouth, I came again with a gush around Jon's cock.

I cried out as both men continued to paint me with their cum, deep grunts accompanied each spurt until they stilled.

My lips throbbed, breasts tingled, and my pussy convulsed in what felt like a never-ending climax. I didn't want the euphoric wave dousing me to recede, but gasping for air, my body eventually quieted.

Jon lay over me, his cheek on my cum-covered breast as we both heaved to fill our lungs.

I tilted my head back, blinking at the dark god looming over us.

Elijah gazed down upon us, his eyes no less intense than when he'd stroked his cock in time with Jon's plundering of my pussy.

I licked along my lower lip again, whimpering over the addictive sweetness of Elijah's seed still there.

"Don't," he murmured, using his thumb to wipe the remaining wetness from my mouth.

Jon suckled at my cum-covered breast, and Elijah grasped his hair, pulling his head away from me. Traces of Elijah's spunk clung to Jon's cheek and his tongue as it flicked out to gather more from the corner of his mouth.

"No—please." Elijah ripped his T-shirt off overhead and wiped Jon's face then the rest of the cum from my chest and cheek.

I should have been exhausted. Should have been a boneless heap on the weight bench, but I was strangely rejuvenated. Wide awake as though having consumed a double shot of espresso. I squeezed my pussy around Jon's softening cock, and he groaned, resting his forehead on my breast again.

My smile came easily as I ran my fingers through his hair while looking up at Elijah. We didn't touch, but I felt as though a band had wrapped around and held us together in a firm yet gentle embrace.

Elijah returned my smile and cupped my cheek in his warm hand, connecting the three of us physically, which felt as beautiful and as right as the night before. "I've never seen anything so delightful as when the two of you are in the throes of passion."

I sighed and pressed my face against his palm, drinking in

his show of affection, his old-world type charm, and the satisfied bliss in his eyes.

"Might I have the privilege of carrying you upstairs?" he asked, his gaze causing heat to shiver over my skin.

"I'm good." I snickered as Jon let out another groan. "But I think Jon could use some help."

Elijah chuckled, one of his eyebrows quirking as he glanced down at the noodle-like body unmoving between my thighs. He ran his hand over mine clasped in Jon's hair and down over his back.

Jon shuddered and arched like a cat before letting out a sigh. "You could probably lift and take me up to the highest point of this damn cave without losing your breath," he muttered against my skin, his exhale warm over my nipple. "If your body wasn't like a damned furnace and your cum so fucking tasty, I'd swear you were one of your robots."

Elijah outright laughed, and as Jon finally pulled out of my body and stood, swaying, what he'd said registered in my brain.

Tasty cum.

I bit back giggles because he'd spoken the truth.

And I wanted more.

"Come along, sweet female." Elijah swept me up into his strong arms as though forgetting I'd stated I was fine.

I didn't argue but snuggled in close, sniffing along his warm neck, inhaling the comforting scent of embers, cinnamon, and sex.

Jon was quiet as he trailed along behind us while Elijah climbed the stairs. Cradled in his arms as though I was the queen of his world, his steady heart beat against my ear in one of the most soothing sounds on earth. The idea of having Jon's chest pressed on my other side, holding me between the two of them rekindled life between my thighs.

I fought the need to squirm to alleviate the growing ache between my thighs.

Elijah pushed open our bedroom door. "What are you thinking about?" Elijah asked as though he could smell my arousal.

"Sex," I stated bluntly since me speaking my mind had so far gotten me all sorts of delicious climaxes.

Jon snickered behind us, and I somehow knew he'd been focused on the same thing. Thankfully, he seemed the opposite of upset over my sudden sexual outspokenness.

There was something about Elijah…

He set me on my feet in the bathroom and started the shower.

Jon hugged me from behind, and I leaned against him, wanting to cuddle and fuck at the same time.

Elijah turned and took us in.

Both Jon and I held our breath, waiting for him to make the next move.

"Care for her," he told Jon.

My husband nodded and swallowed—probably the same disappointment I felt as Elijah strode away from us.

Again.

Jon ushered me into the shower enclosure and crowded close, his hands on my backside. "Holy fuck, you've got one fine ass."

All trace of exhaustion sounded gone from his voice, and I spun, wrapping my arms around his waist. "So now what?" I asked, deciding I was done waiting for him to address that damned elephant we'd been circling for days on end.

Fucking at Elijah's command had definitely loosened my mind and tongue. I hoped Jon felt the same.

"Now," he murmured with a glint in his eyes, "I wash every inch of your body, hoping to get those pussy juices flowing again so I can sink my cock into you. Or I could just use conditioner to lube up my dick and shove it up your ass."

I snickered and pushed him back enough I could see his face. "I'm serious, Jon."

"So am I." His eyes shown with mischief as he once more reached for the bodywash.

"You couldn't get it up for a third time that quickly even if you wanted to," I muttered as he began sudsing up my torso.

"Don't know about that." He smirked and rubbed his flaccid dick against my thigh while turning me slightly to wash my back. "Something about this place—that *man*—makes me feel like a teenager again."

Jon sank to his knees, taking care to wash me clear to my toes.

I ran my fingers over his damp hair. "You like him."

Jon finished before standing and meeting my gaze. "Yes."

"You want him."

He blew out a huge breath but kept his focus on me rather than flitting away as though he experienced guilt over that fact. "So damn much I can't think of anything else. You?"

I nodded and bit the inside of my lip. "It's like...we were destined to meet him. Feels...right. Know what I mean?"

"Yeah," Jon didn't hesitate to agree. "He makes me think about all sorts of things I never considered before."

"Would you let him fuck you?"

Jon searched my face but didn't answer.

"I would be okay with it," I whispered assurance of my consent.

"What about you?" he asked. "Do you want his fat cock filling your pussy? Stretching your ass?"

I studied my husband just intently as he did me but couldn't read what went through his mind. My heart thumped heavy in my chest. "Would it make you upset if I did?"

"Not if I was there with the two of you—watching." He pushed my wet hair over my shoulder and caressed his fingers down over my breast, his gaze trailing along with the movement. "*Or* participating."

A whimper leaked past my lips as his fingers ghosted over my belly.

"Ah." He grinned and lifted his focus once more, dimple popping. "The truth comes out. How long have you been fantasizing about two men taking you at the same time?"

Oh God.

I swallowed but knew honest words needed to flow between us. "O-only since meeting Elijah."

"Hmm." That twinkle lit in his eyes again as his dick twitched between us.

Jon's jealousy from the past? Gone. Fled the building, as though it'd never existed.

There was absolutely no reason for that truth, but I wasn't about to get bogged down with details when more exciting things lay before us.

"Okay." I narrowed my gaze, ready to wield a little more of this brazen sexuality being around Elijah had brought out in me. "How long have you been finding men hot?"

"Only since meeting Elijah." Jon repeated me, word for word.

I let out a sigh and relaxed into my husband's arms. "There's something about him—magical, almost."

"My fanciful wife." Jon's chuckle rumbled beneath my ear, and he squeezed me tight. "He's just a hot-as-fuck, lonely man, that's all."

"That's all?" I said, smiling and closing my eyes while imagining my body impaled between the two of them. My core spasmed with need.

Jon didn't answer, and we stood for a few moments in

silence as I warmed through—and not from the hot water caressing my back.

"His cum," I finally murmured.

"What about it?"

"It's like a double shot of espresso but sweet as candy."

He huffed a snort. "I wouldn't go that far."

"Still. I want more." I felt free to admit.

"My body can't get enough of those goddamned growly commands." He made the statement as though his head wasn't sure of the same.

I took Jon's hand and pressed it between my thighs to keep him from getting lost in confusing thoughts.

One of Jon's eyebrows rose as he slid his fingers through the fresh slickness seeping from my pussy. "Is that cream all for me or because of him?" he asked, no trace of anything but lust in his eyes.

"Yes."

Jon grinned as though pleased with my response, kissed the word off my lips, and lifted me into his arms.

We hadn't talked everything through, but thoughts of further discussion swept from my mind as he claimed my mouth, filling my mind and body with his love.

CHAPTER 27

JONATHAN

I couldn't stop thinking about what had happened. And how much more I wanted to explore. Being dominated by Elijah, allowing him control, had snicked all kinds of feel-goods in my brain into place, laying out a path that I wanted to follow but had no fucking clue where it might lead.

The taste of his cum still lingered in my mouth long after I'd made love to my wife in the shower and we dressed to finish out the day.

Dakota and I sat to eat a late lunch, but Elijah's presence remained in my mind although he hadn't joined us.

"Do you think he's all right?" Dakota asked, her gaze flitting up the stairs to the upper floor where I didn't get a sense he lingered.

I popped the last bite of my turkey sandwich into my mouth and chewed, wondering. He hadn't seemed to regret what we'd done. I shrugged. "Maybe he just needs some time. Seemed fine to me though."

Dakota sighed and stood, gathering our plates. She'd

made him a sandwich as well, and it sat untouched in front of his empty seat. "Guess I'll wrap this up for him."

"Are *you* okay, baby?" I asked, sitting back in my chair, my focus on her downturned lips.

"Yeah." She tried for a smile. "I just..." Blowing out a breath, she fully faced me. "We need to talk this through completely, Jon. I-I need to know what this is." She swept her hand around his house, her troubled eyes welling.

"Shit." I hopped up and pulled her against my chest. "If it's too much, we can light out of here right now. Walk away and put whatever this is behind us. Just say the word, Dakota, and I'll do whatever you want."

"Your job—"

"Fuck the damn job if staying here is going to make you cry."

Dakota clung to me, nuzzling her face against my chest.

I kissed the top of her head, soothing my hands down her back atop Elijah's shirt.

"We're going to stay," she said matter-of-factly, "but promise me we'll talk to him and figure this out when the workday is over—or when he comes back."

"I promise, baby."

Elijah's presence flicked my eyelids up before the thought he'd come home materialized in my half-asleep brain. No noise rose from the hallway from where I'd left our bedroom door wide-open when Dakota and I had finally gone to bed, but I didn't doubt his return.

After showering, I'd finished up what I could in the office regardless of my boss being there to guide me and his team through more paces with the robots.

Dakota and I had eaten dinner—alone. Darkness had

fallen, and we'd shared a bottle of wine while waiting for Elijah to show his face. Dakota had wondered if he'd been called away for work, but there was no way in hell he would have left without telling us.

It was another two hours after lying down in our bed before my wife slept.

My eyes had eventually closed, and I'd ridden the edge of slumber, images of black dragon scales rippling through my mind until a shiver of energy had lifted the hairs on my arms, rousing me fully.

Slipping from beneath the covers caused Dakota to sigh and turn, but she didn't wake. I grabbed my shorts off the floor and pulled them on before heading out our bedroom door. Sniffing the air, I looked left toward Elijah's room, but his scent rose from my right, drawing me toward the stairs.

Darkness covered the open living area, and even though I couldn't see clearly, I could make out the shadowed image of his bulk on the couch.

Without a word, I descended the stairs and walked into the sunken living room. I settled onto the couch a few feet away and angled toward him, close enough I could see a glass of wine in his hand.

"My apologies for leaving without word." He kept his voice low, the deep bass sending a shiver down my spine that curled around to my front and zapped at my balls.

"Are you all right?" I asked, fighting to see his eyes in the darkness while adjusting my junk.

"I am...unsettled," he finally answered, his voice portraying a vulnerability I'd never expected from him considering his usual confidence.

"You regret what we did?"

"No." He quickly corrected where my mind had gone. "It's —complicated."

"We've been ignoring this elephant long enough, Elijah. Talk to me. Let's figure this shit out."

He exhaled deeply. "Part of me longed to make demands that I have no right to speak to either of you, but my other half refuses to push. Consent is of utmost importance to me."

"Do you have, like, a split-personality or something?"

Elijah huffed a quiet laugh. "Not exactly, but I *do* have conflicting desires. My intention yesterday had been to lead us all down a path the three of us seem to want, but part of me began to lose control."

"Seemed as though you had your shit together to me." I shrugged even though he probably couldn't see the action.

"I needed some space to…calm myself."

"Understandable." I sat back, arms along the back of the couch. "So you're feeling better now?"

"Much, thank you."

We sat in silence for a few seconds but far from uncomfortable. Well, except for the bulge in my shorts Elijah's presence always caused.

"You're good with us staying here?" I questioned.

"Yes."

"And I'm still your employee?"

"Hopefully for the foreseeable future."

I grinned into the darkness, loving how easily we communicated when we'd been hoarding our own thoughts for too damned long. Shit was easier this way.

Made my dick fucking hard and the rest of me like a live, strung wire.

Or maybe that was just Elijah's presence.

"I've never wanted to submit to anyone or anything," I admitted, laying myself bare since he'd opened up to me. "But you…goddamn, when you're whispering those lust-laced commands in my ear… Fuck." I shifted on the couch as my dick began to swell.

"You desire to submit to me."

"*I* don't," I clarified, "but my body sure as fuck does. I've never been attracted to a man. Never wanted another man's cock in my mouth. Hell—" I snorted a laugh, "if you'd told me two weeks ago I'd actually like the taste of a man's spunk, I'd have knocked you out."

Elijah chuckled. "You could try."

"Hmm." I peered through the darkness, wishing the damn moon shone brighter outside the massive windows. "That sounds like a good time."

Silence, luscious enough to seize my balls, rose over us as I imagined grappling with Elijah, our bodies entwined and sweaty. Our dicks hard and leaking all the fuck over each other.

"What about Dakota?" His question jerked me back to reality.

"What about her?"

"Does she know your desires, and does she feel the same way toward me?"

"Better fucking believe it. My wife has a lot of fantasies that include the two of us."

Elijah shifted but didn't close the space between us like I half wanted him to do. "Is that so?"

"Call her a good girl, and she'll probably do just about anything you ask."

"And you?"

I snorted. "I won't lie and say I hated you telling me I was a good boy. Not sure I'll follow orders as willingly as she might though."

He muttered something that sounded an awful lot like *we'll see about that.*

I opened my mouth to question him, but he beat me to it.

"You're the bridge between us, Jon. Dakota has seemed to find her voice, but she will still look to you to make decisions when it comes to your marriage—and who you invite into your bed."

"So it's up to me," I reworded what I hoped I had right. "Meaning I get to be in control next time, because there sure as fuck *will* be a next time."

Elijah snickered. "You will be the one to initiate, but never doubt who is the alpha among us."

I should have laughed or at the very least scoffed at the word that would have made my wife swoon.

Nope.

Yearning to kneel before Elijah and worship his fucking *everything* rolled over me at the title he'd given himself. Come to think of it…he'd called me beta when ordering me to come while I'd been buried balls deep inside my wife.

"Goddamn." I adjusted my aching dick, more on board with this fantasy shit than I'd ever have expected of myself. "So, uh, I have this idea."

"I'm open and willing to give you whatever I'm able to." Elijah reminded me of what he'd said not long after we'd met.

Nothing was free. Everything came with a cost.

One positive about my negative outlook—low expectations didn't leave space for disappointment. Internally, I'd given up hope of ever impregnating my wife, and I'd planned on becoming a trash guy once we'd returned to New York in order to provide for my wife.

But now?

I got to game for a living. Sort of.

We might not ever get the family Dakota and I had dreamed about, but Elijah had proved himself enough that I chose to take a risk in seeking out fulfillment of another of my wife's desires.

CHAPTER 28

DAKOTA

Same as the previous morning, I woke before Jon and slipped out of bed, lower lip between my teeth. Instead of making my way downstairs, however, I tiptoed to our bedroom window, hopeful yet filled with fear that Elijah hadn't yet returned to us.

The sight of him glowing in the rising sun, flowing from one pose to the next on the smaller veranda far below, eased tension I hadn't realized rode my shoulders as it'd done for most of the previous day during his absence.

A shuddered sigh of relief swept through me, bringing a smile to my lips. I'd been afraid that what I'd felt for sure had been meant to be had gone awry, and insecurities had hammered at my brain until I'd finally fallen asleep.

Elijah had returned home to us—

"Mmm." Jon ran his hands over my ass cheeks while crowding close in all his naked glory. "You're so damn beautiful backlit in the window like this." He nuzzled my neck with his warm lips while grinding his hard length through my crack. "These delicious curves." Firm hands mapped my front, and he hummed his appreciation a few times, especially when sliding fingers between my thighs and finding me wet. "Watching my hot as fuck boss do his morning ritual?"

No trace of jealousy laced his question.

I tilted my head to the side, giving him better access to my neck and widening my stance so he was free to explore. "Yes."

"Like what you see?"

"Same as you do," I sassed back, pushing my ass against his hard dick.

"Damn straight."

I snorted, and Jon did too.

"Guess I need a new label for myself, huh?"

"Elijah-sexual?" I suggested since Jon had never shown a hint of attraction to another man.

"Yeah." Jon nibbled my lobe. "We'll go with that." He trailed open-mouthed kisses from my ear to my collar bone and back up again, sending a shiver of goose bumps over my bare body, but he pulled his fingers away from my pussy without penetrating me. "Coffee."

He stepped away, and I huffed in annoyance, my core throbbing.

Jon draped one of Elijah's shirts over my back before I could turn and complain. "Here."

Guess he really was focused on that damned cup of Joe.

"I need more clothing than this," I said with light laughter while sliding my arms through.

"No, you don't."

"But—"

"I want you wearing Elijah's shirt, his scent. Nothing else."

Well, hot damn.

I turned, gulping at the need in Jon's eyes trailing over my body as he leisurely stroked himself. My nipples tightened, and I clenched my thighs together.

"Fuck me?" I begged, expecting I wouldn't be able to sit down for breakfast without leaving a wet smear on the chair otherwise. Then again, considering how easily I became aroused in the cavern, I probably still would.

"Nah." Jon smirked, and I glowered. "Coffee first. Fucking later."

"Bastard," I muttered.

"I'll make it worth your while."

One thing about Jon—I trusted him to fulfill his promises and then some.

I made coffee while he put some bacon on to fry, his fingertips trailing over my skin every time he passed, keeping my body heat on high. I cracked the eggs and whipped them into a scramble while he set the table, the muscles of his back flexing along with the ass I loved wrapping my legs around.

Couldn't wait to do it again.

"Did you hear Elijah return last night?" I asked, spatula in hand, turning my focus on the preheating pan.

"No, but I couldn't sleep and came down here after you'd passed out, and he was sitting on the couch."

I glanced over my shoulder, ready to beg for all the hopefully hot details, but Elijah pushed open the slider, letting in a rush of cool, morning air—and the luscious scent of fire and sex.

My mouth watered and knees went weak in a flash.

His naked torso snagged my focus, tanned skin rippling down to the band of his shorts slung low on his narrow hips. I forced my attention off the impressive bulge between his thighs. His gaze held mine as my face heated, and he smiled.

"You're home," I heard myself say.

"Yes, and I apologize for leaving without communicating with you."

"Is everything all right in New York?" My words rushed

out as he walked into the kitchen area, heightening my nervousness. "We'd noticed the helicopter was missing and assumed you'd had to go to the office."

He tipped his head to the side, his smile turning lopsided as he halted beside my husband. "It was…something like that."

"Morning," Jon said, pulling him in for a bro hug as if they'd been best friends for decades.

I imagined all sorts of naughty things they'd been up to during the night, and heat flared to life between my thighs.

"Coffee?" Jon asked, stepping back first.

I stared, lost in a fog of need when I should have been pouting with jealousy.

They appeared completely at ease with each other. What the hell had gone down while I'd been sleeping?

"I can hear your brain working," Jon said with a chuckle, drawing my gaze off Elijah's happy trail I hadn't realized I'd been focused on. "Fantasies got your head jumbled up?" my husband asked, stalking toward me.

"I—"

He plucked the spatula from my hand and reached around me to turn off the stovetop. "I *know* they've got your imagination running wild."

Face hot, I glanced over at Elijah who leaned against the counter a few feet away.

All trace of nicety had disappeared from his eyes, replaced with the kind of heat that turned my insides to glowing embers. "I promise your husband and I behaved last night."

"I wouldn't care if you hadn't," I answered honestly, squeezing my thighs together again.

Jon moved out of my personal space without touching me and sat on a barstool, hands on his thighs. "Kiss him, Dakota."

Blinking, my head whipped toward Jon. "Wh-what? Now?"

"Yes. Let him taste the sweetness of your mouth."

God, did I want to, but I never would have been able to initiate on my own regardless of my new confidence.

My knees shook, but I shuffled to Elijah, instinctive need dictating I take what I craved.

He kept his hands on the edge of the counter behind him, his pale eyes seeming to delve into my soul, stealing my breath as I drew nearer.

I glanced back at Jon.

"Kiss him, baby. I know you want to." His lips lifted in the smile that melted my heart and assured me of his desire for this. "*I* want you to."

I took a step closer, mere inches separating me from Elijah. The heat of his skin seared my palm as I laid it over his thumping heart. Tilting my head back, I gazed up into his face.

"You must make this decision," Elijah whispered, his sweet exhale caressing my face, "and not for anyone but yourself."

"*I* am choosing you, Elijah." I whispered the truth in my soul while lifting onto my tiptoes. I brushed my mouth across the second set of lips I had ever kissed.

Warmth rushed straight into the deepest reaches of me, far beyond my greedy pussy. The empty ache in my chest I only just realized had been waiting to be filled flooded with fulfillment in ways no climax could achieve.

Elijah groaned and grasped at me, his hands nearly spanning my waist, his fingertips digging into my flesh as though fearful I would step away and leave him unfulfilled.

As if. Jon had opened a can of worms that wouldn't ever be hidden from the light of day ever again.

I arched into Elijah, parting my lips in offering to prove *my* want, not just my husband's.

Elijah slid his tongue into my mouth, stroking. Tasting. Thrumming my heartbeat.

My head swam, and I clutched at his shoulders, unquenchable need to have him—*all* of him—to be one with this dark god, causing my entire body to tremble.

I felt tiny in his arms, but somehow, we fit together perfectly, his hard length digging into my belly.

Want.

"Want," I gasped aloud against his hungry mouth.

Elijah cradled my face in his hands, his essence twining with what felt like a newly awakened part of my soul.

CHAPTER 29
ELIJAH

She tasted like spring flowers and sunshine—and she owned my heart the second she opened to my tongue to deepen our kiss. While Jon stirred lust and my violent nature, Dakota soothed, eased the darkness within me, and I wanted to weep from the depth of my need for her.

The evening prior, I'd been desperate to lessen the burn in my blood and had taken to the sky to allow my beast his freedom away from our mates as was safest for the time being. The bond among us had strengthened in our finding mutual release but not nearly enough for me to be completely honest about what I was along with who they both were to me.

I'd lost control in the weight room, or rather, the beast side of me had taken over briefly as I'd painted our female with my seed.

Both she and Jon had tasted my cum again in my weakness, Dakota much more than him before I'd gained control over my impatient beast and stopped them. I'd wondered at her bright-eyed gaze while Jon had lain like a dead man on her breast, lapping at what would deny him free will.

My dragon had roared inside me at the sight, begging my human vocal cords to demand they swallow down every drop, flood their senses with us, begin the process of creating a bond so tight that only death had the power to part us.

My alpha father had done away with the practice of compulsion while I'd been but a youngster who had just learned what sex was, but I'd felt the animalistic instinct deep inside of me, clawing to be set free.

I'd teetered on the edge of losing my humanity but had found the strength to deny my beast and wipe our mates clean with my shirt.

Need.

The beast's word was nothing but a whisper in my head now with the softness in my arms, the sweet breath of Dakota caressing my lips. I held her face in my hands, angling her to deepen the kiss that overwhelmed my mind and sent pulses down through my dick with the yearning to sink into her wet heat and gift her our seed.

Jon and I had made a plan, and his command had set it in motion, but I never expected to be so caught up from kissing her alone. My entire body shook from the potent energy we created, and I lusted to give Dakota the fantasy that Jon said she'd admitted to having.

He approached and moved his wife's hair off her neck, and I slid my hands back down to her waist again, itching to reach behind her for my beta. A sexy moan eased past Dakota's lips against mine.

Jon's hand moved between us, and she gasped, tearing her mouth from mine and tilting her head back onto his shoulder.

"So wet," he murmured while moving his lips over her neck in open-mouthed kisses that left traces of saliva among her skin.

I yanked her body closer, trapping Jon's hand between her thighs and my cock.

"Mmm." He caught my gaze, wrapped his other arm around her waist, and grabbed my length. "Someone likes the taste of my wife."

Dakota wiggled between us, her moan jerking my cock in Jon's hold, but I kept my focus on his face rather than closing my eyes and giving over to his hand moving along the front of my shorts. I released Dakota and grasped at Jon's ass, keeping the three of us connected.

Kiss.

Jon blinked as though he heard my dragon's plea, his lips parting.

Our mouths crashed together over Dakota's shoulder. With teeth and tongue we warred but not for dominance. Lost in a haze of lust at having Jon's mouth and Dakota's lush body pressed against mine, a growl escaped my throat.

"Hot," Dakota whispered, grinding against the hands trapped between us.

Jon and I had come up with a plan to please his wife, but our lust wouldn't allow moving to my bedroom. I tore my mouth off Jon's. "Take off your shorts," I said, moving him back slightly.

As of the same mind, he stepped away and pushed them to the floor, freeing his cock.

I grasped the front of my shirt Dakota wore and ripped it down the front. Her breasts hung plump, ripe, and ready for my teeth, but I desired more. She worked the shirt off her arms, her passion-hazed, green eyes staring up into my face, swollen lips parted.

My claws wanted to expand and shred my shorts, and jaw clenched, I pushed them down with my hands instead.

"Come here," I murmured with a rumble, grasping her waist once more and pulling her up into my arms.

"Yes." Dakota wrapped her legs around me, and I held her thighs, the tip of my cock against her soaked pussy.

She gasped and tensed, but Jon pressed along her back again, his hands snaking around her torso to palm her breasts. "Do you want Elijah's big dick inside you, baby?" he whispered against her ear as she stared up at me, pupils dilated, pulse thrumming in her neck.

She bit her lower lip.

"Be honest, Dakota—tell us what you desire." Jon pushed when she didn't answer.

"Yes," she whispered.

Jon gathered her breasts in his hands and thumbed over her nipples, his attention flicking to my face, blue eyes filled with icy fire. "Fuck my wife, Elijah."

A rush of pure ecstasy rode over me at his command. I wanted her too much to put him in his place. I lowered her slowly, my jaw clenched as her tight heat sucked me in. Soaked and slick, she welcomed my entire length with a low groan, blinking as the base of my cock rested against her swollen labia.

My inner beast shuddered, causing a ripple of goose bumps to erupt over my entire body.

Ours.

Not mine—not his—but ours. Mine and Jon's. Three dragonblood.

My throat went tight, my eyes stinging.

"So beautiful," I croaked, peering deep into the glowing green eyes of the one I'd been dreaming of for close to five hundred years. "Perfect in every way—our sweet female."

"Mmm." Jon reached beneath her spread legs and slid his fingers along where we joined. "He's stretching you good, isn't he?" He pushed his finger in alongside my cock.

She gasped and arched in my hold as I hissed over having his finger stroke over my length. "God, yes."

We were both inside her—

Breed!

I gritted my teeth, focusing on Jon's *finger* pressing against my throbbing length in her tight sheath.

Promising my inner beast we would one day do that very thing, I focused on the present and turning our female's fantasy into reality.

I flexed my hips, nudging deep inside her, and she shuddered, her eyes closing, head tipping back onto Jon's shoulder again. The pulse in her neck caused my mouth to water, made me want to sink my teeth into her soft flesh.

Bite.

Claim.

Jon slid his finger out to play with her clit, and I immediately felt the loss of his touch along my shaft.

Focusing on that thump beneath her skin, the knowledge of what flowed beneath, I lifted her body in a slow, languid fashion and let her sink back onto my aching length. I lusted to thrust, to fuck into her deeply and hard, to fill her with my seed.

Need.

Swallowing hard, I gentled my hold on her thighs and continued to fuck up into the satiny perfection of her body. She'd been made for me, a perfect fit, but I knew she would stretch to accommodate her husband's girth alongside mine when the time came.

And it would.

No doubt troubled my mind.

Fate would have her way, and I would fully claim the two she'd meant for me and the future of the Blood Born.

"Not going to last," Dakota whispered and sucked her lower lip between her teeth as I continued to work her on my cock.

Jon trailed kisses along her neck while continuing to

stroke around where I fucked into her slick heat. "Come if you need to. Soak Elijah's cock with your cum, baby."

"Oh..."

I thrust a few times with slow tenderness, and she whimpered at the combined stimulation from both of us.

"Pinch my clit—" She shrieked as Jon did just that, a gush of wetness rushing over my shaft and down my balls.

My jaw ached, but I continued my slow assault even though she thrashed between our bodies, crying out with each pulse of her pussy around my length.

"You're killing him, baby." Jon chuckled, and I glared at him as Dakota shuddered in my arms. He slid his hand down, smearing her cum all over my balls, and gently squeezed.

"Fuck," I growled the word and thrust hard into Dakota on instinct, pulling another deep moan from her chest. "Don't tease me," I said, piercing my beta with my stare.

He held my gaze and squeezed my balls again, causing a low hiss to leak between my clenched teeth. "You're going to take me too," he said, leaning into Dakota's ear while smirking at me.

She whimpered and dug her fingernails into my biceps as I pulled out of her heat, keeping the swollen head of my cock nestled in its home.

"Such a sticky mess..." Jon wrapped his hand around the base of my cock. "Mmm." He released his hold on me, and I lowered her once more, letting her rest against my groin.

Jon shifted away from us, his attention on Dakota's ass as he fiddled with a bottle of oil.

"Are you all right?" I asked, pulling her chest against mine.

"Yes." Her eyelids fluttered upward, and the passion in her eyes mirrored the desire swirling within me to own her soul.

I licked along her lips, sinking into her mouth when she opened to me. Sweetness burst over my tongue, the spring-like scent of her filling my lungs and soothing the beast prowling beneath my skin, demanding I bind the two of them for eternity.

Soon, I promised him, my heart soaring higher than we had flown in the earth's atmosphere.

"Need to stretch you, baby." Jon's whisper sounded close to my ear, and Dakota relaxed in my arms as he rubbed slick fingers over my firm balls and taint before retreating.

She shuddered, and I groaned at the feel of Jon's finger easing into her body, a mere membrane away from my cock. "Oh, God."

More.

"Okay?" He checked in with her while my dragon prowled inside me, desperate and salivating to become one with my mates.

"Mmmhmm." She hummed, and Jon pressed in deeper, stroking along my length, our female's skin the only thing separating us.

I hissed, pre-cum pulsing from my shaft into her body.

Jon chuckled—and would someday pay for his continual teasing.

Another finger worked into her hole, and she shuddered in my arms, brave in her attempt to remain relaxed against the double penetration.

"Such a good girl for us," I murmured against her ear, holding my beta's eyes.

Heat flared in his, and it was my turn to smirk as I denied giving him similar words. He moved in closer, holding my gaze while licking up the side of her neck and removing his fingers from her ass.

Copious amounts of her continued arousal and my pre-cum leaked around where I filled her pussy.

"Let me in, baby." The slick head of Jon's cock moved over the base of my cock and balls, gathering our combined slickness.

I growled, and Dakota moaned into my mouth when Jon pushed against her pucker.

Her pussy tightened around me as he shoved in past her ring.

She tensed, and her eyes shut tight as she grasped at my hair.

I clutched her thighs, holding her steady, every muscle in my body screaming along with my beast to move. Rut. Fuck and breed. "Give her a moment," I rasped.

Sweat beaded on my brow as all three of us breathed harshly in the stillness. Energy rippled over my skin, doing little to cool the heat of desperation rushing through my limbs. We weren't yet fully in the way I'd been dreaming of but close enough for the time being. We'd taken another step, and I was desperate to reward both of my mates for choosing me.

"I'm g-good," Dakota stuttered and released a shaky exhale. An audible gulp sounded. "Want more."

Jon pushed in a little further, rubbing along my cock but not in the way I lusted for. "Fuck, your hole is a goddamned vise, baby." He pulled out to the head, and I struggled to keep my eyes from rolling back. Fought to keep from fucking up into Dakota with the deep, harsh thrusts my dragon screamed for.

One slow, steady push seated him deep, trapping Dakota between our bodies.

Yessss.

I shuddered and exhaled, grasping her lush ass in my palms as Jon's arms wrapped around us both.

He groaned and dug his fingers into my back as our female laid her cheek atop my heart.

They both owned the thumps beneath her ear—every pulse of dragonblood coursing through my body.

Mates.

I rumbled an agreement, soaking in the moment of finally being one. We weren't yet bonded, but I could feel Jon's energy reaching through our female to tangle with mine.

Dragonblood called to dragonblood, even if he wasn't yet aware the ancient blood swam in his veins.

He was meant to be the bridge between me and our female, but in that moment, she'd brought us together. Her consent to our fulfilling one of her fantasies.

"You're so brave, our sweet female," I murmured against her ear.

A sigh shuddered through her, and I soaked in the moment, etching into memory her wet heat surrounding me, the throb of my beta's cock against the back of mine.

One day, we would share the space I took inside her body, spilling our release together, her climax milking our seed to flood her womb and create another royal Blood Born.

Yessss—need.

I swallowed hard against tightness once more growing in my throat. *Soon,* I promised my beast, *but not until they know the truth and consent to bonding with us for life.*

"Please," Dakota whispered with a ragged exhale.

I nodded at Jon who I realized stared at me, awaiting my command.

A muscle ticked in his jaw as he shifted back. As he slid in, I retreated from Dakota's slick warmth, also needing to clench my teeth to keep from going feral.

She whimpered at the ebb and flow of our lengths gently fucking in and out of her, pressing her lips against my collarbone. "G-God..." Her small gasps ghosted hot exhales over my skin, and the following moans clenched my balls tight against my body much too soon.

"You feel so fucking good, taking us both." Jon thrust in deep as I backed out, his parted lips drawing my gaze. "So damn tight." He shoved in again. "So *fucking* hot. Jesus—Elijah. Goddamn."

I nudged my crown against Dakota's womb, causing her to shudder and grasp at my shoulders.

"Kiss me, beta," I demanded, needing a direct connection with him.

The corner of Jon's lips rose in a smirk, but his eyes betrayed how he fought to control his urge to come.

Our mouths met in a rush.

Take—consume!

The darkness swelled within me at the taste of Jon on my tongue. Our teeth gnashed, and we bit and sucked at each other's lips all the while filling and retreating from our female's body.

Jon dug his short nails into my back hard enough to sting, and I hissed, sinking my teeth into his lower lip.

"Fuck," he panted the word, and I released one hand from Dakota's backside to grasp his hip, keeping him close—his wife fully impaled on both of our cocks.

Dakota groaned against my neck, shuddering.

The combined scents of my mates and the musk of sex swirled in my nose, filled my brain, until all I could feel, all I could sense was their bodies, their hearts beating in harmony with mine.

My shaft throbbed against Jon's, but I kept us still, savoring the moment.

Please.

Please.

Please.

The word echoed, but only one inner voice sounded familiar.

I growled, releasing my hold on the instinct to breed.

Dakota's whimper at my retreat singed my blood, tensing

every muscle in my body as I thrust back in, desperate to shove through her cervix and bury inside her womb.

Jon rutted in time with me as though he too lost his restraint.

"Yes." Dakota cried out between us. "Please...m-more. Need to come."

"We'll take care of you, baby," Jon promised, his tone ragged and breathless. His blue eyes hazed by passion, the pink flush over his cheekbones making his freckles stand out in stark relief, was a gorgeous sight to behold, a memory I would never forget.

He snaked his hand between us, fingers teasing over her folds and along my length as I continued to fuck up into her soaked core.

She gasped and convulsed in my arms, clutching at me. Wet heat erupted around my cock, far beyond a normal female human release.

My dragon roared as her pussy clenched my shaft, her body begging me to give what it craved.

"Jesus fucking Christ." Jon slammed into her ass, both of us buried deep.

We came as one, pulsing and spilling inside her body, grunts and curses echoing in my ears.

Euphoria rushed through me, and even though we didn't spill our seed together against her womb, satisfaction and a deeper emotion swelled inside my chest.

Home.

I leaned in to take my beta's mouth once more, now more than ever determined to keep him and our female forever.

CHAPTER 30

JONATHAN

I did that. Me. Jonathan mother-fucking Ebel.

Satisfaction kept me floating on a high, long after we cleaned up and Dakota lay curled on my lap, truly spent for the first time since stepping foot into Elijah's lair.

Double penetration had been her fantasy, but my thoughts put into words with Elijah last night had gotten us where we'd wanted to be since first meeting.

Fucking like goddamn animals without a single sense of selfishness to be found among the three of us.

Utter perfection, Dakota had whispered once we'd both stilled inside her body, spent and sated.

Yeah, Elijah might have taken the lead the night before, but he'd backed off with his alpha shit, allowing Dakota and I to move on instinct until climaxing.

We'd been three bodies entwined in rapture as one—but it felt like a hell of a lot more.

We were connected, strange and far beyond the magic I was beginning to believe resided in the rock surrounding us.

Dakota, naked in my arms with a light blanket wrapped around her, nuzzled against my neck with a sigh. I tightened my hold on her, breathing in her warm sunshine scent.

Any sense of modesty had long since flown the goddamned coop. I didn't see clothing anywhere in our near future, unless I sat at the desk deep in the bowels of the cave alongside my boss and others could see us on camera.

Elijah stood in front of the stove, a hot as fuck sight with broad shoulders and muscle rippling clear down to his bare ass.

Fuck, what a fine set of globes that man had. Looked hard enough to bounce pennies off of.

Would he ever let me bury my dick inside him? The man was pure top—I doubted he would bottom for anyone. Would he take my ass if I asked?

The thought of him shoving his huge cock up my backside while Dakota watched made my dick twitch, and I bit back a groan.

Even with a little blue pill, I doubted any normal human could fuck as much as I'd been doing since meeting Elijah.

A voice inside me snickered over that truth, and I found myself smirking—and wanting to reach for my cock.

The fuck, man? Give it a rest.

I blew out a breath. So much for our plan where we wooed Dakota up into Elijah's room and romanced her into begging for us both. It was supposed to be a sweet pampering, a gentle loving on her body.

But no. We'd fucked her standing, her poor holes taking a couple of lust-crazed animals.

She let out a sigh and rubbed her cheek against my neck.

"Okay?" I murmured another check-in while trailing my fingertips over her back.

"More than," she whispered rather than the "yes" I'd received the first three or so times I'd asked.

Assured my wife rested easy, my eyes returned to Elijah's

flexing ass as he moved about the kitchen in nothing but an apron.

The scent of bacon had my mouth watering, but it was his naked backside a few feet away that made me hungry in a whole different way.

Dakota placed her hand over my heart. "What are you thinking?"

"That I like hanging out here at our new friend's house."

Elijah chuckled at my answer and turned, a bowl of scrambled eggs in one hand, bacon in the other—and his flaccid cock creating a luscious bulge between his thick thighs. "*Breakfast*, Jon."

I jerked my focus up and grinned. He was one bossy fucker, but I didn't care in the least. "No plans, man. Just enjoying the view. Almost as good as a pair of gray sweats."

Dakota shifted in my arms. "Damn, you two are so hot."

I'd never been so happy in my life. My hot-as-fuck wife who adored me and a man we both couldn't seem to get enough of more than willing to give us anything—who wouldn't be?

The risk of us all finally fucking had paid off, and I was more than here for it continuing.

Elijah tore off the apron and sat. Dakota climbed off me to sit in the chair to my left, between us men right where she belonged. Smiling like idiots, the three of us dug into our food as though we'd just run a marathon.

Twice, I got up to refill our coffee, and the heat of Elijah's stare on my ass made all sorts of butterflies go wild in my stomach. I'd decided to just roll with it, to see where whatever it was happening took us. If that meant me spread out for him to feast on while my wife watched, I wouldn't complain.

Or vice versa.

The atmosphere of Elijah's home had me ready for anything.

I finished eating first and relaxed, draping one arm over the back of my chair, legs spread, and hand on my thigh close to my semi.

The blanket draped over Dakota's shoulder slipped, revealing the top of her breast, but she didn't seem to notice. Hair a rumpled mess, cheeks pink, she damn near stole my breath when glancing up at me through her lashes, her eyes green as spring grass. "What?" she whispered.

"You're beautiful."

The redness in her cheeks darkened.

"Was it better than your fantasy?" I asked, still smiling.

She swallowed and cast a quick look at Elijah. "Yes."

"What else do you have going on in that little head of yours?"

Dakota pursed her lips, but I wasn't about to let my question go unanswered.

"Elijah and I spoke last night, and we both want to continue exploring this attraction drawing us to one another," I said.

Dakota glanced back and forth between the two of us, her tongue flicking out to touch her top lip. "You do?"

Breathless and needy—my favorite tone of voice on her.

"Yes," we both said at the same time, causing her to shift under our combined stares.

"But," I said, trailing my fingers down her neck to the swell of her exposed breast, "I'm not going to take things any further unless you want to."

She blinked up at me.

"This is a decision you need to make for yourself, Dakota, just like when you gave into your desire to kiss him. Don't do it because I'm hot for more. Do it because you want me—and him—for the next four weeks, or however long this lasts."

Forever, the voice whispered in my head, and longing for that very thing sent an ache through my chest painful enough I rubbed a hand over my pecs.

"I'm ashamed to say that I do desire you both," she whispered. "Too much."

"No need to feel that way, baby." I rubbed my thumb over her lower lip to keep her from nibbling on it. "And your agreeing isn't going to hurt me in any way." I stared into her eyes, hoping she read the truth cemented in my heart.

She breathed a heavy sigh, completely relaxing into her chair. "So now what?" She glanced at Elijah, who'd been mostly silent.

"That's up to you, my sweet, sexual goddess who's coming into her own," I spoke before he could answer.

Dakota laughed at my statement, her eyes glowing.

Fuck yeah—I'd done that too.

But she'd been the one stepping outside of her comfort zone, and I hoped she continued down that same path because goddamn, I liked that voracious side of her.

"The guest room is yours for as long as you want it," Elijah said, "but I would love nothing more than if you would both join me in my bedroom. I have plenty of room in my bed and would prefer to have you both as close to me as possible—for as long as possible."

Dakota and I nodded together without consulting each other.

Fuck yeah.

Elijah's focus shifted between us, a smile curving his generous lips I wouldn't mind nibbling on. "There are no expectations on my end, no rules. Enjoy each other, allow me to pleasure you both—the limits are up to you."

"I don't have any," I said without hesitation.

Dakota licked her lower lip. "You don't mind if Elijah

fucks me again?" The vulnerability in her eyes sent that ache through my damn chest for a second time in too short a span.

"Nope—watching him fill up your needy pussy was hot as fuck. Felt good on my finger in there with him too."

She shifted on her chair. "What if he, uh…wants to fuck you?"

I focused on Elijah's pale eyes as he turned his attention to my face.

The heat in his stare, the promise of rocking my mother-fucking world, sent those butterflies all aflutter again. "Then he can," I said, my voice husky.

"*God.*" Dakota half-moaned the word.

"You desire to watch me love your husband, *mon coeur?*" Elijah asked her while holding my stare with lust enough to flood my dick with blood.

Her gulp sounded loud in the cavern while I chuckled over the fact he'd gone for French when he'd already gotten her to pant by speaking English. "Yes."

Elijah noticed me press down on my dick before licking his lips. "Later. For now," he stood, revealing his cock no longer hung between his thighs but bobbed up toward his belly button like mine, "let's clean up and go pack an overnight bag."

"Where are we going?" I stared at the prominent vein running up the backside of his shaft—his very thick and *long* shaft.

Fuck.

My asshole clenched but not from fear of being wrecked. He would definitely rearrange my guts, and I couldn't fucking wait.

"The government officials moved up our meetings, and you're both going to New York with me," Elijah stated.

"Bossy fucker," I muttered even though I grinned.
One of his eyebrows shot up as if to say, "Just you wait."
Bring it, you sexy beast.

242

CHAPTER 31

DAKOTA

Elijah said he'd been to Manhattan and back the day before, but neither Jon nor I had heard the helicopter. It sat in the garage, black and shiny, and I couldn't contain the giddiness in my chest. I'd never ridden in a helicopter before, and the machine reminded me so much of my dream of riding the dragon that my panties didn't stand a chance.

The men had shared me as I'd fantasized about, and it had blown every expectation, every hope for a life-altering climax clear out of my head. Their cocks owning my body had been fifty times better and more potent than my silly imagination.

Becoming one with both men had been so much more than satisfying an itch. I'd been the cheese in their sandwich, the good stuff between two slices of delicious bread. I'd brought them together—and had ideas of doing more of the same in the near future.

Jon had always been enough for me, but before Elijah, I hadn't realized how much my husband and I had been missing out on. And Jon's willingness to explore his sexuality?

So. Damned. Hot.

The insatiable need I'd had for Jon since walking into Elijah's home—and for the man himself—had tripled, and I felt half-mad with lust. Add in the fact we'd finally had the necessary conversation that put my fears of hurting Jon to rest, and I couldn't focus on anything *but* sex and getting close with the two men. Sure, climaxing was beyond belief, but the tenderness, aftercare, and gentle touches afterward?

They'd treated me like a queen, the most desired and appreciated woman on the planet. Who wouldn't become addicted to that feeling? I hadn't wanted to move and not because of being boneless and sated. I wanted to soak in their warmth, be cloaked with all that they were.

Energy had continued to ripple among the three of us over breakfast, and how we managed to shower, pack, and head to the garage without someone getting fucked again was beyond me. Only a slight ache remained from how they'd taken me in the kitchen, but the need for continued intimacy erased any tinge of pain from my thoughts.

I sat on the seat behind the men, our bags on the one beside me, and settled the headset over my ears as the rotor blades started to spin. The noise intensified, but the headset kept me comfortable. I grinned like an idiot, my attention flicking from blond to darker head, my heart melting with every profile glance they allowed me.

Both freshly shaven, golden skin, and my husband's freckles, and all I wanted to do was get them naked again, their bodies pressing against mine while trying to reach the other.

"Damn," I muttered, squeezing my thighs together.

Jon glanced over his shoulder at me, an eyebrow raised.

"What?" His voice sounded slightly muffled in the headphones.

"Oh." My face heated as I realized I'd spoken out loud into the small mic beside my mouth. "Just, um, admiring the view."

He held my gaze as Elijah flicked a few buttons, readying for takeoff. "Are you wet, baby?"

"You two—I can't help it," I answered, breathy to the point Jon's eyes darkened with yummy intent.

"Buckle your seatbelt," he told me before glancing at Elijah. He bit on his lower lip but quickly came to a conclusion.

He reached out, grasped the back of Elijah's neck, and pulled him close. Teeth, tongues, and bruising lips met in a heated kiss that Elijah quickly took over, dominating so damn easily I wondered how I never noticed Jon's natural submissive nature before.

I whimpered as they put on a show to drive me insane, devouring each other's mouths until the three of us were breathless with need.

"Damn you," I moaned, fighting the urge to slip my hand into my pants.

Elijah backed away first, pink flushing his cheeks as he stared at my husband. Need crackled like a live wire between them, and I would have given every last penny along with my prized camera packed in the bag at my feet to see them unbuckle and fuck right then and there.

I waited for Elijah to show his alpha nature, threaten Jon with a good time for being so forceful in taking what he'd wanted. But he glanced my way instead.

I gulped at the fire burning in his enlarged pupils.

"Ready?"

"Yes—more than. Please."

He laughed at my double meaning and turned, focusing

on getting us into the air rather than acting out a live movie of another fantasy I hoped to watch come true.

I sighed and slumped into my seat, anxious to get to New York and details out of the way so we could all climb into Elijah's big bed and get to it already. We lifted into the air, and I let out a squeak, grabbing hold of the armrests. Higher and higher, we rose as the garage platform retracted and doors shut behind it.

From above, one would never know a beautiful, comfortable home lay beneath the mountain. It appeared as though the road disappeared into the hillside, the garage doors made to look like natural rock. The sun shone high overhead offering warmth, and I lifted my gaze to take in the White Mountains.

My breath caught, thoughts of the two men doing a cock tango disappeared from my mind as I imagined I rode on the back of my dragon. The views he showed me brought a tear to my eye. I'd buried my camera in the bottom of my backpack, and I cursed my body's insatiable need to fuck overriding rational thought. But I couldn't tear my attention from the beauty outside to rummage the thing out.

On the way back, I promised myself.

Work chatter—robots and armor, the kind of stuff that would usually make me yawn—buzzed in my ears, but I couldn't be bothered to pay attention to what Elijah and Jon spoke of. Face plastered to the window, I soaked in what an airplane couldn't offer, and until we landed in New York a few hours later, my face hurt from smiling. If only I could have felt some wind on my face and had those warm scales beneath my thighs to rub my needy clit against.

A limo waited for us at the airport, and the second the helicopter door opened, letting in the city air, I grimaced, wishing for the freshness of Elijah's veranda. The air smelled used up and empty. Dirty and wasted on those who didn't appreciate its life-giving force. How easily we as humans got so caught up in working and paying bills that we lost out on the beauty of Mother Nature and her sustenance.

Elijah helped me down and held my hand while heading toward the waiting car and driver. A glance over my shoulder let me know Jon followed, our three bags in his hands and a grin on his face at seeing me clutch Elijah's hand.

Swelling emotion bubbled up inside of me, filling me with that same giddiness and contentment from earlier. My pulse thrummed so hard I found it difficult to breathe properly.

Elijah ushered me into the limo, spoke quietly with the driver, and joined me, his body brushing against mine, shoulder to thigh, keeping my libido on high alert and my panties wet.

Jon slid in the other side, crowding close, sending a ripple of goose bumps over my skin.

Clarity hit me in that second.

The passion among us had *nothing* to do with the cavern we'd been staying in. The need for each other was pure fire crackling in the air, the magical pull of three souls almost... bound together by fate? I'd been sure Elijah had been meant to be our third, but experiencing the non-lessened need for his presence outside the cave solidified the truth in my head.

My fanciful mind enjoyed the idea of us together always, and I rolled with that fantasy, creating all sorts of daydreams about being spoiled rotten while I spent my life caring for the two who loved me to distraction and the babies they would eventually give me.

Each had a hand resting on my thigh, and I shifted in my need to be touched a little higher up.

Elijah nuzzled my ear. "I can smell the sweetness of your arousal, *mon coeur.*"

God, when he spoke like that...

I swallowed hard. "What does that mean? *Mon coeur?*"

"My heart."

I stared into his light eyes, the book cracked open to his soul for me to freely read. The desire to drown in their fathomless depths and never resurface had me leaning in. I needed to breathe his exhales into my lungs, fill the half of my soul up that he owned alongside Jon.

Our lips brushed, a lightning strike of need making my insides glow with desire far beyond a mere seeking of release.

I whimpered as he sat back without allowing me to taste his tongue.

"Tease," Jon muttered, and Elijah flashed him a warning look.

I giggled.

Oh, I couldn't *wait* to watch the explosion between them.

Tension zinged through the limo as we pulled away from the tarmac, a quiet stillness that heightened senses. The kind that made me feel like I stood on the edge of another cliff, watching the rushing wind blow the trees behind me—and I couldn't escape its path even if I'd wanted to.

Which I definitely didn't.

Both men's hands continued to rest on my thighs as though claiming ownership without any hint of competition. Their hot bodies emitted the clean scent of soap with an underlying hint of the smoky fire that clung to Elijah. My mouth watered for a taste of each of them, but my heart was conflicted about who I would beg to be beneath—if I had the guts to even choose.

"You don't have to pick one of us over the other." Elijah's warm breath caressed my ear, sending a shiver down my spine. "No rules, remember?"

I blinked up at him. Could he read minds now?

Jon squeezed my thigh. "What he said, baby. Take what

you want when you want. Him, me, doesn't matter. What-ever makes you happy, Dakota."

"What if it's both of you every second of every damn day?" My question left my mouth in a rush.

He grinned. "Then I'll skip responsibilities to please you and risk losing my new job."

I huffed an exaggerated sigh, my insides all bubbly. "Can't have that."

"Guess you'll just have to suffer in your need every day until we finish work then." Jon's eyes twinkled.

"Am I allowed to touch myself?" I asked, trying and failing to bite back my smile.

Elijah groaned and adjusted the bulge in his jeans, mumbling something in a growl beneath his breath.

"Of course you can touch yourself," Jon said, sliding his hand up to cup me between the thighs, "but no coming until your juicy pussy is filled by us."

The image of the two of them both buried in my body together, the heat of their cum mingling against my womb, sent a shudder down through me, breaking goose bumps across my skin.

Yes.

That quiet voice in my head purred with pleasure, and I was in full agreement. I couldn't imagine the stretch, the full-ness, but I wanted them together like that, even if it hurt like hell.

I hadn't realized the limo had stopped, but the door beside Elijah opened. "We're here," he said, climbing from the car.

Jon opened his door, leaving me a panting, hot mess, and I scowled. By "here", Elijah had meant Jon's and my apart-ment building, which meant it was time to pack up some of our belongings for the month-long stay in the mountain while Elijah went on to the office to get some things accomplished before we joined him.

I'd have preferred to close us all inside, strip down, and beg the men to take me again, but Elijah had responsibilities to tend to—yes, on a Saturday. With the new government contract, he had his people working around the clock to fill orders.

We would only spend the one night in New York, but Elijah had asked us to stay at his penthouse with him rather than sleep separately. While we hadn't yet shared a bed, nothing had ever sounded so good as settling between all that muscle, two warm bodies available for my pleasure before passing out blissfully sated.

"The limo will be back in an hour," Elijah said, helping me from the car. "I'd rather stay, but I must go."

"I know," I whispered, unable to hide the disappointment from my voice or face.

He cupped my cheek in his warm palm, a flood of emotions pouring from his eyes as he gazed down at me. "Tonight, I promise we'll be together again."

My core spasmed, and I wished to beg for him to put us first. I bit my tongue and only got more aroused when Elijah gave his attention to Jon.

Neither spoke, but the look they shared? I had to fan my face.

Elijah climbed back into the limo, quickly disappearing from view.

Silent, I clung to Jon's hand as we walked into our building, needing my husband to ground me against the feeling a part of me had been ripped away as the limo had driven off.

CHAPTER 32

JONATHAN

My dick had been stiff for what felt like hours, long enough my balls ached and I almost wished the magical need to fuck would stop working for a day or two. That part of my body had no issue with Elijah leaving us behind, but my chest sure as hell did.

A different sort of pain knifed at my heart, digging into my breastbone and becoming too damn uncomfortable as Dakota and I climbed the stairs to our second-floor apartment. We'd made sure our car had been returned home from the trailhead by a couple of Elijah's employees as he'd informed us earlier. One less thing to worry about.

The stairwell smelled like trash and stale cigarettes, the roof overhead seeming to push down atop us, smothering the happiness I'd been swimming in for hours on end.

That newfound purpose I'd been contemplating by being the catalyst that had begun to fulfill my wife's fantasies faded into the recesses of my mind as shit from pre-Elijah trickled back in with every step up the stairs. And walking through the creaky, flimsy-as-fuck door that led to the place we called home?

Our apartment was small and could easily fit inside Elijah's living space in the main area of his cavern-like home.

Thinking of what we'd left behind in the mountains, the comfort he easily afforded in spoiling my wife when I'd been able to give her nothing but this shithole, turned my thoughts dark. Old insecurities came rushing in, hitting me from all sides as my foster father had done. Add in my desire to submit sexually to Elijah, and I started to question if I was even a real man. I couldn't fucking provide for my wife. Got hard for another dude. Salivated to crawl for him and kiss his feet for fuck's sake.

A muscle ticked in my jaw.

I hated New York.

Our apartment and everything it stood for and reminded me of.

But one good thing, the *only* good thing in my life, remained the same.

Dakota stood before me, and what a view she gifted my suddenly needy heart.

I wanted nothing more than to rip the damn backpack off her shoulders, slam her against the wall, and bury myself so damn deep in her pussy that nothing else mattered. Where we were, how the past attempted to tear me down, and the fact a piece of me felt like it was missing.

Desperation tensed my body tight, and I couldn't help myself. I dropped my bag and spun my wife around, attacking her mouth, my hands palming her ass and lifting her against my throbbing cock.

"Need you," I growled against her lips, gyrating my hips and showing her exactly how much.

She clawed at my shirt, sweeping her hands up over my pecs to dig her nails into my shoulders with intense hunger I'd never tasted on her tongue before.

"Fuck." I peeled her off me and ripped at my shirt, staring

and salivating as she kicked off a sneaker and pushed down her pants, hopping to get one foot cleared.

Jeans around my knees, I grabbed her again, uncaring that her pants hung off her other leg, trapped by the second sneaker still on her foot. One thrust seated me balls deep in her sopping pussy, and I groaned a few curses while pressing her against the wall and burying my face in her neck.

This was comfort. Dakota was my home.

My lungs sucked in oxygen freely for what felt the first time in hours rather than agonizing minutes, and I buried my face in her hair, frantic for release both physically and mentally.

But an ache remained in my chest, no matter how deeply I burrowed or how harshly I impaled her lush body.

"Fuck, I wish he was here," I said, pumping into her, my hips thrusting in abandon.

"Yes," Dakota whimpered, her hands ripping at my hair, as I tunneled into her over and over. "Oh, God, yes…need him. Miss him."

I licked along her neck, grunting and groaning, trying to split her body in half with my aching cock as visions of Elijah's intense gaze seared my brain.

"Want his hands on me," I gasped. "On you."

I swear to fucking God the scent of him filled my nose, and Dakota cried out, her nails in my scalp, pussy clenching down on me hard enough stars exploded behind my eyes as my balls let loose.

Each spurt up through my shaft sent a shudder through my spine, caused a groan to rumble in my chest, and I clenched my jaw to keep from biting my wife's soft flesh.

"Goddamn!" I growled between my teeth as the last pulse of my cock broke my body into goose bumps. Buried deep, I stilled, sucking wind with my mouth plastered to Dakota's neck. "Holy fuck, that was intense."

"Mmm." Dakota's hold on my head loosened, and she ran her fingers through my too-long hair. "We're both sex-crazed lunatics." She giggled, and I squeezed her plump ass cheeks, trying to push my semi deeper into her warmth.

We'd always been insatiable for each other but not with such intensity.

"That man has turned us into fucking nymphos," I muttered, her soft skin caressing my lips as they moved to form the words.

Dakota pulled my face away from her neck, her eyes still hazed by passion. "Do you think…" She bit her lip, a frown marring her brow. "I mean, this can't be healthy. This level of desire—it's constant."

"I don't know what the fuck it is." I peered into her eyes, praying she could read the truth in my words. "It goes beyond the lust and fucking, baby. It's like…"

"Like falling in love all over again?" she whispered, tears filling her eyes.

I blew a breath between my lips and held her gaze, knowing I could tell her anything—*anything*—and she would still love me. "Yes, but it's almost more. It's like he owns a part of me or something. I wish I didn't feel guilty about it, but I do. And this place?" I couldn't even bear to look around and be slammed again with memories of my shortcomings. "It's not home, Dakota. Feels…wrong."

Dakota sucked her lower lip between her teeth and nodded, a tear sliding down her cheek. "Same."

I kissed the wetness from her satiny skin, slightly relieved to know we faced the same emotional turmoil even though it killed me she suffered in the same way I did. We'd done everything together. Falling in love with someone else should be as unsettling as it was regardless of how right inviting Elijah into our marriage seemed. "It's going to be okay."

"I'm scared, Jon. Afraid something is going to go wrong. That you'll be heartbroken. Angry with me."

I kissed her lips, gentle and slow, tasting the sweetness of her stuttered exhale. "Not gonna happen this time around, baby."

"But what if it does?"

I refused to let her think that way even though I felt insecure as fuck too. "Then we face it together like always, but it'll be three of us. There's safety in numbers, baby. One step forward a day, and we talk shit out at the first hint of something not sitting right with either of us. Honesty and openness is going to be key to seeing us through this."

She heaved a sigh and rested her body against mine as I tried to believe my own words.

"I know in my heart that we're meant to be together, but what if he tires of us and sends us away?"

My mind blanked at the thought. Fucking emptied, creating a gaping hole in my chest that hurt worse than anything I'd experienced before. All I could do was hold my wife tighter, my arms and lips offering the assurance my mind couldn't voice—or believe.

An hour later, we sat in the limo, hands clasped as the driver took us into Lower Manhattan. The traffic, the buildings rising high overhead, smothered me in a way they never had before. All I could think about was returning to the mountains, the peaceful quietness of Elijah's cavern the next day where his energy soothed even while making me horny as fuck.

Dakota and I had been desperate to get the hell out of our apartment. I'd tossed my shit into two duffle bags and had been ready to jet within twenty minutes, but she took more time to gather her photography things and laptop after emailing the contracted images to *North Wood Living*. My skin itched with the need to be gone and get back to Elijah's side.

The limo slowed, and I glanced out the window.

The building housing Tolzman Industries disappeared into the sky above us, and although I expected I'd be spending a lot of time there for work in the future, the ruckus, the city scents assaulting my nose, caused a frown to dent my brow. Even the promise of soon seeing the dude I couldn't get enough of didn't ease my scowl.

A receptionist showed us into Elijah's office fifteen minutes later. He still sat in his meeting, but the scent of him, the peacefulness of his spirit, filled the empty room. The second the door clicked shut behind his receptionist, I breathed a heavy sigh, most of the tension that had been riding me since he'd dropped us off at our apartment fading.

"I want to go back," Dakota grumbled, wrapping her arms around herself. "I—I mean to Elijah's. It's quieter."

"Peaceful," I said, falling into one of the chairs in front of his desk.

"I don't remember hating the city this much," she said, starting to sit beside me.

I grabbed her waist and pulled her onto my lap instead, tucking her against me where she fit so perfectly. "Same."

"Really?" She snorted a laugh. "I thought you enjoyed the hustle and bustle."

"I did." Frowning again, I glanced around Elijah's spacious office. It sat tidy same as everything else about the man. Bookshelves, computers, pieces of art that must cost a fortune created a very Elijah-like room. "Where's the classical music?" I wondered, noting the overhead speakers—and cameras—and actually missing the stringed instruments he loved to listen to. "Sybil, music," I commanded.

A quiet piece, slow and boring as shit, filtered through the speakers, and I almost smiled as another part of my insides settled.

Dakota let out a snicker and melted against me. "Love you."

"Love you more," I said but couldn't find it in myself to grin like usual.

She snuggled against me, her cheek on my chest as I drew circles on her arm with my fingertips and considered where the road we traveled might lead. We were both deeply connected to Elijah in some strange way, falling in love with him it felt like, and I feared the pleasure of being with him wouldn't be worth the pain in the end. Fucking around and having an affair worked for a lot of people in the world, but actually having a poly relationship of equal status and shared…everything? Especially when *nothing* about him and I were equal to anyone with eyes.

I'd been upbeat in trying to ease Dakota's worries, but how would it actually work? How *could* it? Dakota and I had been together since childhood. What man wouldn't become jealous over that bond no one could match? What third party wouldn't be filled with insecurities when trying to build a relationship of three atop one already cemented in place as firmly as ours regardless of my shortcomings?

I chewed on the inside of my lip before realizing it, released the tender flesh from between my teeth, and heaved a heavy exhale as the music overhead built into a crescendo.

I fucking *hurt* at the thought of being without Elijah at the end of our affair.

A knock sounded, and not sure what else to do, I called out for them to come on in.

"Sorry to intrude."

Dakota stiffened in my arms at the young woman's voice, and she sat up, her gaze whipping toward the door.

A petite, dark-haired young woman smiled and moved toward us, a tray with a carafe and mugs on it. "Mr. Tolzman thought you might like some refreshments."

I studied Dakota while she watched the woman cross the room, that sixth sense of hers raising the hairs on my nape and causing a low growl to build in my chest. Swallowing it down, I attempted to dissect the difference between her draw to Elijah, which didn't bother me in the slightest, to the female sharing the room with us, which sure as fuck did—almost as much as that blond douche all those years ago.

No pulse thrummed in Dakota's neck, no hint of hardened nipples poking against her shirt, but the pull toward the woman was intense enough I could almost sense the tug on my own insides. Jealousy slithered through my veins, heating my blood and not in a good way.

It'd been a long time since I'd felt that green giant rear its ugly head so harshly inside my guts, and I hated it. Despised whatever it was that drew my wife to others without a care of how it would make her husband feel.

I exhaled loudly through my nostrils, attempting to calm myself the fuck down, but Dakota didn't seem to notice with how intently she seemed captivated by the gorgeous woman.

"I'm sorry. Do I know you?" my wife asked.

The woman's smile faltered as she glanced at Dakota, revealing purple-blue eyes so vivid I wondered if she wore contacts.

I hated her for her beauty all the more.

"I don't believe so." She set the tray on the table along the far wall and moved toward us while I fought to keep from clutching Dakota close and growling.

Mine.

That voice in my head—the fuck was going on with me? Not giving a shit about Elijah drawing my wife's attention but feeling threatened over this sprite of a woman when I knew without doubt Dakota's sexuality wasn't nearly as fluid as mine was.

Then again, I hadn't been into dick until Elijah.

"I'm Ashley, one of Mr. Tolzman's secretaries." The woman clasped her hands in front of her as though trying to curl in on herself rather than stare with blatant hunger at my wife as I'd expected. "He should be here shortly. Can I get you anything else?"

Dakota shook her head, her gaze glued to the woman who I wanted to hiss at like a pissed off iguana.

I bit my tongue until the woman turned away from us.

It wasn't until the door snicked shut behind her that I could breathe again, and even then, I struggled to chill the fuck out.

"I—" Dakota huffed, her brow furrowing even further as she continued to study the shut door.

The woman was gone. No need to worry, no reason for my insides to be stewing.

I studied my wife, hating how her forehead dented, how troubled her eyes appeared, never mind the she totally missed how I'd been tense as fuck since Ashley had entered Elijah's office.

"Jealous that gorgeous little woman has known him longer than you have?" I asked as the thought entered my head.

I hated that Ashley had access and enjoyed proximity to our Elijah before we had.

Were they involved? Had he fucked her over his desk? Had she wrapped her lips around his cock and swallowed down his sweet cum? Had he kissed her lips and cradled her face in his hands while tilting her world off its axis?

Dakota opened her mouth as if to agree with me, but she pursed her lips, her eyes darkening as they continued to stare at the door Ashley had disappeared behind.

I glanced that way, hairs rising along my arms and on my nape. "Elijah is—"

He stepped into the office, cutting me off from telling Dakota he was outside the door.

Damn spidey senses. What was it about him that drew me into harmony with his every move when he was nearby?

His smile caused all my unrest to skitter away like cockroaches with the flip of a light switch. My stomach filled with goddamned butterflies, and Dakota's wiggle on my lap made my dick think about a fuck fest right there in my boss's office.

"You two are going to be the death of me," I groaned, staring as Elijah leaned down to kiss my wife.

"I missed you," he murmured against her mouth, resting his hand against the back of the chair beside my neck to kiss her again.

She sighed and relaxed against me but whimpered when he pulled away.

"Missed you too," he said, his pale eyes peering deep into my soul and making everything about the city and his secretary just peachy in my mind. He brushed his lips across mine, the soft pillow and gentle caress like fucking kerosene to the flames licking at my skin thanks to his energy.

He made me want to burn with the same intensity as that jealousy from seconds earlier over his secretary.

Ashley.

Lingering insecurities of his tiring of us flitted through my brain again, scattering the breezy thoughts of happiness into the wind. My stomach clenched, and good old fear slithered along my spine, slamming walls back up into place that I hadn't realized Elijah had turned to rubble.

I could trust Dakota with my heart, but him? Could I believe the emotions in his eyes, the window into his soul he seemed to leave wide open as he pulled back and smiled down at me when he had women like that violet-eyed secretary nearby and at his disposal?

Self-preservation said hell no even though I longed to say yes.

I would give him access to my body, hell, even my wife, but I had to be careful in sharing my heart—no matter how much the emotions he stirred in me felt like the kind of love that lasted a lifetime.

CHAPTER 33
ELIJAH

Like a veil of mourning falling over his face, Jon shut me out.

No!

My smile faded, and I stood, clearing my throat. Powerless to read his mind, I considered asking what bothered him but couldn't begin a conversation that would erase the beautiful smile off his wife's face as she gazed up at me.

"Sorry to keep you waiting," I said, my body tensed up tight along with the dragon inside me.

"It's okay," Dakota all but cooed, her eyes full of every emotion I felt deep inside my soul radiating back and forth between us.

Tchaikovsky's "Waltz of the Flowers" filled the room as I rounded my desk, and my smile returned while considering which of the two had asked Sybil to play music.

For some reason, I didn't believe it had been our sweet female.

"How'd it go?" Jon asked as I settled in my chair. He obviously wished to focus on things other than his apparent unrest, so I wasn't going to push against his boundaries.

"Quite well." Not finding what I needed after a quick scan of my desk, I hit the intercom button on my office phone. "Ashley?"

"Yes, sir?"

"Did you print out the files for R5872 like I asked for earlier?"

Her muttered curse came through loud and clear. "I'll have them shortly, sir."

I didn't respond but turned my focus on my lovers, giving them my full attention.

Dakota still lounged on Jon's lap, relaxed, her happiness reaching across my desk to soothe my annoyance over Ashley's forgetfulness.

Jon, however, frowned and emanated a swarm of emotions, of which distrust hurt the most. What had transpired in our short separation? If a simple conversation, Dakota seemed unaffected by it. Perhaps a wayward thought had sent him spiraling in some way? A reminder of past trauma? Some wound from before we'd met that demanded he put those walls between us back into place?

Regardless of what went on in his mind, they both smelled delicious and made me crave to have them naked and kneeling before me.

They'd had sex while at their apartment—the slight scent of their cum clung to them—but I wasn't bothered by their shared intimacy. I hated to miss watching or possibly participating but couldn't fault them for trying to slake their thirst for what they really yearned for, even if Jon no longer seemed to be open to the progression of submission he'd seemed so graciously accepting of.

He needed assurance, of which I would gladly give him.

Eventually. Once we had complete privacy.

I focused on Dakota. "I'm sure a tour would bore you,

mon coeur, but perhaps you would at least like to see the robots Jon has mastered with his dexterous fingers?"

Jon's gaze lightened and flared with heat, exactly as I'd hoped for. Just short of a *good boy* I expected he might enjoy hearing, but I hadn't wanted to sound manipulative. I'd merely spoken truth, nothing that Dakota hadn't already declared about her husband.

For the next hour while touring the lab rooms, my thoughts raced. As much as Jon wished to keep me from burrowing into his mind and heart, I'd already lodged myself there. If not by the taste of my cum and the draw of our shared dragonblood, then by his submitting to my kiss, his body to my leading.

Like me, I expected he feared being hurt. Trusting the wrong man with his heart.

I needed to show him I desired more than just his body, that I wanted his every thought, his faults, and insecurities, to bear them all so he wouldn't have to.

I longed to set him free, but I feared what seeing him on his knees again in such an act might require of him. I'd told myself after Dolyn's disappearance that I would never trust a man who seemed to willingly present himself before me in an act of submission.

Dolyn claimed he had given himself fully while kneeling before me, and he'd ripped my heart out.

No. Jon's act of laying his heart and body at my feet would be different than Dolyn's untruthful act. There would be no question when my beta submitted himself fully to me. I would make sure of it one way or another.

Neither of my mates had the required authorization from the government to see half of the things I showed to them, but the two humans belonged to me—and I owned the items currently in my lab, so I didn't fear showing them all I'd created and accomplished.

The armor, black and scalelike, drew them both to the glass enclosures the items were kept inside like a museum's greatest treasure. Fingers pressed against the glass, they both stared. Dakota's mouth parted as she took in how the overhead light glinted like a rainbow on the armor's surface.

"What do you think?" I asked, wishing I could watch them both at the same time—see what emotions played on their faces, if they recognized what I'd fashioned for my robots. Both had admitted to dreaming about their alpha in our true form, a dragon covered in black scales like those they stared at.

Jon shook his head, his lips pressed tight as he stepped back. He seemed doubly wary. Scared. Unsteady as reality and fantasy clashed in his brain. Did he guess at the truth of what I was? Who *he* was? Having stood before the cross in my dungeon I'd covered in the same scalelike material, I expected a riot of words clambered in his brain.

Dakota's pulse thrummed in her neck, and she couldn't seem to tear her gaze off what I had fashioned after my true form.

Shoulders tensed and hands shoving into his pockets, Jon glanced back at me, his gorgeous blue eyes shut down completely to any delving I might wish to do into his thoughts. "You dreamed of a dragon like I did as a child, didn't you?"

"Something like that," I found myself murmuring rather than giving him the truth as he deserved.

Oh, how I longed to tell them of our fate since their birth, lay every last inch of my soul bare to them, but until Jon knew my heart and trusted me, he would probably see me keeping the truth from them as a lie. That was something I couldn't afford him to think if he learned of the other fibs I'd told in attempts to keep them close by.

Manipulation.

I gritted my teeth.

"It's beautiful," Dakota whispered, her fingertips trailing down the enclosure. "Just like the dragon I dreamed about."

The heat of Jon's stare was like a lick of flames across my face, and I swallowed against the thickness in my throat over her willingness to state her thoughts aloud. She would have to be my focus, and hopefully, Jon would in time see I meant them no harm.

"We could go to my apartment and order some dinner, or we could eat out," I suggested, my voice ragged and torn over what might lay ahead when I'd been so sure of having made progress in bonding with my mates.

"Takeout sounds good to me." Dakota flashed me a smile, her huge pupils letting me know she wanted more than just dinner.

"Jon?" He still peered at me, unsmiling yet a hint of vulnerability thankfully showing in his eyes.

"Yeah. Sure," he muttered, but Dakota didn't seem to catch onto his unease.

She slid her hand into his, leaned her head on his shoulder, and brushed her knuckles over mine.

While I would have loved to claim her, let every person who worked for me see the three of us physically connected even if only holding hands, Jon wasn't yet ready.

I laced our fingers together, offering the back of her hand a quick, chaste kiss, before releasing her. "Come." I led them, keeping my hands to myself lest my employees have something to gossip over. Rarely did I spent much time in the New York office, and with things wrapping up on the morrow with one last early meeting, I looked forward to returning home where there would be nothing to distract me from assuring Jon of his place for a handful of weeks.

"Mr. Tolzman!" Ashley's raised voice pulled me up short of the office exit. She hurried toward me, a file in her hands.

Both of my mates stiffened beside me as my secretary drew near.

"I've been looking everywhere for you!"

My inner beast purred at her nearness as he always did. Not in a sexual way but more along the lines of how I might have felt connected to a sister if I'd had one. It was the only reason I'd kept her on staff, since she had the memory of a toddler.

And same as every time Ashley came into close proximity with me, I thought of Dolyn. Why, I wasn't sure. They looked nothing alike with her dark hair compared to his golden. Her height would have been dwarfed by his as well. Even their personalities were opposites, although Ashley did seem to carry a sense of heaviness about her as my ex-lover had.

When she'd arrived for her interview, both halves of me recognized the woman needed looking after. It'd been that tortured look in her eyes that had made the decision an easy one even in knowing I would be reminded of all I'd lost every time I set eyes on her.

"The files you needed." Ashley's smile hid something as it always, but the usual sting of remembrance of Dolyn while in her presence didn't prick at my chest with the same intensity.

Perhaps the final aspect of healing from my grief had begun—thanks to Jon and Dakota.

Heart lightened, I took them from her hands and stepped back, motioning Dakota into the elevator. "Thank you, Ashley."

"Of course, sir. It was nice meeting the two of you." She smiled at my mates before turning away, not waiting for Jon or Dakota to state the same.

I glanced down at Dakota to find her gazing after the woman, a frown denting her brow.

Jon stared after the woman as well, an even deeper dent

between his eyebrows. He glanced at Dakota and snaked an arm around her back, tucking her close against his side in a possessive hold as if wishing to shield her from the smaller, unthreatening woman.

Had something happened between the three of them earlier in the day?

"Is everything okay?" I asked, following them into the elevator.

"Yeah, just fucking starved," Jon answered first, seeming to force feigned relaxation onto his face. "Any place around here we can pick up a steak and some loaded potatoes?"

Choosing his redirection of our conversation for the time being, I pulled my cell from my pocket. "I know the place—and they'll deliver."

"Thank fuck."

While en route to my apartment, Dakota once more sat between us, her fingers laced through Jon's on her thigh, her head resting on my shoulder. A subtle hint of springtime flowers filled my nose, Jon's wilder, fall-like wind beneath.

My mouth watered to taste them, to feel their bodies beneath me, but something unsettling had definitely changed the atmosphere around us. I'd promised Dakota we would be together that night, and I had no plans to disappoint our female, but would Jon still be willing?. The sexual energy between him and I would demand he play a part, but would he open his heart? Would he submit his body once more to my command, or had whatever insecurity that had set him on edge close him off to the intimacy we needed to experience together in order to strengthen our bond?

Once inside my suite and surrounded by his alpha's scent, Jon's tension visibly eased in his shoulders as well as smoothing the line he'd had furrowed between his eyebrows.

Still, dinner at my small table proved a silent affair. I'd expected more unrest, but the quietness zapped with energy and filled with heated glances, ripe with an aroma of arousal. Every second not touching my delicious mates heightened my awareness of their pulses. My inner beast roamed restless beneath my skin, desperate to become one with them.

Whatever had set Jon on edge earlier in the day no longer mattered as my mind focused on moving forward.

Soft classical played from the overhead speakers, and even Jon seemed so wrapped up in his own mind that he didn't mention my lack of taste or tease me about my choice of music. No easy grin lifted his lips, no smirk of arrogance, but I made myself content with the way he stared at my lips, with his enlarged pupils in the candlelight of my penthouse suite.

He couldn't hide or deny his desire for his alpha, same as I couldn't for him.

Dakota, in her usual display of servitude that gave her great joy, insisted on cleaning up our dinner things. Jon and I sat before the windows overlooking Manhattan, me with a glass of wine, his hands empty and resting on his thighs. We studied each other, him with an inquisitive stare while I allowed him to seek out the truth of what he longed for in my eyes. The tension between us went beyond sexual, and while we'd once been vulnerable with each other in the dark of my home, the wall he'd erected to keep himself safe once more sat like a literal mountain between us.

I considered ordering him to kneel at my feet so I could touch his hair, his face, assure him with gentle caresses that he held half of my heart forever and always. I considered crawling across the space between us and resting my cheek against *his* knee, showing my beta that he owned my soul, and I would go to any lengths necessary to prove it to him.

Torn between figuring out exactly what he needed, I held my silence and remained in place.

Dakota approached but hesitated from sitting beside either of us.

She was our buffer, I realized in that moment, a bridge to span whatever distance Jon's mind had placed between us.

I set my wine aside and stood, holding out my hand. She moved toward me and slipped her palm against mine, eyes luminous in the dim light. Dakota would be my focus, our female's desires all that mattered. Knowing Jon would follow in whatever way I led, I decided to take advantage of that fact. Maybe he just needed to fuck his thoughts from his mind and find the peace he'd been experiencing earlier in the day when I'd dropped the two of them off at their apartment.

"Tell me what you want, *mon coeur*," I murmured brushing her hair away from her flushed cheeks.

She licked her lower lip, her gaze flitting to Jon and back. "I want to watch," she whispered, her cheeks tinging pink at the confession.

Yessss.

Lust sprang to life inside me as my dragon rumbled his approval. Stomach tight in expectation of refusal, I focused on Jon's face—his parting lips, the slight widening of his pupils as I allowed my desire for him to show on my face. Perhaps he would allow me to love him, but if not, I would give him all of me, everything he desired if it meant easing his fears.

CHAPTER 34

JONATHAN

My body fucking froze at Dakota's confession. I'd expected her to want us both, and I was fine with fucking her with Elijah on the other side. Making myself available to him alone after the shit day I'd had didn't sit well with me. Well, my damned dick was *definitely* on board. Aching and leaking, the fucking appendage couldn't wait for his touch and whatever else he might have in mind.

"Jon?" he questioned quietly, and hearing my name on his lips melted me like I did with Dakota whenever I pulled her into my arms.

Fucking hell, this man.

Swallowing my groan, I nodded.

Heat flared in his pale eyes, the singe along my skin making my blood burn as I stood to follow him and an excited Dakota into his bedroom.

Hands fisted at my sides, I stayed back a few feet as Elijah pulled a plush chair close to his bed and Dakota curled her legs beneath her on its seat. He whispered in her ear, and her face flushed. She nodded up at him, the desire in her eyes, the smile on her lips a mirror of what I felt coursing through my damn body even though I tried to squash the need.

My brain remained shut tight behind a thick wall, safe from manipulation and hurt.

Seeing Ashley and Elijah face to face with each other didn't suggest jack shit as far as my wondering over if they'd fucked or not. But Dakota had stared with renewed interest, and I fucking hated it more than I did my ex-best friend's desire for my wife.

I felt both Dakota's and Elijah's stare on me.

I stood at a fucking crossroads that led into the unknown. It was dark down both paths and scared the fuck out of me.

Would caving in to fear and retreating make me lose what I shared with Dakota? She'd definitely gotten in over her head with Elijah—would I take a backseat, considering everything he could offer her that I couldn't?

Giving her my full attention, I searched long and hard.

Her smile slowly faded. "You don't have to—"

I held up my hand, having heard all I needed to.

Dakota put my feelings first. Every. Time. There was no need to fear seeing as how we'd been through a dumpster fire countless times and had come out unscathed.

Breath held, I turned my focus on the dark god of a man who reminded me of my childhood imaginary friend even though he didn't sport wings or have claws at the ends of his fingertips. I remembered the feel of his owning grasp on my nape, his hold while tasting my mouth.

A whimper escaped me, and I moved forward as though powerless to withstand his draw.

He can own my body, I told myself, stepping closer to him, his stare burning my skin, electrifying every nerve ending with the energy snapping between us.

A mere two feet separated us, and I had never been so aware of my nerve endings. The blood rushing through my arteries, my heartbeat thrumming in my ears. A loss of saliva in my mouth, and goose bumps covering every inch of my skin. Tension locked my muscles rigid, need drawing my balls tight against my groin regardless of the lingering wariness lingering in my mind.

Elijah slid his warm palm along my cheek, pushing his fingers through my unbound hair to cradle the back of my head with a firm, comforting grip I sank into with a relieved sigh. No commands, no words, just gentle pressure pulling me close as he leaned in to kiss me.

Fucking hell...

My eyelids slammed shut, and my hands reached for him as though moving on their own, grasping his dress shirt tight, desperate to hold onto him. I groaned as he slid his tongue between my lips. Whimpered as he caressed my cheek with his thumb and angled my head to lay claim to my mouth with a tender kiss that rocked my world, tilting it haphazardly enough I felt my legs sway beneath me.

The need in me was too much, overwhelming in its pull toward him, to let him burrow so deep inside me we became one where I felt sure I wouldn't have to fear jack shit any longer.

"Let me love you, Jon," he whispered against my mouth, holding my head still in the cradle of his hands.

Goddamnit all to fucking hell.

My pulse raced, and dread wanted to claw up my throat, demanding I couldn't trust him with my heart.

But his eyes... Jesus, the vulnerability he showed made my stomach swoop and throat tighten.

"Yes," I heard myself whispering exactly what that voice in the back of my head begged for.

Elijah stepped close, an overflow of tenderness emanating from his steady gaze. "I promise not to hurt you—unless you ask me to."

Fuck.

Why did that bring back all those flashes of balls and chains, gags and floggers? The memory of the cross in his dungeon and how hard I'd come on the floor before hit me like a freight train that couldn't be slowed.

I panted while he pulled my shirt off overhead. Moaned when he mapped out my entire upper body with his hands, fingertips searing every inch of skin they touched.

I needed him so fucking badly that my body trembled. Fucking knees knocked. I kicked my sneakers off, but he grabbed my hands when I reached to undo my jeans.

"Let me unwrap the gift of you," he commanded quietly.

"Jesus, Elijah." I swallowed hard and nodded, knowing and not caring hearts rested in my eyes.

Dakota whimpered, but I couldn't tear my focus off Elijah's face as he sank to his knees and made short work of my jeans, pulling them down. Heartbeat throbbing in my throat and dick aching like a motherfucker, I stepped out of them, damn near collapsing as Elijah ran his palms up the sides of my thighs.

He licked up the underside of my dick.

"Ah fuck!" My eyes rolled into my head at the same time Dakota moaned. My hands gripped Elijah's hair, to yank him close or push him away, I didn't know. I hung on for dear life as he closed his mouth over my leaking head and took me deep into his throat.

"Fuck…oh, Jesus fuck." I groaned and whimpered, gasped as he swallowed around me, taking me straight to the edge in five seconds flat. "Christ, fucking stop before I blow my load. Please, Elijah—mercy!"

He hummed and backed off slowly, his tongue swirling around my length, gathering the pre-cum oozing from my swollen head as though trying to coax my climax from my balls regardless of my desire not to come all over his face just yet.

"I've never done that for a man," he rasped as though taking my dick into his throat had left him hoarse.

"Never?"

He shook his head while glancing up at me, kissing the insides of each of my thighs.

Goddamn. He was a total alpha, definitely didn't bow to any man…but he'd gotten on his knees for me. "Jesus, Elijah."

Slowly, he rose to stand before me, the intensity in his eyes, the blackness swirling in his pupils weakening my knees and making me delirious with the need to drop to his feet and worship him like he'd done for me.

Yes.

I sank onto the edge of the bed rather than giving in to complete submission, unable to tear my gaze from Elijah's face as he began unbuttoning his shirt. Awareness that Dakota sat a few feet away, watching us—probably soaked between her thighs—wasn't enough to distract me from Elijah unwrapping the gift of *him*.

He didn't reveal anything I hadn't already seen when he pulled the white shirt off his arms, his pecs flexing and abs rippling, but I drooled like a motherfucker.

I reached for him on instinct, needy as fuck, and he stepped close, allowing me to unclasp his belt. The snap of his slacks, the teeth of his zipper slowly descending sounded loud in my ears atop my panted breaths.

His groan as I freed his erection and wrapped my hand around it was better than any music I'd ever heard. I wanted to play that shit on repeat until it echoed for eternity in my head. I didn't bother pushing his slacks all the way off but leaned in and licked the wet trail glistening down to his balls. The man leaked like a goddamned faucet, his pre-cum as sweet as I'd remembered.

"Christ." I swallowed and went in for more, moaning while lapping up his flavor that swarmed my taste buds, tingling my tongue. I wanted every drop lying in wait in that heavy sac of his to shoot into my throat. Fucking longed for it. Needed it—

"No." His stern command stopped me from closing my mouth over him, and he grasped my chin, forcing me to look up at him. Darkness warred with the pale irises, swirling enough I blinked to focus on them. "Lie on my bed," he rasped as though barely holding back from ravishing me. "Let me pleasure you."

I did as commanded, telling myself it was my body obeying, not my head, but fuck if that damn wall I attempted to keep erected between us didn't tremble as he crawled atop me, gaze latched to mine, his eyes begging me to submit.

Yes.

He took my mouth, and I told the damn voice in my head to fuck off. I lifted up to fuse our mouths together better. Nipped his lower lip. Trapped his hips between my thighs, my feet resting on the bed, and fought to ignore the size of his hard cock pressing against mine and how badly I wanted his girth to defile me.

Elijah gyrated his hips, and I groaned, my dick jerking alongside his, slick from his pre-cum.

I wasn't going to fucking last.

"Fuck me, Elijah," I hissed through clenched teeth.

Fuck me already so I can get you out of my fucking head, my system.

He planked over me, propped on his hands, his massive shoulders and pecs above me. "Dakota," he said, keeping his focus on my face although he was definitely more aware of our surroundings than I was in that moment. "Are you wet?"

"S-soaked," she whispered, shifting on her chair.

"Come show me."

In my peripheral vision, she moved to the bed and slid her pants to the floor.

"*Show me*," Elijah repeated, and she dipped her fingers between her thighs.

He glanced at her and licked his lips, sitting onto his haunches, his hand outstretched toward her.

She climbed onto the bed on her knees, thighs spread, and I finally turned to look at her as Elijah slid his hand down over her bare pubis and up into her glistening pussy.

"So slick and warm, *mon coeur*." He pulled out, his fingers dripping, and palmed his dick, smearing her and his abundant arousal down his length. "More..." Twice, he gathered her moisture and slickened his dick, and the third time, he reached between my bent legs and cupped my balls.

My eyes rolled back into my head again as I growled a curse, my dick bobbing and leaking on my stomach. Jesus fucking Christ, his touch—the quiet sounds of his exhales, the scent of fire clinging to his scent and surrounding me...

I fisted the comforter at my sides and clenched my jaw to keep from losing control and coming completely untouched. His proximity was life. Fucking euphoria and all mine for the taking.

Or rather, receiving.

Elijah smoothed his hands down over my ass, and I relaxed, so damn ready for his touch I swallowed down a sob of neediness. He breached my ring of muscle with one fingertip, and I whimpered.

"Okay?" he whispered, and I swallowed hard while nodding.

Who knew a finger up the ass would feel so goddamned good?

He slid in another soaked with their combined juices, and I bucked my hips, tossing out curses like a madman as he pushed deeper, stretching my virgin ass, readying my poor hole for his huge cock.

"L-Lube," I gasped, knowing that would at least make things a little easier on me even though I was all but panting to be wrecked by his dick.

"Relax," he half-cooed, gliding his fingers in and out in an abundance of slickness that didn't make sense. "What we produce in our need is more than enough for me to own you."

Own.

Jesus, *fuck.*

That sounded so goddamned right yet scary as hell. But I wasn't about to stop this train barreling toward losing my ass's virginity. Nope. Needed him to dick me down and leave me boneless, Dakota's fantasy come to life.

"Just do it," I said through clenched teeth, opening my eyes to meet his gaze and grabbing hold of the back of my knees to widen my legs.

He caressed my thigh, watching as he pulled his fingers from my hole.

I clenched around nothing, the absence of his presence in my body like a knife to my damned chest. "Please—Elijah." Begging wasn't hot in my mind, but my wife thought so.

A deep moan rolled from where she remained planted on the mattress beside me, fingers up her pussy. The musk of her arousal flooded my lungs alongside the scent of brimstone. A delicious combination that made my mouth water.

Holding my gaze, Elijah crowded close and pressed the head of his wet dick against my pucker.

I bore down as I'd seen Dakota do hundreds of times, knowing it would make penetration more bearable. He pressed, and I let out a steady breath, hissing against the burn of intrusion.

"God—fuck!" I gritted my teeth, fighting against the need

to clench. "Ah, Jesus!" The head of his cock lodged inside my ass, and I panted, struggling to stay relaxed.

"That's it," he murmured, the caresses of his hands up the backs of my thighs soothing enough I shuddered a huge exhale.

"So hot, Jon..." Dakota whispered, her fingers making squishing noises while she fucked herself with them inches from my trembling body. "Relax and let him in, baby. I promise it gets better."

"More," I demanded, staring up at Elijah with determination to take every goddamned inch of his massive cock up my ass because it was what my wife wanted.

I want.

Elijah palmed my flagging erection and squeezed, causing my eyes to roll back into my head.

"Fuck—"

He shoved in what felt like a fucking foot—probably a goddamn inch—and I bucked, crying out against the pain burning through my asshole.

"Look at me while I own you, Jon."

Goddamn mother*fucker*. I didn't *want* to submit.

My eyelids popped open without consent of my brain, and Elijah pushed in a little farther, sliding his other slick hand over my thickening cock.

"Breathe, baby," Dakota suggested, her voice so damn breathless that my dick jerked in Elijah's hold.

I released my pent up exhale and relaxed, not having realized every muscle in my body had tensed to the point of eruption, and not the good kind.

Another nudge, another stroke on my rigid length, and I hissed through my teeth. No fucking way he could fit another inch—

He pulled out and slid back in, and the burn shifted into pure fucking *gold*.

"Oh, *fuuuuck.*" I groaned the word through clenched teeth, my balls drawing up tight. Another withdrawal, a slow sink into my body, and Elijah's balls rested against my ass, filling me completely. Fucking stretched to capacity—and so goddamned fucking perfect I wanted to sob.

"Oh my God." Dakota moaned from beside me, but I couldn't open my eyes. Couldn't fucking move, or I'd either start crying like a baby or blow my load prematurely all over my stomach and prove what a slut I was for Elijah's cock.

Not that I would really care about the latter. His dick had been crafted by the gods to fit inside my body and hit my prostate just right.

"Sit on his face, *mon coeur,*" Elijah murmured, squeezing the base of my dick while rocking into my hungry ass and rubbing where I needed him. "Give him something to focus on so this doesn't end before I thoroughly enjoy the gift of him."

Internally, I whimpered like a cowering dog, and the desire to once more crawl for him, rub my face on his thigh, and feel his hands on my head and fingers running through my hair swept over me. I should have been flattened, taken out by the powerful energy emanating off the god buried balls deep in my ass, but every cell rejuvenated, coming to life with renewed outlook and hope for the future.

I'd always wondered why Dakota enjoyed a good dicking up the ass, and now I knew...or rather, almost did.

The sweet scent of my wife's pussy wafted over my nose, jerking me back to reality and reminding me I wasn't alone in my blissed-out state of waiting for the climax of a lifetime.

I grabbed hold of her hips and dove into her slick folds like a starved man, delirious with need, like I floated a breath away from being swept into oblivion. I hadn't even realized she'd settled atop me facing Elijah until her hot mouth closed over the tip of my dick.

"Fuck!" I garbled against her pussy lips, panting and sucking at her swollen labia hard enough she flinched.

I dug my fingertips into her thighs and shoved my tongue up her hole as far as it would go.

Elijah pulled out to the crown and thrust into my ass.

Stars exploded behind my eyelids.

Had to come. A deep growl rumbled my chest. Had to fucking *come*.

"Please...fucking *please*," I begged against Dakota's satiny skin, unable to do anything but *feel*.

"No coming until I say so," Elijah said, his low voice rippling over my skin, his hand a vise around the base of my cock to stop me from nutting.

I cursed through clenched teeth, thrashing in my need to fucking come already. A deep craving for Elijah's spunk all up in my guts swept through me, taking control of my mind. Everything but the friction of him thrusting in steady rhythm inside my hole escaped my consciousness. I grunted against the exquisite torture of his hard cock rubbing against my prostate, making me mad with the need to bust.

No way would I be able to keep quiet—

Dakota took me deep, the head of my dick hitting the back of her throat.

My balls erupted without permission, jerking my cock against Dakota's tongue, shooting, pulsing, spurting as she hummed around my length, her pussy muffling my hollers. She swallowed down every drop, but my dick didn't soften.

I groaned a few f-bombs, Elijah's stroking on my inner walls jacking me back up to the edge again before my climax ended.

Dakota lifted off me, and I forced my eyelids up to find her sprawled beside me, fingers in her pussy, lips parted, watching as Elijah fucked my ass as though hell-bent on wrecking my insides.

But there was no pain, nothing but the insatiable need to be closer. Fuller.

"Elijah," I croaked, and he planked over me on his hands beside my shoulders, the black of his eyes swirling—maddening in its darkness.

"You're going to pay for coming without my permission," he murmured.

Why the *fuck* was the idea of that so goddamned hot?

He thrust deep enough I saw stars again and captured my mouth, obliterating all thought but him.

Elijah owned me, every atom inside me. Every breath that filled my lungs smelled like him, every lash of his tongue sweet along mine. He dominated me with ease, and I sank into submission, greedy for everything he gave. The onslaught of his alpha nature, the unspoken demands he placed on me to conform to his will, was hot as fuck.

I willingly handed over my body, my mind, but my heart cowered behind crumbling rock of determination.

"Fuck me, Elijah," I growled against his lips, desperate to take us back to distracted need rather than the over-whelming desire for deep intimacy I craved. "Hard. Fast. Want your cum inside me."

Two words tore from his mouth in a language I didn't understand, but they faded from my ears as his dick throbbed, shooting tingling heat into my guts.

"Oh, fuck!" My jaw clenched and spine arched as he continued to empty, every spurt of his cum ratcheting my need to spill again.

But this time, something in me denied my body release.

I waited his permission, his guidance.

Jesus, what was wrong with me?

Still pulsing, he pulled out, leaving me empty, his hot seed seeping from my hole. I panted, strung with the need to fuck. Would he let me—

"Take her."

I rolled between Dakota's thighs without finishing my thought, obeying Elijah's command and filling my wife's pussy with one savage thrust. My inner animal unleashed, I hollered and fucked into her with no intent other than coming again. Taking. Devouring.

My ears rang, muffling her cries and my grunts while I attempted to rail into her deeper than I'd ever done in the past. Her nails dug into my back, but the sting didn't hinder me from trying to split her in two—pushing her toward the headboard with every savage thrust of my hips.

"Jon!" Dakota shrieked, and her pussy clamped down on me, pulling, milking a second climax from my aching balls in a matter of minutes.

A guttural cry flew from me, and I shoved my face in her neck, arms wrapped around her body. My release rushed through me like a euphoric wind, my soul soaring through the sky as though I had wings.

CHAPTER 35

DAKOTA

Jon's eyes had been closed almost the entire time Elijah had fucked him, and with how he whimpered and moaned as if in pain, I wondered if he'd only agreed because it was what I wanted. His brow remained dented with a frown long after we cleaned up.

While we'd snuggled on the couch and enjoyed some wine, Jon making his jokes about his no-longer virgin ass and acting all carefree, I swore an unsettled energy emanated from him, causing me to believe he wasn't as comfortable as he made out to be.

Climbing into bed between the two men a little while later seemed so right, felt so perfect. Having Elijah at my back, Jon against my front, nothing sexual but gentle caresses and languid kisses…I couldn't have asked for more, physically. I felt cherished, but the emotion couldn't override my sense that something was off.

Jon and I stared at each other in the dim light filtering in through the drapes attempting to shut out the city.

I'd been satisfied in so many ways that night, but same as always when near Elijah, my mind refused to rest. He spooned my backside, his breath hot on my neck, hand rubbing my thigh and revving me back up as his cock swelled and dug into my leg.

Sure Jon hurt somehow, I opened my mouth to stop what was bound to happen again, but my husband pressed his fingertips to my lips and scooted away, taking his body heat with him. "I want to watch," he whispered what I had earlier, and my pussy pulsed in response.

"May I love you, *mon coeur*?" Elijah murmured against my ear and reached between my thighs.

Wetness seeped from my needy pussy, and I nodded even though my mind considered saying no.

Elijah teased my opening, rimming and pressing in slightly, but didn't give me what my body craved.

My lips parted as my breaths heightened, and I continued to stare at Jon while Elijah's hand drove me near to destruction. The hardness of Elijah's cock promised what I needed, and I pressed against him, whimpering.

Elijah rolled me to my back, breaking my gaze from my husband.

Pale eyes glinted in the darkness, piercing me with so much emotion my breath caught. Elijah cradled my head in his hands and dipped low, sweeping his soft lips across mine. I made another small noise, and he slid his tongue between my lips.

Heat flushed through me, and all thought fled except for the need to be filled by him. I clutched at his back with my hands, my heels digging into his ass. "Please."

He flexed beneath my hold, notching his cock inside me with a groan. "*Mon coeur*, so perfect." A groan rose from his chest as he slowly sank into my pussy, his mouth capturing my lips once more.

"Goddamn." Jon's low, breathless voice flitted through my mind, and I reached for him.

He grasped my hand with a tight squeeze, keeping us together.

Elijah withdrew to the crown and sank back in, drawing a groan from all three of us. I yanked with my heels, desperate for him to lose control and fuck me like he'd done with Jon. Bridled lust, *passionate* fury, trembled the muscles beneath my hold.

"Let go, Elijah," I whispered against his lips as he backed out again, leaving me so damn empty tears welled in my eyes. "I want it all."

A growl rumbled the chest pressed against mine, and he thrust in deep, pulling a gasp from my lips. "Again."

He gave what I asked for, bruising my cervix and capturing my mouth, devouring as though I belonged to him, body and soul.

I dug the fingernails of my right hand into his back and held on, lifting my hips to meet his driving hips while grasping Jon with the other. Pleasure, hot and bright, slid along my spine, breaking across my skin, and I moaned my hunger for him to fuck me harder. Deeper.

Need.

As though hearing the thought echoing through my head, Elijah plowed into me over and over, the wet sound of Jon jerking himself beside us adding fuel to the fire smoldering inside me. Flames burst to life, and I arched beneath Elijah, my climax shrieking through me with hurricane force.

"God! Oh…*God!*"

Elijah buried against my womb and growled, his cock swelling impossibly large before releasing. Hot spurts coated inside me as he continued to fuck into me with abandon, and a second climax rushed over me, stealing my breath, same as the first time he'd filled me so perfectly.

Jon's loud groan, one I well-recognized, barely registered through the ringing in my ears as Elijah stilled, and I fought to keep my footing in reality. His forehead resting on my mine, Elijah breathed heavily, his sweet exhales caressing my mouth.

"So lovely," he whispered, cradling my head again. "So beautiful." A few French sayings flitted past his lips, but he pressed his mouth against mine, stealing my thought to ask what he'd said.

Jon released my hand and rolled from the bed.

Elijah lifted his head, trailing a thumb over my bruised lips. "Was it too much?"

"No." I squeezed my inner walls around his softening length, drawing another groan from him.

"You need to rest, *mon coeur*."

Releasing a heavy sigh, I loosened my hold on his body, biting my lip as he pulled away. Coolness from the air-conditioning slid over my damp skin, and I shivered at the loss of both men.

"Okay, baby?" Jon asked, wiping between my thighs with a warm towel as Elijah strode toward the bathroom.

"Yeah." I smiled and turned my attention on him, guilt over not realizing he'd returned to my side twisting my stomach. "You?"

"Mmm." He tossed the damp towel aside and pressed his lips to mine. "Fucking exhausted."

I hummed my agreement even though I felt the need to push for an answer to my question. He stretched out on his back beside me, lacing his fingers through mine again.

Elijah returned and spooned my backside, and although both men soon breathed heavy with sleep, my mind refused to rest. My worry over Jon's growing distance had started earlier in the day, soured my stomach, and haunted my mind. Sure I had unintentionally hurt my love, I lay in bed long after both men slept, thickness clogging my throat, nausea roiling in my stomach.

Jon rolled away in his sleep, curling in on himself like a child. A mere two feet away, but it seemed a mile.

I chewed the inside of my lip to death, and tears slid down my cheeks, but I didn't stir from Elijah's gentle hold. Couldn't. Didn't want to. I needed Jon to return to me, to *us*. Come back to what we'd agreed to, because I wasn't nearly ready to let go of the growing emotions that had burst to life in my chest as Elijah had made love to me.

I woke, bleary-eyed and groggy. Groaning, I rolled toward Jon, but cold sheets met my hand. Jerking upright, I blinked, bringing into focus the empty bed on either side of me.

"Hey, baby."

I whipped my head toward the other side of the bedroom to find Jon lounging on the chair in nothing but shorts, a cup of coffee in his hand.

"Hey," I whispered back, swinging my legs to the edge of the bed.

No Elijah, I noted after a quick scan. "Where is he?"

"Gone to his meeting."

"Already?" I sighed and padded across the large room, naked as a jay and relieved, loving how Jon's gaze roamed down over my body, lingering on the apex of my thighs as I moved closer to him.

He sipped his coffee, glued gaze sending a tingle of warmth through me. Sitting his mug aside, he reached out a hand toward me.

My heart settled, mind rested as I curled against his hard chest and breathed in the scent of fallen leaves and earth that seemed to cling to his skin. His unbound hair tickled my cheek as I burrowed my face in his neck.

"You were sexy as fuck last night," Jon murmured against

my hair, wrapping his arms around me, and every last trace of anxiety fled my mind. "And Elijah..." He shifted beneath me.

"Are you okay, Jon?"

He expelled a heavy breath and fully relaxed into the couch with a sigh. "Yeah."

"Did he hurt you?"

Quietness lingered between us long enough my heartbeat sped back up, and I pressed my hand against his chest, eyes clenched shut and searching as though I could read the energy beneath my palm.

"Not physically, no," Jon finally answered.

The unsettled energy I noticed the evening before from him tingled along my skin, and I worried my lip between my teeth. I could feel his pain. His confusion. His need to keep himself safe.

We had always been close, but never had I ever experienced in my own heart and mind what he did. It was like being one with Elijah had opened up some deeper connection between Jon and I, and I refused to call it fantasy. I could *feel* my husband's pain far beyond what I often empathized with.

Brow furrowing, I wished to send him some of my peace about Elijah. Share my trust of the man's heart and intentions toward us, for I didn't doubt him with a single cell in my body.

Elijah loved us both. Deeply and unconditionally. I'd held his gaze while every flex of his ass pushed his cock into my husband. I'd sucked Jon and saw wave after wave of Elijah's devotion pouring from his eyes as we stared at each other while pleasuring our lover. I'd felt his caress deep inside my body hours later, his passion and love as though his hand reached inside me and placed his heart in my care.

But how did I speak such thoughts without sounding like

a crazed lunatic? How did I tell Jon that I understood his pain, that I literally experienced it with every breath he exhaled?

"Talk to me," I whispered instead, imagining my inner peace flooding from my chest, through my arm and hand, into his spirit.

"I'm fucking scared."

"We can go home, right now." I told him the same thing he'd offered me, even though my heart broke. "We can leave this all behind and start over."

"No—"

"We can move to another city, Jon. Head south where it's warmer like you've always wanted to do. I'll—"

"No, baby." He pulled me tight against him, muffling my mouth against his neck. "This job—it's too important. Think of everything we can gain from this. The experience, the contacts I'll make. Hell." He snorted a laugh that didn't sound the least bit like happiness. "The fucking salary for *gaming* is ten times what I could find doing design work. We're staying."

I pulled back and peered into his troubled eyes, the vulnerability he shared with me squeezing my heart. "Don't do this for me, Jon. Please. You heard what Elijah has said. We need to choose for ourselves what we want."

His dimpled smile, however swoon-worthy, didn't ease or melt me like it usually did. "I'm doing this for *us*."

"I'd rather if you did it for *you* because it's what you desire. I know you do. I can feel it as deeply as my own need." Jon didn't reply, and I rubbed my thumb along the patches of his scruffy jawline, choosing to let the matter lie quiet for now. "Did you speak with him this morning?"

"No." His gaze flitted around the apartment. "Being the chickenshit I am, I pretended I was asleep until he left."

"You're not a chickenshit." I hoped he read the truth of my

thoughts in my eyes when he finally looked me full in the face. "You just need to figure out how you feel. What you want."

"I want to submit so fucking bad," he whispered and swallowed, his Adam's apple bobbing. "To give him every goddamn inch of me, inside and out, and to lay my entire fucking life at his feet and tell him to do with me what he will." A frown furrowed his brow as he peered down at me. "What kind of spineless man does that make me, Dakota?"

The words had come straight from that fuckface of a foster father who'd raised him.

I cupped Jon's cheek in my hand as my eyesight grew hazy from the sudden tears clogging my throat. "It makes you a man who loves deeply. The kind every single person on this planet is searching to find. Faithful. Devoted and honest."

His gaze lightened although he didn't smile. "You just say that because you don't know anything different than me."

"I have no wish to either. You're it for me, Jon. You have been since we were kids."

Along with Elijah, both of us I felt sure wished to tack on.

Neither of us spoke the truth aloud though.

We stared at each other in silence for a few moments, and I needed to bury the hatchet once and for all.

"I'm sorry for hurting you all those years ago," I whispered, my throat tightening.

He huffed a snort. "You've said it a million times already, baby, and I'll tell you again—I forgave you the second you walked away because of how I reacted over that blond douche. There's nothing you could do to change how I feel about you, Dakota Taylor Ebel, okay? I'll be yours forever and always, no matter what."

A half-sob, half-laugh escaped me, and he pressed his lips against mine, soothing the guilt I couldn't rid myself of.

A heavy sigh shuddered his chest, and he tipped his head back against the couch, eyes closing as he pulled my head against his neck once more. "Love you, baby," he murmured.

"Love you more," I whispered, closing my own eyes and praying to whatever god existed above that Jon would find the strength to give in to what both he and Elijah longed for.

Because living without one or the other and hoping to find containment or happiness was no longer an option.

CHAPTER 36

JONATHAN

Dakota always quieted my inner demons, but I held tight to the wall I'd built, the imaginary line I couldn't cross even though my body begged me to do so.

More coffee, breakfast, shower together, and cuddling—without sex—on Elijah's bed, surrounded by his scent would have been fucking heaven if it weren't for the damn ache in my chest that no amount of rubbing or scratching eased.

I wondered over my well-founded fear and the sexual high Elijah had taken me on the night before. Considered the cum he'd filled me with and its ability to hit me like the sweetest drug and make me crave more as I'd done with Dakota from the first time we'd had sex. And watching my wife surrender herself to him without me involved in their coupling turned me the fuck on rather than pissed me of.

I hadn't slept worth a shit the night before, and I finally drifted off in peace, Dakota wrapped around my body. When I woke, Elijah sat on the couch in his suit and tie, Dakota still naked—and straddling his thighs.

I should have seen red, my stomach souring, but found

my cock swelling and my hand sliding down my stomach to wrap around it, same as the night before when Elijah had made love to my wife.

He lifted his gaze from her face, the emotions in his eyes hitting me like a rush of wind and stealing my breath.

Goddamn him and whatever that energy was reaching out to me with desperation I couldn't say no to.

His slow smile caused my dick to jerk in my hand. "Good morning." The low rumble of his tone pebbled my skin. "Or should I say afternoon?"

I didn't stand a fucking chance of preserving myself. Protecting myself from hurt.

Fuck if I was going to stop trying though.

At least he didn't demand I crawl to him and sit at his feet like a trained dog while he fingered Dakota and enticed her body to climax all over his hand and slacks. I busted a nut at the same time as she did, my hand milking my shaft until my balls sagged in relief.

I swore to fucking God, Elijah's *good boy* was whispered after in similar praise to my wife.

But I refused to acknowledge his words or how they swelled my chest with fulfillment and shit ton of pride over pleasing him.

An hour later, the chopper packed full with a bunch of our shit and a dozen or so bag of groceries including boxed mac and cheese at Elijah's insistence, we headed back to the cavern for the rest of our four-week stay.

Elijah suggested we move into his room, and I carried our stuff there without bothering to double-check with Dakota. She wore her heart on her sleeve even if she glanced at me with a question in her eyes.

Settling into a routine came easily enough. We cooked together, showered together, slept together, Dakota more often than not a writhing, panting mess between us. Still,

Elijah wouldn't allow either of us another taste of his cum. He also didn't try to fuck me again, and I couldn't decide if I was thankful or pissed off about that fact.

Any kisses shared between the two of us weren't the gentle sort but pure fucking war—and I refused to back down and melt at his touch as my body seemed desperate for.

The sexual tension swarming like hornets in the tech room while working raised the hairs on my neck, heightened my pulse to the point of needing to talk myself out of hyperventilating and panting for my boss on a daily basis.

Elijah had said I would pay for coming without permission that night in New York, and every heated glance, every stare that singed my skin, promised he would hold true to his word.

So what the fuck was he waiting for?

Me to ask for his undivided attention?

Not happening.

I dreamed of the dungeon. The cross. The chains dangling from the ceiling and the cane that would probably hurt like a goddamn son of a bitch. Desire to kneel at his feet and beg for him to hurt me—love me—had me hard as a rock more often than not. I jerked off more than a horny teenager in the bathroom, and I swear to fucking *God* that Elijah could tell I didn't gift him those orgasms. Like he could smell the cum on me even though I cleaned up thoroughly every time, his knowing stare promised I would pay.

Coming without his permission haunted my mind but fuck if I could stop.

No amount of burying myself in Dakota's ass, pussy, or throat eased the ache inside me. Like a darkness leaching into my soul, a hazy sheen of *something* latched onto my innermost being, demanding I soothe its need with whispered pleadings in a voice I didn't fully recognize as my own.

What was that all-important piece, what link that would set my world right again, the same as it was when I'd first met Dakota? Had meeting Ashley caused the unrest? Did Elijah's continued show of dominance in his steady stare? The idea of leaving him and his lair fucked with my reality to the point I didn't consider it any further.

What part of the puzzle that would make sense of everything in my head was I missing?

Two long-ass motherfucking weeks, and no amount of beer, good wine, fucking, or pouring myself into my job eased the unrest beneath my skin.

Elijah had disappeared an hour into the workday, the tension snapping between us probably finally catching up to him.

Dakota had gone off down the mountainside, camera in hand, to get some images for a newly contracted White Mountains travel brochure, and I slaved away, putting the latest robot model to the test in its seventh or eighth different suit of armor. My eyes burned. Throat itched. Backside fucking ached from sitting on the goddamned chair for too long.

Tossing the controller onto the desk, I sat back and pinched the bridge of my nose.

Something had to give.

"Can't fucking do this anymore," I muttered to myself and shot up from the desk, stalking out the door. The hallway lay empty, and no sounds rose from the garage or stairs leading to the upper floors.

Like a string tied to my head and tugged, my gaze swiveled toward the door directly across from me. My hand lifted before I thought, punching in the key code same as I'd done supernaturally once before. The lock clicked, and I pushed inward.

Soft light rose, and I stepped over the threshold.

Silence reigned as I glanced around the room that had been tidied since my last visit. Although coated in a bit of shadow, I noted the cleanliness of the floor, the various benches, and peg boards and tables with their precisely lined toys. My feet moved me to the left, my fingers trailing over various instruments, some of which I had no clue about how one wielded them or the pain level they might inflict.

Floggers, crops, whips…a cane that made my backside clench and rushed the blood to my cock. My breath echoed in my ears as I lifted the wooden rod, its smoothness and unnatural warmth reminding me of the scale-like armor Elijah had created.

Holding the cane closer to my face revealed tiny scales.

It had definitely been designed by Elijah.

I slid my hand along its length, and like I'd stroked my stiff dick, pre-cum oozed from my slit, smearing in the jeans near-choking my balls.

The cane would hurt when wielded by Elijah—I had no doubt—but his touch would bring pleasure in its wake.

And fuck if that thought didn't make my cock jerk and my heart rate accelerate.

A rush of that *something* swarmed over me, catching my breath a second before Elijah's presence registered in my lust-filled brain. The darkness in me rose, tingling my hands, my feet, and my balls.

Yes.

Breath held, I turned.

Elijah hovered in the doorway, tensed like a dragon ready to leap at whoever had dared to touch his treasure. Pale eyes, dark pupils swirling—I didn't fucking imagine the other-worldliness of his strange stare. The dude was not thoroughly human. No fucking way.

I swallowed but couldn't tear my gaze from him. Couldn't

breathe as he stalked toward me, shoulders hunched, chin lowered, gaze piercing. "The beast inside you calls to me."

I didn't know what the fuck he meant, but it sounded like truth with how the words rumbled deeply from his chest and caused my arms to erupt in goose bumps.

That voice in my head? Yeah—it fucking agreed whole-heartedly, almost…cackling in glee.

"Let me show you." Elijah stalked close with his sugges-tion, clasping his hand around mine, which still clutched the cane. Our chests bumped, and he tipped his head to the side, his gaze roaming down my neck and back to my lips. "Let me set you free."

Please.

My balls seized, and I released my hold on the cane as Elijah stepped back, taking it with him.

"Strip." His low command didn't allow argument, not that I'd have attempted one.

Every inch of my tingling skin, every zapping atom inside my body, craved what I somehow *knew* what he and he alone could give me.

My hands shook while pushing off my jeans and kicking them free from my bare feet. I pulled my shirt off overhead and dropped it to the floor where it landed with a soft swish. Our heavy, panted breaths echoed in the cavernous room of melted rock and kinky toys meant to set a tortured soul free.

At least, I hoped that would be the truth.

Fists clenched at my sides, I stood before him, dripping pre-cum and shivering even though lava seemed to boil inside my soul.

Elijah took his time sizing me up, his gaze lingering here and there, and until he circled me, I wanted to beg him to just get on with it already, same as when I'd offered up my virgin ass to him. Lifting his arm, he trailed the end of the cane up the inside of my thigh, over my cock, and up my abs, leaving a trail of fire in its wake.

I hissed between my teeth, my nerve endings alight and ready to fly.

"I know you want me to strap you to that cross," he said, his voice as strained as I felt, "but you lost that privilege by disobeying me while in New York."

A frown dented my brow as he set the cane aside and reached overhead to the dangling chains I hadn't realized I stood beneath. "Give me your hands, beta."

My fear squashed by need, I obeyed, and soft leather caressed my wrists, shackles attached to the chains.

Elijah moved away, and my gaze trailed over the ceiling, to the other end of the chains against the far wall. He pulled them upward until my arms stretched overhead. I was strung up, balancing on the balls of my feet and stretched taut, but not enough that my muscles screamed for relief.

"I'm going to do what I dreamed of doing," he said, pressing his once more against me, his mouth on my ear, the heat of his skin like a brand on my chest. "You're hung at my mercy," he murmured with a deeper rumble, and I whimpered. "Mine to torment, mine to *pleasure*."

He wrapped his hand around my cock and squeezed.

I swallowed hard. "Jesus—Elijah."

"You've offered yourself, so now I'm going to break down every fucking wall you've built to keep me out."

Yes.

I shook my head but couldn't voice the argument in my head. I wanted to shout a resounding no, to tell him to stop, but found my lower lip between my teeth instead.

He left me chilled through, striding toward one of the tables. He returned with a blindfold, his black pupils still swirling in that ungodly...*hotness* that made my balls throb.

"To help you see better," he said, wrapping it around my head and shutting out the strange, gorgeous sight of him.

"D-don't I get a safeword?" I managed to ask past the tightness in my throat I figured to be fear regardless of the lust swarming beneath my skin.

The tip of the cane moved down my spine, bringing a shiver along with it.

"Do you want one?" Elijah asked while sliding the cane down between my ass cheeks.

My hips pressed toward him, and a moan escaped my parted lips rather than the yes I'd intended on giving. But I ought to have one regardless of my desire to be wrecked by Elijah's toys.

"Oatmeal."

Elijah chuckled, trailing the cane back up my spine. "I promise once we begin, that word will never cross your lips. Your desire to submit is strong regardless of how much you fear doing so."

He spoke the truth.

The warm tip of the toy he wielded disappeared, and a whoosh sounded.

Crack!

Pain fucking exploded across the top of my thighs, and I jerked forward, cursing and jerking the chains.

Crack!

Another landed above the first, and I bit my lip so goddamn hard the coppery tang of blood hit my tongue.

"Jesus fucking Christ." I breathed through the searing pain, having something all-consuming to focus on that made my mind quiet exactly as I'd always hoped it would. Why the fuck had I thought starting off with a goddamned cane was a good introduction into this pain/pleasure shit though?

I didn't even know if the agony would morph into something I might find pleasant. Fire raced through my blood, but rather than shrinking from it, I leaned into the pain, soaking the clarity and mind-blowing awareness it brought.

Like my eyes had been opened, my senses heightened—flooded with fucking *life*…

"Again," I whispered.

A third whoosh, and pain lanced across my left ass cheek, another across my right before I could gasp.

"God—"

Elijah's cane hit me like a million bees' stings, right above the backs of my knees, and I stumbled, breathing heavy. It took me a few seconds to get my feet beneath me, my breath escaping in pants, my dick leaking so much it dripped off my balls to the floor.

"More," I heard myself say through the buzz rising in decibel between my ears.

He landed hits up my thighs, over my ass, every crack lessening in agony until what I longed for snuck in quietly on its heels. Pain evolved into gloriousness, so goddamn heavenly, so fucking *luscious*, I found myself drifting toward the darkness in my soul.

I floated. Flew free, exactly as Elijah had promised.

CHAPTER 37
ELIJAH

I didn't hold back but gave Jon all the strength of my arm, taking care to not hit him in the same place twice. Red welts rose across his freckled skin, and my dragon squealed in delight—shuddered with every stripe across our beta's flesh. I trembled with the need to release fully to my beast and shift with every moan leaking from Jon's lips.

The scales on the cane would recognize his dragonblood and keep his skin from breaking but would also make his recovery ten times faster than a man-made cane beating would. Even as I made my way up over the tops of his ass cheeks, the lowest welts began to fade.

My heart pounded, and I fought for breath. Sweat coated my body, and I ripped my shirt off, the cotton restricting my movements.

Jon sagged in the chains, his head hanging forward, sweat dripping from his body. His brow smoothed over, and I stepped close, rubbing my jean-clad, aching dick against his ass. He moaned and pushed back against me, even though the friction of my jeans against his raw ass waiting to heal had to sting like hell.

"So perfect," I murmured, and his moan caused my length to jerk against his backside. "You're everything I could ever want in a mate."

Yessss.

Sweetness hit my nose, jerking my head to the door I'd left open on purpose. I dropped the cane and reached around Jon's waist to grab hold of his straining dick.

Dakota stepped into view. She pulled up short, her breath catching and eyes widening as her gaze flitted over her strung-up husband and the leaking dick I slowly worked. She licked her lips, and I smiled over Jon's shoulder when her focus finally landed on my face.

Jon groaned and tipped his head back against my shoulder as I smeared my hand around his crown and down to the root.

"Your wife is here," I murmured against his ear since the blindfold cut off his vision and I wasn't yet sure if he could scent her as easily as I did.

He groaned, his length pulsing in my grip but not spilling.

"I'm going to fuck you now," I said while kicking off my shoes. "And you aren't going to come until I say so."

Jon whimpered and nodded, and I put distance between us, tearing at my jeans with a hint of my talons since Dakota stood on the other side of my beta and wouldn't see the action. I shoved the nearly ruined material off me and pressed against my beta once more, lubing my hand with the slick mess oozing from my dick.

I wanted to thrust into Jon's ass with one shove, demand he submit not just his body but his heart to me as well. I lusted to pull his hair, tilt his head at an angle, and sink my fangs into his neck.

Mark.

Claim.

I hissed against the darkness barely restrained beneath

my skin and held Dakota's gaze while crowding close against our lover. I rubbed against his puckered hole.

Take.

Teeth clenched, I pressed forward, breaching the ring of muscle in Jon's ass without any prep. He groaned and found his footing enough to arch his spine.

My little pain slut. My beta.

I grabbed hold of his hips and glanced down to find the welts nearly gone from his backside. "Relax and let me in," I murmured and watched while I sank my shaft slowly into his hole.

He grunted but didn't tense, so blissed out from the pain that had shifted him toward subspace.

I leaned forward and bit his lobe to remind him where he remained shackled by my chains and was mine for the taking. "*Such* a good boy for me."

He whimpered and fucked himself deeper onto my shaft.

"Yes," I hissed along with my inner beast, pushing into Jon until my drawn-up balls rested near his.

Mine.

"This ass belongs to me," I growled against my beta's ear, my gaze once more on his wide-eyed, panting wife.

Us.

Jon gasped and whined, unaware my dragon claimed him along with my human form. A few curses muttered past his lips as I pulled out to the head and slowly slid back in, my cock bucking hard at being fully sheltered in our beta's heat.

"Give in to what your heart desires, Jon," I said, reaching for his cock once more. "Say you belong to us."

My dragon growled his approval over being included in my request even if Jon wasn't yet aware of that half of me.

Jon shuddered and swallowed a gulp of air.

I continued my slow assault even though he didn't offer us what all of us wanted.

Manipulation.

The fuck it was. I was simply giving him what his body craved. It was Jon who refused to voice the submission he felt deep in his soul, same as I did my place as his alpha.

"Harder," he said on a gasp as I bottomed out in his tightness.

"My kinky pain-whore." I chuckled and bit his earlobe harder, fighting against the swelling tingling in my balls. "We're doing this my way." I whispered my reminder and slowly withdrew again, backing off enough my cock sprang loose from his ass.

"P-please. D-don't stop."

I reached between us and lined my cock up for another slow glide deep inside him. Reaching up, I grabbed hold of his neck and squeezed my other hand around the base of his cock.

His chest rose and fell in rapid succession, his body trembling against mine.

"How badly do you need to come, Jon?" I murmured, my gaze seeking out Dakota, my entire body still, tensed, and ready to explode in release at the sweet scent of her arousal flooding the dungeon.

"So fucking b-bad," Jon rasped, his voice barely audible. "Christ. *Please* move."

I jerked him slowly, swirled my palm over his slick head and grasped his girth once more. Dakota's gaze followed my hand's every move, her pupils huge and black.

"Tell me you're mine," I whispered in Jon ear for him alone, buried deep inside his ass.

He gulped, another shudder rippling down over him.

"Speak what's in your heart, and I'll set you free."

Still, he hesitated.

Choke! Claim!

I squeezed our beta's throat but not nearly enough to satisfy my beast's demands.

We would do no such thing.

Slow gyrations of my hips ground me deep into Jon's body without thrusting like he begged for, and my harsh grip on the base of his dick kept him on the brink of eruption.

"Jon."

"I-I can't."

Dolyn had said the same, unable to allow vulnerability that would have set him free.

My eyelids slammed shut as the reality of why Jon refused to submit to me hit me hard. "You don't trust me."

Jon didn't respond, and I knew I'd spoken truth.

I slowly backed out, my chest aching, but couldn't bear to pull free from the warm clasp of his body around my glans. Doing so would end the connection between us, same as it had with Dolyn on our final night together.

It had also broken the tenuous bond between us, allowing him to leave me while I'd slept.

The melted rock on my left called to me, the tears of dripping granite that shouldn't have been possible but was a heavy reminder of the grief I'd suffered over Dolyn's abandonment.

I would not lose Jon. Refused to.

"Jon." Dakota's whisper pulled my focus toward her. She didn't attempt to give herself release like she usually did while watching us but stood firm in the doorway like a gorgeous goddess of golden flame and flashing eyes.

Jon groaned, his head shifting as though look for her past his blindfold.

"You told me you wanted him," she declared quietly, her tone firm, owning every word.

He grunted an agreement.

"That sixth sense of mine?"

A nod of acknowledgment moved his head.

"It tells me we *can* trust him—and I know you feel it too. Search inside for the truth, baby," she whispered, her voice pleading without a hint of coercion. "He's not your foster father. Not that asshole ex-best friend or that blond douche. This is *Elijah*. The man who took us in and offered us shelter, asking nothing in return. The lonely soul who has showered us with nothing but affection, care, and compassion. His offer of a job wasn't manipulation in attempts to get you to submit to him. He's selfless. Giving. Loving exactly how your heart has always longed for, how I won't ever be able to fulfill."

Jon choked on a sob, his head tipping down, sweat-dampened hair hiding his profile from my view.

Dakota met my eyes in a silent pleading for help to make him *see*.

Submit.

My dragon once more whispered a word I'd been taking in the wrong way. Same as I was the alpha in our triad, I, too, needed to submit to my lovers.

I wrapped my arms around Jon, placing my cheek against the back of his neck. "I give you every piece of me she doesn't own, sweet beta of mine. I'm yours to do with as you please," I murmured and sank into the tight confines of his body that welcomed me like a worn glove.

Home.

Swallowing hard, I clenched my eyes shut. "Yield to me in return—I'm begging you, Jon. Please."

"You…have my consent." The ragged whisper spilled from his lips, and I choked on a sob.

My inner beast roared, scales rippling down my back.

I clutched Jon harder, teeth clenched to keep from biting into his succulent skin. "Thank you. Thank you," I choked on the words, pulled out of his ass, and thrust in fully, unable to bury as deeply into his soul as I longed to do.

"Please."

Jon's choked begging had me reaching for his dick. He leaked pre-cum as freely as mine, slickening my hand.

"Submit to my love, *mon coeur*," I whispered, and he melted against my chest, every muscle in his body limp.

A guttural groan escaped him as I held him upright and fucked into his tight ass, my dick straining to go deeper, harder. I slammed into him while working his length in time with my thrusts until both of us gasped for breath, rattling the chains overhead.

The scent of sex flooded my nose, overcome by the sweetness of our female who still stood in the doorway, lower lip between her teeth and one hand palming a breast beneath my shirt she'd replaced her hiking outfit with.

"Fly free for me, Jon."

He tensed in my arms, twitching and groaning as his cum shot toward Dakota in long ropes from my jerking grasp.

Holding still in his ass, I allowed myself release, my cock pulsing deep inside him, filling him with my seed. Eyes clenched shut, I gave him all that I was as promised, everything I had—my heart, my mind, and my soul—until I emptied. Spent, I wrapped my arms around his sagging body, cradling my beta to my heaving chest as our hearts thrummed in time with each other.

"Thank you," I whispered, my voice broken.

CHAPTER 38

JONATHAN

I fucking soared through the air, wind whipping at me, flooding my heart, my mind with relief. Black scales rippled beneath where I sat as we shot across the sky. My dragon. I recognized the balm-like effect he had on me, quieting my thoughts. Making all things right again. We rose and fell through darkness, our bodies pure light as pinpricks dotted the night sky, waking tingling warmth inside my body.

I could taste Elijah's cum on my tongue even though he'd released inside my ass. He overrode everything, every sense, until all I could feel, smell, and see was him becoming man from the creature I'd dreamed of for as long as I could remember.

"Elijah," I tried to whisper but couldn't hear if I'd managed to speak aloud.

"Shh." His hot breath caressed my ear, my neck, as the blissful tingling in my ass spread through my torso into my limbs and up my neck to my mind.

His cum was more than just tasty. Like Dakota had

claimed, it hit like a shot of espresso even though I hadn't swallowed it down..

Clarity returned like a breath of fresh air, like that first sip of strong coffee peeling open my eyelids in the morning, pulling me from my dreamlike state where reality and fantasy evolved into one.

Darkness coated my vision, and I realized the blindfold meant to help me focus on Elijah's touch still prohibited my sight.

His arms remained around me, but he slowly backed away, his cock slipping from my ass.

I groaned, wanting him to press back in, but he left me empty and dripping his cum. My hole pulsed as though desperate to close up tight and keep his seed inside my body until it soaked in, became one with me.

A low growl rose behind me, and Elijah used two thick fingers to push his seed inside me as though wishing he could breed my ass.

My dick attempted to revive, and I moaned in disappointment that the appendage remained drooped, flaccid between my thighs.

Regardless of my limp dick and wrists remaining shackled overhead, the chains clanked as I twisted slightly in their hold to fuck myself on Elijah's probing fingers stroking over my oversensitive prostate.

Sweetness wafted past my nose.

Dakota...

Her scent flooded through me, and I sucked air deeply into my lungs, having forgotten she'd witnessed my finally giving over to what Elijah and she both wanted.

What I'd been desperate for yet feared.

No such emotion worried me now. I hung suspended although sagging in my bonds, still riding out that sense of freedom Elijah had gifted me. Even after his touch eased from my hole, I felt connected to him, at total peace.

"The chains," Elijah said, and I listened as Dakota shuffled across the room.

The sound of metal ratcheting hit my ears, and my limp arms lowered.

Elijah caught them to keep them from dropping to my sides. He quickly released my wrists, and the chains clanked to the floor as he wrapped his arms around me once more, holding me tight against his chest. "Are you okay, *mon coeur?*" he whispered in my ear while pulling off my blindfold.

My heart.

The meaning of his words flitted through my brain. He'd been calling Dakota that for days, as though to assure her of his feelings for her, but he'd spoken to me—I had no doubt, same as he'd done before releasing me from my mental restraints—to send me soaring. My lips turned upward from the happiness rising inside me.

"Better than," I managed to croak as he pressed a kiss to my neck, his lips warm and branding.

A shudder ripped through me at the thought of wearing his mark, and I blinked in the dim light, breathing in the delicious scent of our combined cum—and my wife's arousal.

She moved in my peripheral vision, drawing my focus. Eyes luminous and green as spring grass, she stared at me with such love and devotion my heart attempted to shatter from the sweetest pain imaginable, one I never wished to escape.

I held her gaze as Elijah gathered me in his arms, and just as I'd always expected, he carried me with ease to the large bed on the far, tear-droplet-like wall.

He sat against the headboard, cradling me in his arms as he had with Dakota countless times. Strong hands clutched me close, possessive fingertips caressing my hair and thigh.

Rather than feeling like less than a man as I'd have done even an hour earlier, I sank into his comfort, soaking in the aftercare he offered.

Dakota approached, her face radiant.

I'd done that—my motherfucking submission.

Chest puffing up, I held out my hand to her.

She settled on the mattress beside us, tucked against Elijah's side, her fingers twining through mine.

We sat in silence for a few moments, our breaths perfectly in tune, making me wonder if all three of our hearts beat at the same time—and for the same reason.

"What held you back?" Elijah broke the stillness.

While at the apartment, I'd promised Dakota that everything would be okay as long as we talked shit out. That we were honest with each other about our feelings. Elijah asked for mine, and him wanting to know more of me settling another piece of my soul into place.

He cared, exactly as Dakota had claimed, perhaps, even loved me as she did.

"Fear," I answered honestly. "Of trusting but also losing you—or my wife. She's…drawn to people." Flashes of faces in her strange file sprang to life in my head, the most prominent being that blond douche and the latest who'd severely snagged her attention, Ashley. As usual, unrest snaked through my guts, but I no longer questioned why it hadn't with Elijah.

We had been meant to meet him. Fate had brought us together, and I had no choice other than to submit to her will, which would bring us nothing but joy in the future I no longer doubted.

I closed my eyes and rubbed my face against the light dusting of hair on Elijah's chest.

A low rumbled growl of contentment sounded beneath my ear.

"You're the first person she's felt that for who didn't rouse…darkness in me, I suppose you could call it," I continued. "Maddening jealousy, a possessive insecurity I don't usually experience with her. Same with Ashley."

"My secretary?" Elijah asked, his slow strokes on my skin and hair stilling.

"Yeah. Not sure why that pissed me off. Dakota only likes dick."

She squeezed my fingers. "Only yours and Elijah's."

"They're the only two you've had," I reminded her.

"The only two I'll ever *want*," she tossed back.

I rubbed my thumb over the back of her hand before lifting our clasped palms to my mouth to brush my lips over her knuckles.

"There's nothing wrong with finding someone beautiful or experiencing attraction," Elijah stated quietly. "It's who you've chosen to attach yourself to, who you remain *loyal* to, that matters in the end."

"Who you *love*," Dakota whispered.

I shifted to sit atop Elijah's lap rather than melting into him, needing to see my wife's face. "You have nothing to be ashamed of, baby. No more wallowing in guilt when you feel that draw, when that strange tingle in your head telling you're somehow connected to these strangers. They don't matter."

"Connected?"

Dakota nodded at Elijah's asking for clarity. "It's more than simply a sense that I've seen them before—or even know them. It's…deeper than that. Something on almost a primal level. I can't really explain what it is." She shrugged, her shoulders sagging.

A second later, her head whipped to the open dungeon door.

Jesus fucking Christ.

"Talking about *gifts*," I muttered, recognizing the aware-ness stiffening her body and wary as fuck since everything had seemed to be going perfect for a change.

"What is it?" Elijah set me off his lap, his instincts rising to the surface, same as mine.

"I..." Dakota toward us, and I recognized the confusion on her face.

"Someone is here," I stated what she questioned, consid-ering the lair we hid inside that no one else knew about according to Elijah. "A strange one."

She turned back toward the door. "Yes."

Elijah hopped off the bed and grabbed his jeans off the floor. "No one can get past my security system."

"Dakota wouldn't lie," I said, sliding off the bed with the intent to follow him, realizing as I did so that there was no residual pain, no lingering ache from the cane he'd wielded to bring me the greatest pleasure I'd ever known.

A few muttered curses flew past Elijah's lips, and he started toward the door, only half-dressed and in bare feet. "Stay here."

His growled command didn't slow my instinctual need to remain on his heels, but he halted in the doorway and spun. Darkness swirled within his pupils, and I blinked as the image of my dragon flickered around his body.

Guess a part of my brain still lingered in that floaty place he'd spirited me away to.

"Please." Elijah pleaded, and I fucking *felt* his unease, his worry for us as he laid his hand on my bare chest. He touched his own with his other hand. "I can sense your desire to protect me but remain here where it's safe. I beg of you. If anything happened to either you or our female..."

Lips pressed tight, I dipped my head once, loving how he'd claimed my wife as *ours*.

He turned and sprinted up the hallway.

The ache that had knifed at my chest when he'd left us to collect our things in New York didn't radiate pain through my sternum like I'd expected. Elijah was no longer in sight, but his essence remained in my head and gut, like he'd taken up residence there.

"Who do you think it is?" Dakota asked, her voice small and shaking.

I turned to find her huddled on the bed, arms wrapped around herself and trembling.

"Dakota," I said, striding to grab her up in a comforting hold, her feet dangling in the air. Face buried in her neck, I breathed her in as she melted against my chest. "Baby—it's going to be all right. There's no person on the face of the planet that mountain of a man of ours can't handle. I can promise you that."

"You love him, don't you?" she whispered, and I shifted so I could meet her gaze.

Even if the truth hurt her, I had to speak it. Loving Elijah as I did my wife, couldn't be helped or ignored even if the word might sting. "Yes."

Tears glistened in her eyes. "Is it wrong of us to love two people at once? The same need and deep longing to be one with them?"

"Fuck, no." I'd never felt so damn sure of anything in my life. "Is it wrong of me to like being chained up and beat half to death—and get off from it?"

She attempted to hold back a smile. "You're hot as fuck when you submit like that, but next time, I'm going to be on my knees in front of you."

The image in my head of the three of us connected in that way brought back what had landed us in Elijah's dungeon to begin with.

"I lost my job because I refused to share you with my asshole ex-best friend."

"*What?*" Dakota's eyebrows furrowed.

"He wanted a threesome, and I said no."

"My God, Jon—*that's* why you feared giving into this pull toward Elijah?"

I nodded. "His lust for you dissolved my only friendship outside of what you and I have. My ability to provide for us was taken away because of it. I'd been manipulated and lost everything out of loyalty to you—*not* that I'm blaming you." I swallowed hard. "That asshole told me to make the decision for you, that you would do whatever I asked of you."

I hadn't wanted a threesome with him, but those final words in his pleading had haunted me. Still fucking did.

"That's why I pushed you to decide for yourself, baby. Couldn't bear the thought of forcing what my body desired with Elijah and find ourselves in even deeper shit than we already were."

"We can still leave, Jon."

I whipped my head up to find her eyes troubled. "Is that what you want?"

She shook her head without hesitation. "But if that's what you need—"

"No. This thing we have going on with Elijah makes me feel...whole. Complete. Remember how you said you thought something was missing back when that blond douche drew you away from me and I got all insecure and pissed off?"

Dakota cringed. "As if I could ever forget."

"I finally understand. It was Elijah."

Her eyes welled with tears as she stared up at me. "We're staying."

"Exploring this triad and hopefully strengthening whatever this is binding us together with him," I tacked on.

"We have to tell Elijah. Right now."

I understood her need for haste but glanced at the open

doorway, the silence deafening. Unease itched my feet, but I didn't want to ignore what he'd laid down as a clear command. "He told us to stay put."

"Disobedience usually means punishment," Dakota stated, her tone suggestive as fuck.

One of my eyebrows jacked up, and she bit her lower lip. "Do you want to see me strung up again, or are you just curious as hell what strange person managed to slip into our home undetected?"

"Think it's Ashley? She's his secretary, so surely she knows where he lives."

"He said *no one* knows."

Dakota chewed on the inside of her lip, and I brushed my thumb over the abused flesh.

"None of that."

"Let's go, Jon—I have this weird feeling growing in my stomach, and I don't like it."

Hurry.

Trusting her instincts and that goddamned voice in the back of my head, I grabbed my pants and quickly yanked them up over my junk before reaching for my wife's hand.

As one, we chose to follow after Elijah, and with every step closer toward him, a sense of urgency moved my feet faster.

CHAPTER 39

ELIJAH

Only one being—one *person*—knew about my home and how to get through the wards and my home's defenses without Sybil alerting me of an intruder.

I sprinted up the stairs, my stomach in knots, hoping like hell Dakota's senses lied while the beast inside me lay quiet but poised, ready to strike in defense of our mates. I would have preferred to remain in the perfection of how things had fallen into place among the three of us, how fate had steered us through to the point of readiness to bond fully. Jon's complete submission had been a gorgeous sight to behold, as equally fulfilling as having Dakota connect with her true self and gift her love to me.

But our moment had been interrupted, and I feared what —*who*—I would find. Memories dragged to the surface of my mind, causing piercing grief to cut me open and make me bleed. I'd hoped gaining my beta's consent to own him fully would have erased what I'd been desperate to be rid of for years.

I threw open the door leading into the kitchen, and it banged against the wall.

I stumbled to a halt as though I'd slammed into a slab of granite, my dragon hissing his displeasure at the man I'd expected and hoped to never see again after having met my fated mates.

There was a single dragonblood who had the ability to enter my lair without Sybil alerting me.

He'd owned my heart for over seventy years.

"Dolyn." His name left my lips in a rush, turning the naked man from facing the slider he shut behind him.

The light in his amber eyes, the perfection of his golden body, and his gorgeous yet hesitant smile slammed into me with the force of a sudden gale, leaving me on unsteady ground. "Elijah."

His voice hit me like a punch to the sternum, ripping the air from my lungs. Why now? Why show up after I'd pined for a decade for his return and had just grabbed hold of what fate finally gifted me?

My heart attempted to pound from my chest, but I couldn't move. Couldn't blink. "You—you're..."

Dolyn started toward me, his shoulders broader than I remembered even though they appeared rounded by defeat, his dirty blond hair cut shorter than I'd ever seen. He was still achingly beautiful as ever regardless of the heaviness that hung over him that seemed doubled than when last we'd stood before each other.

He paused an arm's length away and sank to his knees, head bowed in a show of true submission he'd denied me for our entire time spent together.

My beast growled, but it sounded more like disgust than bitterness to my inner ear. At least the other half of me offered the strength my suffering human side lacked in that moment.

"Where have you been, and what are you doing here uninvited? Walking back in here like you didn't leave without a trace ten years ago?"

"I—I needed time."

"Time for *what?*"

He lifted his broken expression upward, the agony radiating off him drawing on my empathy I hated in that moment, same as the beast did inside me, calling me weak. "To find her."

The hurt Dolyn had caused fell over me once more like the weight of a mountain. I fought to keep from buckling beneath its heaviness.

How could he possibly forget the truth considering all we'd been through together?

"There is no *her* for us Dolyn. We searched together for years. *Years* and found no trace of a dragonblood female to force a bond with."

"But I just hoped…" Dolyn's eyes implored me to hear him out. "You yearned for her more than anything, including me, and I felt sure that if I could just locate a female, gift her to you, that you would finally relent and accept me as your alpha. That we could live out the rest of our years as we are meant to."

"You were never born to lead, Dolyn," I stated, my voice finding some of its strength at his audacity to continue to insist he was my alpha.

A shuddered sigh wracked his body at my feet. "I'm home and ready to submit to what fate has demanded, seeing as we're the last two Blood Born to walk this earth," he whispered without a hint of true submission or joy in his voice.

No. Not ours.

The scent of Jon and Dakota wafted up the stairwell from where I'd left them, sending another harsh ache through my chest but one that flooded my soul with peace instead of pain.

Dolyn and I had never experienced the kind of connection I did with my intended mates. Yes, I'd cared for him, attempted to help him accept who he was, but he'd denied me at every turn, refusing to accept his place, which would have brought a sense of fulfillment he still fought hard to find.

He had never been meant for me, merely a companion to pass the time while Jon and Dakota became of age. Still, my heart hurt at the memory of all the years Dolyn and I had shared and how neither of us had enjoyed a hint of true satisfaction in playing the roles as we had with each other.

"Our stations in this life are determined by dragonblood," I reminded him with a soft tone, hoping to ease the further disappointment awaiting him. "There's no changing what has been destined by fate."

Another musk and sweet scent ghosted past my nostrils.

Yessss. They *are ours.*

Dolyn's nostrils flared as though his heightened sense of smell had alerted him we weren't alone. He scrambled back to his feet, his gaze flitting over my shoulder. I didn't doubt he sensed my two lovers down in the dungeon. His eyes hardened, erasing what little light he'd had left shining in his amber orbs, but I couldn't rouse a single shred of empathy for the pain I was about to inflict on his heart.

Hands fisted at his sides, he glowered. "What—"

A low growl rumbled my chest, and I moved to stand in front of the doorway, although no trace of aggression lined Dolyn's face, no suggestion he readied to sprint down the stairs and hurt my lovers or take for himself what belonged to me.

He raised his nose and sniffed, brow furrowing deeper.

The confusion dissolved as he blinked, his eyes widening. "You've actually allowed others into our home?"

"*My* home," I corrected him, my tone firm.

Dolyn ignored the truth I'd spoken, his focus intent over my shoulder. "They're...*human.*" His golden eyes I used to get lost in hardened like stone as they jerked toward me. "You've chosen them? Over me? They're...they're *nothing*! Completely unworthy of you!"

I bared my teeth, my body tensing with the need to shift, the need to rip Dolyn limb from limb for saying such things about Jon and Dakota. "I've not yet claimed them," I growled, "but I will—if they'll have me."

"They aren't of the same blood!"

"They *are*," I snapped as awareness they approached swept over me. "They are my fated mates, Dolyn." I fought off the dragon shrieking beneath my skin with every ounce of strength I possessed. Shifting and revealing my real shape before telling them the truth of who we were could ruin everything. "They're mine. My beta. My female. A trace of the dragonblood flows through their veins—"

"It's not possible!"

"It is *truth*," I spat, my insides burning like the earth's core. "Perhaps you can't recognize it because they aren't yours to love!" As for me, I could sense the ancient blood approaching, and it called to me on a primal level. To cherish and bring pleasure.

Protect.

Dolyn snorted, his chin lifting in a tilt haughty enough he peered down his nose at me. "Even if they *do* carry a trace of our superior DNA, they'll never shift. We are the only two left of the original lineage, Elijah. Whoever they are, they're not good enough. How can you possibly believe them to be—"

"No. Fucking. *Way*." Jon swore from behind me at the same time a horrified gasp left Dakota's lips.

My inner beast whimpered at the sudden flare of emotion swarming my senses from Dolyn in front of me and both of my true mates behind me.

I was alpha, the one meant to lead us, but in that moment, I knew nothing but bafflement and complete unrest.

What cruel trick had fate played?

CHAPTER 40
DAKOTA

"You!" Jon stormed forward, hands fisting like he readied to pummel the naked blond douche for once more intruding on our peace.

Elijah grasped his arm so he couldn't stride past, halting my husband in his tracks. "You know him?" Careful wariness laced his question.

"Not personally, thank fuck." My husband spat the words with unmistakable disdain.

"Jon, Dolyn," Elijah stated, barely restrained anger simmering beneath the proper graciousness he offered to the naked man who'd let himself into our home as though he shared in ownership. "Dolyn, Jon."

Tension and energy radiated throughout the cavern, strong enough to raise the hairs on my forearms and not in the usual delicious way the nearness of my two lovers enticed. Shivering and arms wrapped around my trembling core, I stared at the man who had almost ruined my relationship with Jon years earlier.

Recognition came easy as he had a face I would never forget, same as it must have been for Jon when first laying eyes on Dolyn. The man had strong features as perfect as Elijah's. Golden skin and hair and the most gorgeous amber-like eyes. His body was built similarly to Elijah's, right down to the length and girth of his heavy cock between his thighs, but nothing about him aroused me like either of my lovers did. The pull toward him wasn't as strong as it'd been once before either, but this time I realized the truth of why I'd been drawn to him as though his soul pulled me in like a tractor beam.

The scent of fire and brimstone—*Elijah*—clung to Dolyn.

It'd been our lover's aura and energy lingering on the stranger long after it should have faded that had drawn me so intensely, even though we hadn't spoken a single word to each other. Not his blond perfection, not the stunning smile he'd flashed at me while striding past and leaving me breathless as only Jon had ever done. This was the man that had made me notice something was missing in my life, but it hadn't been *him* I'd been desperate for.

It'd been the scent of Elijah, the third meant to fill the emptiness I hadn't realized resided in my soul.

And the golden god known as Dolyn? I had no doubt in my mind that he was the man who'd left and broken Elijah's heart, the one I knew Elijah still pined for regardless of my husband and I becoming involved with him.

Fear flared in my head at that knowledge pinged to life, burning clear down to my legs and causing my knees to weaken.

I'd finally become comfortable in who I was, and this man's arrival stirred up a hornet nest of emotions, a complete upheaval of that happily-ever-after triad I'd dreamed about. My mind set on staying in the cavern with my lovers until my heart beat its last, but Elijah's connection with the man ran deeper than that which he shared with both me and Jon. I feared Dolyn would attempt to replace my husband in our dynamic. Or perhaps his return would erase all of Elijah's interest in both Jon and me.

I mean, the intruder had the body of a god and was Elijah's match in almost every way except for their opposing energy.

My gaze snapped from one man to the next—Elijah's stare on the blond, Jon's scowl focused on the same place.

And Dolyn?

He studied *me*, ignoring both Elijah and Jon who stood like a warrior wall between us, both tensed and seemingly on the verge of pouncing like a couple of lions to defend me if needed. "I've seen you before."

I swallowed hard, nodding, baffled why Dolyn couldn't care less about the two men ready to rip him to shreds should he speak the wrong word.

Safe.

Twin, low growls sounded from my lovers, and warmth flooded through me regardless of my fear, a sense of belonging—a promise that nothing would tear us apart.

"New York," Dolyn suggested, although he sounded sure rather than posing a question.

"A mere passing on the street," I whispered, my insides still a riotous mess. How did I know it'd been Elijah on him that had drawn me to follow him up the street? Why would I even think that?

My fanciful imagination, most likely.

No. Truth.

The quiet whispers assured me I wasn't losing my mind, even though the fact I heard a voice to begin with suggested I did.

"You followed me for two blocks before that man—" he gestured at Jon "—caught up and caused a bit of a scene."

I cringed at the memory of how Jon's low hiss of anger hadn't mirrored the devastation in his eyes when I'd told him that the man somehow had what I'd been missing. The words had spilled without thought. I hadn't considered how my claim might make my other half feel, the devastation it would wreck on his already insecure nature.

It hadn't been a sexual draw to Dolyn but one of energy, which I'd tried to explain to Jon, but his jealousy had overshadowed all ability to think rationally. I'd been his, the only person that had ever belonged to him, and Dolyn had proven a threat to the peace he'd found in sharing his life with me. Because of his upbringing, Jon had always been cautious with others. Never acted impulsively either. But that situation I'd placed him in was a scenario where there hadn't been time to plan. He'd simply reacted on instinct, which called on anger to shield his heart that I'd broken without intending to.

He'd been unkind. Spewed words I hoped to never hear ever again—feared it to the place I'd submitted to him in every way once we'd made amends. I'd looked to him to make all our decisions which I'd recently learned had almost torn us apart again. Some would call it codependency or perhaps toxic, but something far beyond natural tied me and my husband together.

My request for space from each other due to the Dolyn incident had simply been for me to gain clarity and lick my wounds from pure embarrassment, but Jon hadn't taken it as anything but a breakup, considering his abandonment issues. He'd been heartbroken, as had I, and it hadn't been more than a handful of days before I'd begged for forgiveness, pleading with him to take me back.

Never had emotions wrecked me so thoroughly, but in that moment, I recognized I faced even sharper heartache, regardless of the assurance both men had offered me.

Jon had basically admitted that his cynicism of all strangers drawing me in atop his asshole ex-boss's treatment was what had hindered him from giving himself fully to

Elijah. And now this blond douche, as he'd been named by my husband, had to show up and potentially ruin the best thing that had ever happened to us.

Rather than sit back this time, I needed to be proactive.

Connect.

At the voice whispering in my head, I stepped forward to stand behind the men and grasped Jon's right hand in my own. He clutched at me like a lifeline, and I reached around to wrap my other hand around Elijah's left fist, which hung at his side.

Both men shuddered as though they'd been desperate for my soothing touch, and I swore gentle energy rippled through the circle I'd created even though they both stood facing away from me. Shoulders relaxed. Breaths came easier. But most of all, the tension thickening the air lessened, allowing my heartbeat to slow and mind to rest. We were meant to be together, of that, I had no doubt.

Dolyn's brow furrowed as he watched the three of us intently, and I tilted my chin up while peeking between my men, silently telling Dolyn to do his worst. We three would stand the test of time.

Elijah was our home, our true family, and I could only imagine the struggle of wondering what the fuck was going on inside Jon's head, the insecurities that must be screaming for him to replace the walls Elijah had recently torn down.

I longed to fight further for what we had found with him, but there was only one person who could assure Jon of his place.

It was Elijah who would need to still the overwhelming upheaval of emotions Jon must be feeling facing Elijah's ex-lover.

Dolyn gave Elijah his full attention, his amber eyes burning bright with what seemed like golden flames. "These are the two you claim belong to you? Common humans who bicker on the streets without a care of what others might think? They have no *class*, Elijah. No proper bearing. Your parents would be ashamed."

"What the actual fuck, man?" Jon attempted to bolt forward, but Elijah held him steady with his grip on my husband's forearm, his focus never wavering from Dolyn's face.

"*I* belong to *them*, Dolyn," Elijah stated quietly when I'd expected a roar of anger, and strangely, a flash of claws. "My heart, my soul, my mind. Every part of me I would lay at their feet every day until eternity passes if they'll have me."

CHAPTER 41

JONATHAN

Elijah's words hit me like a kick to the gut, stealing my breath. Warmth spread through me as I clutched at Dakota's hand.

Mate.

The word whispered in my mind as I studied the naked asshole in our home. Some hidden piece of my soul lusted to rip through my skin and shred the intruder, slice his big dick off and shove it down his throat until he choked. He was the man who had broken Elijah's heart. The one who'd almost ended me and Dakota years earlier.

Easily the same size and width of Elijah, the douche's presence filled the cavern like Elijah's did, but he didn't draw me in like our lover—even if most women would find the blondish god-like man to be hot as fuck, which even I couldn't deny. But no magnetism reached across the distance, no awareness of his body or scent filled me with need.

Only Elijah.

Mine.

A low growl rumbled my chest so reminiscent of what I'd heard from Elijah a few times that a desire to laugh welled up alongside the possessive sound leaving my lips.

"You would give yourself to these...*humans*." The man spat the word like a curse, his brow furrowed, shoulders tensing. "Seriously, Elijah? You're royalty. Far above these..." He waved his hand, grimacing at me and my wife with disgust in his eyes.

Another low rumble rose from Elijah's chest, pulling my full focus.

The dark shadow of my dragon flickered around Elijah's shoulders, causing other memories of to click into place like perfect puzzle pieces, and suddenly, I *knew*.

"Holy motherfucking mother of God—dragonblood," I whispered, my mind fucking *blown*.

Elijah's breath caught, and he stilled.

I stared at his profile, willing him to face me, to tell me the truth he had withheld from us.

"My God," Dakota whispered, her small hand squeezing mine as she realized her daydreaming perhaps *wasn't* fantasy.

"Elijah, is it true?" I rasped, staring at the hair which was the same color of the scaled armor, the crop—and my dragon with the pale eyes.

His shoulders slumped. "Yes," he finally said but still didn't take his gaze off Dolyn.

Flashes of memories assaulted my brain from early childhood of the dragon had been my constant companion. I'd simply needed to close my eyes, and he had been there to carry me away from pain and sadness. Even before I learned what emotions were and how to attempt to regulate them, my imaginary friend carried me through, cradling me against his warmth, his low rumble—almost like a cat's purr—steady beneath my face when I'd clung to him.

All in my head, of course. Concocted as a means for my mind to help me deal with shit.

Or had he been?

"Was it you?" I asked, my voice ragged as fuck, my pulse thrumming in my ears. "Those nights..." I swallowed hard, my eyes stinging. "Seeing me through the shit of my childhood until I met Dakota? And even after, you visited me in my dreams."

"I have no recollection of these actions, but perhaps fate allowed future memories of your alpha to lead and offer you strength in your time of need," Elijah confessed, finally giving me his full attention.

His large black pupils swirled same as I *swore* I'd glimpsed on occasion since meeting him, but a shit ton of vulnerability and wariness I still experienced filled them as he carefully watched me.

Did he fear my reaction to the truth of who—*what*—he was?

For some reason, the fact he wasn't purely human didn't surprise me like it should have. Too many unnatural things had gone down since he showed up in our camp, including how his energy along with my wife's radiated through me as though Dakota taking our hands had somehow linked our emotions.

But I sure as fuck couldn't decide what I felt about him lying to us.

I had promised myself to offer nothing but honesty in figuring out this triad shit and perhaps naively expected the same from him.

"Explain, Elijah," I demanded, hating how my voice shook and betrayed my apprehension.

"The dragonblood..." He paused, and I bit my tongue to keep from ordering him to quit stalling, to tell us everything he'd been withholding before I blew a fucking gasket and lost my shit. "A mere drop flows through both of you."

Yes.

I blinked at the whisper, that goddamned voice that had insisted from the beginning Elijah had been brought into our lives for a purpose.

Elijah's gaze flickered over my face as though drinking in every line and freckle, like the sight of me alone filled a part of his soul.

Warmth spread through my chest, a desire to step closer, but I held still and waited for further explanation.

"I could feel you, see you, on the breeze, and I sought you out."

"Our camp," I said.

Elijah nodded. "The dragonblood in you spoke to the beast inside me, and I knew you were my fated mates. Both of you. The beta and female I have longed for my entire life." His breath left in a rush, and his shoulders slumped. "I am not human, Jon. I am a shifter, a dragon of old, an ancient soul almost five hundred years of age."

"My God," Dakota whispered again, and I glanced over at her to find her eyes the size of saucers, staring at Elijah. She clutched his fist as though needing the connection between them to keep her grounded.

She held tight to the man—the dragon shifter—who wanted us, *both* of us, even though according to the blond douche, we weren't "good" enough. And royal blood? What a fucking joke. She and I were far from it, mere orphans, hicks from the sticks of upstate New York.

And yet Elijah had told Dolyn he belonged to us.

He may have withheld truth—hell, outright lied a few times from what I could recall in that moment—but I couldn't deny the naked honesty in his voice and the magnetic pull between us from the second our gazes had first collided.

"You are the bonding gateway between an alpha and female, Jon," he continued, searching out my eyes, imploring me to understand. "That is the gift of a beta—they're necessary, their purpose as essential to our bond as the precious female who will carry our seed. An alpha is nothing without his beta."

"Elijah—"

I shot my head toward Dolyn and growled, stilling his vocal cords. Possessiveness flooded through me, and in that moment, I would stare down a hundred golden dragons in order to protect what belonged to me.

He ignored me, his focus on Elijah. "Did you feed them your seed that would bind them to you without their consent as our people of old practiced? Did you manipulate these two worthless creatures into submission as your beast wanted to do with me?"

"I would never!" Elijah's voice raised. "Yes, I had the opportunity but denied my baser instincts as is right!"

Dolyn continued to glare, disbelieving, although why he gave a shit about our consent, I had no fucking clue.

"He offered us the freedom to choose at every cross-roads," Dakota whispered. There was no coercion involved."

Connect.

I realized Elijah still clutched my left forearm, but it wasn't enough.

Squeezing Dakota's fingers with my right hand, I twisted from Elijah's grasp.

He whimpered as though I'd physically hurt him, but I quickly laced my fingers through his.

My throat tightened as a ripple swept through Elijah. His eyelids fluttered closed, and he filled his lungs with a shuddered sigh. As though the press of our palms opened a gateway, I caught hints of his emotions and energy creep up my left arm, across my chest, and down my right toward Dakota, who stood behind us. Nothing had ever felt so right in my life. So *fucking* good. Even better than soaring after having my ass handed to me while strung up in the dungeon.

I lifted my head and stared Dolyn in the eye while swallowing away my outward emotion. "Elijah belongs to *us*. He is our mate." I inhaled until it hurt. "My lover. My alpha, and that seed you seem jealous about him denying us so far? I'm gonna gobble that shit up and feed it to my wife. Let her suck it off my tongue the second your unwanted ass is gone from our home."

Elijah's breath caught again, and Dolyn's gaze narrowed once more as it settled on him as though I didn't exist. "You would choose the half-breeds over the last full Blood Born on this earth?" he asked Elijah as though I hadn't spoken a word.

"Fate has destined what is to be among us three," Elijah stated quietly. Kindly, even, when I was ready to physically kick Dolyn out of the space he had no business being in. "I won't give up her gift of my two mates for anything—royal blood or no."

"You would leave me stranded?" His voice rose, his hands fisting at his sides, whiskey-colored eyes widening. "Alone in this world where my years of searching has proved that I have no hope of finding another?"

"Isn't that exactly what you did to me a decade ago?"

Point to Elijah.

I had to bite my tongue to keep from hissing my pleasure.

"I'm sorry fate hasn't been as kind to you as it has to me after the choice you made to break my heart," Elijah continued.

Dakota shifted behind me, drawing my focus over my

shoulder. Brow furrowed, she peered at Dolyn with a look I recognized.

One I knew well—but this time, clarity lit in her eyes.

That sixth sense?

It *was* real, and I felt sure shit was about to get a whole lot more interesting.

That strange voice in my head snickered, and I relaxed fully, ready to see what my wife was about to reveal.

CHAPTER 42

DAKOTA

The revelation that the paranormal wasn't fiction made my head spin. And the ease with which Jon submitted to what Elijah called being fated mates almost knocked my feet from beneath me. I wanted to pinch myself but couldn't release my hold on Jon's hand or Elijah's fist as a wave of emotions far beyond my own trickled through my mind. Heartache, love, unbelievable joy, trust… all radiating through the tenuous bond I felt through touching them both.

I stared at Elijah's ex-lover, the one who had broken his heart in order to search out their female and had ended up alone because he couldn't be patient and wait for his own destiny.

Believing in fate also meant he had to leave the White Mountains so that Elijah could find the two who belonged to him as he'd declared Jon and I did.

My emotions tumbled over the more muffled ones from both Jon and Elijah—for I was sure the circle my husband created had somehow swept away the veil that kept us from connecting completely.

As for Dolyn, although his close proximity didn't pull on me like it had the first time, his presence alone still drew me in with more strength than any other face I'd caught on camera and tucked away in my strange file.

He claimed to be the only other dragonblood.

Perhaps…

"Dolyn," I whispered, breaking the stillness among the four of us.

His gaze swung my way, and he didn't bother hiding the disgust from his eyes. Darkness swirled in his pupils, same as I'd seen in Elijah while in the basement—the beast within.

Half-giddy over the reminder I lived a real-life fairytale, I considered pinching myself again but knew without doubt I would feel the pain if I did. "There are more of us than you believe."

He scoffed, massive arms crossing over his chest, but I wasn't interested in drinking in the sight of how his muscles popped in a show of strength. Façade, I realized, *not* confidence. The man hurt, suffered already, for the choice he'd made in abandoning Elijah. "And you know this *how?*"

"I—" I blew a breath from my lips. "I'm drawn to some people, like we connected in a past life or something. It's like if I look long enough, focus harder, that I might see them— what and who they are inside."

His lip curled as he glanced down over my body. "Elijah claims a 'mere drop' of dragonblood flows in your veins, and you believe that's enough to give you one of the gifts of our kind?"

"Gifts?"

"Mythical abilities long before my parents' time," Elijah said, but his voice didn't hold the disbelief Dolan's did. His fist relaxed beneath my hold.

Me—us.

I blinked at the voice in my head, the soft words bringing

clarity to my mind of what I truly was. I no longer had to submit myself to guilt, that the draw toward others in my heart was cheating in some way.

I held the power within myself to set us all free.

Something compelled me forward, and I released my grasp on both Elijah and Jon to skirt around my husband.

"What are you—" Jon's question shut off at Elijah's shushing him.

"Her choice, *mon coeur*."

I glanced back at Elijah to find his eyes overflowing with love and pride for me stepping forward of my own volition. Heat rushed through me at the memory of warm scales rubbing between my thighs. "I dreamed of your true form countless times since touching you."

"Then perhaps you *are* gifted—one drawn by dragonblood," he murmured, his eyes glinting with blue fire.

Truth.

Strengthened by the inner voice I accepted wholeheartedly, I turned.

Dolyn's light brown eyes narrowed as they settled on me. Disgust still radiated from his stare but a hint of insecurity as well.

My shaking legs took me toward the man who had set something in motion so profound, so *otherworldly* that my brain still wanted to argue my new reality.

A quick pinch to the back of my hand promised that I *wasn't* dreaming. Insides fluttering with combined fear and excitement, I shuffled close to the man I'd once chased after through the streets of New York because he had something I wanted but hadn't known it at the time—the scent of my alpha clinging to him.

Dolyn eyed me warily but didn't flinch when I lifted my hand.

Both men behind me growled quietly, and I swallowed a

giddy snickering that would make me sound like a cackling hyena who'd lost her marbles.

Neither of my lovers made a move to stop me though.

"May I?" I whispered, holding Dolyn's stare.

He hesitated, a muscle ticking in his jaw.

"Dolyn." Elijah stated his name quietly but with authority.

The golden god dipped his head in agreement, his face flushed.

Warmth radiated from Dolyn's chest before I even laid my hand on him. Heat snaked between the slight distance separating us but not in a sexual manner. The draw I'd felt so often with others before intensified, and his frown dissipated, eyes widening as though he too recognized the connection between us.

My palm pressed against him—skin to skin.

A flash of absolute recognition swept through my mind, the *thing* that had always been at the edge of my consciousness whenever coming across a strange one. I saw Dolyn's golden dragon with its glowing amber eyes flashing in sunlight. The spines along his back down to the tip of his tail. His roar blasting from a massive gaping jaw didn't fill our cavern or my ears, but I experienced his pain, his anger, his *disbelief* at what flowed between us.

Other pictures wavered through my mind, settling the underlying continual unrest that the man I touched might still find a way to replace Jon as Elijah's beta.

That sixth sense I'd hated about myself?

It was the answer to us all finding true contentment.

"Not possible," I heard Dolyn whisper through the sudden rush of wind in my ears.

I closed my eyes against the feelings my touch invoked in him and radiated back to me, determined to pull the grainy images in my head into better focus.

Another black dragon but smaller, lither than my Elijah—with eyes as brilliant a green as dew-kissed grass.

A tiny dragon with grayish scales and purple-blue eyes...

"Ashley." I breathed a mere whisper for him alone, my eyelids popping open to land on a disbelieving gaze with swirling pupils. "She is the one you've been searching for."

Dolyn blinked down at me, and I realized he had clasped his huge hand over the back of mine, holding my palm tight against his chest. "I saw her in my mind," he croaked. "How—how is that possible?"

"She's mostly human," I whispered, peering up into his troubled gaze as he fought to believe what I had seen, what our connection had shared with him. His heart beat heavy under my hand, and I held his gaze without fear or unease until his tumbling emotions settled slightly.

He inhaled deeply as though hoping to scent her through my memory. "My female."

He hadn't asked a question, but I found myself nodding. "She belongs to you. The other I didn't recognize."

His exhale left in a rush. "Nor did I. But the female—how is it you know her?"

"Ashley is Elijah's secretary."

"What?" Elijah's gasped word broke the bond between me and Dolyn, and I turned, my hand dropping from his chest.

Elijah stared at me, eyes wide. "That's impossible! How could I not have known she is Blood Born?" He breathed the question as though to himself rather than asking me for an explanation.

I tried for a smile, which wobbled at best.

"*Mon coeur,*" he whispered and beckoned to me with his free hand.

Two quick steps and I pressed against his chest, the scent of fire and the warmth of his skin against my cheek settling the riot that had initiated the second I'd lost contact with him.

"You're so fucking fierce, baby. Goddamn, do I love you." Jon's arms wrapped around me from behind, trapping me between my men, settling everything inside me.

Home.

I breathed a heavy sigh at the quiet whisper, so overwhelmed that my eyes stung.

"Ashley O'Connor," Elijah said, his low voice rumbling beneath my ear. "She's an absent-minded, timid little thing—much more fragile than the female humans we used to share, Dolyn. Don't hurt her."

The command from my alpha rang out with a finality that promised retribution if ignored.

"I—I'm sorry, Elijah," Dolyn murmured, his own heartache once more reaching to caress my mind, but a sliver of hope had seemed to ease his pain. "I apologize for abandoning you without a word even if my intentions had been pure. I—I thought I was doing right in leaving, hoping to locate what we were both so desperate to have."

Sorry I wasn't enough, I felt sure Dolyn wanted to add.

I turned my face from where I'd burrowed against Elijah's chest in order to connect with Dolyn's eyes.

Emotion poured from him, complete conflicting chaos.

"Go to her," I whispered, smiling through the tears hazing my vision, "and find your alpha mate together."

"You mean our beta," he corrected me—but I wasn't so sure he spoke truth.

"A gifted one of the ancient blood has revealed your destined mates," Elijah assured him while squeezing me tight. "Do as she says and claim them as fate intended."

Dolyn's gaze roamed over the three of us pressed together as Jon nuzzled against my hair.

Lips pursed, Dolyn nodded and spun. I buried my face

once more in Elijah's chest. He didn't speak, but the slider opened and closed with finality.

Elijah's chest heaved a heavy exhale. "Are you all right?" he murmured.

I nodded, eyes clenched shut.

"The fuck is he doing?" Jon asked, releasing his hold on us. He took a step forward, and I turned from Elijah, my gaze following my husband's toward the massive windows over-looking the veranda.

Dolyn's stood on the edge, his back covered in rippling muscle and tattoos. He glanced over his shoulder and dipped his head even though he couldn't see through the one-way glass.

He threw himself off the edge

I shrieked, clutching at Elijah's arm.

"Fuck!" Jon took a quick step forward, but Elijah grabbed his wrist.

"Wait, *mon coeur*."

A golden, scaled body shot upward, disappearing within a heartbeat as though becoming one with the blue of the sky.

Jon jolted back, bumping against Elijah's shoulder. "Holy fucking hell!"

A hysterical gasped giggle burst from me. "Somebody else pinch me. Please—this can't be real!"

"I would rather love you—both of you—if you'll have me?"

Elijah's murmured confession tore my focus off the window. The vulnerability in his stare stilled the giddiness, begged me to accept the gift of his heart, and made my eyes burn. I laced my fingers through his, clutching tight.

Jon ran his hands through his hair and mumbled beneath his breath. "Think you better fucking pinch *me*."

"I owe you both an apology and an explanation," Elijah said rather than pushing us for an answer. His pale eyes revealed the guilt and hope for forgiveness I felt trickling through our bound hands. "I withheld the truth from you."

"For good reason," Jon muttered, crossing his arms over his chest in a show of insecurity I hadn't expected considering all that had happened. "If you told us the truth when we first met you, I'd have dragged Dakota away before the damn magic of this place pinned us down like I did her body every other hour of every day we've spent here."

Need kindled between my thighs, and I swallowed hard against the rush of saliva flooding my mouth.

"While my scent's pheromones linger inside these walls, there's no enchantment over our home," Elijah said with a soft chuckle as though well aware of my arousal, "but the connection between our souls that fate intended—*that* can't be put aside as anything but magical."

The two men stared at each other, and I shivered over the growing tension. Energy slid over my skin but with a complete lack of anger or hurt.

Elijah squeezed my fingers and held his other hand out toward Jon. "Will you..." He swallowed as though unsure if my husband's submission freely given before Dolyn's arrival was still on offer.

Jon didn't hesitate to move close and grasped Elijah's hand, sending a shuddering sigh through our lover. "I didn't lie to Dolyn about who you are to us, Elijah." My husband peered into our alpha's eyes, the truth of his words shimmering through the energy connecting the three of us. "I love you—have for a while, just didn't have the fucking balls to admit it."

Elijah's throat bobbed, and a sweet ache swept over me.

"Same," I managed to whisper past the thickness in my throat. "So much."

Without a word, we stepped in toward one another, closing the circle. As though of the same mind, we pressed inward, the men leaning down enough for all our foreheads to touch. "You are mine," Elijah whispered, his voice ragged, "and I am yours."

"Yes," both Jon and I said at the same time—a decision that didn't need thought but came straight from our hearts.

Whispers poured from Elijah's lips, words I couldn't comprehend but ones that resonated deep inside my soul. I gasped as flames licked up along our legs. Flames without heat, blue and beautiful, flickering, reaching upward as Elijah continued to speak, surrounding us with his love.

CHAPTER 43
ELIJAH

I despised that Dolyn had arrived at the most inopportune time. My mates and I had been on the cusp of reaching a pinnacle moment of aftercare where I would have been free to unveil my lies no matter the fear they would leave me.

But it had taken Dolyn's return for me to fully set the past behind, allowing me complete freedom to bond with the two fate had gifted to me. Being in my ex-lover's presence had revealed nothing lasting had bonded him and I together. Our energies didn't mesh, our thoughts hadn't ever aligned, nor had our wants been the same. We'd pushed and striven to create something that could never be.

Jon clutched my left hand with firm assurance as ancient words poured from my lips.

Dakota cradled my right in her soft, nurturing hold.

And my dragon freely spoke power into every syllable beginning the bonding between us, pale fire the color of my eyes gently wrapping around our bodies.

I lifted my head from where our foreheads had pressed together, my heart overflowing with joy and affection.

Dakota's eyes glowed green, swirling with a fire of her own. Jon's a blue so vivid, so rich I wanted to weep. Shimmering images rippled over both of their skin, almost as if they *did* possess scales that wanted to burst forth from within.

Yessss.

Mine—ours.

"You are worthy," I murmured as the flames receded and their eyes returned to normal. "My mates."

Dakota gazed up at me, her face radiant with the love she had declared.

"The fuck *was* that?" Jon asked, peering down at our bare feet, lifting his toes to wiggle them as though checking for burns.

"I set our bonding into motion."

He jerked his head up, a hint of a dimple denting his cheek. "A bonding like in those novels she reads?" he asked, tipping his head toward Dakota. "The kind where we can feel each other from a different room? Smell the sweetness between her thighs and the pre-cum dripping from our dicks?"

Dakota gulped, and all the blood in my body sped to my groin.

Jon glanced down at the growing bulge in my jeans as I fought for words to answer his question. "Pretty sure that part of the bond started a few days ago," he said, shaking his head, his grin widening. "Pretty fucking sure I like that part of this bond thing too."

A groan rumbled in my chest at the blatant lust in my beta's eyes.

"So now what?" Dakota asked, her voice small yet lust-laden.

Claim.

Own.

I shuddered at the desire rushing through both halves of me, what my beast had been begging for since first scenting our mates on the late summer breeze. "Now we complete our union. If it is indeed what you both are willing to submit yourselves to."

"Yes." Again, they spoke as one, their answer like a gentle caress meant to ease the last of my worries.

Elation roared through me, making my soul soar as high as our dragon half had ever taken us into the sapphire sky.

"Come." I released Jon's hand but held Dakota's while heading toward the stairs leading to the second floor. We would need a bed for the requirement to complete our connection as fate intended.

Blood rushed to my groin at the promise of things to come. Fulfillment for what I had longed for my entire life lay within my reach—but only because of mutual desire and love, not because I'd coerced either of my mates into agreeing to become one with me.

"Shit," Jon muttered from behind us, and I sensed his hesitation.

Stumbling to a stop, I glanced over my shoulder to find him peering outside.

"Can we, uh, see you in all your scaled glory?" he asked before swiping his tongue over his lower lip. "Take a ride through the friendly skies?"

Dakota backhanded him playfully. "Are you kidding me right now?"

"What?" He appeared offended, rubbing his shoulder. "If anyone, you should be asking that question!"

"Yeah, I want to see our alpha's other half. Trust me, I lust to ride him just like you," Dakota breathed, "but let's deal with this bonding business first. Our luck, someone else will show up and try to keep us from tying Elijah to us for life."

Amusement flooded through me. "Oh, *mon coeur*," I

murmured, tracing my thumb over the back of her hand. "Business couldn't be further from the truth. I promise pleasure like you've never tasted before—"

"Let's go." Jon crowded close, slapping my ass as he passed us and bounded up the stairs.

Snickering, I allowed him to lead, actually turned on by his sassy nature.

My beta would prove *more* than a pleasure to put in his place.

But first.

The lights in my bedroom rose as we entered, and I turned to face my lovers, all silliness taking a back seat to the seriousness of what we were about to partake in. "The beta is the bridge between an alpha and their female," I said, my gaze flitting from one hopeful gaze to the other. "The mating act reflects that, and when we're connected and spill our seed, the emotional link will settle into place. There is no breaking of the ancient bond of my people—*our* people."

I found myself smiling, knowing so many more with dragonblood walked the earth than I had ever dreamed possible, but the trust in Dakota's eyes—the lust in Jon's—wiped the thought clear from my head.

"You fuck me while I fuck her," Jon said, grasping the physicality of the required mating without my needing to explain.

"Yes."

Mischievous interest lit his eyes. "Jesus fucking Christ. I get to be in the middle."

My attention roaming down over his smooth chest to the hard ridge trapped inside his jeans along his left thigh. "You're hungry for it."

"Goddamned right, I am," Jon rasped, pressing the heel of his hand against his bulge.

Dakota whimpered, her tangy sweetness teasing my nose.

She nibbled on her lower lip and glanced between us then at the bed, her nipples hardening beneath my shirt, the pulse in her neck thrumming in time with my own heartbeat.

I released her hand and undid the buttons hiding her milky-white breasts from us. Large nipples, a dusky red hue, furled tight beneath my gaze as I slid the shirt off her shoulders, and it fell to the floor. "Will you allow me to love you through our beta?" I murmured, rubbing my thumbs over her budded flesh.

She moaned and licked her lip, her eyelids fluttering shut. "Yes. Please, yes."

"On the bed, *mon coeur*."

Her obedience caused my chest to swell, rousing my dragon's glee—and our combined desires to fuck. With him backing my body's natural reaction to Dakota's submission, I feared keeping hold long enough to complete the bonding.

As though reading my mind, Jon shoved his jeans off and crawled across my bed toward her, his plump peach of an ass in the air drawing a groan from my chest.

My hands shook while pushing down my own half-shredded jeans, and Jon settled between Dakota's thighs, capturing her mouth, both of them emitting the kind of whimpered moan that made my already leaking cock twitch.

"Hurry the fuck up, alpha," Jon growled, "or I'm going to blow my load without you stuffing my ass."

The darkness in me chuckled at his impertinence—his very *intentional* impertinence. "Speak to me that way again..." I warned, the unspoken threat lingering.

"Can't fucking wait." Jon's declaration sent another dribble of pre-cum oozing down over my length.

Palming myself, I moved to stand beside the bed, readying my cock for his ass with the slickness my body provided. "Wrap your legs around his back, *mon coeur*. Let him in."

Her ankles wrapped around his waist, and one flex of

Jon's ass pulled another moan from them both, my skin shivering as they slotted together.

"Slow and easy," I murmured more to myself than them, climbing onto the bed behind my mates.

Already on his knees, Jon slowly fucked in and out of Dakota, the scent of their combined arousal, the sounds of their feasting on the other's mouth enough to make my eyes want to roll back into my head. Nostrils flaring, I breathed them in deeply and crowded in close, using my knees to press Jon's legs wider.

He stilled as I rubbed my slickened crown over his puckered hole. Pre-cum continued to slip from my dick, and I pressed forward gently into his still-opened hole.

Jon cursed, his face burying in Dakota's neck.

Her eyelashes fluttered, and she peered up at me with eyes hazed by passion, sucking my soul into hers, moving me forward without thought. Jon's tight heat clamped down on my cock as I slid in without resistance.

"Oh, *fuck*," Jon groaned, pinned between the two of us. Gaze locked on my female, I pulled out, keeping my crown notched in Jon's body, and slid back in, the friction of his clasp on my cock making my jaw clench.

"Christ." He swore a few more times and pushed up onto his hands, planking over Dakota, the muscles along his spine rippling. "Not going to fucking last." He moved with me as I pulled out again, both of us pressing forward with a grunt.

My dragon clawed at my insides, roaring to be set free. I allowed enough of the wall containing him down so he might share in the taking. The time for our desperate need to claim had arrived.

CHAPTER 44

JONATHAN

"This is your place, my beta." Elijah's declaration throbbed my dick inside my wife. "I want no other between me and our female."

Wrong fucking time for my throat to go tight, but I couldn't help the emotions his words roused in my chest.

I'd always wanted a man in my life. Didn't have a father and certainly didn't want a *daddy* in the kinky sense, but I'd always hoped for a best friend who would have my back with loyalty like Dakota's. Someone to stand beside me. Encourage me. Recognize me for who I was and remind me I had worth regardless of my shortcomings.

I didn't have to be everything. It was okay to not be enough—

"Even if our female didn't exist, I would still need you, *mon coeur.*"

I shuddered, a strangled curse ripping from my lips. He buried inside my body as though making himself at home deep in my guts.

"We three make a whole," he continued, working his cock in and out of my throbbing hole.

Truer words had never been spoken because fuck my insecurities up until that point. Elijah and Dakota were the other parts of my soul, the pieces created to make me feel complete.

Elijah ran his hands up along my spine to clasp my shoulders.

My ass fucking burned even though he had stretched me to the max while down in the dungeon. "Jesus—fucking hell." I groaned, attempting to arch my back so he could bury even deeper.

Dakota clenched around my dick, and I cursed again. "Please," she whispered, tugging on my heartstrings, my desire to fulfill her every wish.

"Fuck me, Elijah." I groaned as he gyrated his hips, grinding his dick into my ass. "Make us yours."

A low growl rose from behind me, his shaft bucking inside me.

"God, yes," I groaned in response to what could only be his dragon purring its pleasure.

Elijah pulled out, the tip of his flared head still embedded inside my body. Copious amounts of his sweet pre-cum leaked around his girth and over my taint. "So slick and warm," he murmured in his low bass, sending a ripple of goose bumps along my arms.

My wife's sweet exhales bathed my lips, and I licked into her mouth as she wound her arms around me.

"Fucking love you baby," I murmured before sucking on her tongue.

Elijah shoved in with a harsh thrust, ramming me into Dakota's tight pussy.

A grunt ripped from my lungs.

"Oh God," Dakota whimpered, clutching at me tighter. "More."

Like a bridge, Elijah had said I would be. He used me to

fuck Dakota, setting a slow yet relentless pace in wrecking me.

My balls ached like a motherfucker. Firmed against my groin and dripping Elijah's arousal, they brushed against the wetness leaking from Dakota's core with every combined thrust of Elijah's and my hips. I'd never felt such perfection, such sheer fucking bliss-like *torture* in my life. His cock alone stroking along my prostate was delicious as fuck, but combined with Dakota's soaked pussy clenching around my dick?

Goddamn.

I groaned and lowered onto her fully, my arms useless. Face buried in her neck, I clung to her as Elijah and I moved in steady, perfected rhythm. I needed more, to fucking blow the load brewing in my balls.

"Harder," I said, remembering the strength of his thrusts, the pain/pleasure of him shoving deep inside me less than an hour earlier.

We picked up the pace in retreating, but it was all Elijah's thrusting that buried me against Dakota's womb. She grasped at my shoulders, her gasps and moans pushing me closer to the damn edge of something in the horizon of my mind. My soul longed to reach for it, to be swept up into whatever it was that simmered between us.

Elijah swore, plowing into my ass, banging the headboard of his bed against the wall.

Dakota gasped beneath me, and I grazed my teeth along the tender skin of her neck, the desire to bite her swelling, flooding my mouth with drool.

"Please, Elijah," she whimpered, wiggling and scratching the fuck out of my shoulder blades.

He lay over me, the heat of his chest searing my back, and Dakota released her hold on me to clutch at him if his hiss was any indication of her nails digging in. Another thrust made the bed thump, and she lifted her head, their mouths coming together in a rush inches from my face.

"Aw, fuck." I groaned and tried to move between them, but he held me pinned. Impaled and full to overflowing in every way. I wanted in on that kiss though, determined to get my share. My neck ached, but I twisted my head to reach them just right, bringing all three of our tongues together in a messy, wet tangle of flesh.

Sweat slickened our bodies, the heat on the verge of combustion into flames. The scent of brimstone and sex filled my nose, the softness of my wife cradling my front, the hard muscle pressing along my back.

"My loves—my life."

Elijah and his fucking declaration made my eyes sting, the harsh thrusts of his hips slamming the air from my lungs.

"Ah, fucking—Jesus—Christ—Elijah. Fuck!" His pistoning ripped curses from my lips, and I went boneless between my lovers, submitting my body to his actions, his desires.

"*Yessss,*" his otherworldly growl in my ear made my spine tingle. "*Mine. Ours.*"

Dakota cried out, her pussy clamping down on my dick like a goddamn fist. Without a single flick to her clit, she came around my cock, pulsing and milking.

"Fuck—fuck—fuck." I panted with Elijah's thrusts, stars lighting up behind my eyelids. Groaning, I buried my face in Dakota's neck.

My taint spasmed, and cum rushed up through my shaft, spurting inside her.

Elijah roared, his cock bucking inside my ass—a flood of heat filled my insides, and I swore to fucking *Christ* his cum shot through my dick into my wife.

Motherfucking...

Dakota's pussy pulled along my dick with a sucking motion as though desperate to drain us both dry.

I wasn't deep enough. Needed more.

"Elijah," I groaned at the prolonged climax, every spurt from my balls against my wife's womb like a wrecking ball to my soul.

That goddamn growl rose again as he nosed along my neck.

I tipped my head, my own lips sliding along Dakota's sweet flesh.

Bite.

I obeyed the command, not sure where the fuck it came from—my own goddamned head or Elijah's lips where my neck and shoulder met.

Dakota gasped as I sank my teeth into her, the slight coppery tang of blood hitting my taste buds—

A sharp sting from Elijah's mouth ripped all thought from my head, causing another pulse of cum to shoot from my balls.

Heat rushed through me like a wave, searing my body. Awareness of my lovers' emotions, the overwhelming euphoric release from both of them, flooded through me as though I'd become a conductor between their bodies.

A gleeful hiss radiated through my head as what seemed like a handful of voices whimpered in my ears.

I could feel both of my lovers in the deepest parts of my soul and hints of shadows beyond the physical. My blood lay rich and thick on Elijah's tongue. Dakota's limbs tingled with mine as her climax ebbed away, leaving only elation in its wake.

Breathless, I licked at the wound I'd made in my wife's neck as my dick finally shot its last bit of cum inside her.

Elijah shuddered, suckling on my skin, his tongue soothing until the burn beneath his mouth dissipated.

I'd found heaven, beyond any Elysium every fucking religion promised in the arms of my two lovers, my mates.

Yes.

I agreed with the voice inside my head even though I wasn't sure whose it was. We'd found our place—our home.

CHAPTER 45
DAKOTA

I still felt like a limp noodle, but Jon insisted he couldn't wait another minute to see Elijah in his true form. His childlike excitement tickled me, filling my heart with joy similar to the kind etched on his face and what I could sense rolling off him in waves through the intensified bond between our emotions.

Weak-kneed and barefoot, I followed both him and Elijah outside onto the veranda, the cool air licking at my still-heated skin. Elijah had cleaned Jon's cum from between my thighs with his tongue, the salty musk of both my husband and I thick in my nose. He'd worked my clit to a second climax before greedily lapping up yet another orgasm from my slit.

Only then had he agreed to Jon's insistence that our alpha show us his other half.

Naked, Elijah clutched my hand, strolling steadily after Jon who'd tugged back on his jeans and T-shirt. The late afternoon air didn't seem to bother either men as they stopped near the edge Dolyn had tossed himself off of what felt days earlier but had only been hours.

Elijah lifted my hand to ghost his lips over my knuckles, his contentment flooding through me and brightening my smile that hadn't dissipated since our full bonding. My facial muscles ached, but I didn't complain. He tucked blonde strands of my hair flying in the breeze behind my ear. His eyes darkened as though he saw the explicit images from my dreams flashing in my head.

"Next time, *mon coeur,*" he murmured and winked, sending an eruption of butterflies through my belly. Turning, he glanced over Jon's body, appreciation in his gaze. "I believe I'm going to fashion a saddle of sorts so I can strap you both to my back—tied down tight."

"Fuuuuck," Jon groaned and shuddered even though Elijah hadn't suggested anything sexual in nature.

Arousal, thick and sweet, seeped between my thighs. I heaved a sigh, thrilled by the promise of all my fantasies that my men, my *mates*, would one day make come true.

"You're wet as fuck," Jon stated, his blue eyes bright in the sunlight falling on his face.

"At the thought of riding you while riding our alpha?" I almost giggled with glee. "Damned right I am."

A low growl slipped from Elijah's lips, silencing both of us.

The black of his pupils swirled. "Stand back, my loves," he murmured.

Jon and I clasped hands, stepping away as we'd done when Elijah had climbed into his helicopter. But this time, there was no whine and roar of an engine, no slow whirling of blades whipping up wind.

Elijah stood on the veranda, eyes on us, the cliff at his back.

Silence settled except for the rustling of fallen leaves scattered over the stones separating us.

"Be careful," I whispered as sudden fear flooded through me.

Jon clutched my hand tighter, concern matching mine radiating in our bond.

Warm assurance flooded through us from Elijah, even though we weren't physically touching. It was going to take a while to get used to all the emotions that weren't my own filling my chest. Regardless of their newness, a lack of discomfort in their appearance gave me hope for the days ahead.

"Don't blink," Elijah whispered.

He tipped backward, and a gasp ripped from my lungs as he disappeared from view over the cliff's edge.

"Jesus—" Jon's curse hissed away in the wind as a black scaled head appeared then shot higher as a flap of wings lifted Elijah's true form directly into our sight. He hovered as our breath caught. Inky black scales rippled with shimmering color as though a rainbow imprinted over his bulk. Spikes lined his back, clear to the tip of his tail. Even the edges of his long, nearly translucent wings ended in sharp tips.

Another flap kept him from gravity's pull and blasted us with air nearly as strong as his helicopter's blades.

He was terror and beauty incarnate. A perfect blend of danger, deliciousness, and all ours.

Mate.

The whisper purred through my mind but wasn't the voice I'd heard when confronting Dolyn.

"It's really you," Jon choked in disbelief, but I couldn't tear my gaze off Elijah's pale eyes and the elongated pupils, the filmlike eyelids that blinked shut from the sides rather than vertically.

Yessss.

It was our alpha beast speaking, I had zero doubt.

A smile seemed to stretch the dragon's gaping jaw, and he shot upward with a harsh flap that rushed even harsher wind into our faces and blew my hair back.

A shriek then laughter burst from both Jon and I as we stepped away from the force, our heads shifting toward the sky to keep Elijah in sight as long as we could.

He disappeared in a bend of light as he'd told us he must do, lest anyone hiking the mountains catch sight of him. It had been days and days since he'd stretched in his true form, and both Jon and I had insisted he take a few minutes of complete freedom when we'd felt his inner pull to do so.

A shiver slid down my spine as the day's coolness made itself known fully on my skin.

"Pinch me, baby."

I did so on Jon's forearm, harshly enough he hissed. "Guess we aren't dreaming, huh?"

"Nope." He shook his head, scanning the sky. "Definitely not. This is weird as fuck."

"But are you happy?"

"Fuck yes." He didn't hesitate to answer even though the bond wouldn't allow for lies.

"Is it scary to you that we won't have any thoughts that are fully our own? Emotions we might wish to hide?" I asked, wrapping my free arm around my core to stay warm.

Jon's head whipped toward me. "What do you have to hide?"

"Absolutely nothing," I quickly assured him even though he would heart the truth in my heart. "I initially thought it might suck when PMS strikes—you both will feel my bitchy side—"

"Ah, fuck." Jon rubbed his hand over his face.

"—but then I realized that you'll both be aware of my grumpiness long before I lose the ability to hold it back."

"So that underlying...whatever it is I feel coming off you,"

Jon stated slowly, finally turning my way to study my face. "Is that…"

"Yeah." I grimaced. "My breasts are sore, and I'm a little bloated too. But look on the bright side." Jon's brow rose at my smirk. "You'll have something more than my hand or mouth to take care of your animalistic needs for those five to seven days."

Heat flashed in Jon's eyes along with a rush of warmth between my thighs that wasn't purely my own.

"Oh." I blinked. "This bond thing is seriously kinky—"

Awareness of Elijah's return to close proximity pulled both of our gazes off each other. We searched the sky, and my nostrils flared as the scent of him filled my lungs.

But where was—

Black scales flickered back to life, taloned feet settling directly in front of us. His entire body shimmered into existence atop the veranda. Elijah in his true form barely fit on the stone outcropping, crowding us against our home's front door.

I bit the inside of my lip to keep hysterical laughter from bubbling out of me.

A massive dragon stood feet in front of me, warmth along with the scent of brimstone and that cinnamon-like spice scent filling the air.

Jon reached out first, his fingertips trailing over what appeared to be impenetrable scales, same as the armor Elijah had crafted for his robots.

A low rumble huffed over my face as Elijah turned his long neck toward us.

I placed my palm against Elijah's face, completely at ease with the wide mouth and sharp teeth displayed, regardless of how they appeared more than capable of ripping a human head completely off with one chomp. "You're deliciously warm." Humming, I ran my hand along his jaw and down over smooth scales.

Pale eyes blinked at us, and I stepped in closer, releasing my hold on Jon's hand to wrap my arms around Elijah's neck. Eyes closed, I breathed him deep into my lungs, no longer chilled by the late summer breeze.

Mine.

I chuckled over the possessive, deep voice tumbling through my mind and the whimper those words brought to Jon's lips.

Breed.

A shot of need rushed through me. Mine, my husband's, or our alpha's, I couldn't tell. Probably all three, considering how insatiable we were for each other.

Breed…

Longing far beyond being filled by my lovers and finding release beneath their touch flooded through me as the meaning of the word clarified in my mind.

I wanted a family. A child—*children*—of my own to nurture and love unconditionally.

It takes three dragonblood to create life.

I blinked at the full sentence whispered in my mind, something Elijah had warned us his beast rarely used to communicate.

"Well, fuck." Sweet relief rolled through our bond from Jon, and tears smarted my eyes at the truth he'd kept from me for years.

He'd blamed himself for our inability to have a baby when all along it'd been fate that had been biding her time.

I reached for my husband, and he took my hand, moving close to wrap his arms around Elijah's neck alongside mine. "Love you, Jon."

"Love you more."

A blasted hot exhale snorted from Elijah's nostrils.

Love you both forever.

EPILOGUE - ELIJAH
A HANDFUL OF BLISS-FILLED WEEKS LATER...

I sniffed the wine Jon had poured into my glass, my gaze glued to his naked ass as he bent to set the bottle on the coffee table. Earlier that afternoon, I'd had him shackled to the cross with cane slashes lining his backside and Dakota tied to a bench, a vibrator bound against her clit and chained to the clamps biting her nipples.

The marks on Jon had faded as they always did, but the lust inside them hadn't. They had both pleaded with me to let them come. Begged for relief.

I'd denied them, removing the vibrator from between Dakota's legs before her body could take over her mind.

Such sweet submissives, my mates, always aiming to please me and do as I said even when it brought the most glorious pain from being edged for hours.

I'd promised to satisfy them—but in my time, after finding my own climax across Dakota's breasts. I'd unstrapped Jon to watch him crawl to her, his tongue lapping at my cum and sharing it with her, their mouths greedy for the life-giving nourishment.

The memory of their moans, the wet sounds of her

sucking my cum from his tongue, sent a fresh rush of need through me. We were insatiable for one another and had experimented in the dungeon and the bedroom, learning delicious means of pleasuring one another. Twice since our bonding, I'd felt Jon's desire to mate in the same way, and I'd gladly given him his wish to be the bridge between his alpha and female.

Dakota's inner desire, one she hadn't yet voiced aloud, swelled me to the point of pain every time I considered what she longed for, what my beast often pushed for without words our mates would hear.

She snuggled against me, naked as always inside our lair, her sweetness tickling my nose as Jon settled on her other side, his gaze dropping to my swollen dick.

Clothing rarely remained on our bodies outside of work or when hiking through the cool fall air that invigorated our lungs and limbs. Unhindered access seemed to please us just fine when hidden away from the rest of the world.

I sipped my wine, waiting for my beta to voice the question in his head. While I was their alpha, the one they'd both submitted themselves to, I still refused to manipulate.

My inner beast submitted but growled his displeasure over my continued mindset. I watched my beta's gaze roam over both my and Dakota's bare flesh. Heat always rested in the deepest parts of me, but Jon's hunger never ceased to kindle ember to flame.

He trailed his fingertips up Dakota's thigh, stopping just short of the apex of her thighs before sliding them back to her knee. "What are you thinking about, baby?"

On a sigh, she spread her legs slightly.

Jon glanced at my face, but he didn't move his hand upward.

I nodded and hummed my appreciation at the hint of a purr coming through my bond with him. While both Jon and

Dakota heard whispers of their inner beasts, neither could yet fully converse with them or had experienced the flexing of muscle and bone to take on their true forms.

Perhaps one day.

A shudder rippled over our female as Jon slid his fingers deep into her core at my approval.

Denied for hours on end, I knew her climax lay a breath away.

"What do you desire?" I murmured against her hair since she hadn't answered Jon.

"I—I want you to breed me."

Yessss.

I groaned over what my inner beast had been desperate to do from the moment of our bonding, what I'd prohibited him from speaking the afternoon I'd shown them my true form for the first time. The mere thought of both Jon and I filling our female together caused slickness to ooze from my slit. Setting my wine aside, I considered the pain—the assurance of life from taking our female in such a way while she was fertile.

And I could scent the ripeness of her womb and the egg lying in wait.

On our trip to New York the week before, Dakota had visited her doctor to have the IUD removed. The decision had been hers alone even though our connection allowed her to feel both my and Jon's beast's desire to procreate as well.

They hadn't been able to become pregnant in all their years of trying, and I had assured them that it took three with dragonblood to produce offspring, same as they'd both heard that day on the veranda. Their relief, Jon's especially, had made me want to breed her immediately, but I held onto patience for Dakota to make the decision for herself.

Her body, her choice.

But fear tingled in the base of my spine—

"You won't hurt me," she said, tilting her head back, pleading with her eyes. "Please."

I caught Jon's gaze, and the trust and devotion in his stare tightened my chest.

"We'll go slow," I said, returning my attention to Dakota, my heart full to overflowing with love for them both.

"And if it becomes too much," Jon tacked on, "you gotta let us know, baby."

"I will," she whispered while flashing a radiant smile up at me then our beta.

Breed.

I chuckled at my inner beast's vocal demand I allowed him to voice so both Jon and Dakota would hear through our bond, I stood and swept her into my arms.

"Your dragon is a bossy fucker," Jon said even though his desire to do the same came through loud and clear through the energy connecting us.

I'd done nothing but dominate when mating with my lovers as said fucker ordered over and again, but it was time to show Jon that I belonged to him just as much he did to me.

Creating life together would be the second most important act outside bonding the three of us could take part in.

And in this, I would submit myself to him.

Lying on our bed, I shifted Dakota atop me where I wanted her. "Give me your mouth, *mon coeur*," I murmured, my grip on her hips keeping her from backing herself onto my hard cock.

"Elijah," she whispered before lowering her soft chest to mine and flicking her tongue over my lip. A few languid licks, gentle nips, and I ended our kiss, holding her gaze as my taint pulsed a stream of pre-cum over my rigid shaft.

"Jon," I beckoned, allowing the bond to speak the rest of the words in my head directly to his mind.

"Fuck yeah," he muttered, climbing onto the mattress and

straddling my thighs. He grasped the base of my cock and pulled on Dakota's hip from atop my hand, shifting her backward. "Fill her up with that thick dick. Soak her insides so she's nice and slick for us."

My dragon growled at being told what to do even though Jon's demand was exactly what he lusted for.

Jon guided my cockhead into our female's already wet heat and pulled her firmly onto my shaft until I buried against her cervix.

I fought to hold still and groaned as another pulse through my groin flooded her insides, readying the way for us to breed her properly.

"Oh my God," she breathed as my pre-cum oozed from her hole to drip off my tight sac. Her attempt to wiggle and grind her clit on my pelvis ended at a slap of Jon's palm on her backside.

"Wait."

She hmphed and pouted.

Snickering, I lifted my head to lick over her lower lip. "So impatient."

"You know how long I've been fantasizing about this?"

"Too long," I answered since nothing she thought on could be hidden from me or our beta.

"Hurry, Jon," she demanded, and I grasped her hips once more to make her obey. "I can feel how badly your balls are throbbing to bury inside me—oh fuck." She whimpered and went boneless at Jon's finger probing her entrance.

I hissed through clenched teeth as he slithered his index finger along the back of my length inside her body.

"Mmm, so tight," he murmured, shifting closer. "Goddamn soaked, baby. Fuck yeah. Gonna feel so good shoving my dick up inside you with this thick cock."

Dakota moaned, arching as he pushed in a second, stroking along my throbbing shaft.

Breed!

Jon chuckled, his pupils blown wide so that only a ring of blue remained as he stared down at me. "Patience, mate. We need to make sure she's ready for us."

I hissed at him along with my dragon but didn't argue.

"I'm good." Dakota hastened to assure us on a gasp.

Please, three beast-like voices echoed through our bond.

Jon slid his fingers free from her body and shifted closer on his knees. "Slow," he said as though commanding the six halves of us about to become one. "Easy." He rubbed the slickened crown of his cock over my balls to gather my pre-cum, and I growled. His lopsided smirk popped his dimples free, and I shuddered at the swell of emotion in my chest. "Love you too, sexy beast," he said with a wink and pressed forward.

Our female's body gave way, allowing his tip to slip inside. A guttural moan sounded as she pushed up onto her elbows and arched deeply.

"*Mon coeur?*" I cradled her face in my hands, her panted exhales hot on my wrists.

"I—I'm find...don't stop, Jon."

He pressed in deeper, stretching her around our combined girths.

She moaned her discomfort I could feel burning through my own groin. "Don't you *dare* fucking stop," she said, her voice determined, "or I'll be the one wielding that damn cane next time he chains you to the cross, Jon Ebel, swear to *fucking* God."

A shot of lust from my beta accompanied my chuckle.

One day soon, I would sit on the sidelines and enjoy watching our fierce female dominate our beta.

"Jesus," Jon hissed, sinking in halfway until another hint of stinging zapped through my veins.

Silence hovered as though all three voices and those of

our beasts were at a loss of words. Time stood still as pain gave way to pleasure and we hovered on the edge.

"At your leisure, my love," I murmured, holding Jon's gaze.

With a groan, he breached her entirely, his dick sliding alongside mine, filling her completely.

"Oh, God. Oh, *God!*" Dakota tensed and shuddered, panting between us.

I released my hold on her face and caressed my hands along her sides, tremors in her body causing the skin beneath my palms to shiver.

Thrust.

Fuck.

Own!

I clenched my jaw.

"Tell me you're okay, baby," Jon said, his voice a ragged whisper as he clutched at her hips as though fighting off the command I refused to voice even though he'd heard my inner beast's pleadings.

Tension radiated through my muscles, keeping me rigid beneath her.

Dakota pushed up onto her hands in a full plank but kept her eyes clenched shut. Her nipples pebbled tight, their ache lancing through my own chest. I soothed my thumbs over them. *"Fuck,"* she moaned, shifting her hips.

Both Jon and I hissed as her pussy moved over our shafts.

"Fill me up," she begged on a choked sob.

Jon pulled her upright, snaking his arms around her body, one hand grasping her breast, the other her throat. But his eyes focused on me. "Touch her clit. Make her come around us." He pulled out partially, the friction of our clasped cocks sending a rush of exhilaration and adrenaline through my bloodstream.

My dragon roared, and I fought to keep from fucking into

Dakota like the animal beneath my skin was desperate for. I found her hardened nub with my thumb, stroking lightly when I'd rather sink my teeth into the sensitive flesh until she bled on my tongue.

She shuddered. "Yes—oh please, more."

Jon thrust along my cock, and a guttural groan spilled from her lips.

"Just like that, oh shit. You feel so good."

"Jesus," Jon murmured against her ear before grazing his teeth over the scar he'd left on her neck when we'd bonded. "So wet and hot. You're a goddamned vise stretched around our dicks, baby. So fucking perfect for us."

Our beta stroked a few more times while I feathered my fingertip over Dakota's bundle of nerves. Wetness smeared over my entire groin, the scent of sex thick in the air. I could taste her sweetness in the back of my throat, the heady musk of the arousal from all three of us in my lungs.

A low rumble from my inner beast swelled inside my chest, and I couldn't contain his groan.

Jon shuddered at the sound.

Dakota whimpered.

"Give in, Elijah. Fill her. Fuck her like you've hungered for since day one. Flood her with your cum along with mine so we can plant that baby we're all desperate for inside her womb."

I pulled my hips into the mattress and thrust upward with a roar, my hips bucking them both. Hands tight on Dakota's thighs, I fucked into her pussy while Jon did the same in opposing action.

"Need—" Her voice cut off on a gasp, and she licked her lips, letting out a moan as instinct took over, allowing our beasts to own our bodies. "H-harder." She gasped again as I stabbed against her cervix, needing to burrow deeper where her body had no choice but to accept our seed.

Dakota panted, her body jolting in Jon's hold, and her climax tingled through my mind and straight to my ball sac.

"Now," Jon said with a growl, thrusting alongside me. Buried as deep as physically possible, our cockheads throbbed against each other.

Dakota shrieked, her pussy clenching down on us.

White light ripped through my mind at the first shot of cum releasing up through my shaft. Jon's cock pulsed, spurting in time with mine. Fire shot through my blood, igniting along the three of us, blue flames licking, slithering inside Dakota to mingle with our seed flooding her womb.

She cried out again, her core milking us, greedily soaking up every drop of our essence we offered.

I felt the continued heat she did deep inside her womb.

Jon's lightheaded bliss rushed through my brain.

I sent out wave after wave of my love to them both throughout the prolonged climax.

Dakota sagged in Jon's arms, completely spent, one final pulse through her core causing both Jon and I to shudder and jolt.

Yessss.

I groaned, reaching for my lovers and yanking them down atop me. Soft flesh pressed against my entire front, Dakota's warm breath on my left pec. I stroked my fingers through Jon's sweaty hair and tucked his face into the right side of my neck.

"Mmm," he hummed his pleasure, licking the saltiness from my skin.

Dakota clenched around our softening lengths.

Jon grazed his teeth over my neck.

I hissed at his action as loudly as the inner beast inside me. "Don't get any ideas, beta."

He chuckled, causing his cock to slip from our female's hold. "Fucking love you, baby." He planted a hard kiss on her shoulder before lifting his gaze to mine. Sated blue eyes as vivid as an afternoon sky peered into mine. "Love you too."

"Love you more," I assured him in the same way he always did his wife.

Emotions radiated through us. Words weren't really necessary, but they felt damned good to say.

"Don't go anywhere," Jon murmured before brushing his lips across mine.

As if I could even if I'd wanted to.

Our female draped over me, her slight weight enough to pin me in place for as long as she needed my body as a pillow. My gaze trailed after Jon's peach of an ass flexing with every step toward the bathroom.

He'd led our coupling in the bed, and I trusted him to see to the aftercare of our female.

He returned from the bathroom with a warm, wet towel to tidy up Dakota—something I usually did for both of them. I hated to pull from her warm embrace but gently shifted her off my shaft and onto her back.

I lay on my side and stared into her sated, sleepy eyes as Jon cleaned between her thighs. "Are you all right, *mon coeur?*"

"Mmm," she hummed her contentment I already felt and lightly stroked a fingertip over my lower lip.

I nipped at her, causing her smile to widen.

"You've made all of my dreams come true."

Hopefully.

Jon tossed the towel across the room to land on the floor —that he would pay for, I promised him through our bond.

Smirking, he lay on Dakota's other side, tucking in tight against her body.

I shifted closer, bracketing our female between us, my hand on Jon's hip to roll him so he faced me.

"Do you think Dolyn found his mates?" our female asked, staring up at the ceiling.

"The fuck you thinking about him for?" Jon grumbled, shoving an arm under his head to better see the two of us.

Dakota sighed, and I rubbed my face in her hair, breathing in the scent of spring and sunshine. "I don't want him to be alone. I hope he gets to feel what we do—find what we have."

Jon snorted. "If he gets within ten feet of Ashley, she won't stand a chance of denying him."

"Is that how it was for you?" Dakota asked, amusement in her tone.

"Fucking right." His dimples flashed, and my love for his carefree attitude bounced through our bond, deepening his smile—and my own.

I turned my attention to the beautiful woman between us, the precious gift fate had given us. "You're the rays of morning's first light. The twinkling of stars in the dark night. I love you with every breath that fills my lungs."

"I can feel the truth of your words in my heart." Dakota's green eyes shimmered with tears, and she reached over to press her fingertips to my lips. "I still don't know how it's possible to have two loves, two men, *dragonblood* I can't imagine living without. You are my life, Elijah. You and Jon." She laced her fingers through his, and contentment—to a point—flowed between us.

"What is it you still desire, *mon coeur*?" I whispered in her ear, fighting a smile.

"I'd like to put that saddle you finished up this morning to use," she said in a rush, pulling away from me enough to see my face. "I want to ride on your back and glide over the mountains."

"More like you're aching to ride me while riding him," Jon said, and she gasped, jerking her head toward him. "Don't bother denying it, baby." He grinned again, his dimples on full display. "You talk in your sleep."

"I do not," she breathed.

"You do," I said, biting back my chuckle. "Always have."

"Damn." She blew out a breath and faced the ceiling once more. "So you both know all about that dream I keep having."

"Hot as fuck, and I'm game," Jon said, raising an eyebrow my way, "if our alpha doesn't mind my being strapped to his back while you fuck yourself on my dick."

I chuckled. "Fucking right."

Jon snorted on laughter at my word choice.

"Tomorrow, though," I said, too comfortable to move—even if the thought of Dakota's cum coating my scales caused my cock to twitch and had my dragon's claws clicking together in his glee.

Jon's inner dragon hummed his approval through our bond, and even Dakota let out a shuddering sigh of arousal.

Perhaps they would soon be able to fully communicate with their dragons in the way I did. I hoped they would grow in strength and learn from me, becoming more dragonblood than human. Maybe one day, we would soar the skies together, all our wings extended in complete freedom.

"Do you think it worked?" Dakota whispered, turning her gaze once more to the ceiling.

I slid my hand from Jon's hip to her belly.

Jon placed his atop mine.

Both of Dakota's wrapped around ours. "Oh!" She lifted her head and blinked at her stomach. "Oh!" she repeated and glanced between the two of us, her eyes wide. "I—I can feel..."

"Holy fuck." Wonder laced Jon's voice. "How the *fuck*?"

"She'll have my dark hair," I said as our daughter's self-conscious whispered of her existence through the bond. "Green eyes like her mother's. Jon's dimples and stubborn chin."

"She?"

I nodded firmly what my being a royal Blood Born allowed me to see unhindered. "In three months, you'll see the truth I speak."

"Three *months*?" Dakota's eyes widened further.

Jon's muttered curse brought a chuckle to my lips.

"Dragonbloods have a much shorter gestation period."

"Guess we better get busy readying for the little shit."

Dakota backhanded her husband. "She's going to be an angel and have you wrapped around her little finger the second her shriek first pierces the air."

He grimaced but didn't argue.

I could feel my mates' pleasure, their absolute joy deep inside my soul.

Warmth radiated from Dakota's belly up through my hand and beyond, and my vision hazed.

The three of us had found love—and we had created dragonblood life.

ABOUT THE AUTHOR

Spicy romance author Lynn Burke believes everyone deserves healing and a happily ever after. She loves writing hot, inclusive stories of various pairings or triplings and creates characters who will steal your heart.

She is a USA Today Bestselling author, a wrangler of her three spawn, and a farmer's daughter who grows organic food. To escape reality, she hides in a quiet corner with her nose in a book.

You can find more about Lynn at her website: www.authorlynnburke.com

Also by Lynn Burke

Abel's Obsession

Divulging Secrets

Healing Storms

In Between

Reluctant Lumberjack

Resisting his Mate

Billion Dollar Love Anthology

Blood Born Series

Bonds of Worship Series

Dark Leopards MC

Darkest Desires Series

Devil's Outlaws MC

Elite Escort Series

Elite Escorts MM Series

Fallen Gliders MC

Forbidden Obsession Duet

Found by Fate Series

Midnight Sun Series

Missing Link Series

Risso Family Series

Sandy Ridge Series

Sinful Nature Series

Vicious Vipers MC

www.ingramcontent.com/pod-product-compliance
Lightning Source LLC
Chambersburg PA
CBHW070238200726
48293CB00005B/1679